KID SAVAGE

image

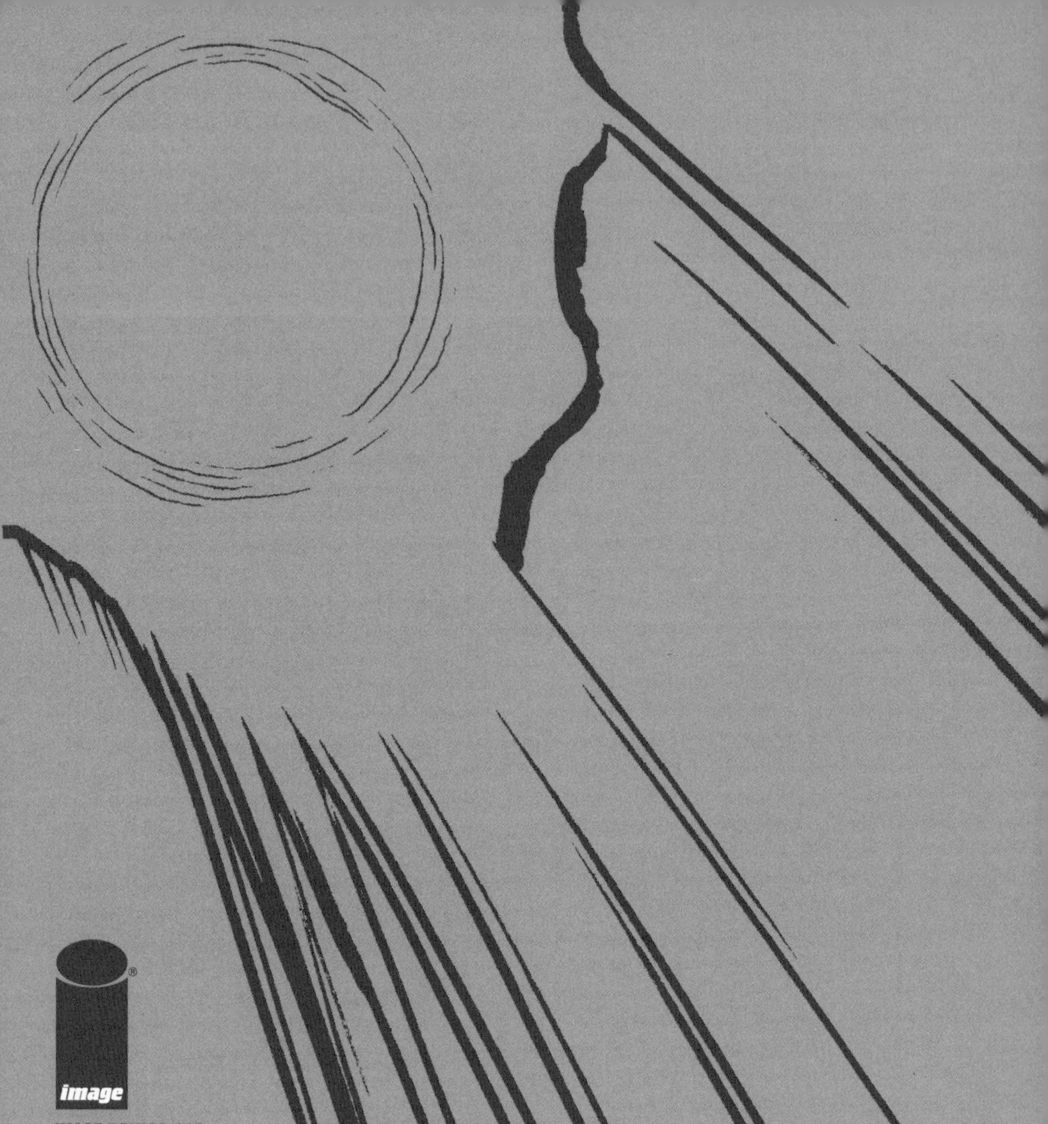

IMAGE COMICS, INC.
Robert Kirkman—Chief Operating Officer
Erik Larsen—Chief Financial Officer
Todd McFarlane—President
Marc Silvestri—Chief Executive Officer
Jim Valentino—Vice-President

Eric Stephenson—Publisher
Corey Murphy—Director of Sales
Jeff Boison—Director of Publishing Planning & Book Trade Sales
Chris Ross—Director of Digital Sales
Kat Salazar—Director of PR & Marketing
Branwyn Bigglestone—Controller
Drew Gill—Art Director
Brett Warnock—Production Manager
Meredith Wallace—Print Manager
Briah Skelly—Publicist
Aly Hoffman—Conventions & Events Coordinator
Sasha Head—Sales & Marketing Production Designer
David Brothers—Branding Manager
Melissa Gifford—Content Manager
Erika Schnatz—Production Artist
Ryan Brewer—Production Artist
Shanna Matuszak—Production Artist
Tricia Ramos—Production Artist
Vincent Kukua—Production Artist
Jeff Stang—Direct Market Sales Representative
Emilio Bautista—Digital Sales Associate
Leanna Caunter—Accounting Assistant
Chloe Ramos-Peterson—Library Market Sales Representative
IMAGECOMICS.COM

KID SAVAGE, Volume 1
First Printing. April 2017.

Published by Image Comics, Inc.

Office of publication: 2701 NW Vaughn St., Suite 780, Portland, OR 97210.

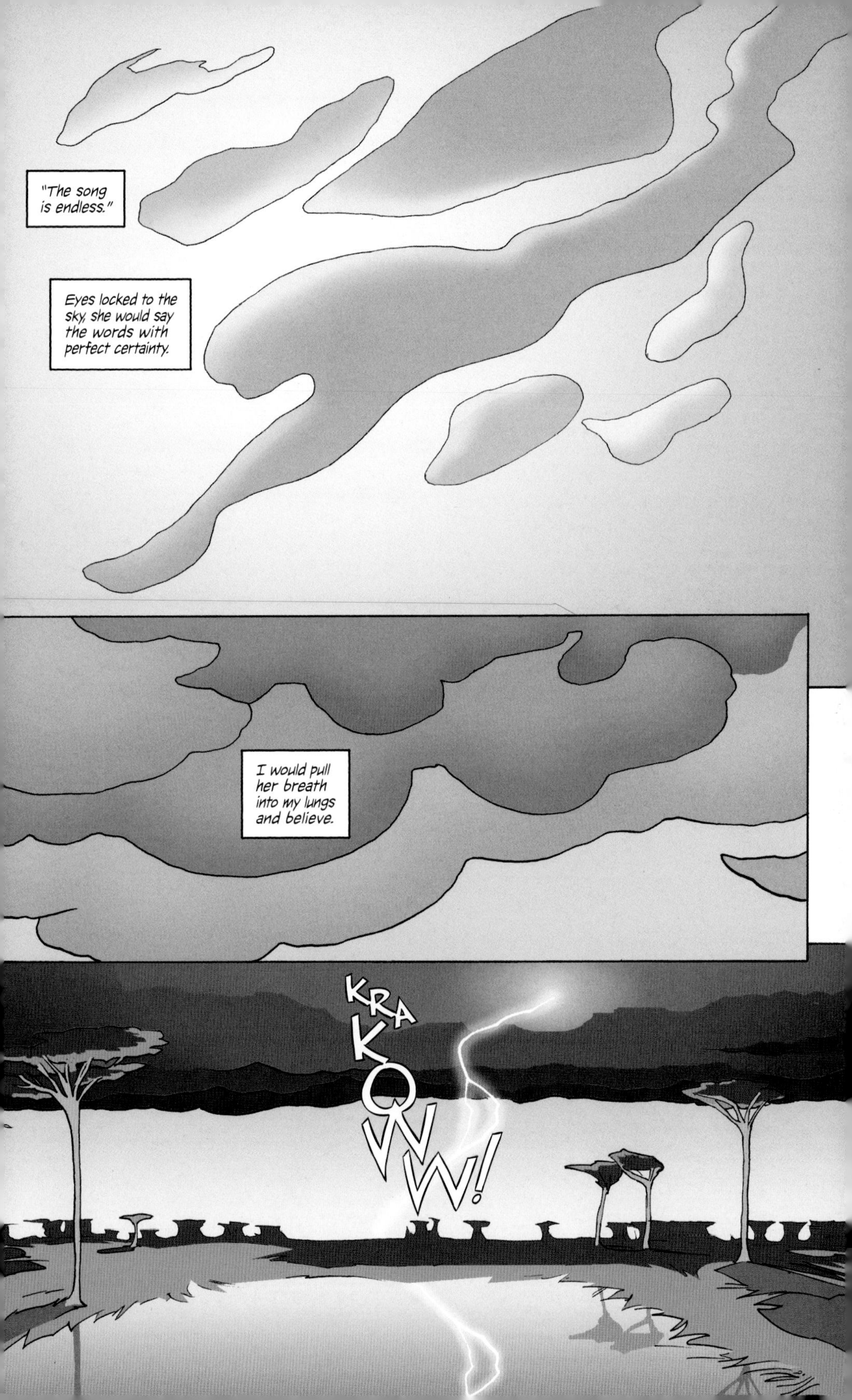
"The song is endless."
Eyes locked to the sky, she would say the words with perfect certainty.
I would pull her breath into my lungs and believe.
KRAKOWW!

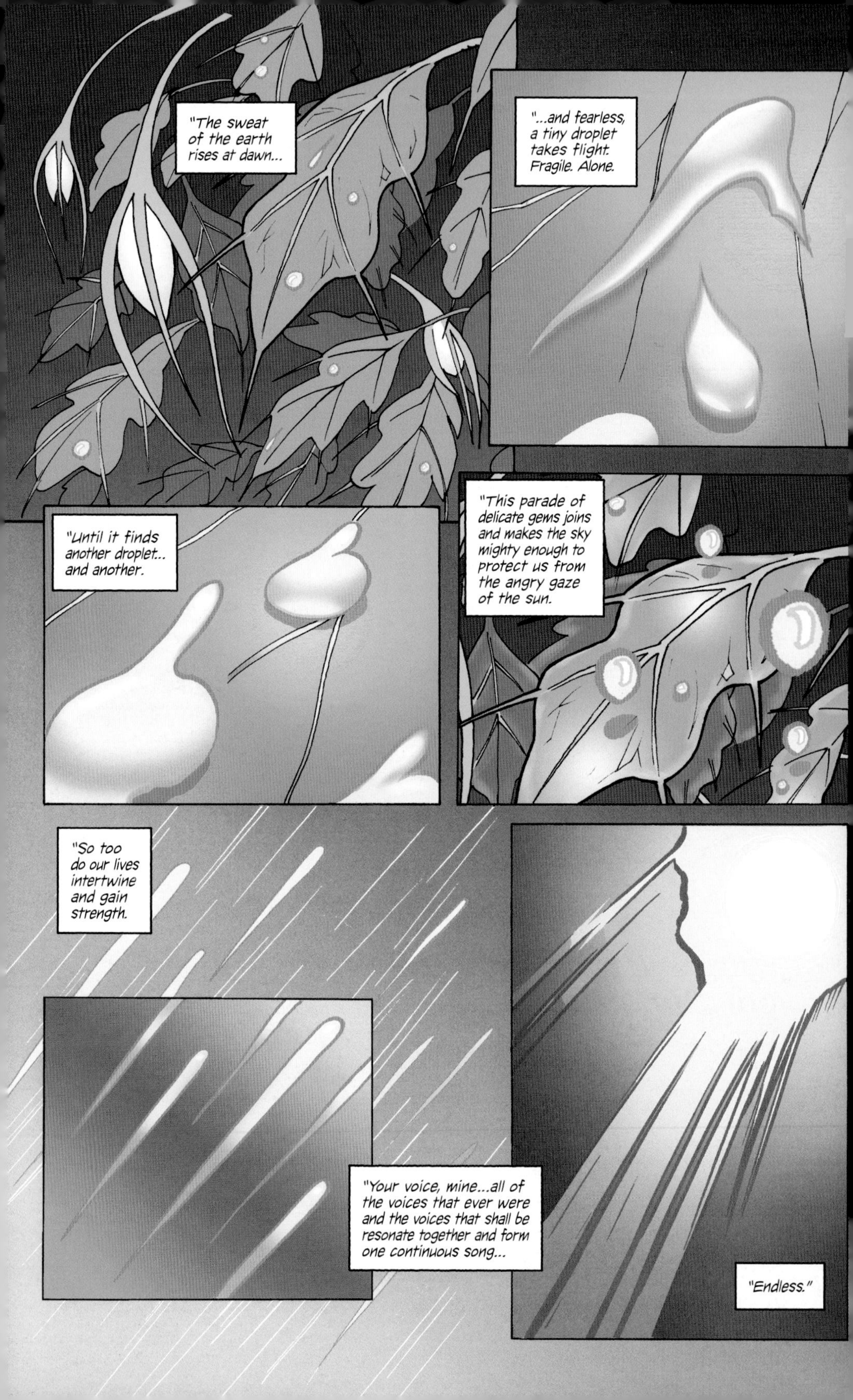
"The sweat of the earth rises at dawn...
"...and fearless, a tiny droplet takes flight. Fragile. Alone.
"Until it finds another droplet... and another.
"This parade of delicate gems joins and makes the sky mighty enough to protect us from the angry gaze of the sun.
"So too do our lives intertwine and gain strength.
"Your voice, mine...all of the voices that ever were and the voices that shall be resonate together and form one continuous song...
"Endless."

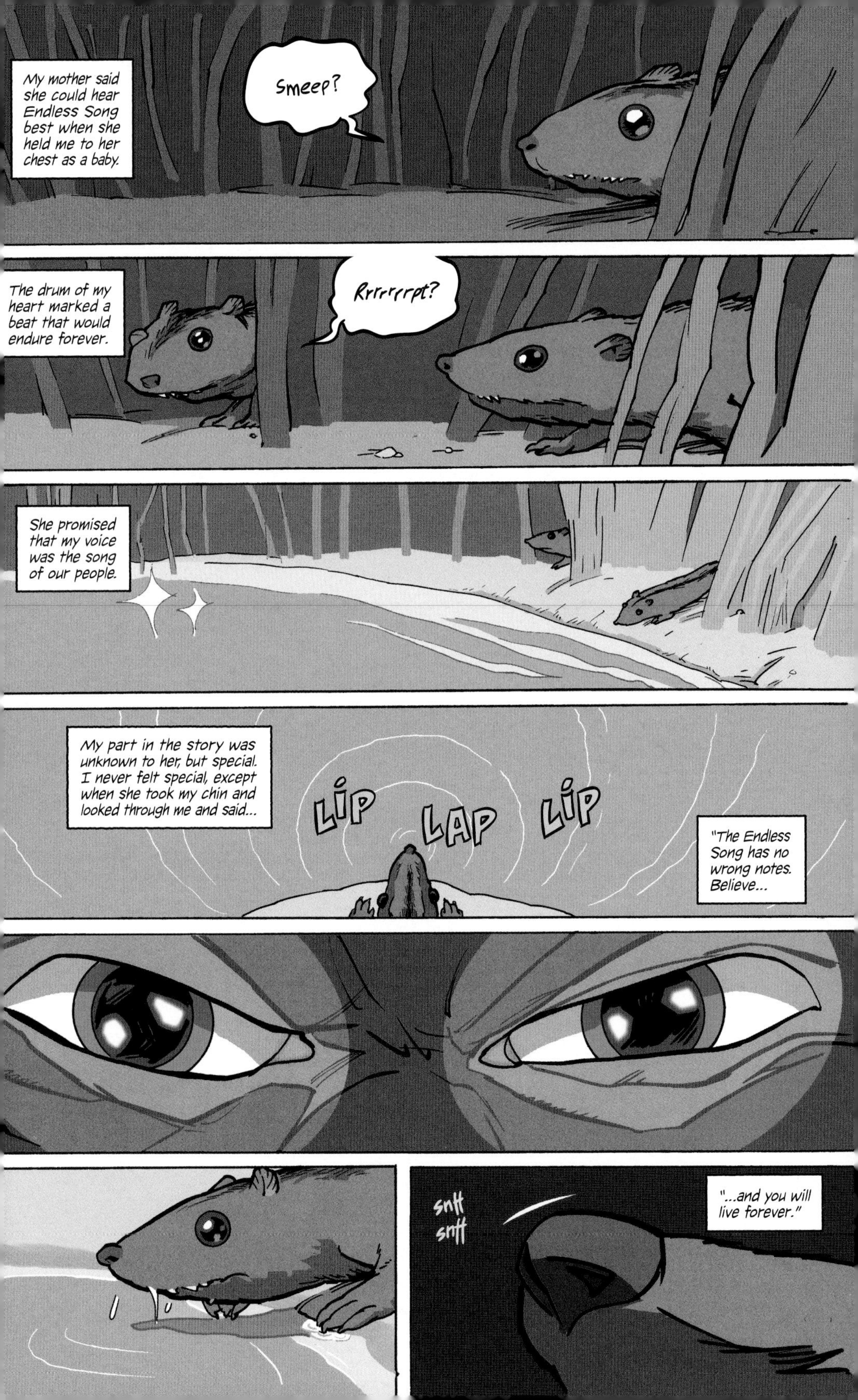
My mother said she could hear Endless Song best when she held me to her chest as a baby.
Smeep?
The drum of my heart marked a beat that would endure forever.
Rrrrrrrpt?
She promised that my voice was the song of our people.
My part in the story was unknown to her, but special. I never felt special, except when she took my chin and looked through me and said...
LIP
LAP
LIP
"The Endless Song has no wrong notes. Believe...
snff
snff
"...and you will live forever."

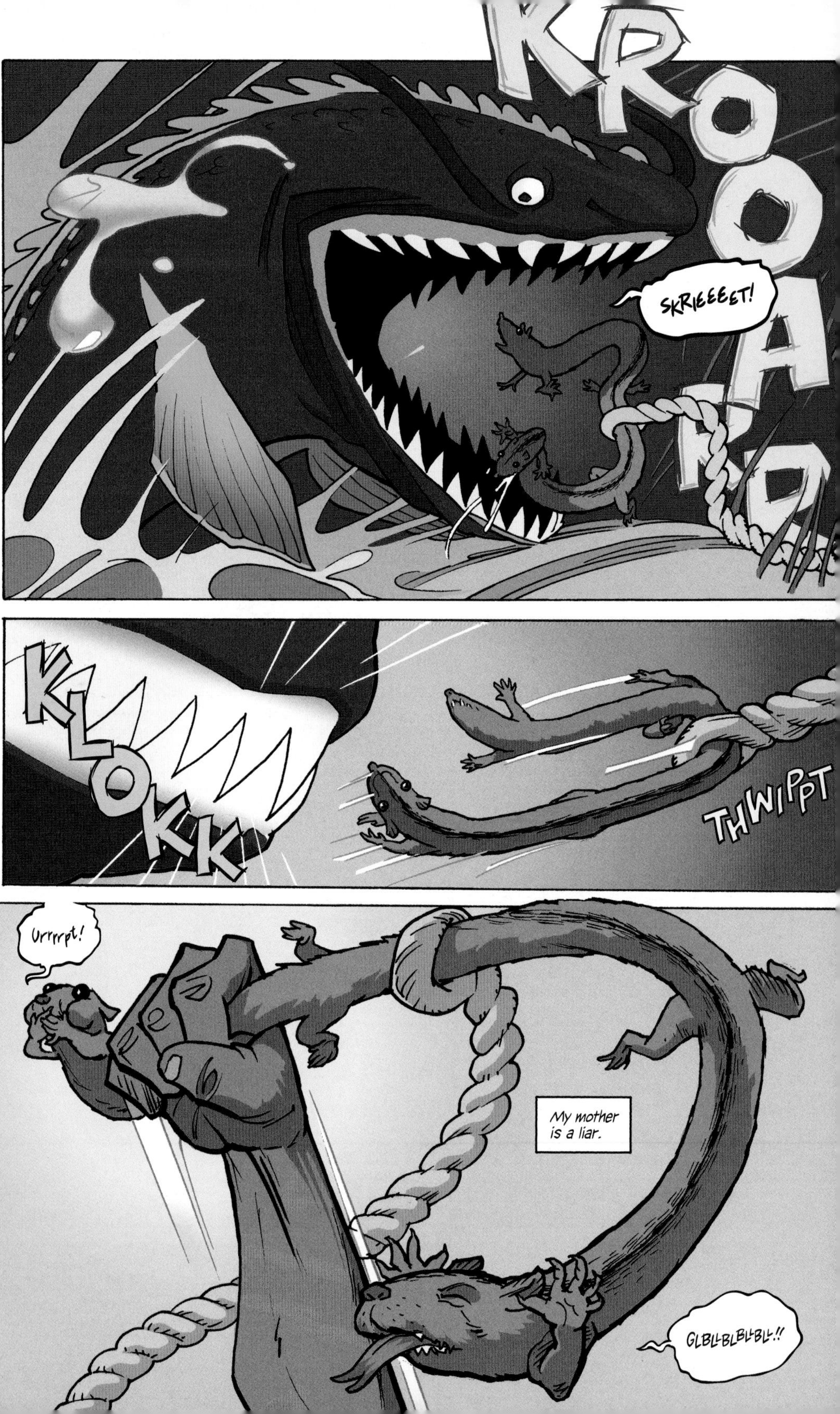
KROOAARD
SKRIEEEEET!
KLOKK
THWIPPT
Urrrrpt!
My mother is a liar.
GLBLL-BLBLL-BLL-!!

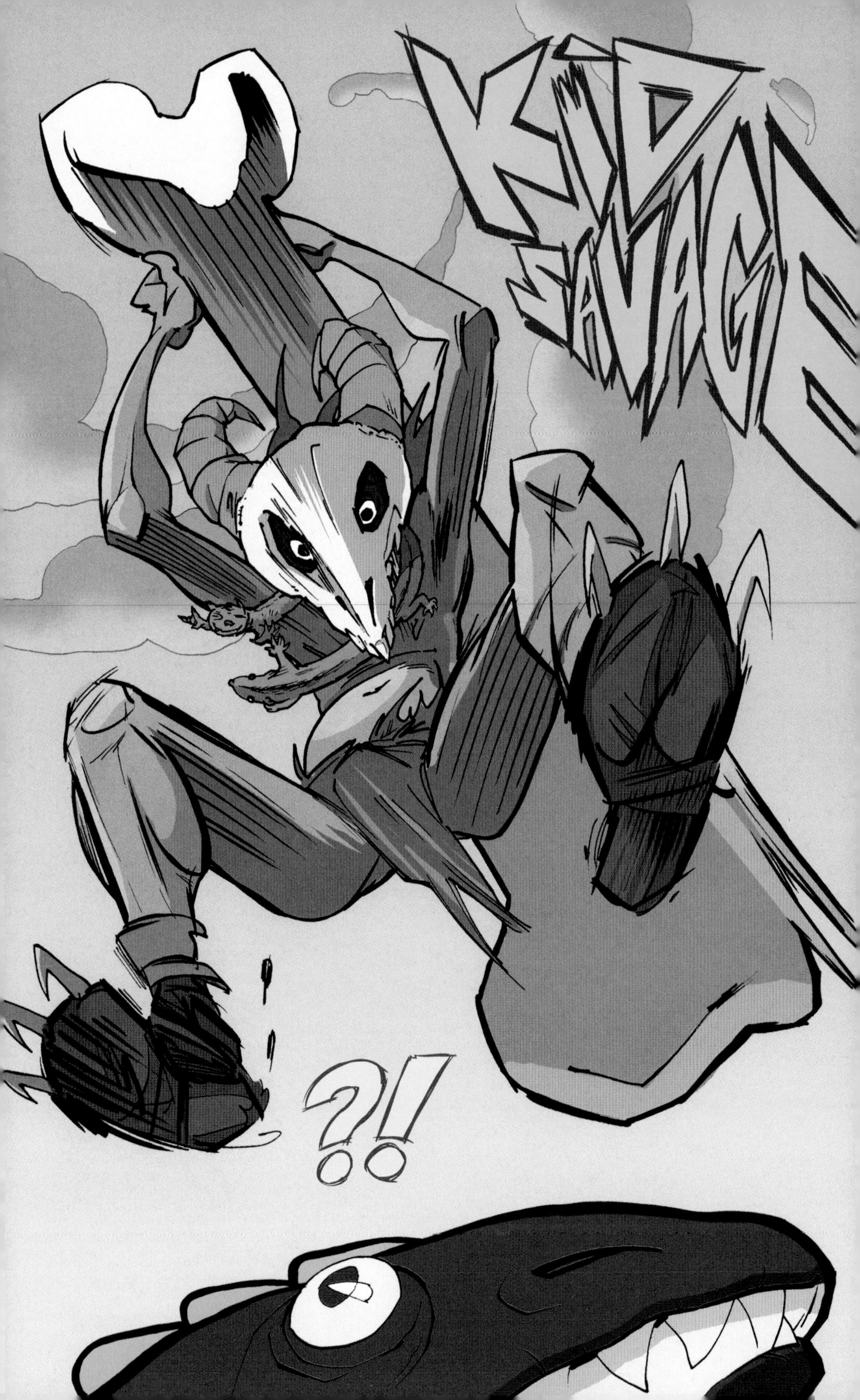
KID SAVAGE!!
?!

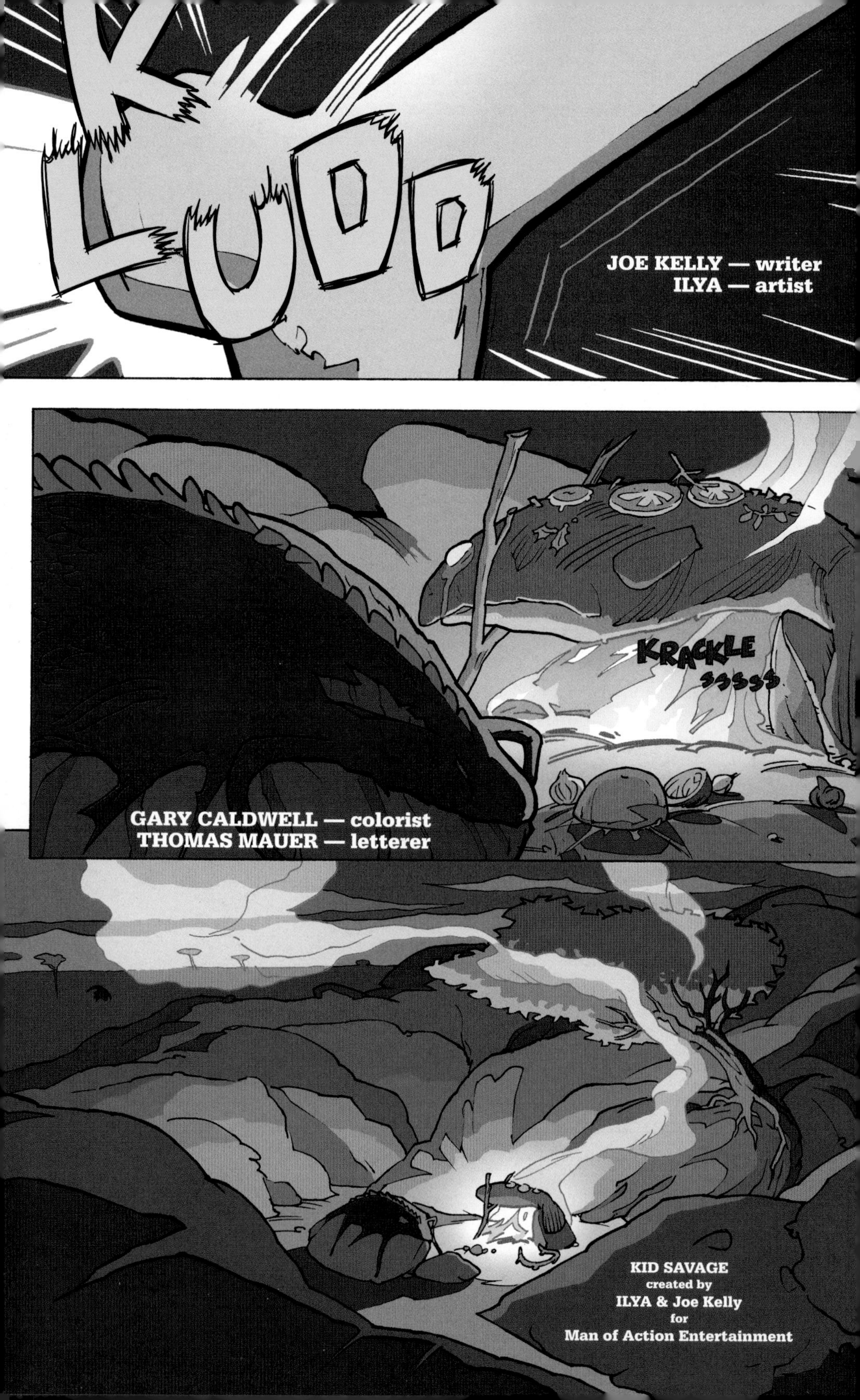
KLUDD
JOE KELLY — writer
ILYA — artist
KRACKLE
sssss
GARY CALDWELL — colorist
THOMAS MAUER — letterer
KID SAVAGE
created by
ILYA & Joe Kelly
for
Man of Action Entertainment

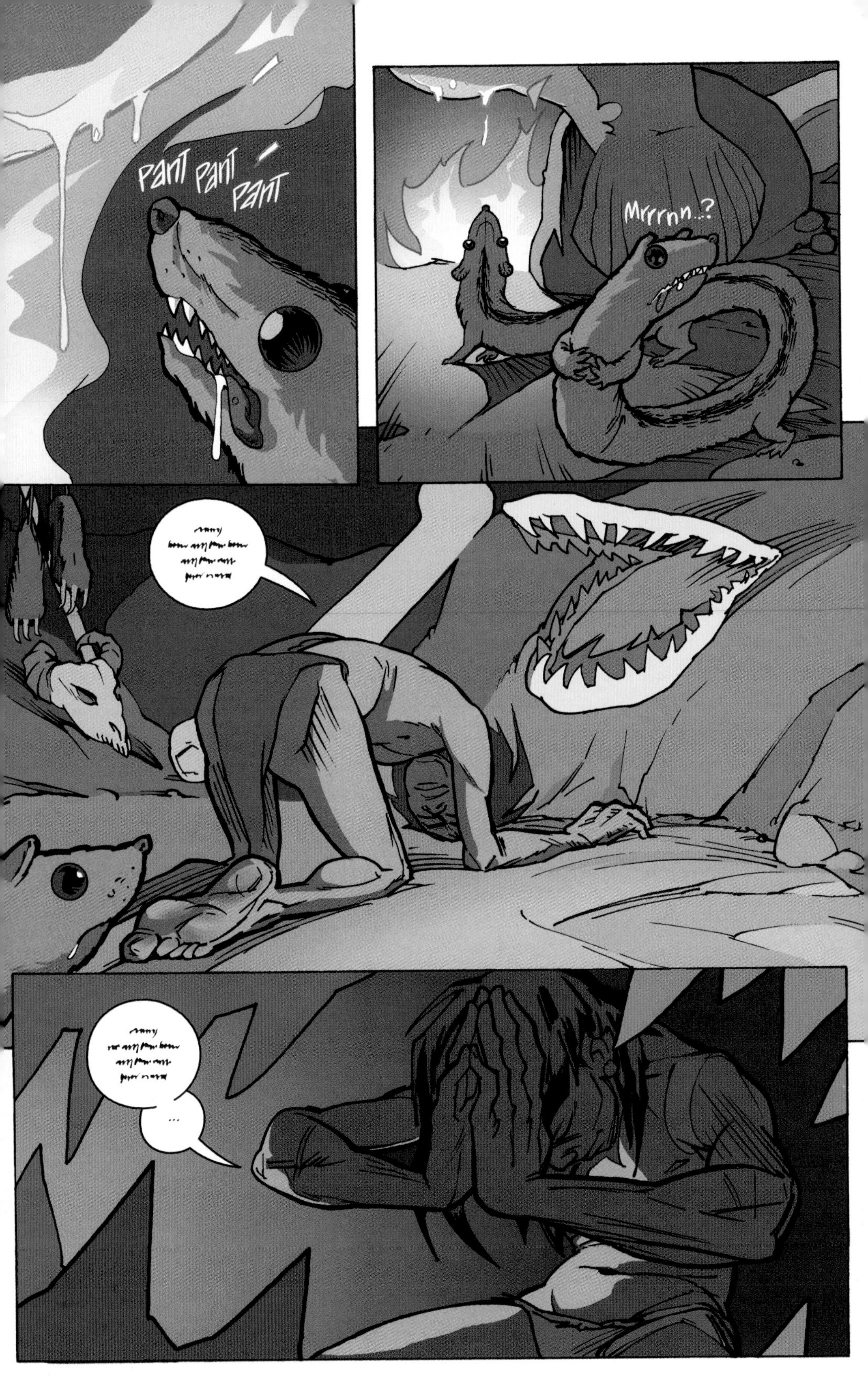
PANT PANT PANT
Mrrrnn..?
...

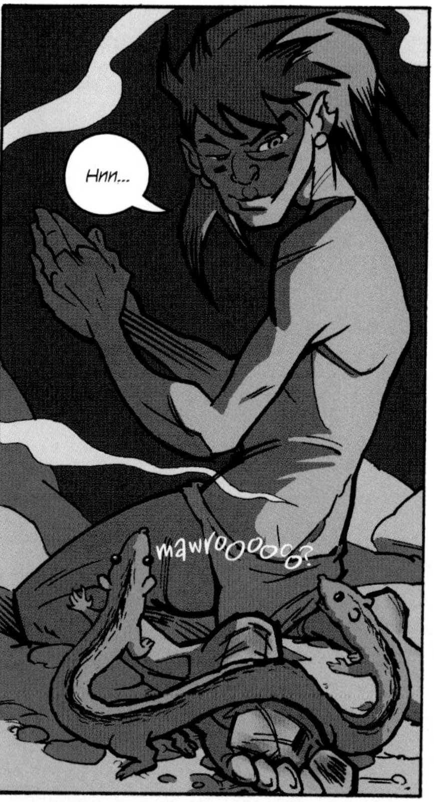
Hnn...
mawrooooo?

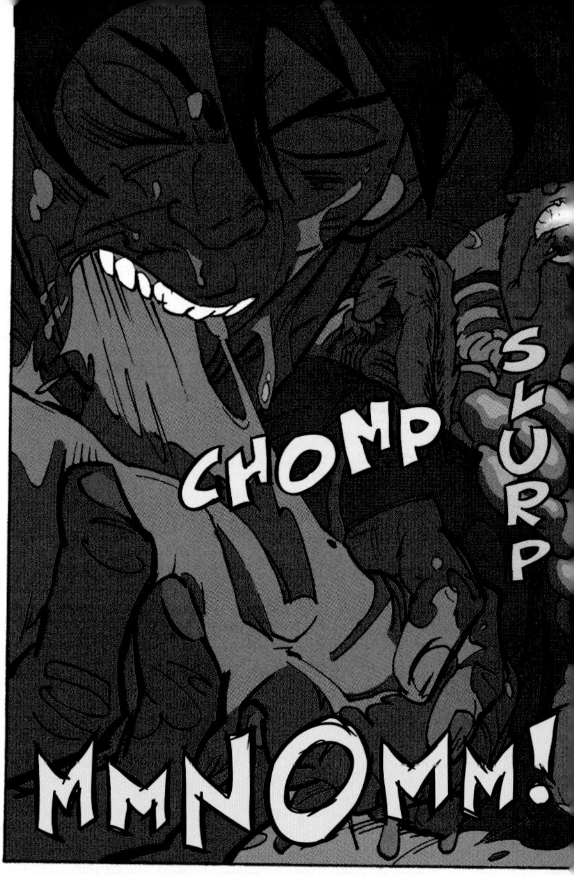
CHOMP
SLURP
MMNOMM!

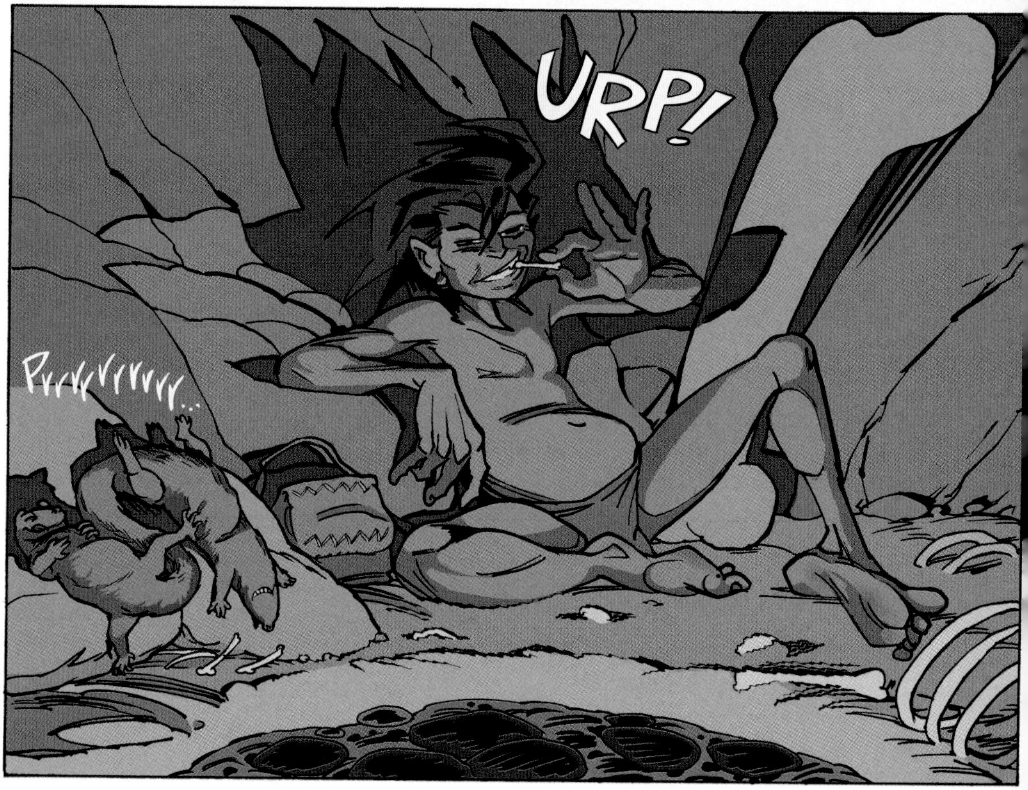
URP!
Prrrrrrrrr...

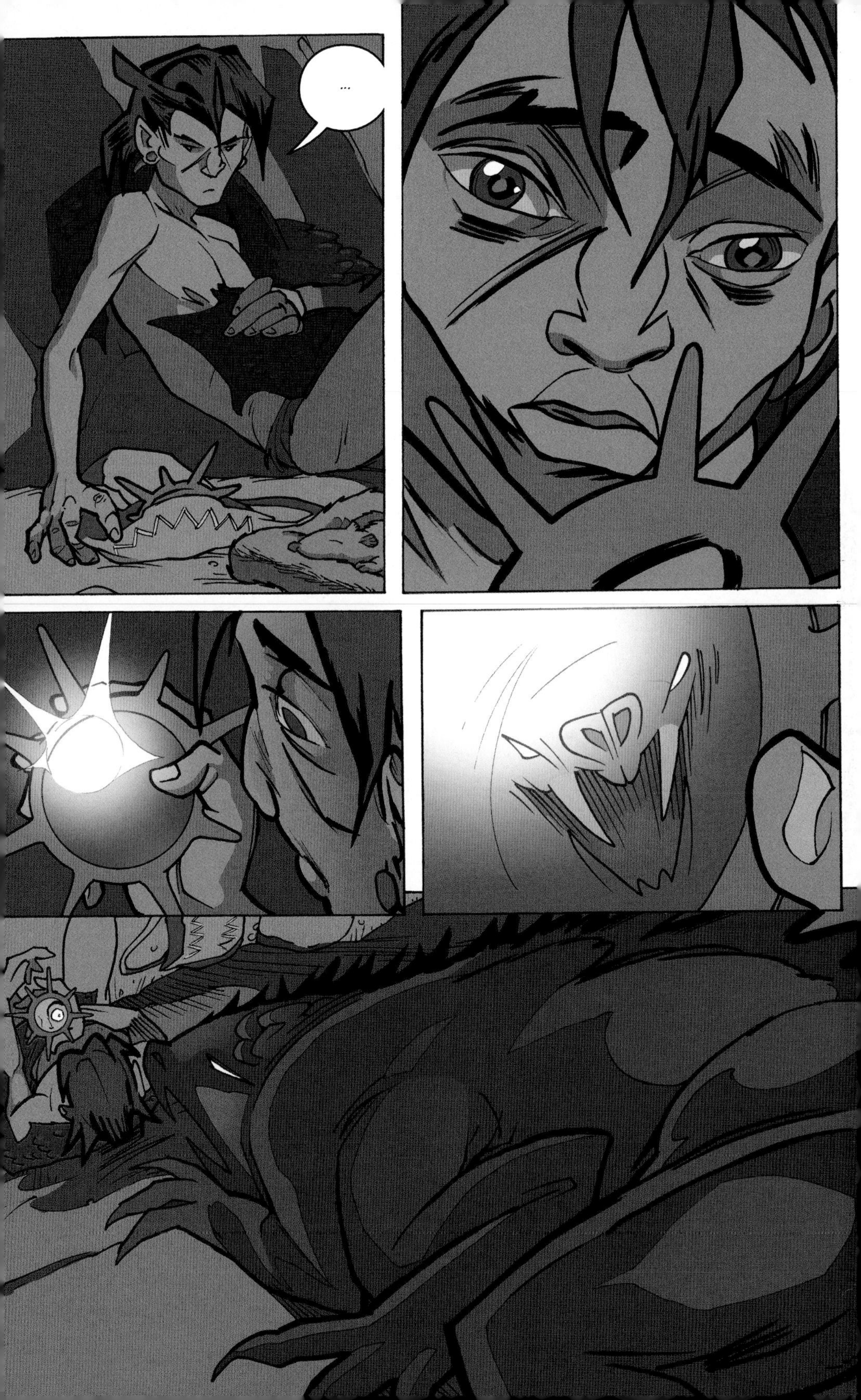
...

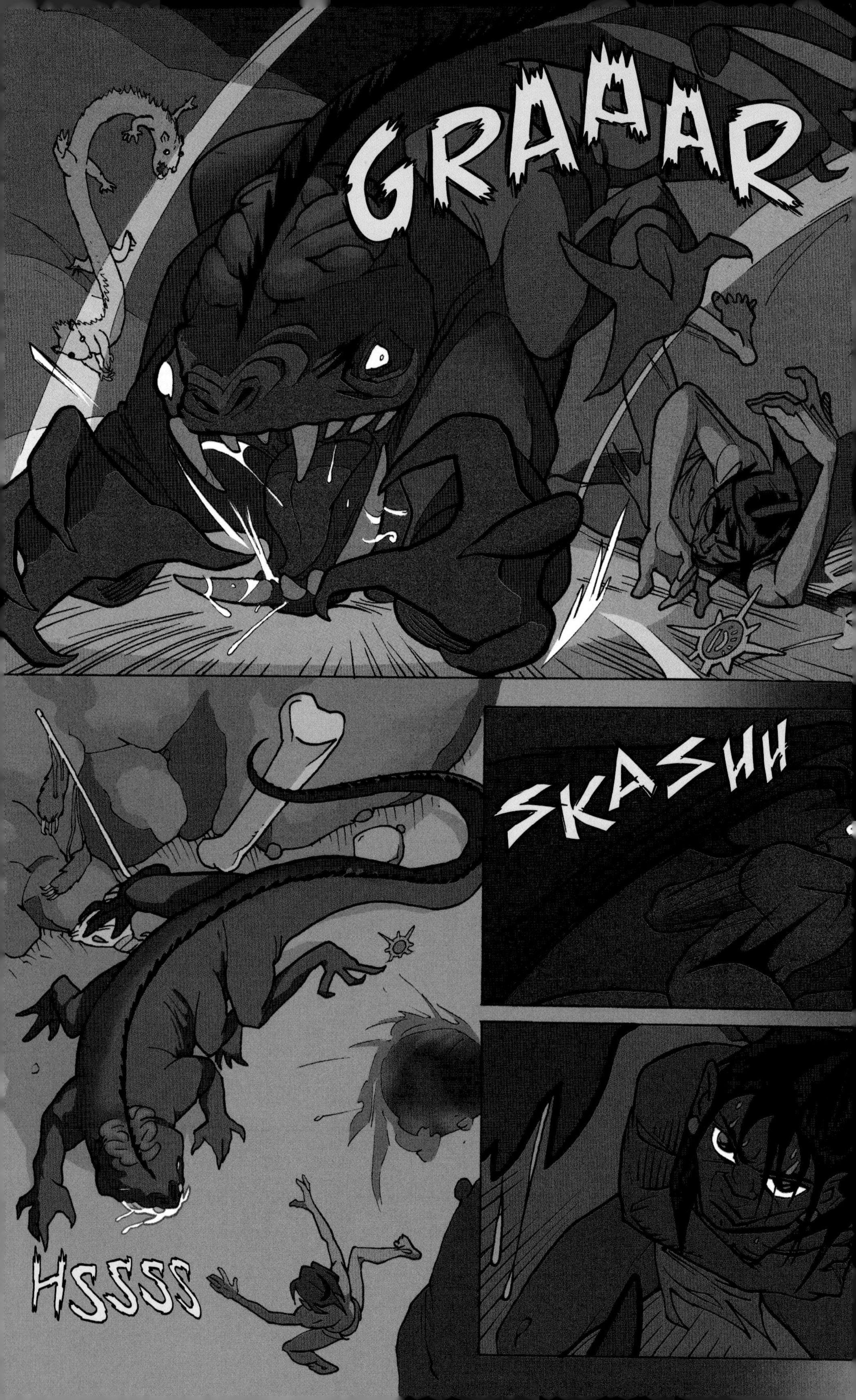
GRAAAR
SKASHH
HSSSS

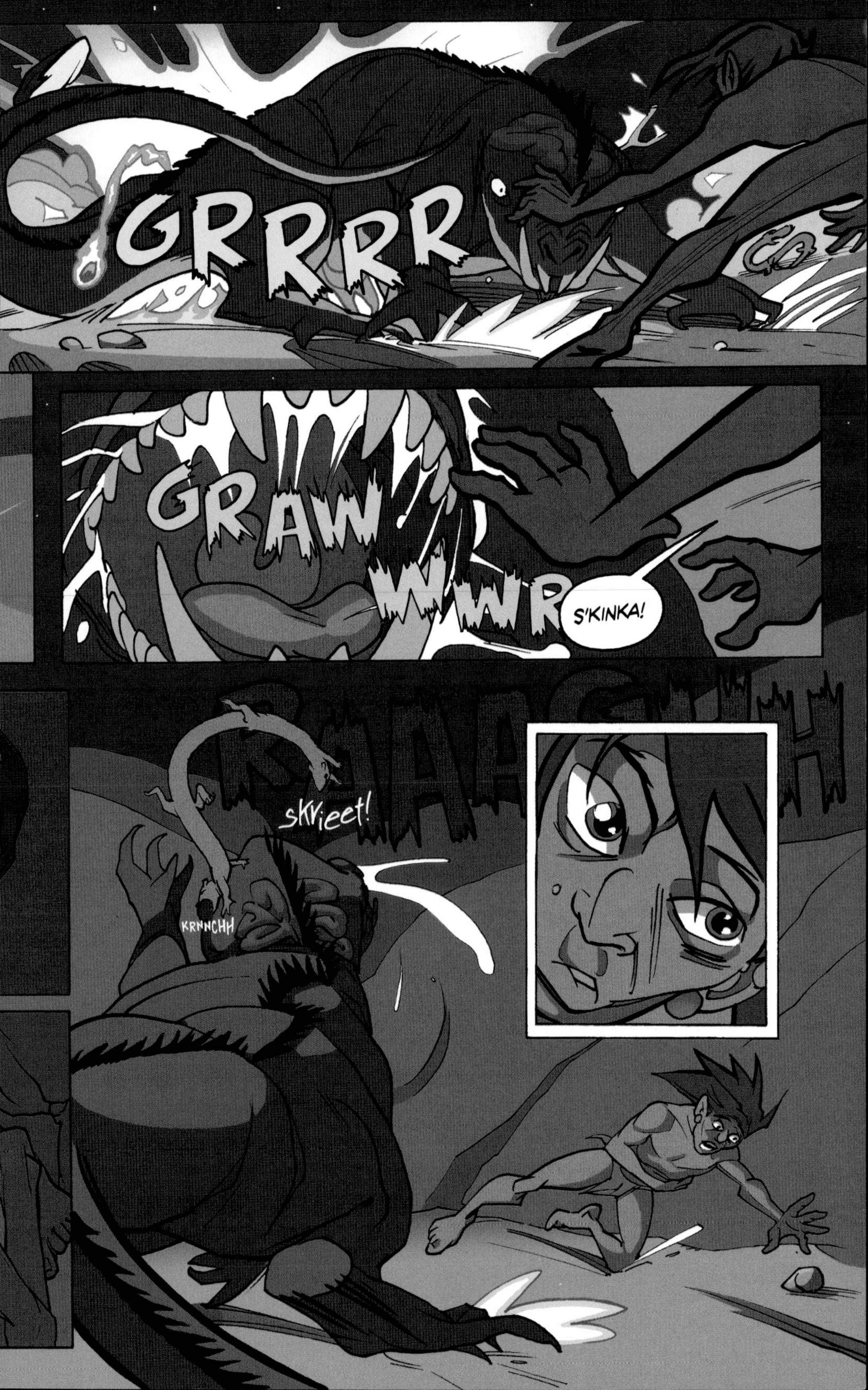
GRRRR
GRAW
WWR
S'KINKA!
skrieet!
KRNNCHH

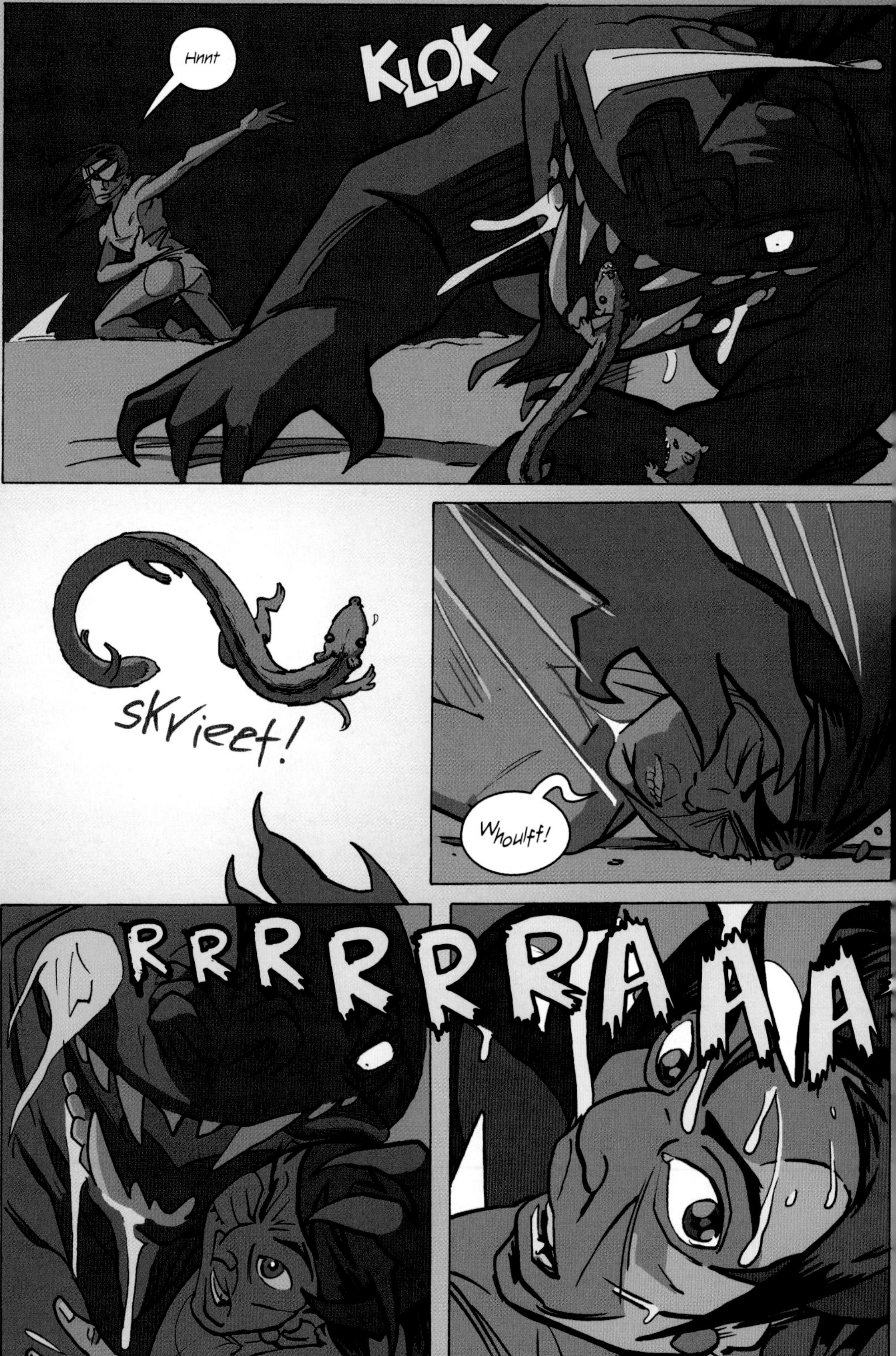
Hnnt
KLOK
sKvieet!
Whoulff!
RRRRRRAAA

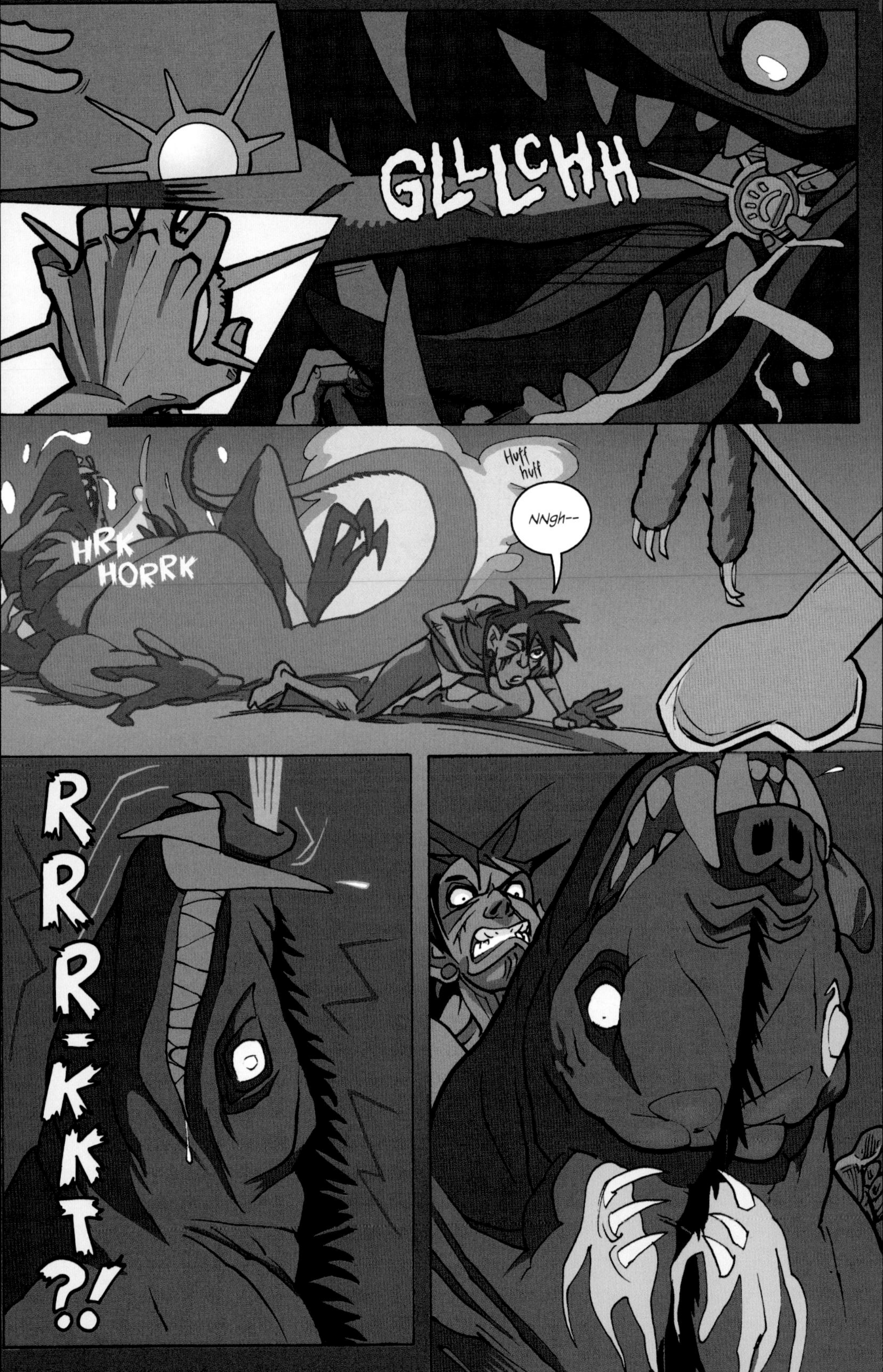
GLLLCHH
HRK HORRK
Huff huff
NNgh--
RRR-KKT?!

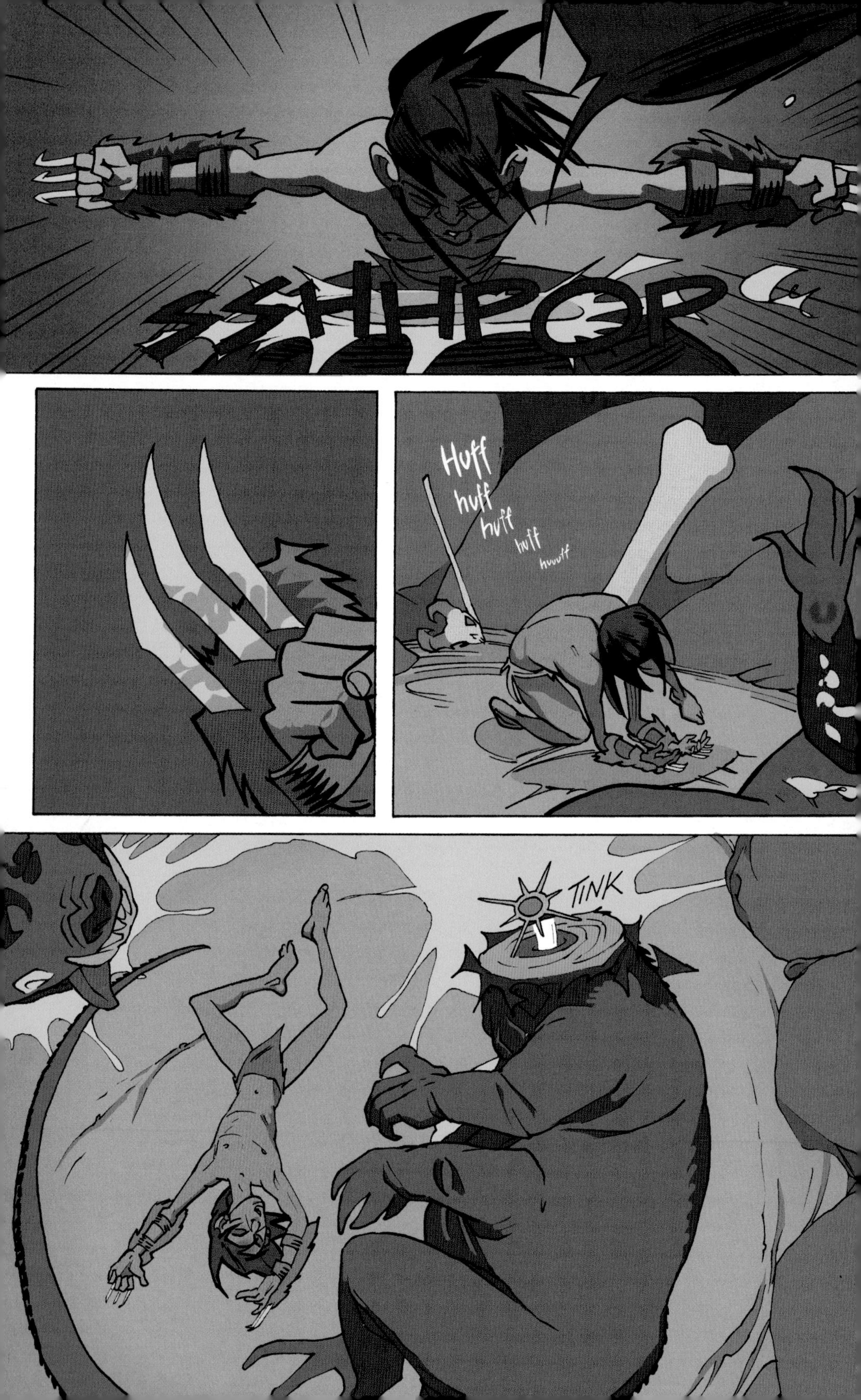
SSHPOP
Huff
huff
huff
huff
huuuff
TINK

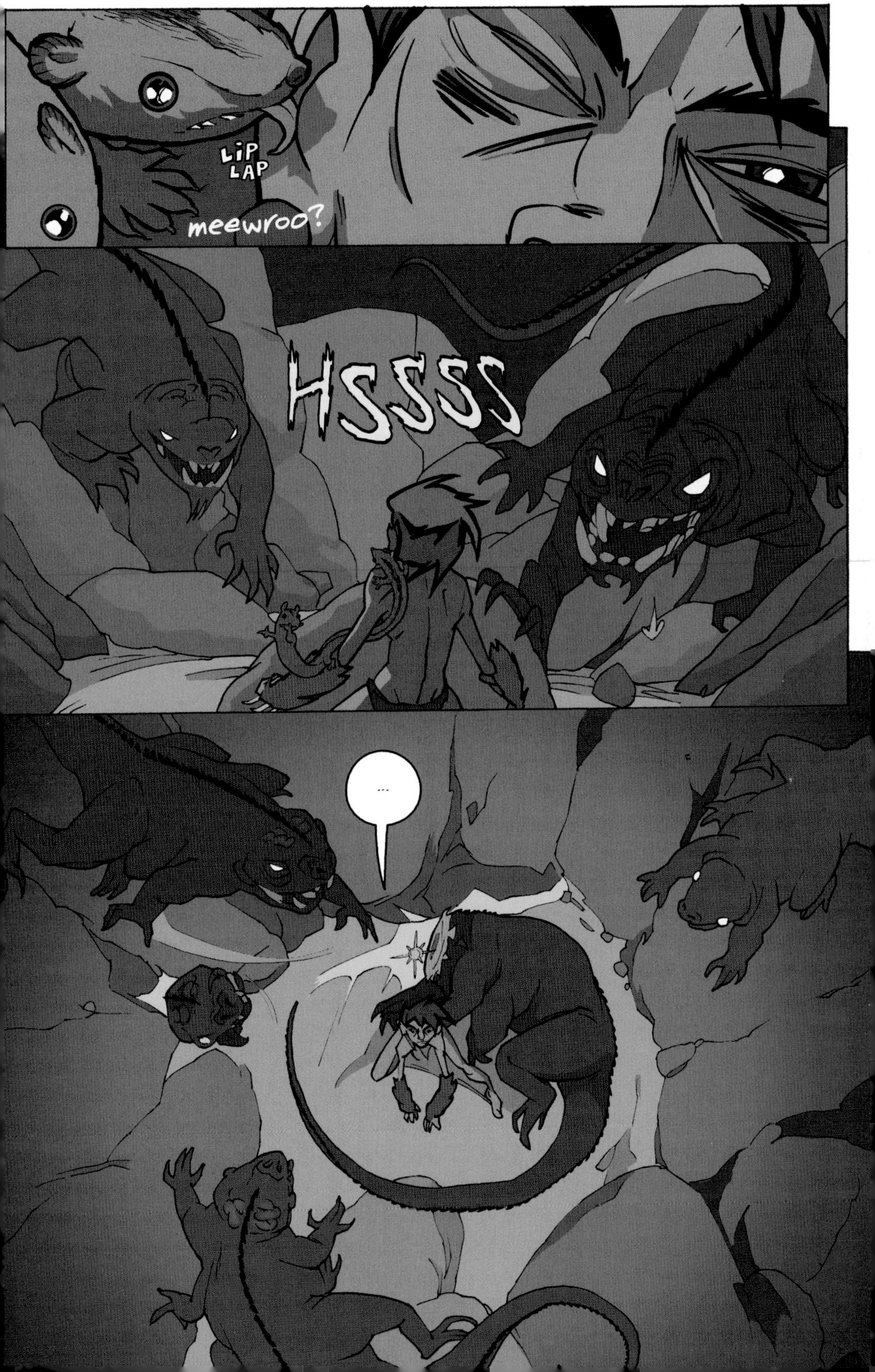

LIP
LAP
meewroo?
HSSSS
...

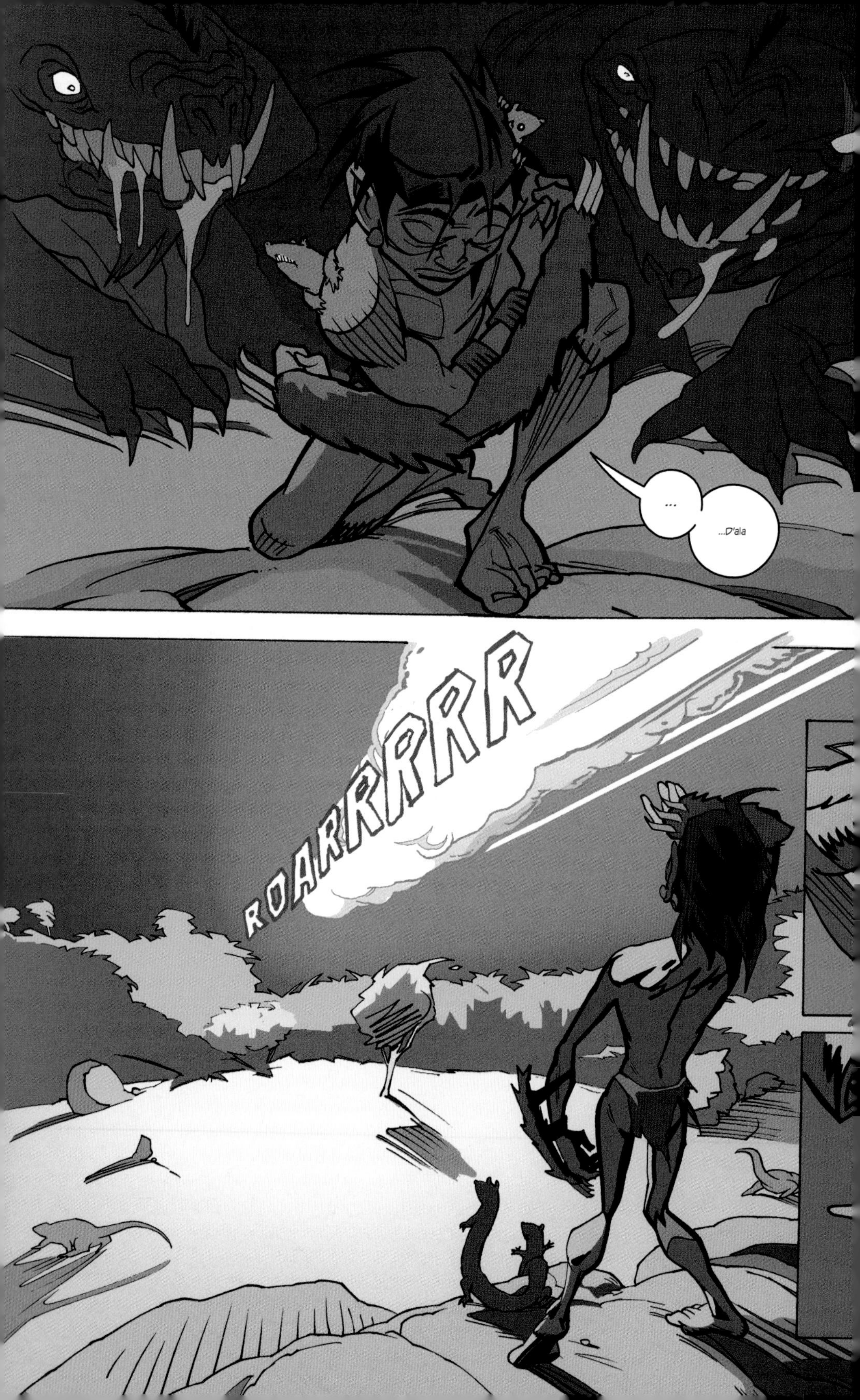
...
...D'ala
ROARRRRRR

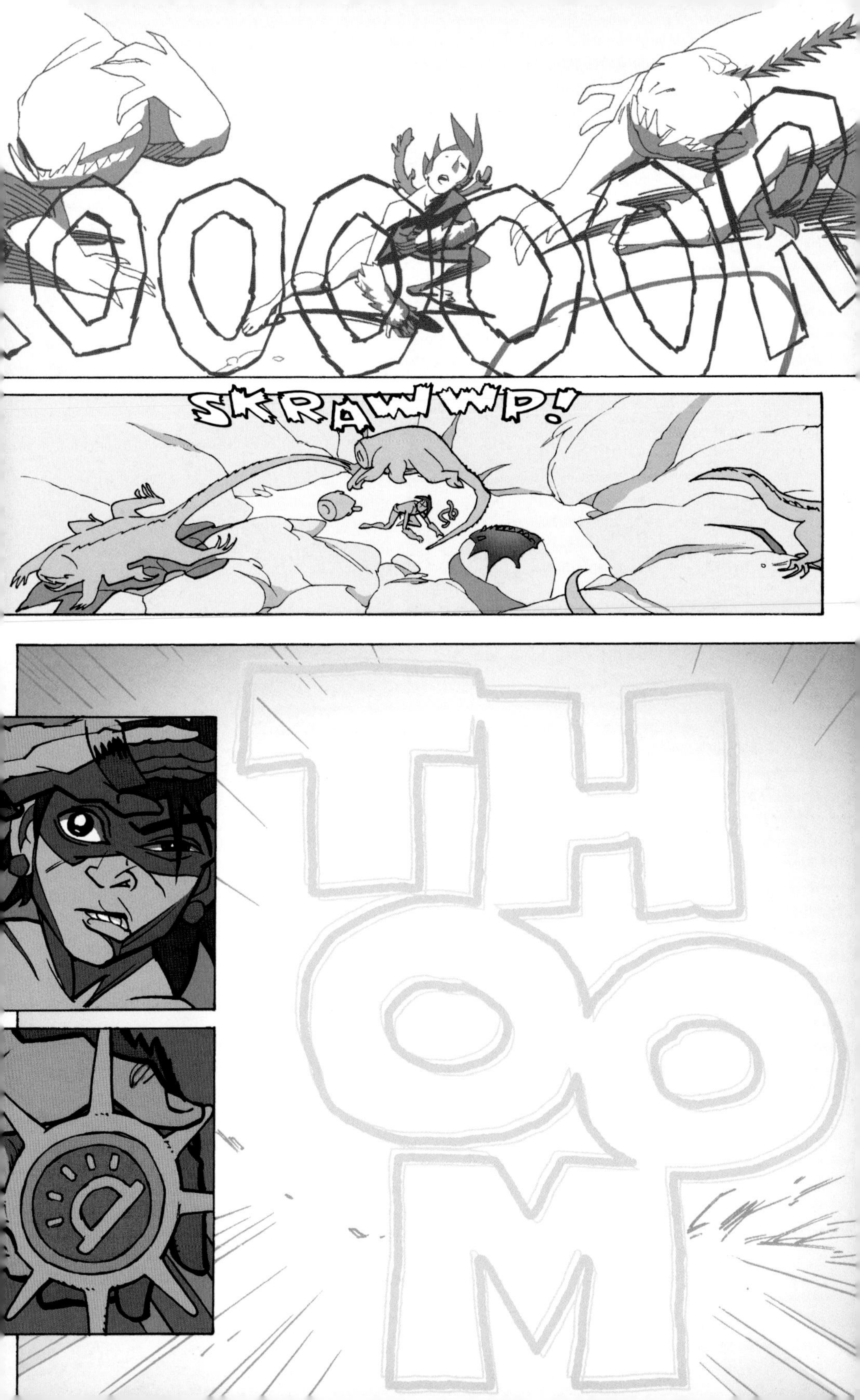
SKRAWWP!
THOOM

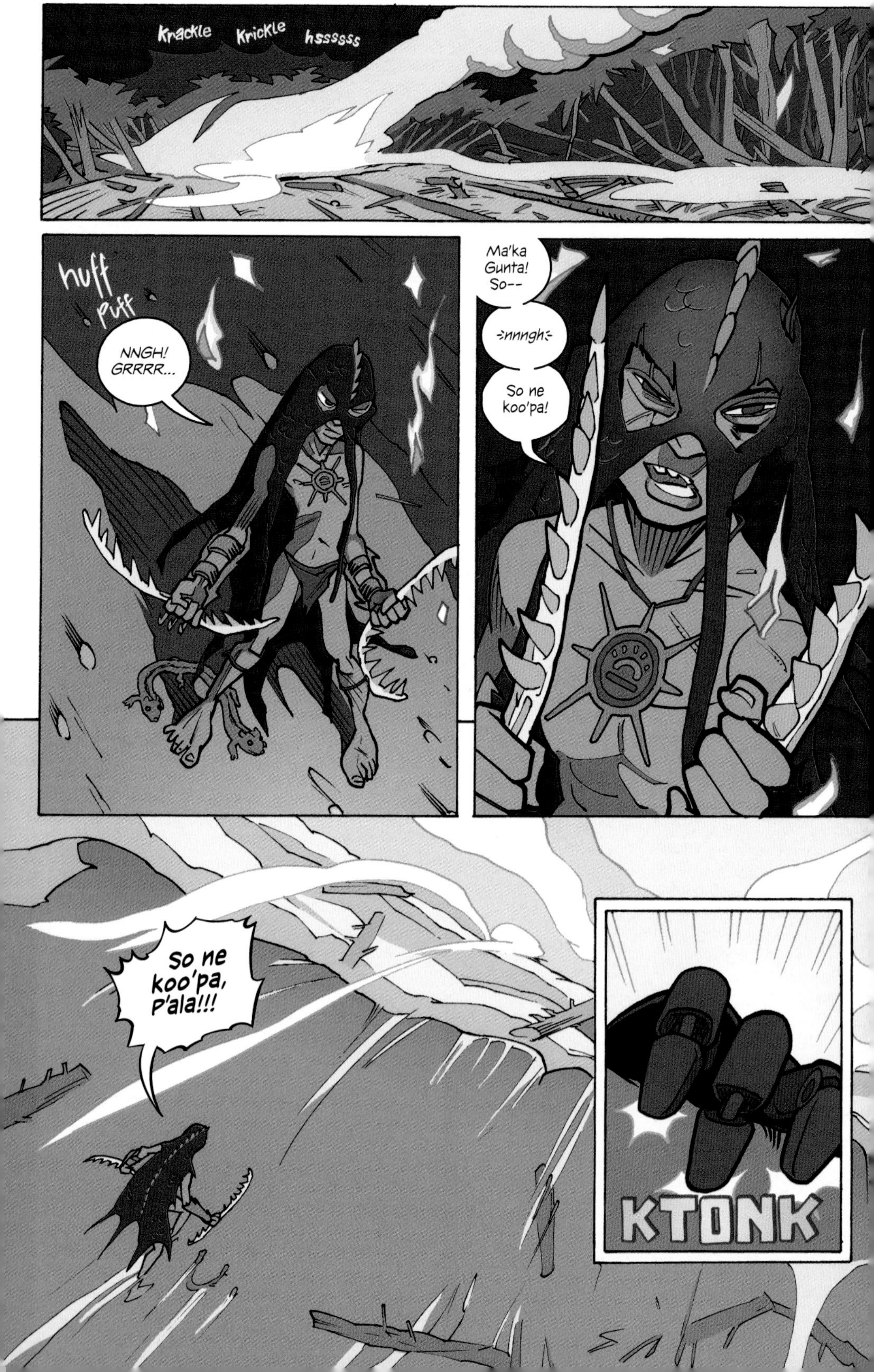
Krackle
Krickle
hssssss
huff
puff
NNGH! GRRRR...
Ma'ka Gunta! So--
nnngh
So ne koo'pa!
So ne koo'pa, p'ala!!!
KTONK

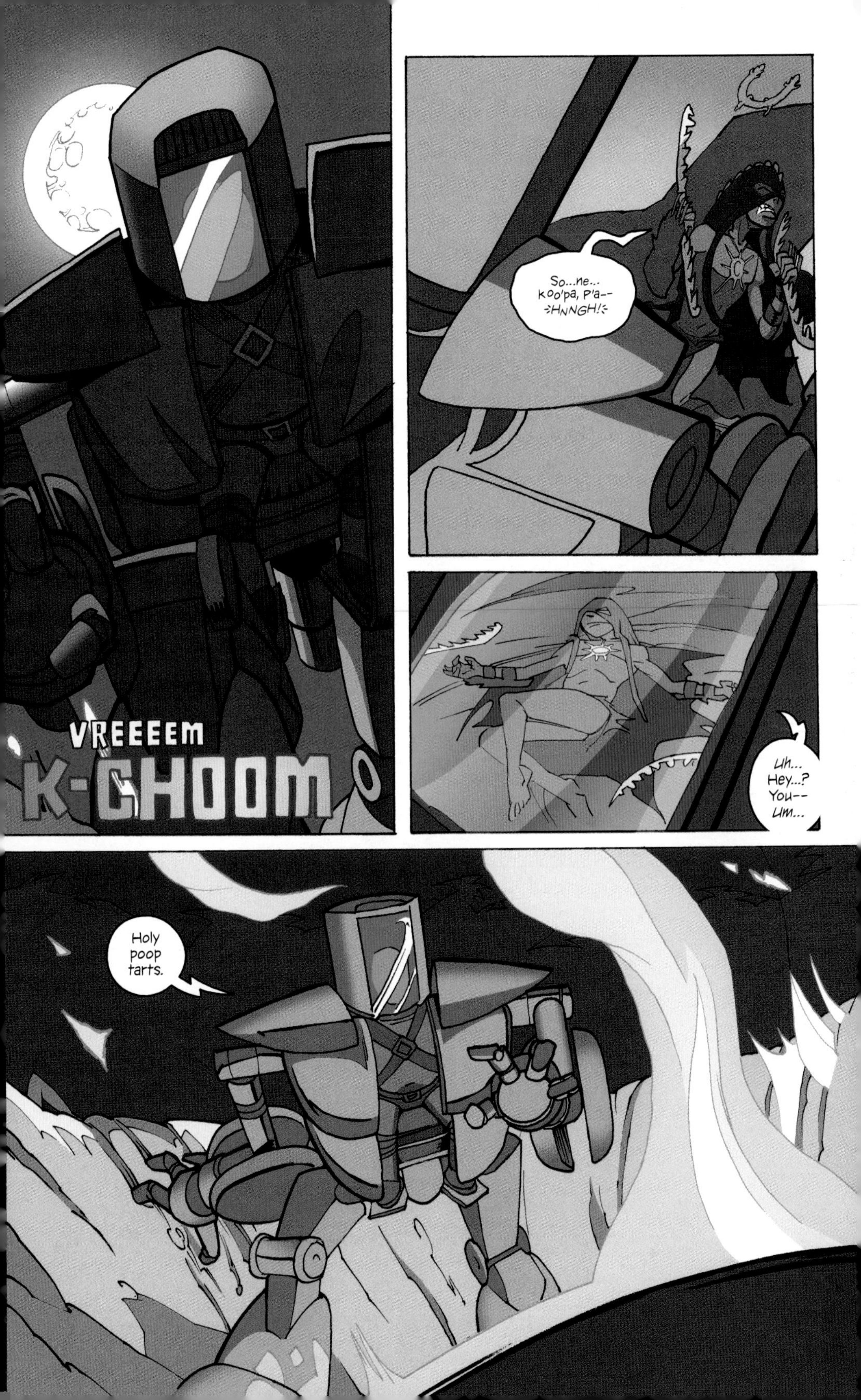
VREEEEM
K-CHOOM
So...ne... koo'pa, p'a-- HNNGH!
Uh... Hey...? You-- um...
Holy poop tarts.

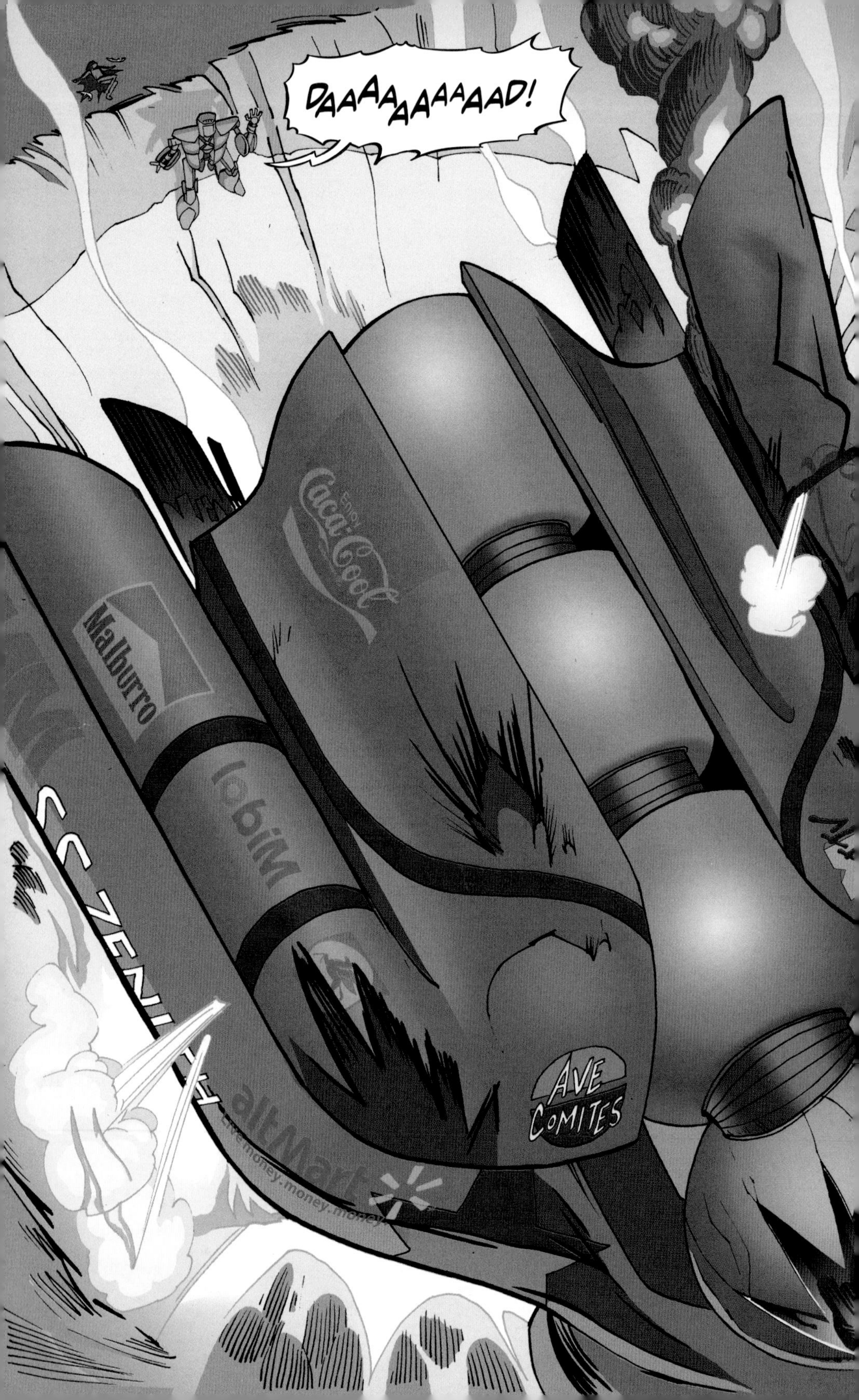
DAAAAAAAAAAD!
Malburro
Enjoy Caca Cool
AVE COMITES
altMart

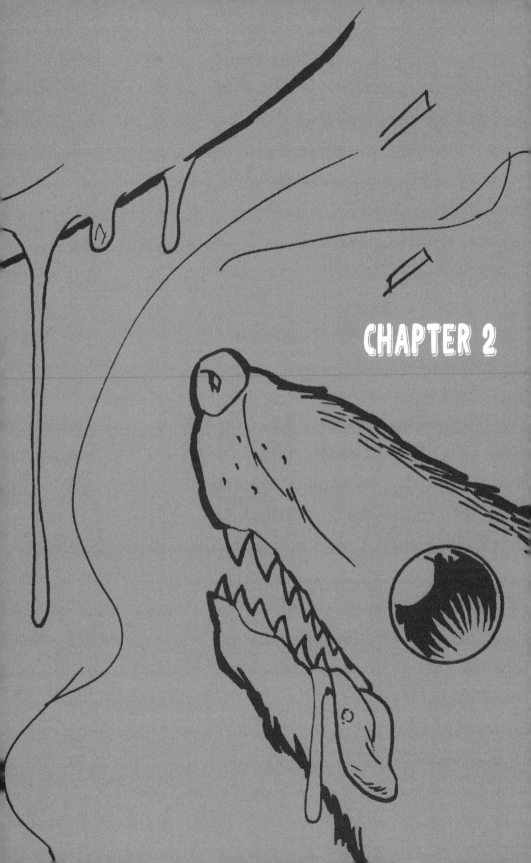

CHAPTER 2

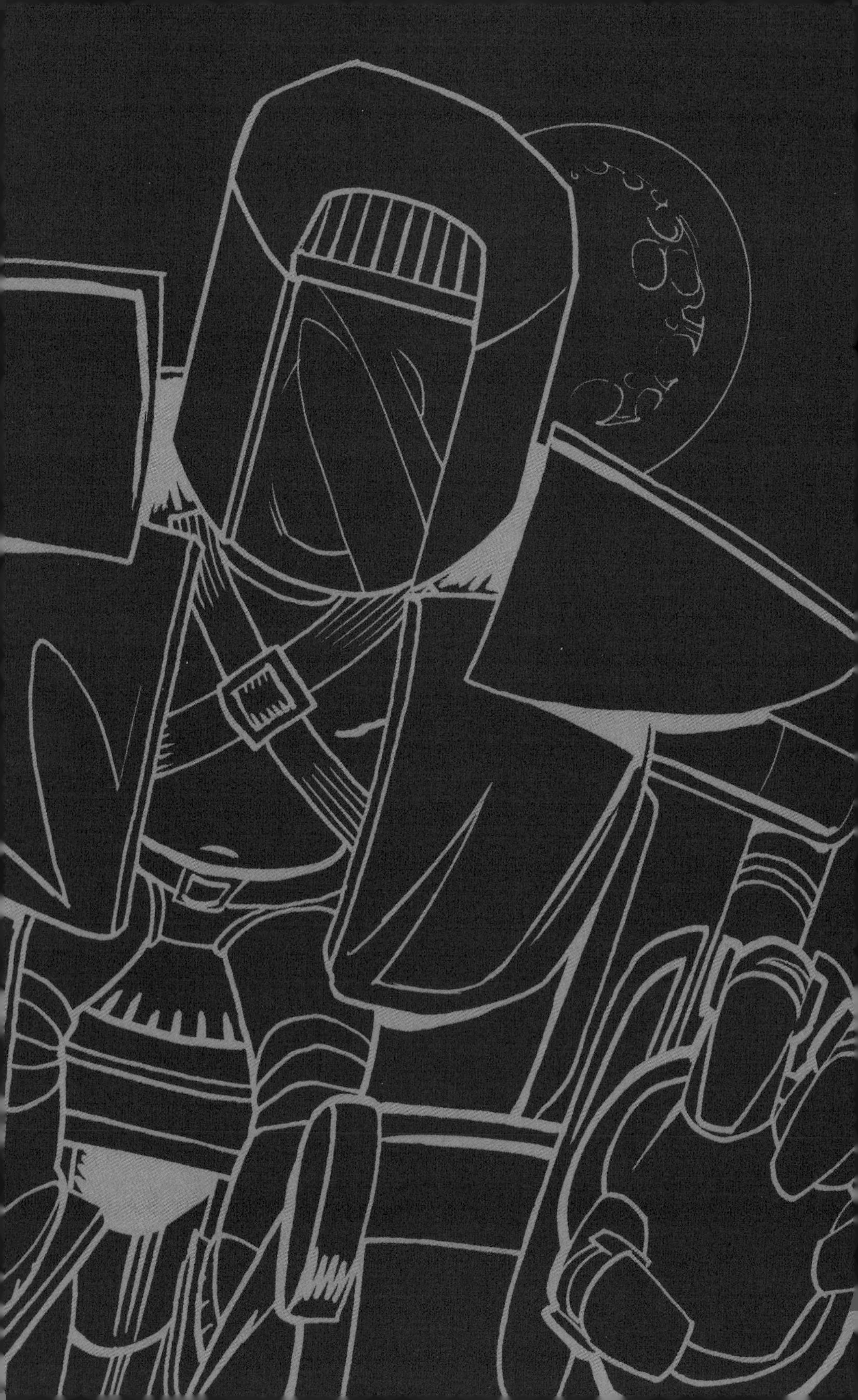

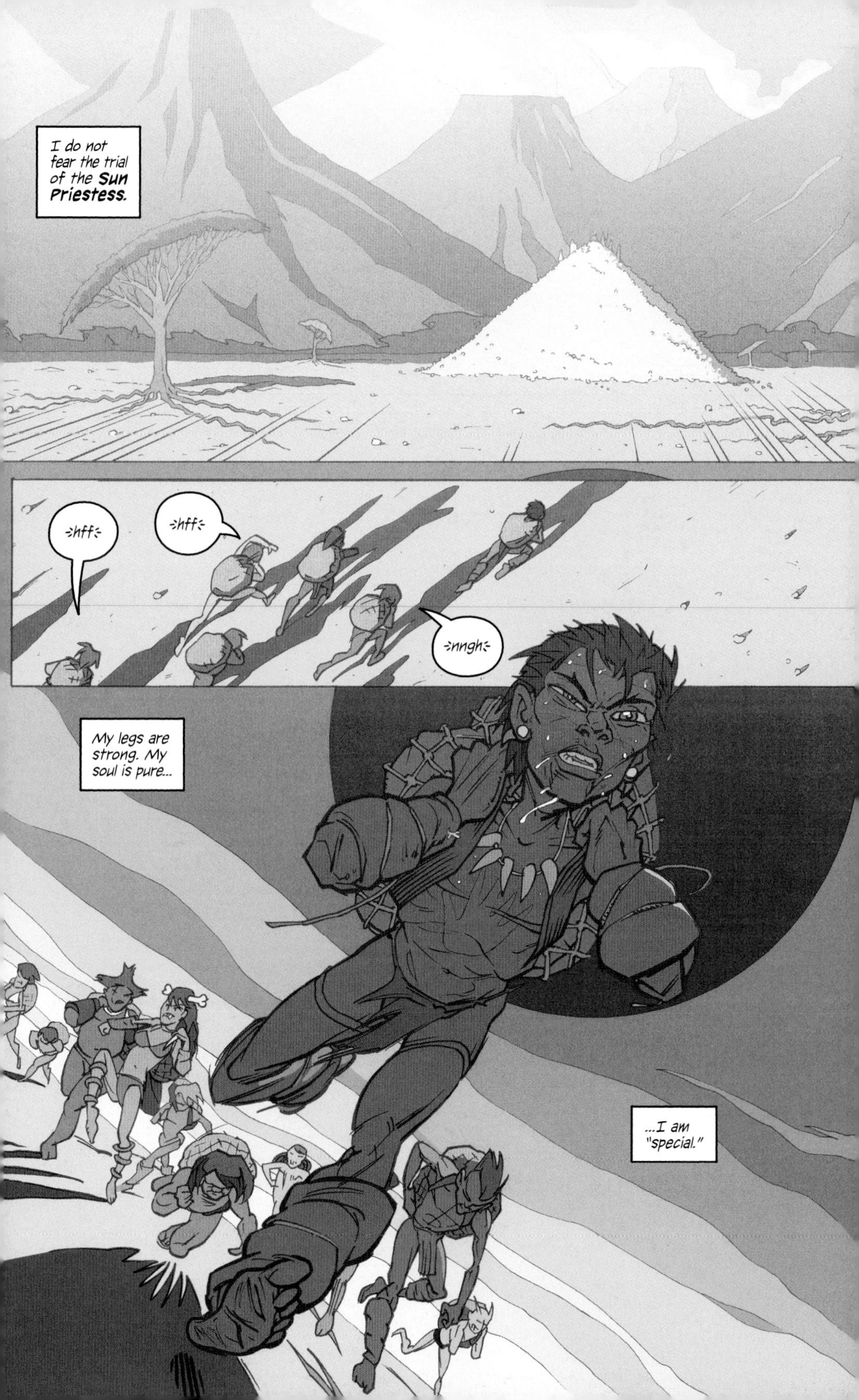
I do not fear the trial of the **Sun Priestess.**
hff
hff
nngh
My legs are strong. My soul is pure...
...I am "special."

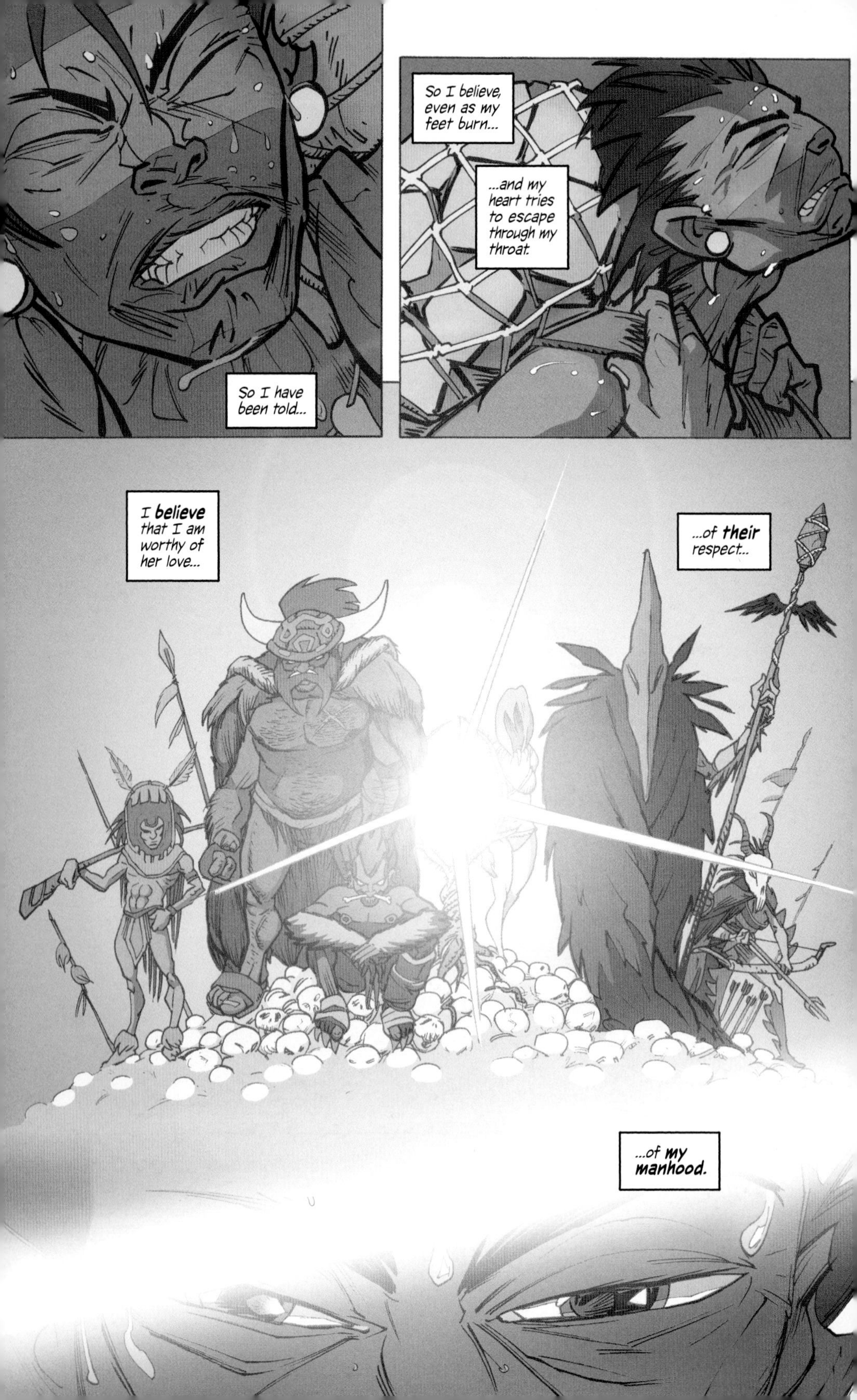

So I have been told...
So I believe, even as my feet burn...
...and my heart tries to escape through my throat.
I believe that I am worthy of her love...
...of their respect...
...of my manhood.

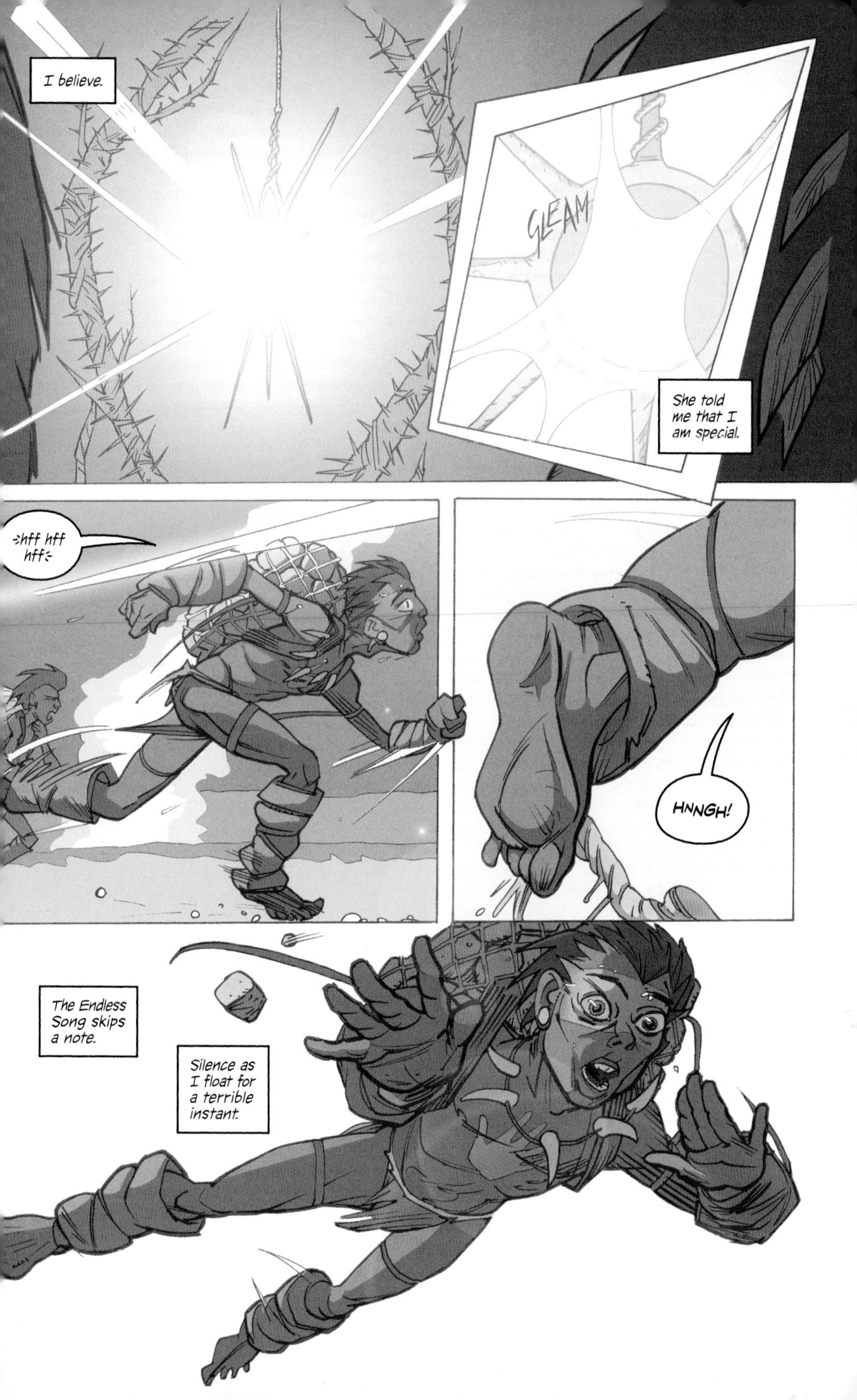
I believe.
GLEAM
She told me that I am special.
hff hff hff
HNNGH!
The Endless Song skips a note.
Silence as I float for a terrible instant.

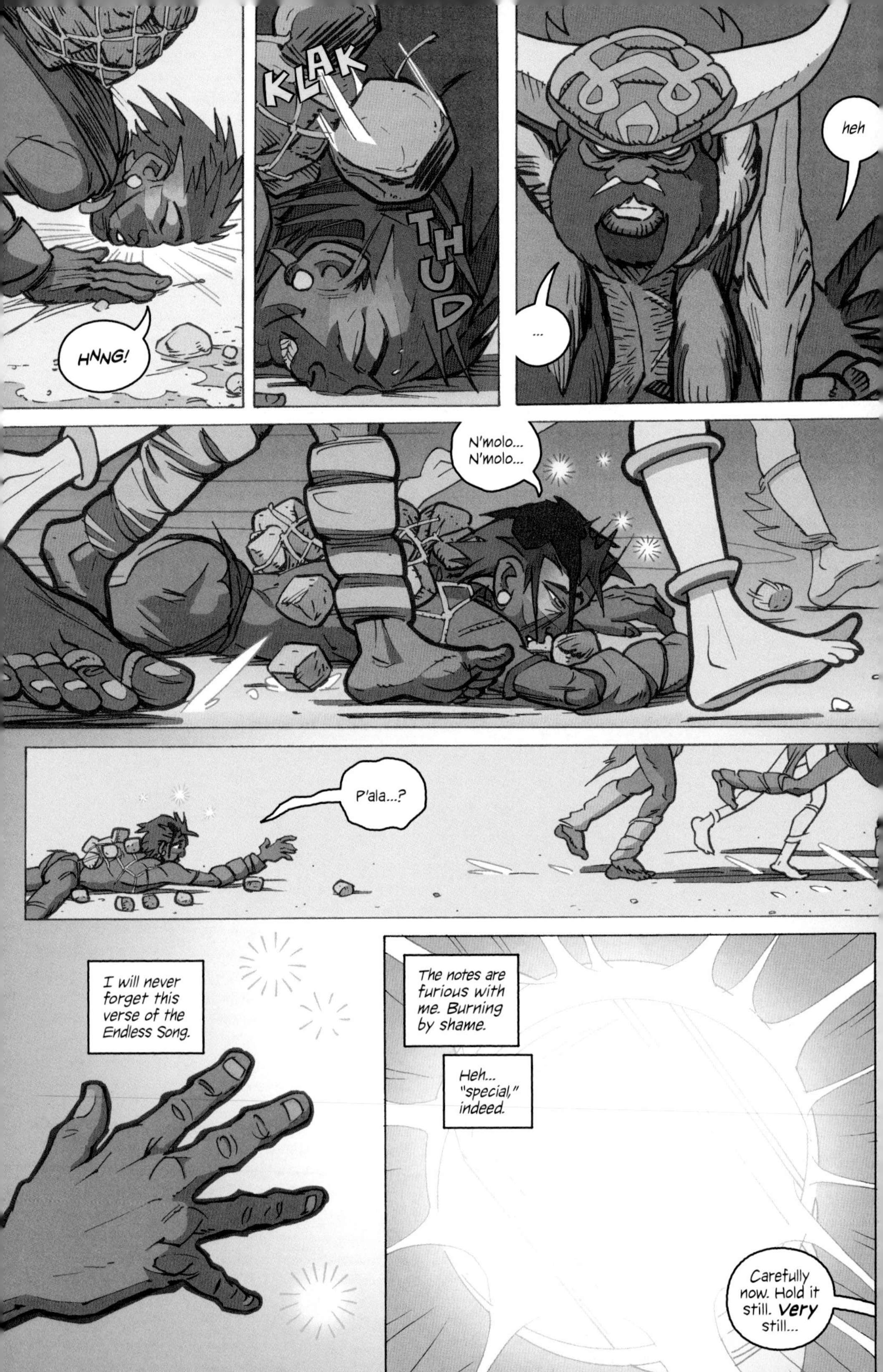
HNNG!
KLAK
THUD
...
heh
N'molo... N'molo...
P'ala...?
I will never forget this verse of the Endless Song.
The notes are furious with me. Burning by shame.
Heh... "special," indeed.
Carefully now. Hold it still. Very still...

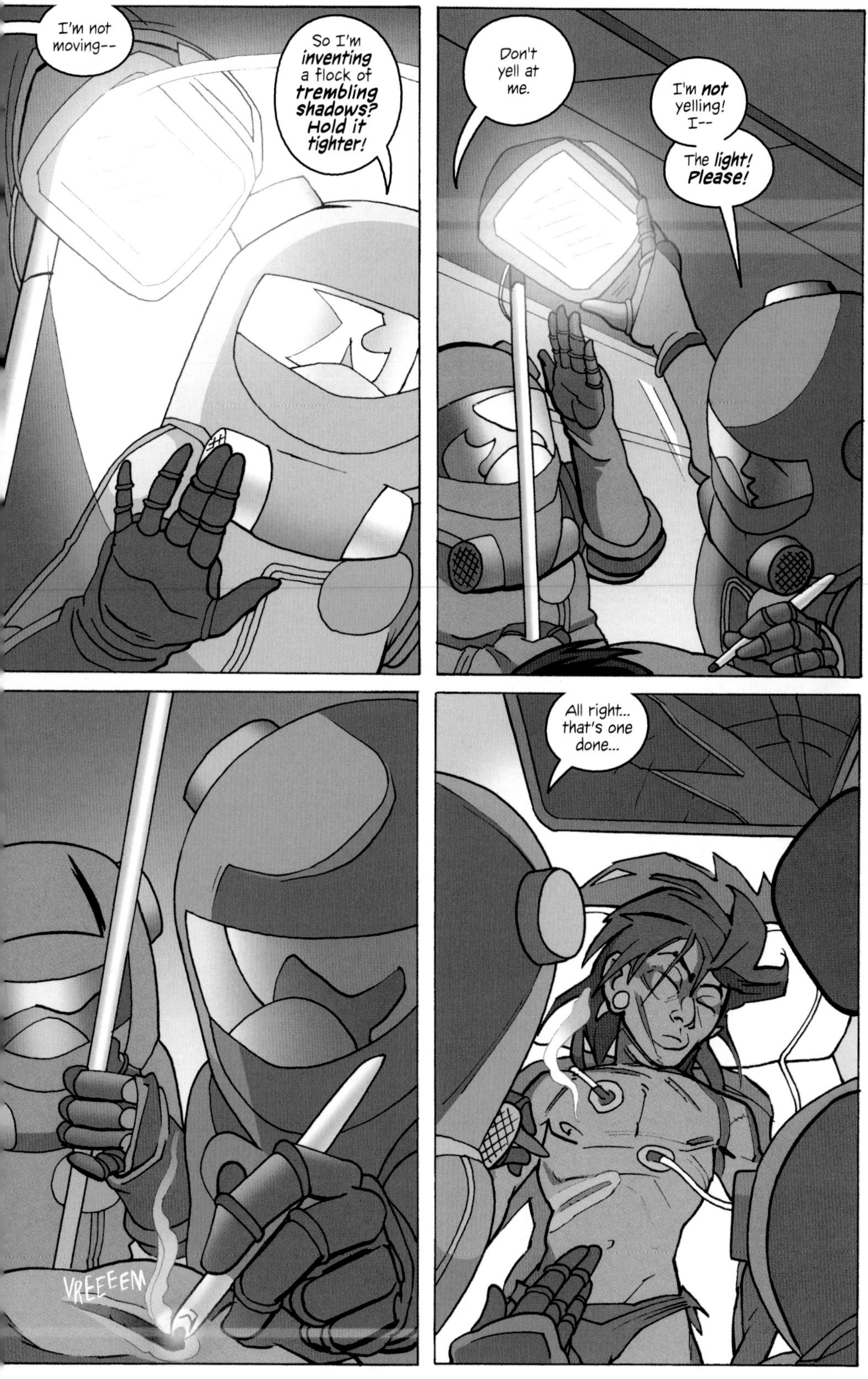
I'm not moving--
So I'm inventing a flock of trembling shadows? Hold it tighter!
Don't yell at me.
I'm not yelling! I--
The light! Please!
VREEEEM
All right... that's one done...

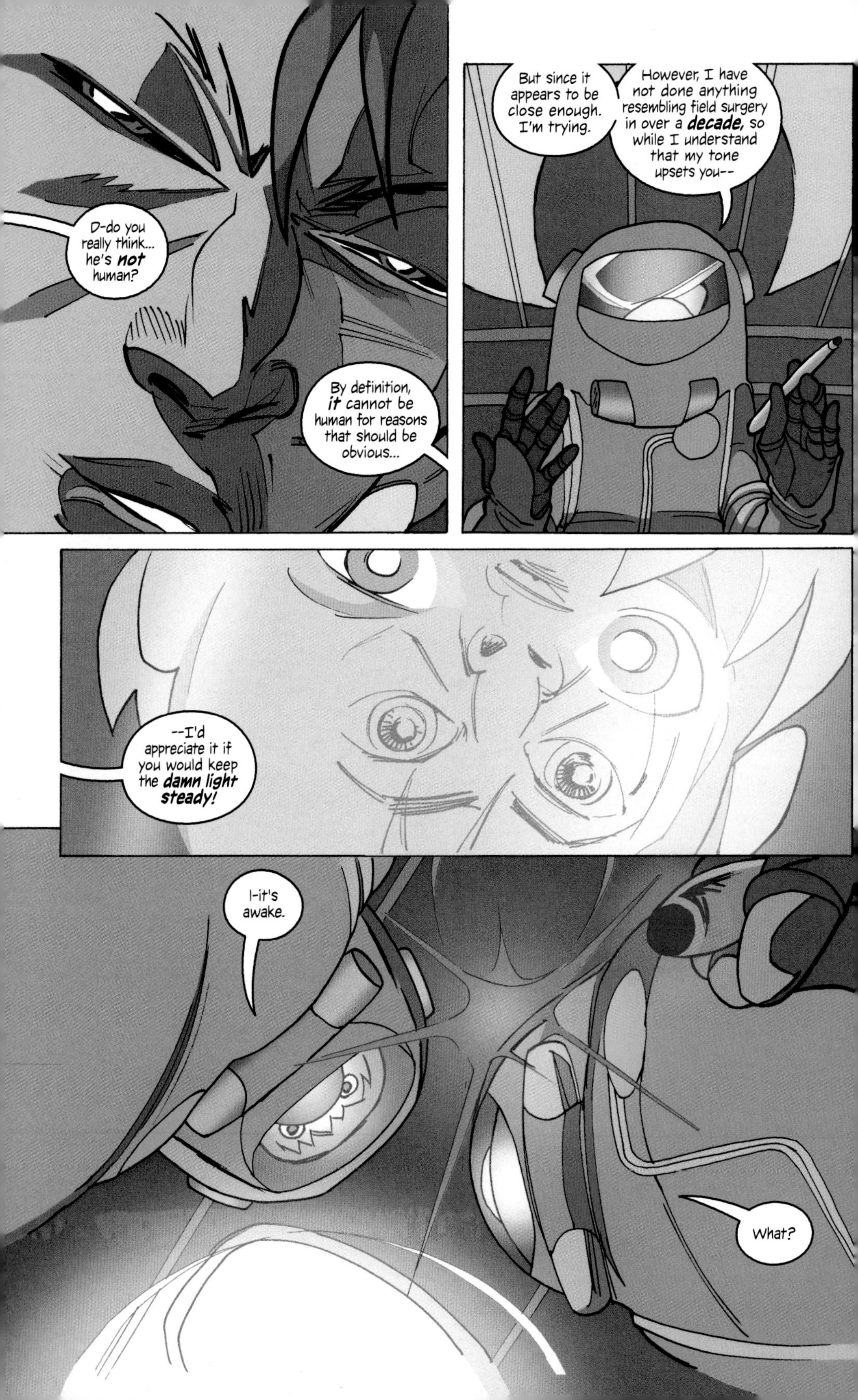

D-do you really think... he's **not** human?
By definition, ***it*** cannot be human for reasons that should be obvious...
However, I have not done anything resembling field surgery in over a ***decade,*** so while I understand that my tone upsets you--
But since it appears to be close enough. I'm trying.
--I'd appreciate it if you would keep the ***damn light steady!***
I-it's awake.
What?

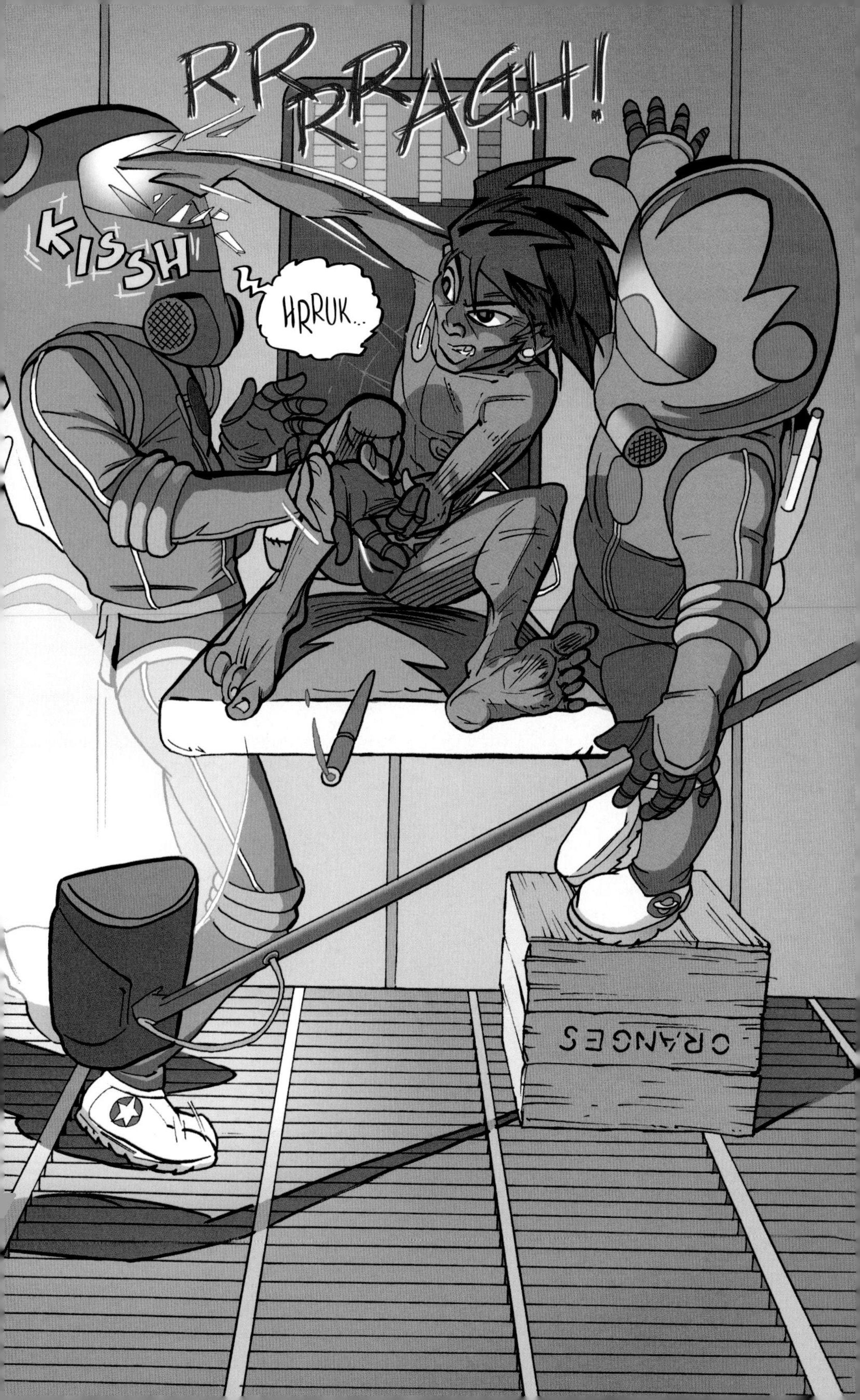
RRRRAGH!
KISSH
HRRUK...
ORANGES

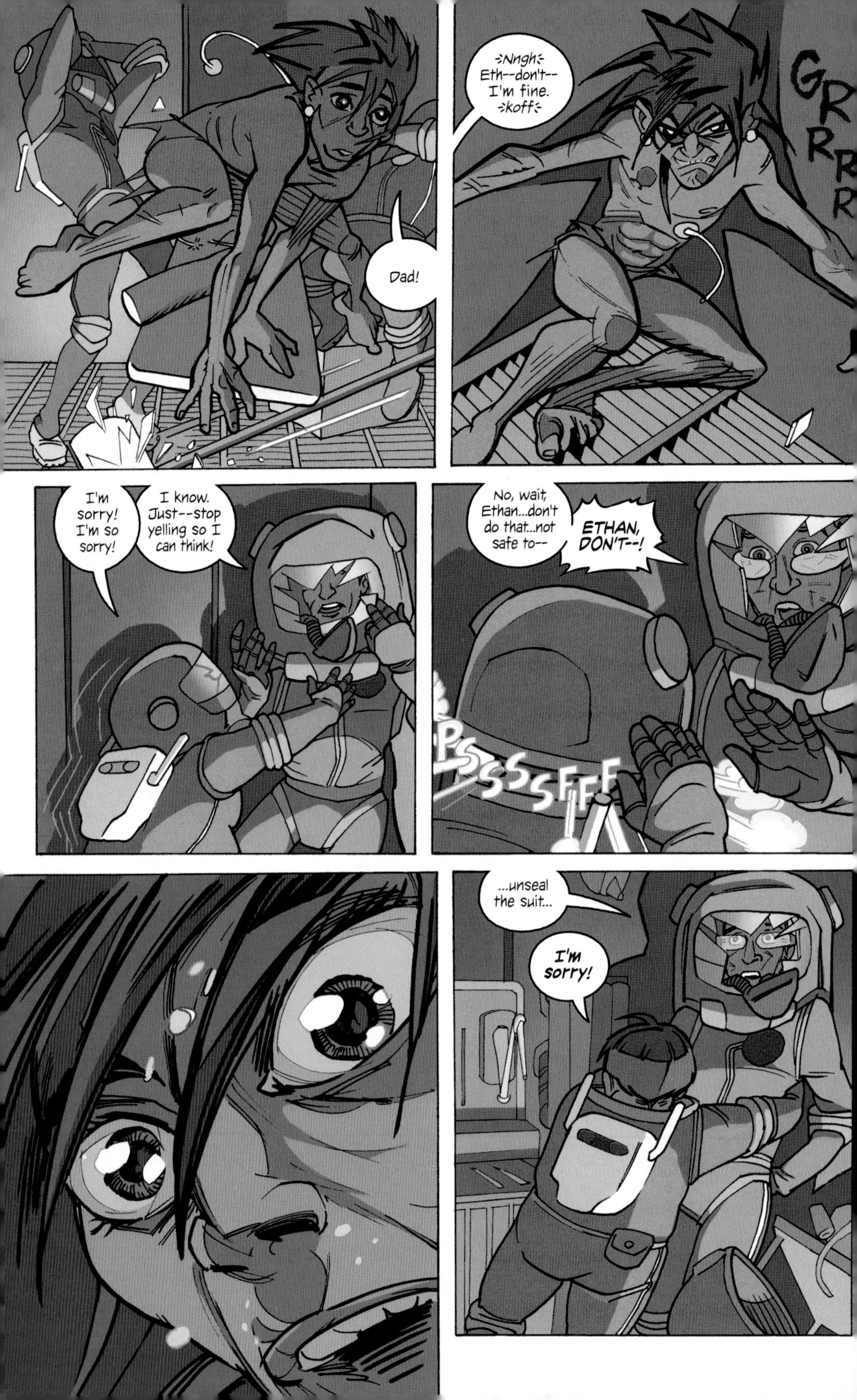
Dad!
-Nngh- Eth--don't-- I'm fine. -koff-
GRRRR
I'm sorry! I'm so sorry!
I know. Just--stop yelling so I can think!
No, wait, Ethan...don't do that...not safe to--
ETHAN, DON'T--!
PSSSSFFF
...unseal the suit...
I'm sorry!

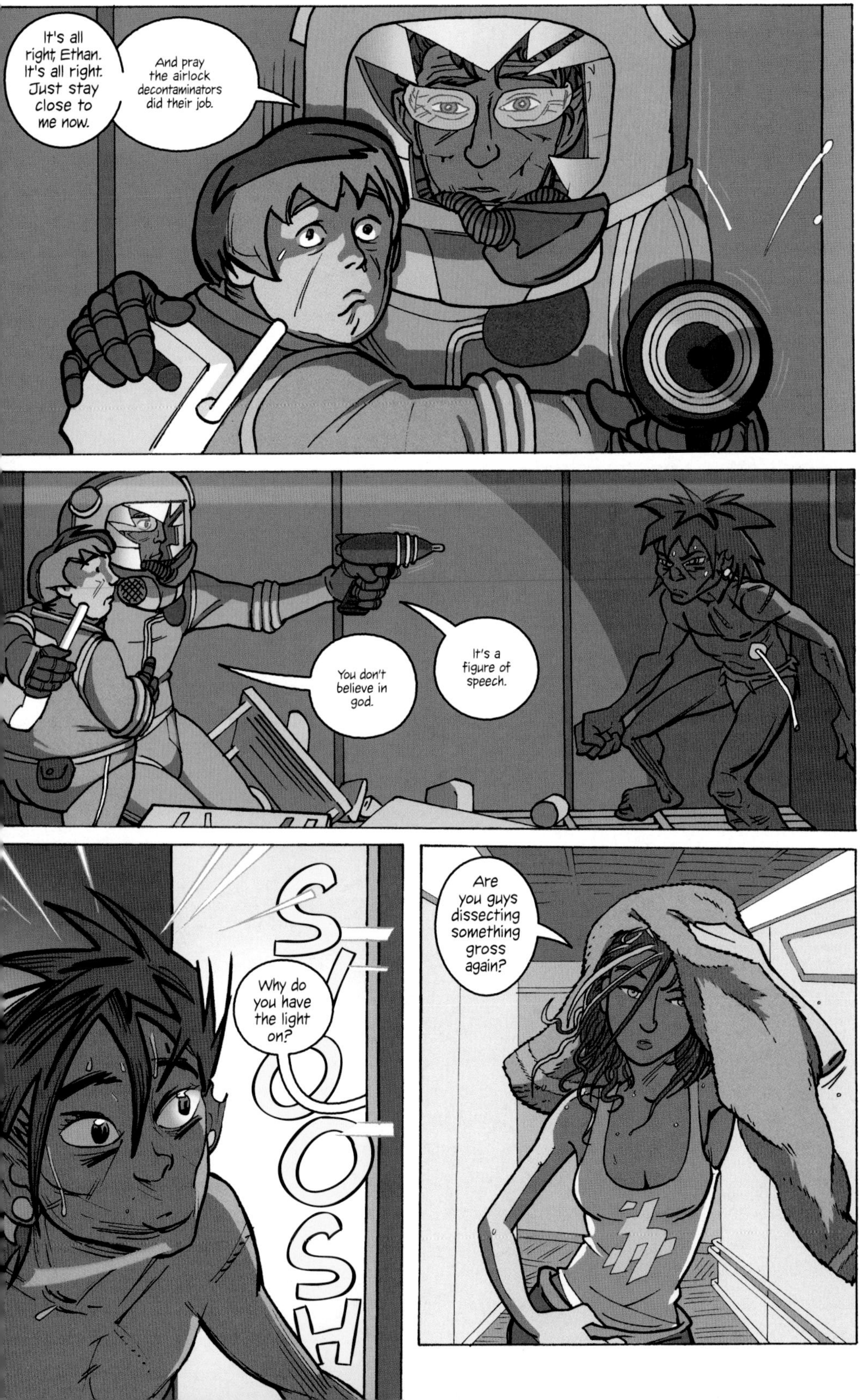
It's all right, Ethan. It's all right. Just stay close to me now.
And pray the airlock decontaminators did their job.
You don't believe in god.
It's a figure of speech.
SHOOOSH
Why do you have the light on?
Are you guys dissecting something gross again?

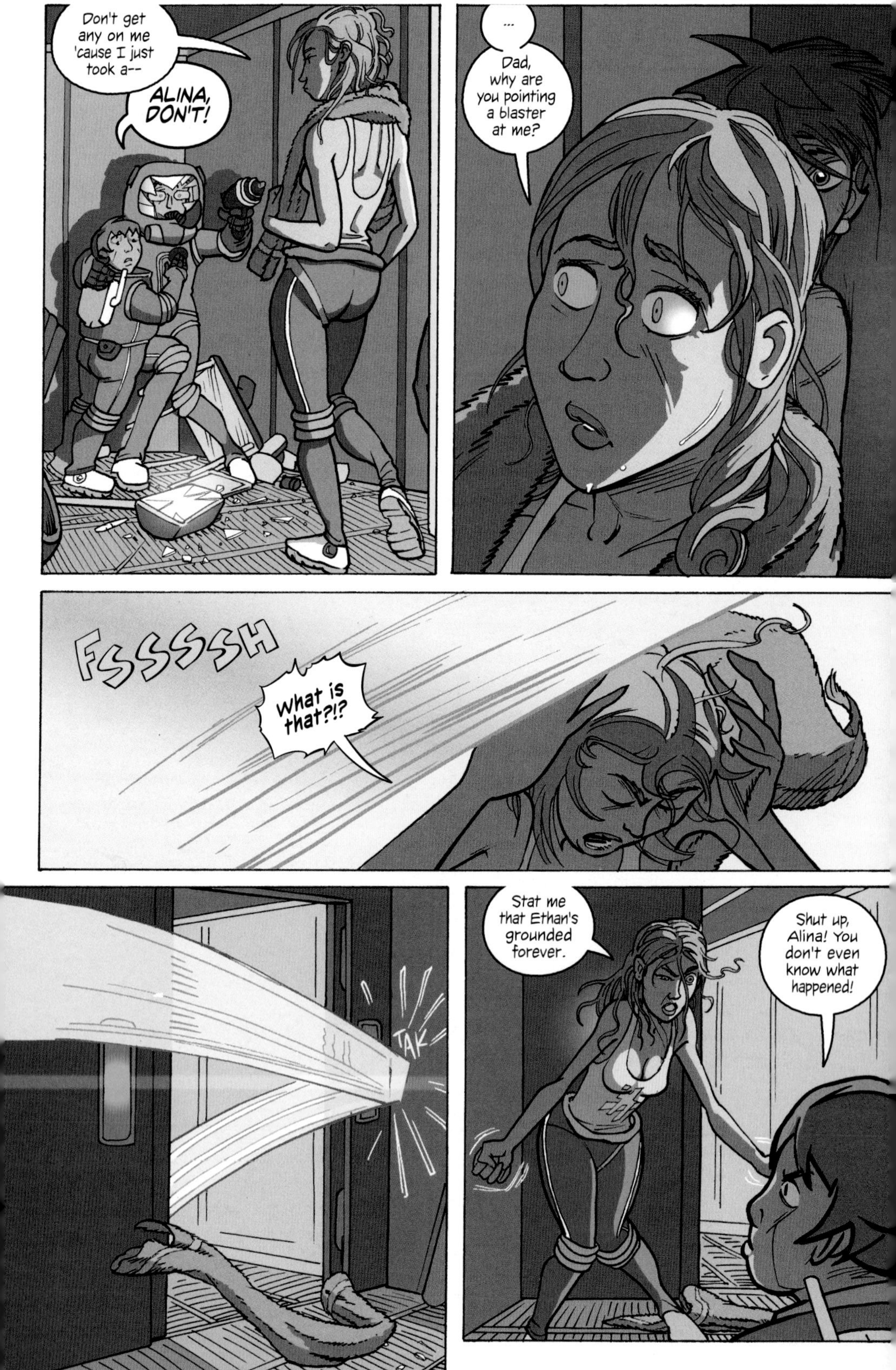
Don't get any on me 'cause I just took a--
ALINA, DON'T!
...
Dad, why are you pointing a blaster at me?
FSSSSH
What is that?!?
TAK
Stat me that Ethan's grounded forever.
Shut up, Alina! You don't even know what happened!

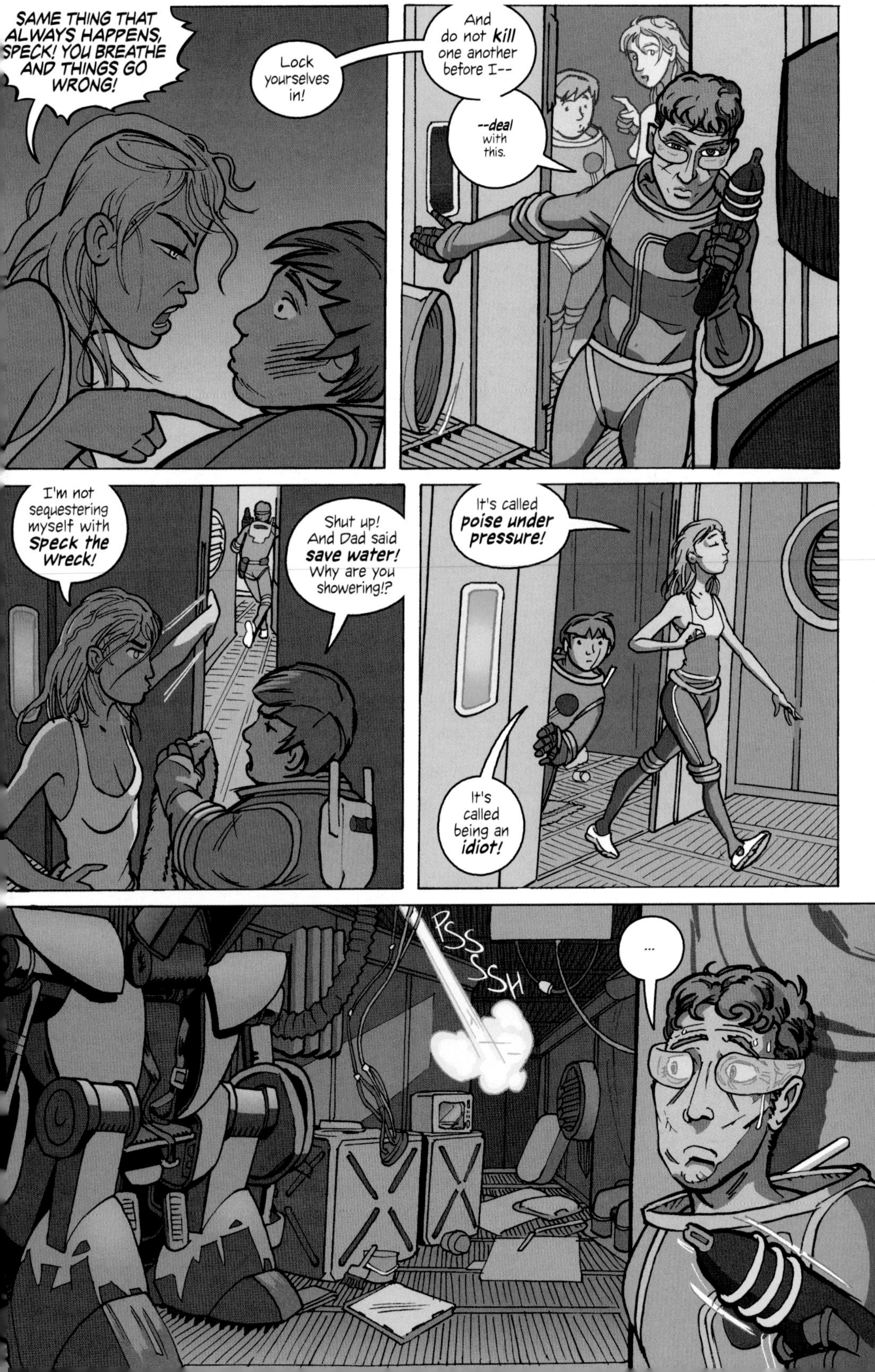
SAME THING THAT ALWAYS HAPPENS, SPECK! YOU BREATHE AND THINGS GO WRONG!
Lock yourselves in!
And do not kill one another before I--
--deal with this.
I'm not sequestering myself with Speck the Wreck!
Shut up! And Dad said save water! Why are you showering!?
It's called poise under pressure!
It's called being an idiot!
PSSSSH
...

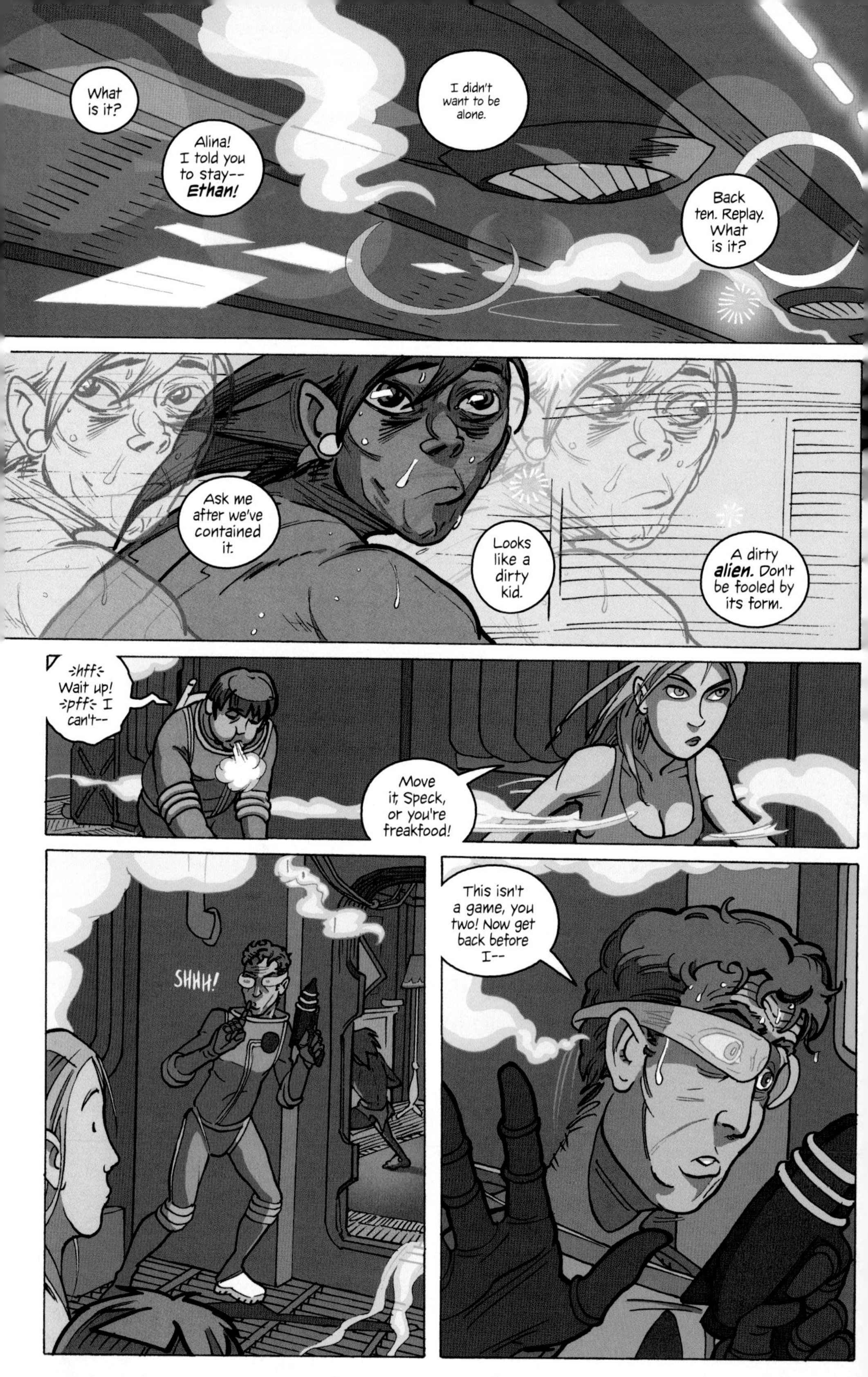
What is it?
Alina! I told you to stay-- *Ethan!*
I didn't want to be alone.
Back ten. Replay. What is it?
Ask me after we've contained it.
Looks like a dirty kid.
A dirty *alien.* Don't be fooled by its form.
hff Wait up! *pff* I can't--
Move it, Speck, or you're freakfood!
SHHH!
This isn't a game, you two! Now get back before I--

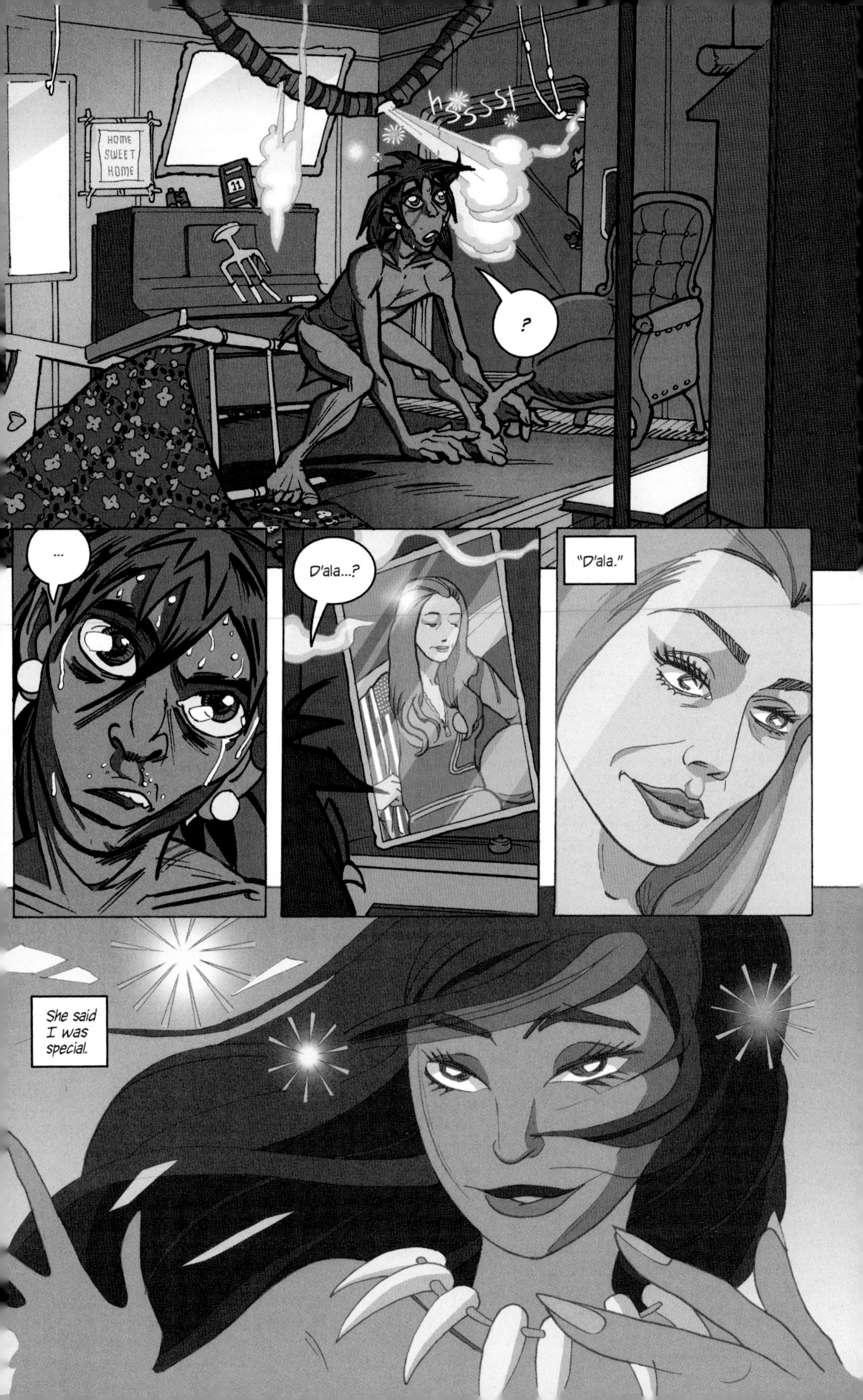
HOME
SWEET
HOME
11
hsssst
?
...
D'ala...?
"D'ala."
She said
I was
special.

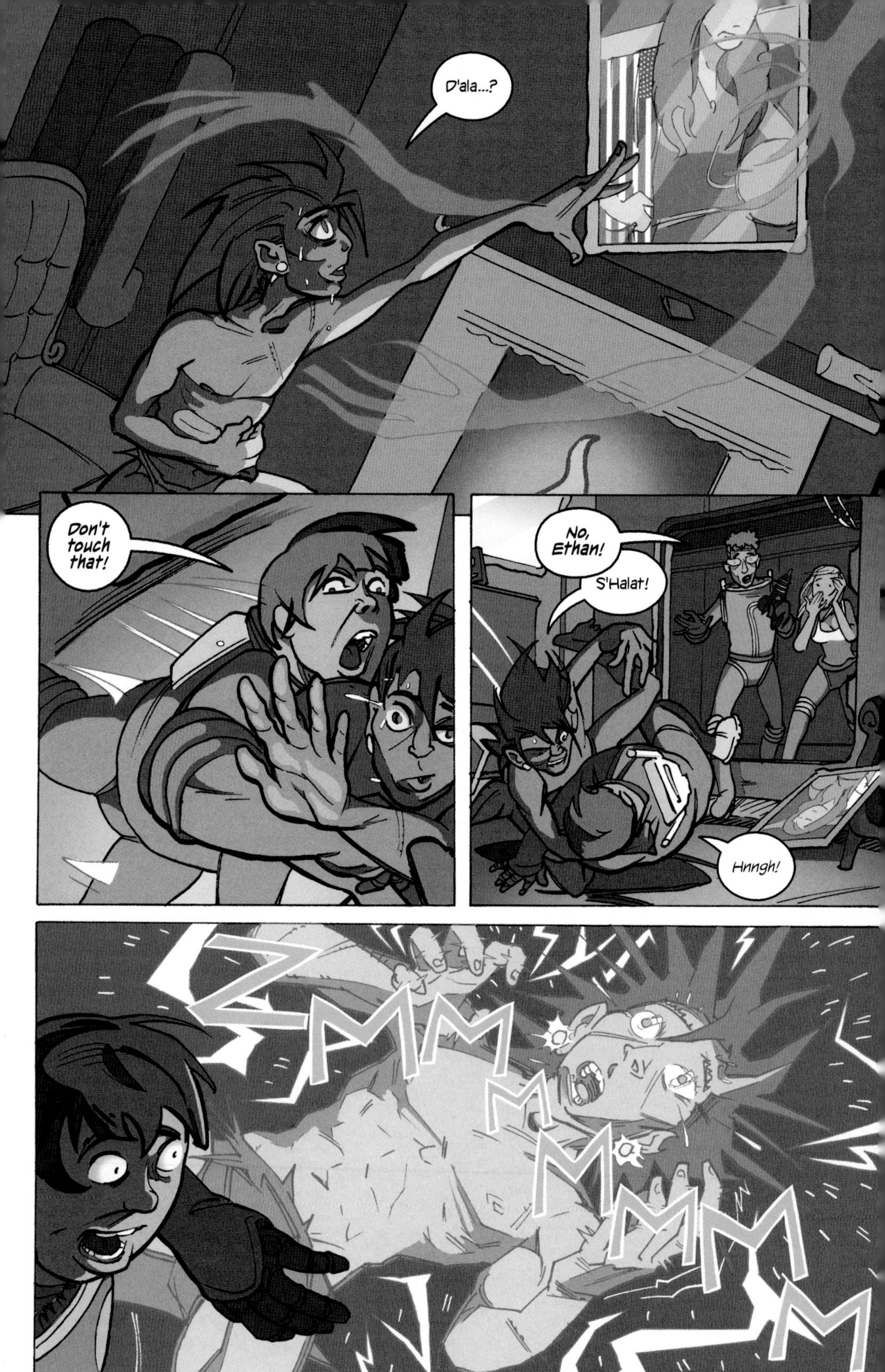
D'ala...?
Don't touch that!
No, Ethan!
S'Halat!
Hnngh!
ZMMMMMMMM

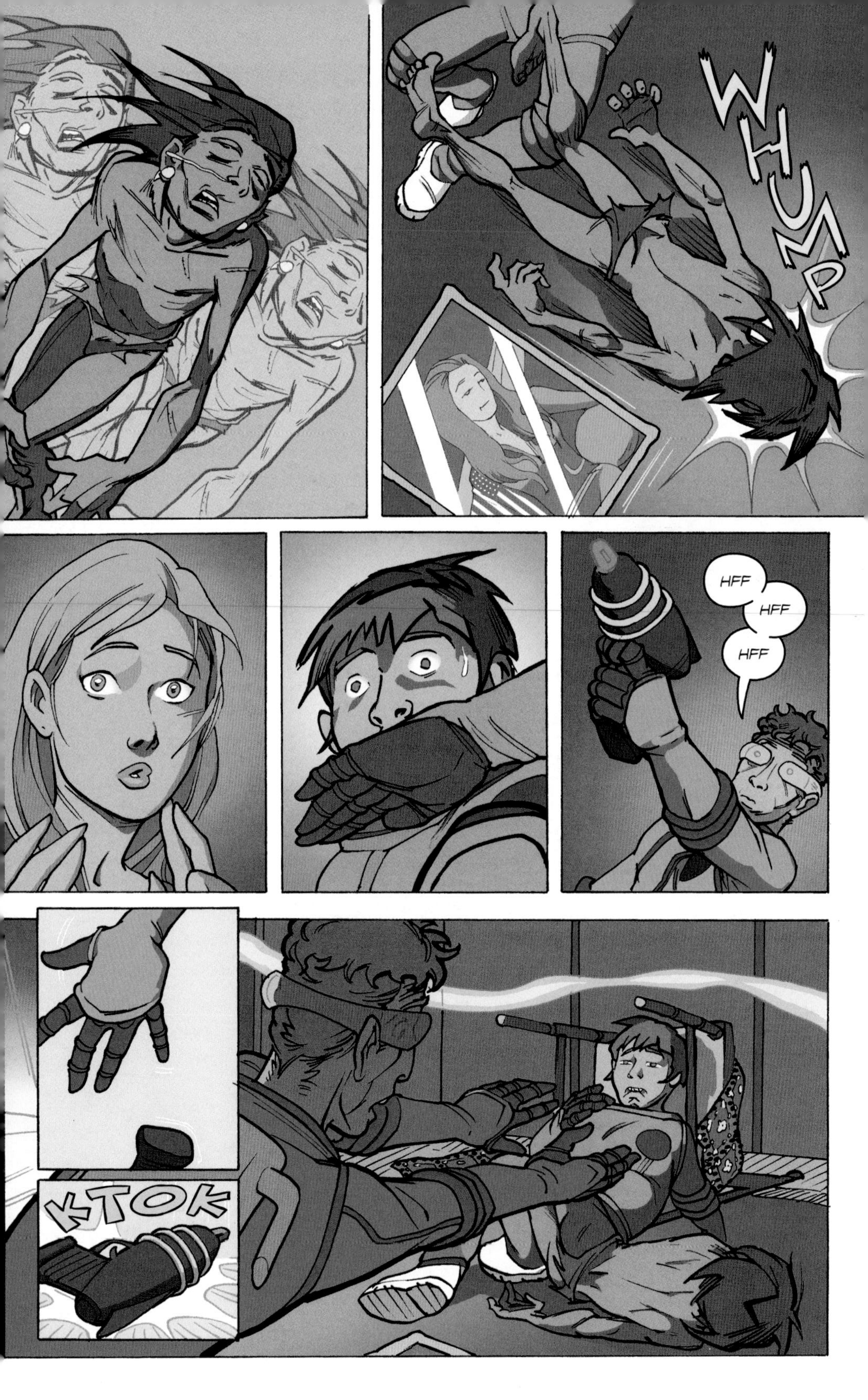
WHUMP
HFF
HFF
HFF
KTOK

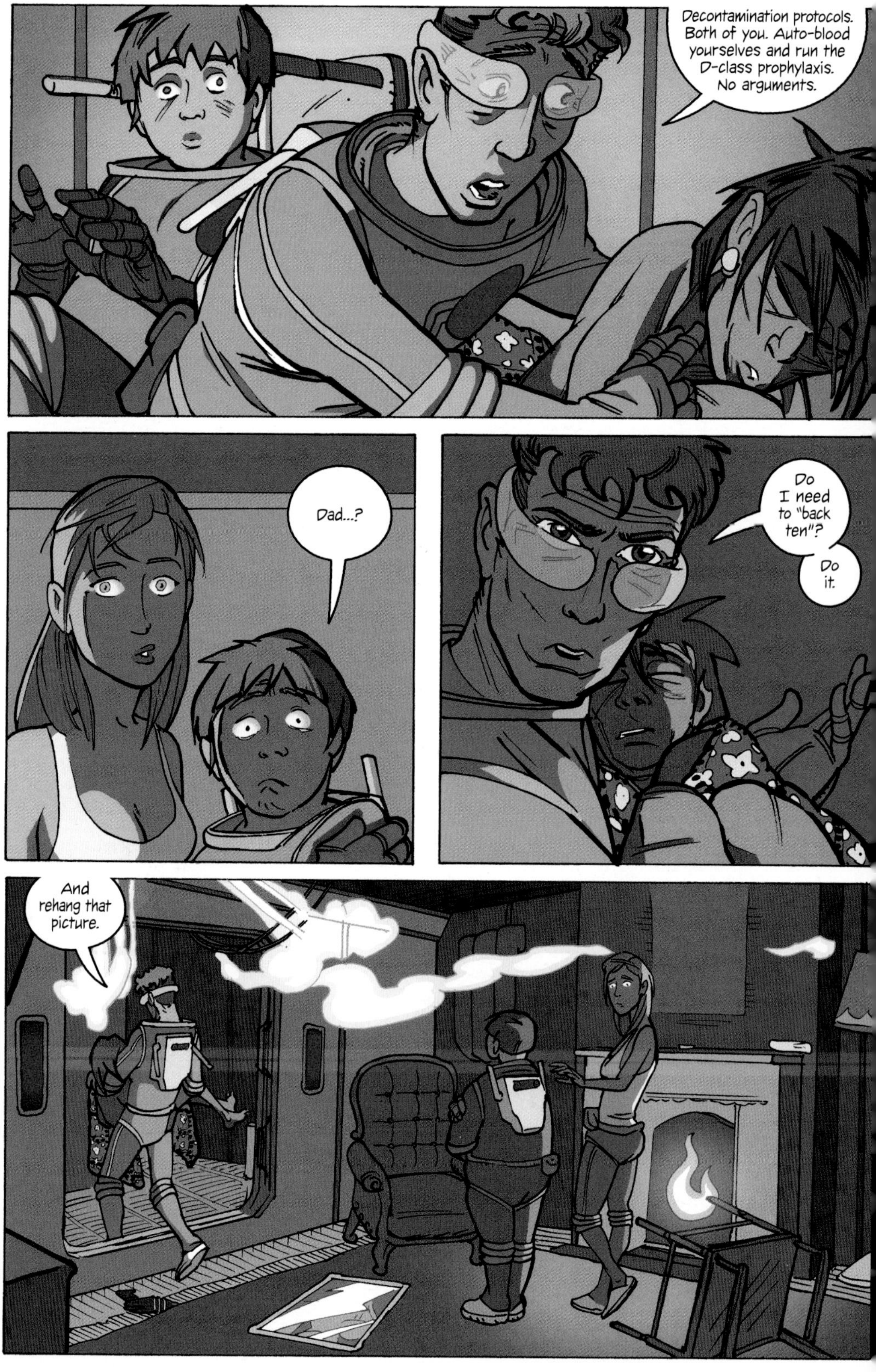
Decontamination protocols. Both of you. Auto-blood yourselves and run the D-class prophylaxis. No arguments.
Dad...?
Do I need to "back ten"?
Do it.
And rehang that picture.

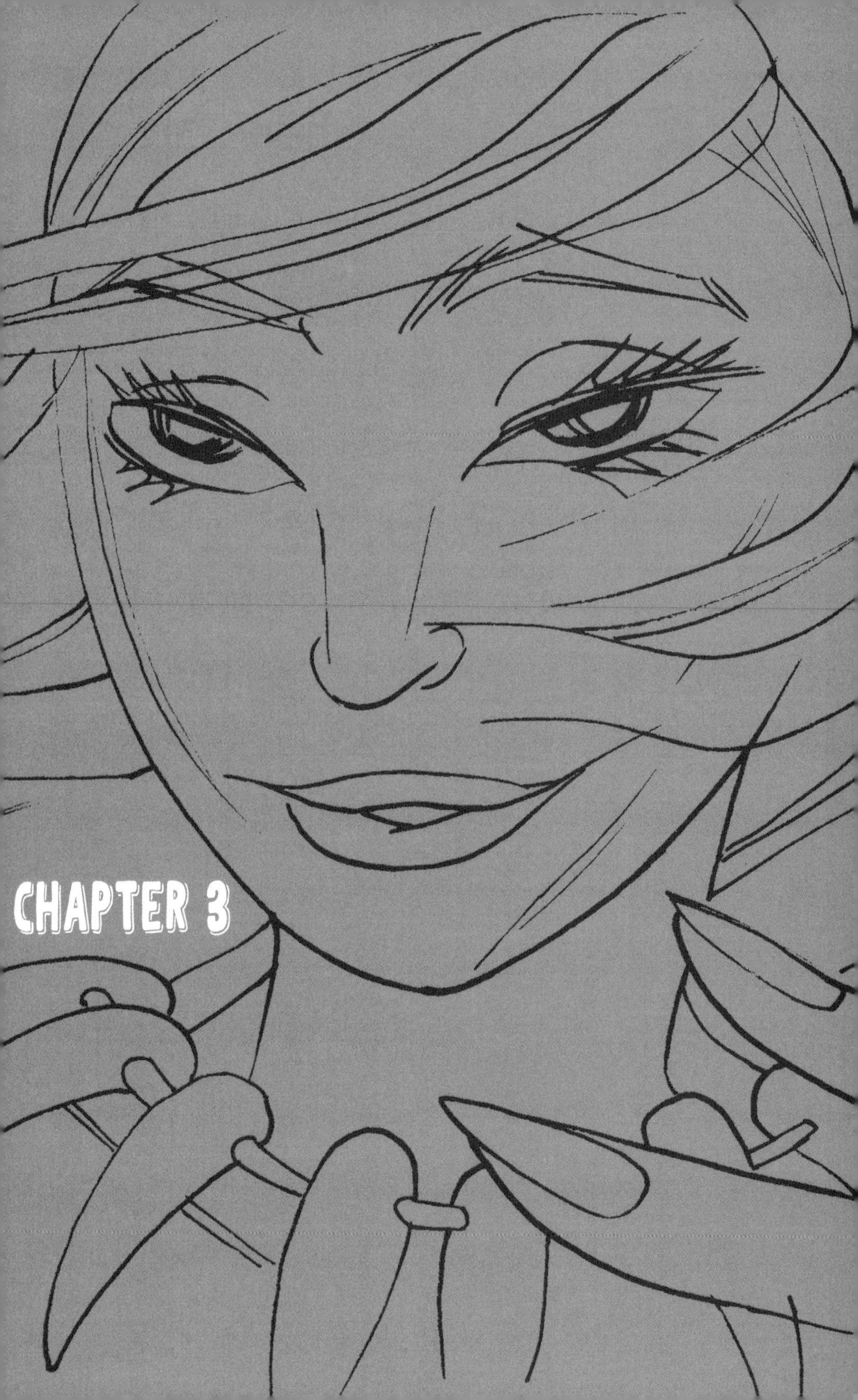
CHAPTER 3

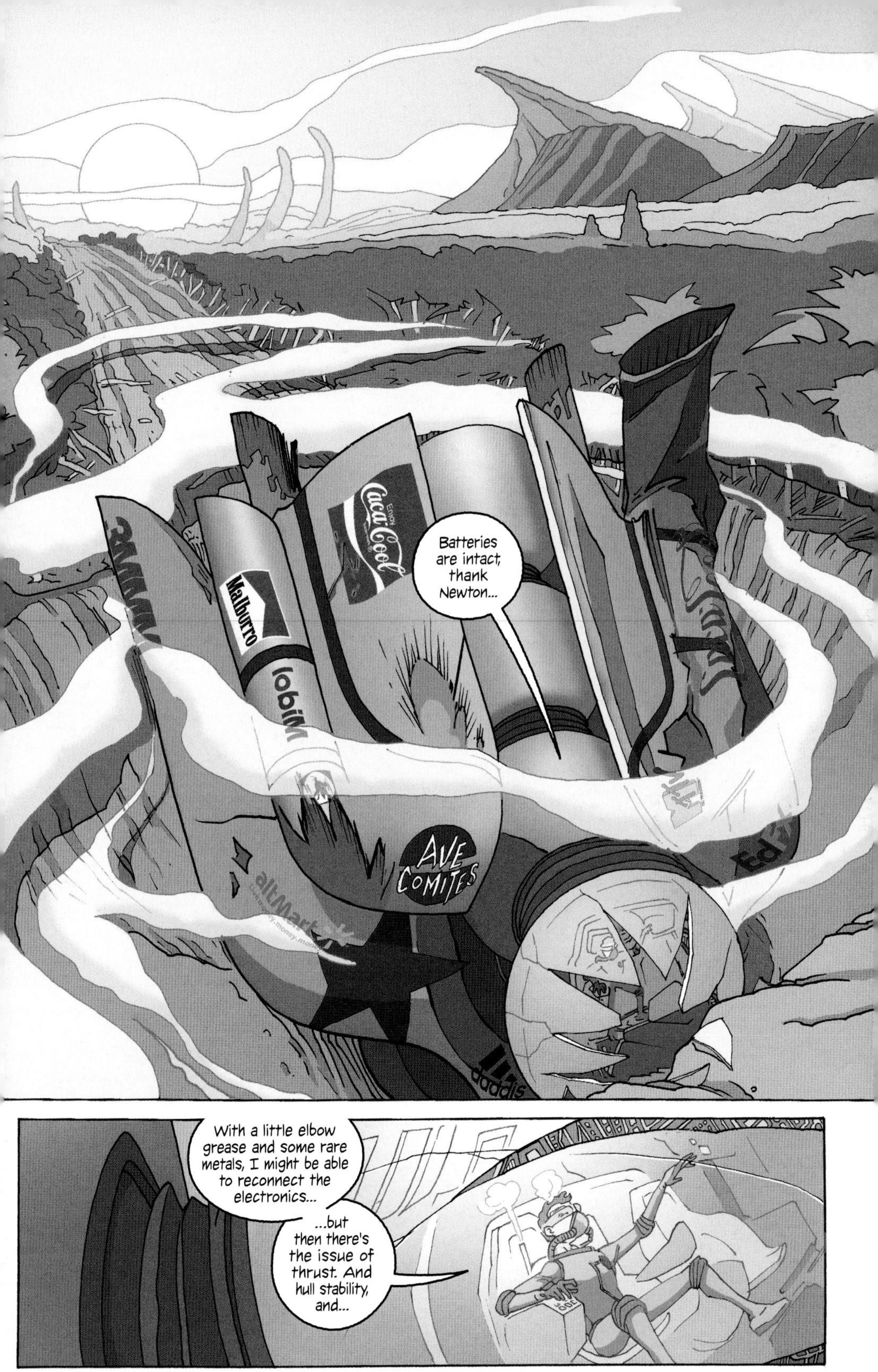
Batteries are intact, thank Newton...
With a little elbow grease and some rare metals, I might be able to reconnect the electronics...
...but then there's the issue of thrust. And hull stability, and...

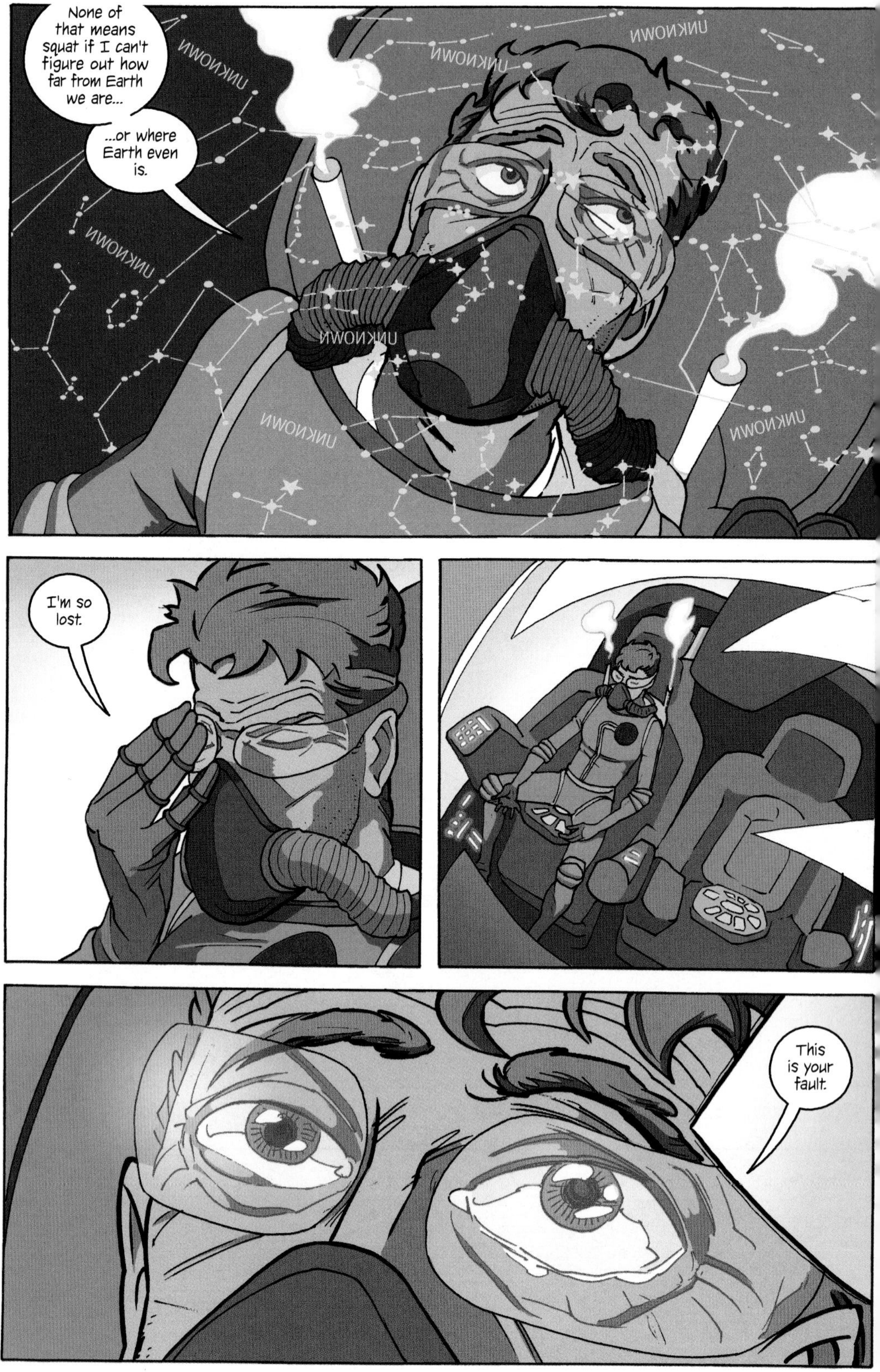
None of that means squat if I can't figure out how far from Earth we are...
...or where Earth even is.
I'm so lost.
This is your fault.

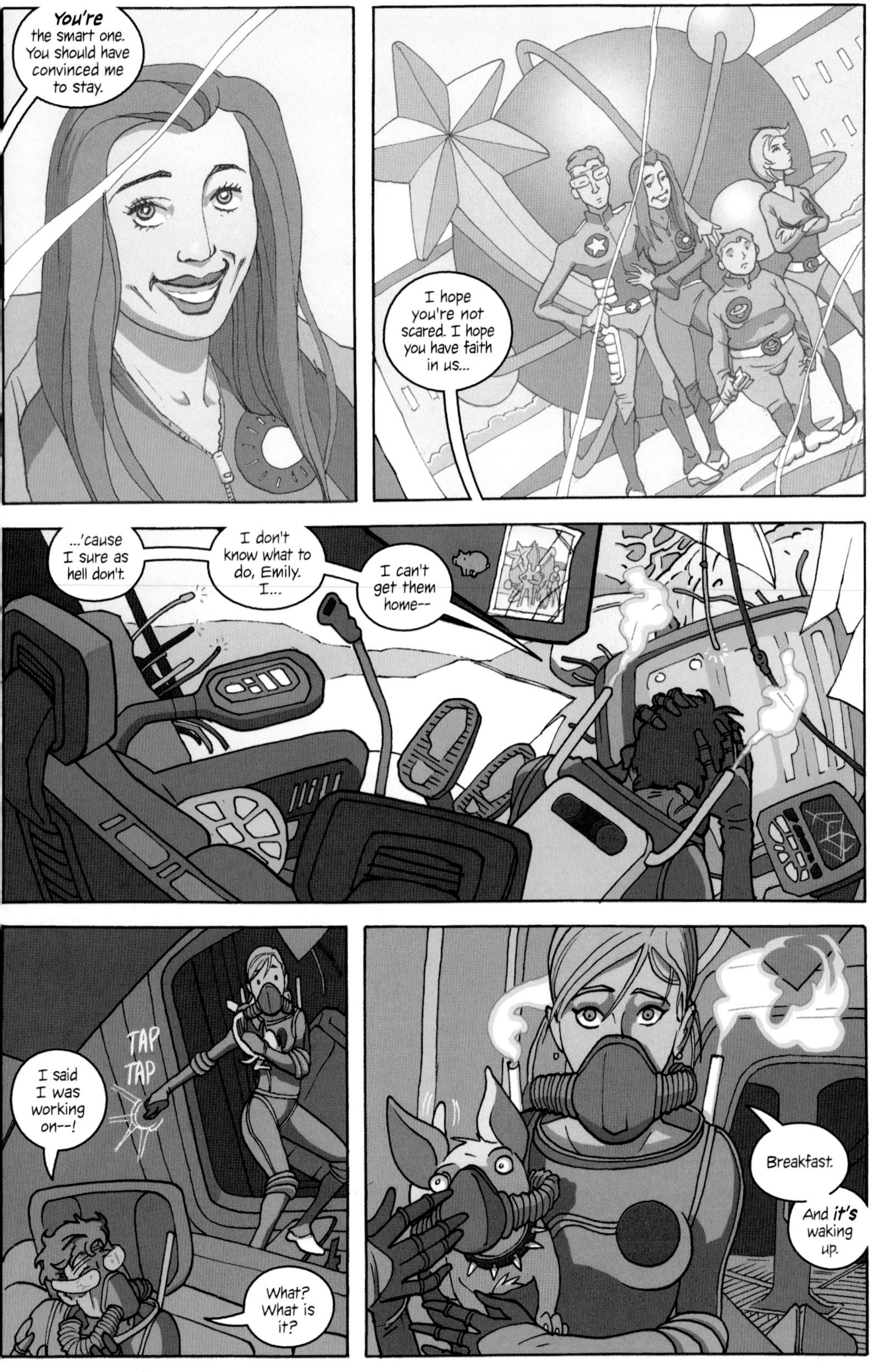
You're the smart one. You should have convinced me to stay.
I hope you're not scared. I hope you have faith in us...
...'cause I sure as hell don't.
I don't know what to do, Emily. I...
I can't get them home--
TAP TAP
I said I was working on--!
What? What is it?
Breakfast.
And *it's* waking up.

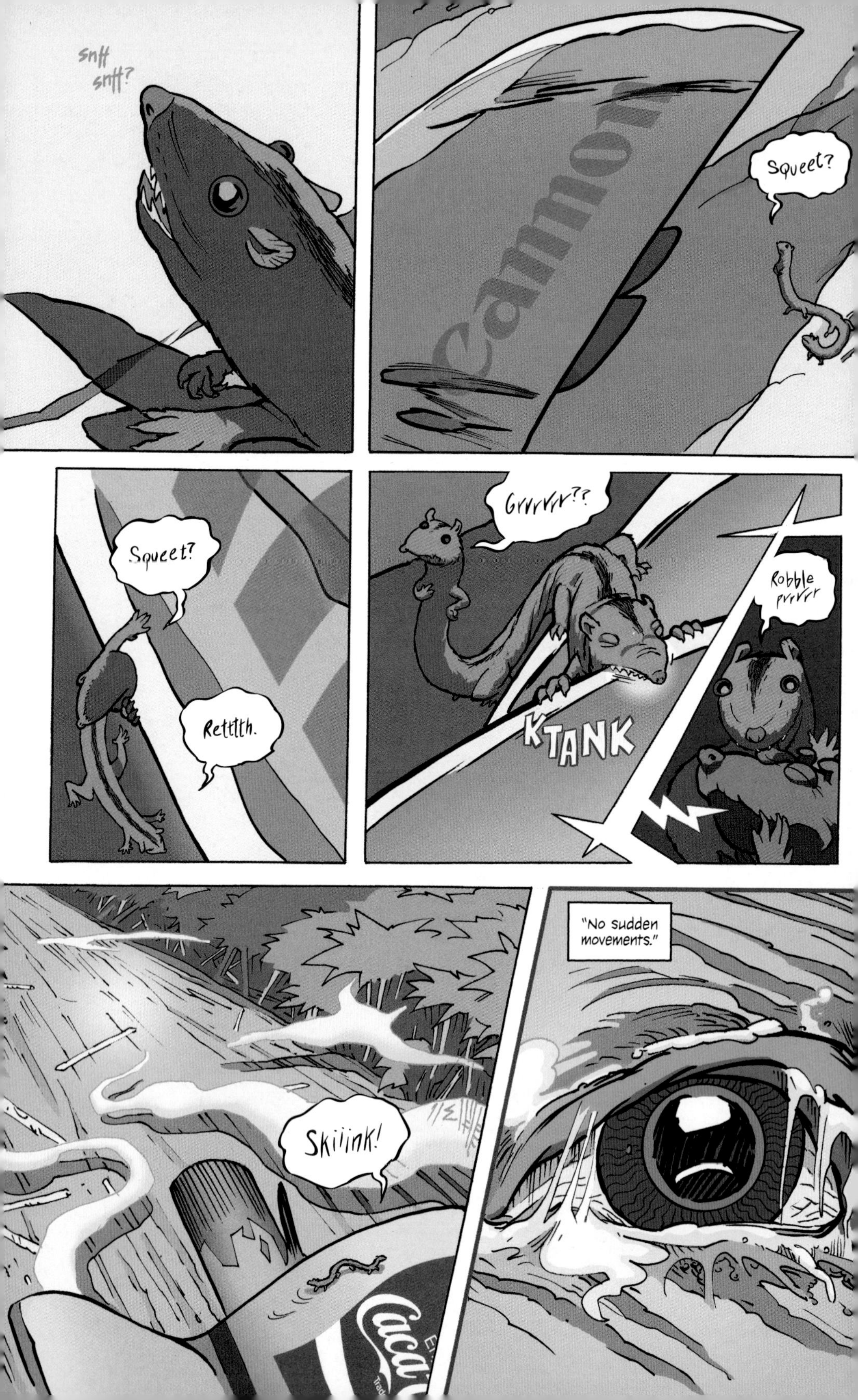
snff
snff?
Squeet?
Squeet?
Retttth.
Grrrrrr??
KTANK
Robble
prrrrr
Skiiink!
"No sudden movements."

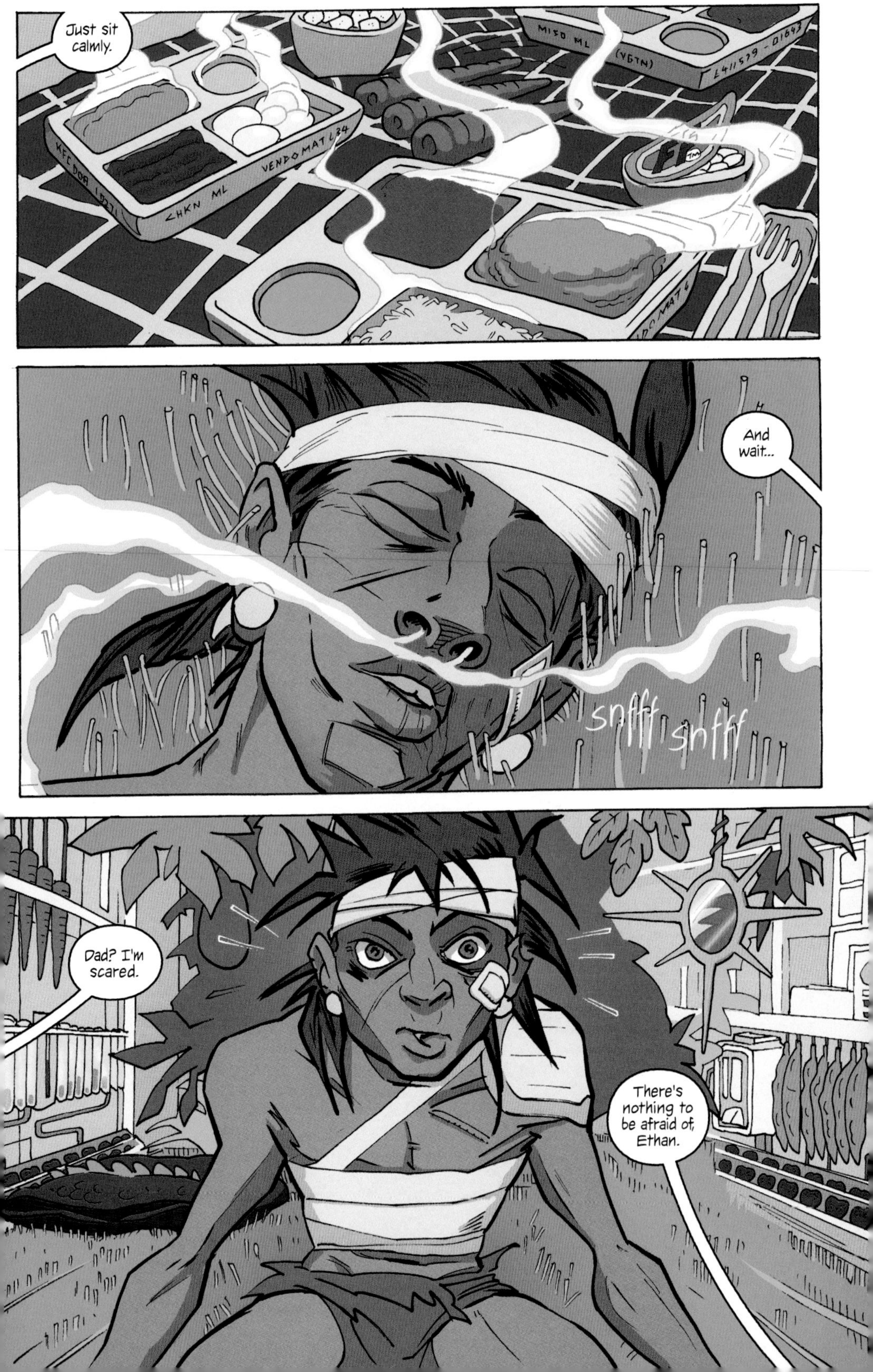
Just sit calmly.
CHKN ML
VENDOMAT L34
MISO ML
(VGTN)
And wait...
snfff snfff
Dad? I'm scared.
There's nothing to be afraid of, Ethan.

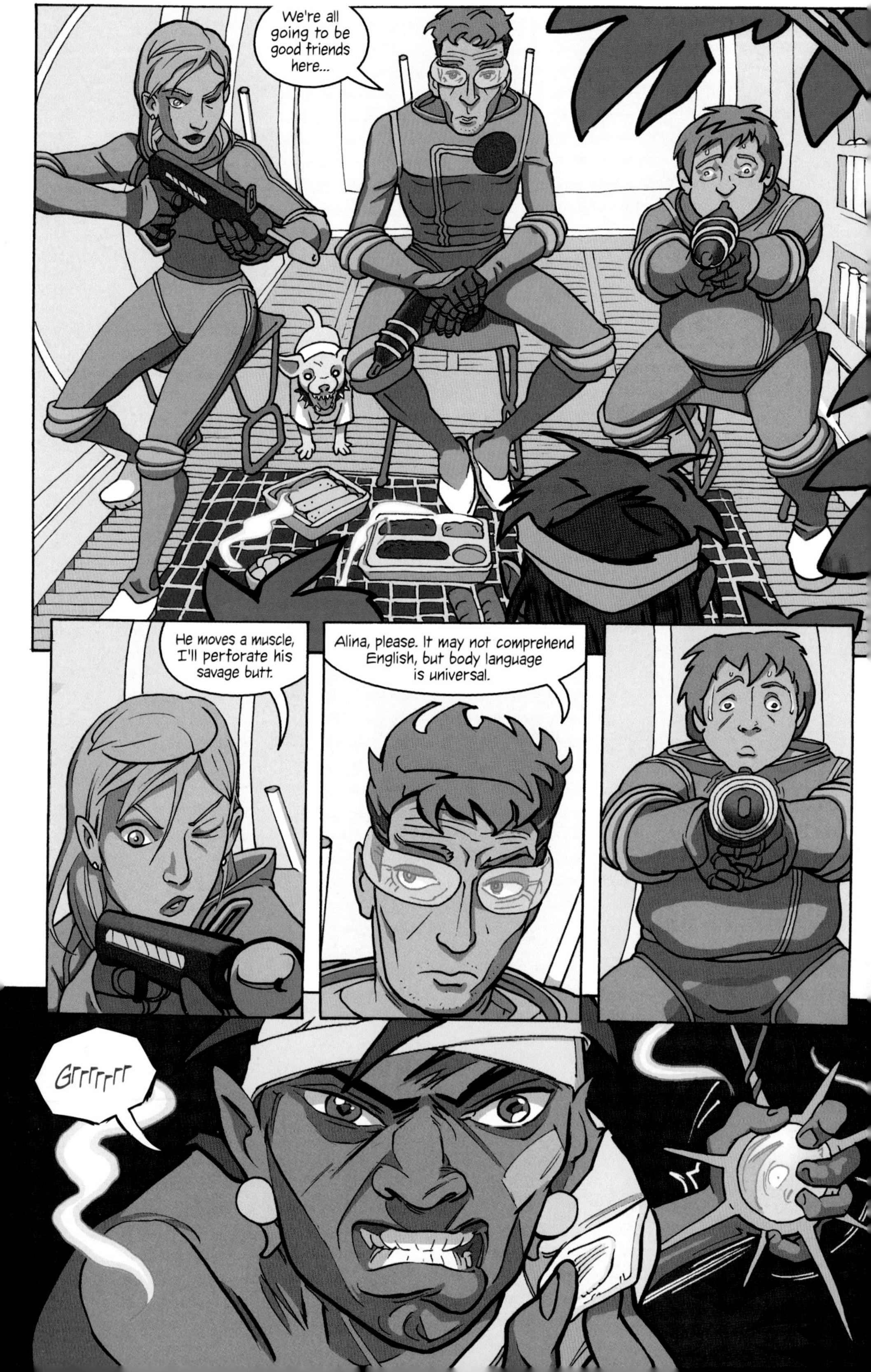
We're all going to be good friends here...
He moves a muscle, I'll perforate his savage butt.
Alina, please. It may not comprehend English, but body language is universal.
Grrrrrrr

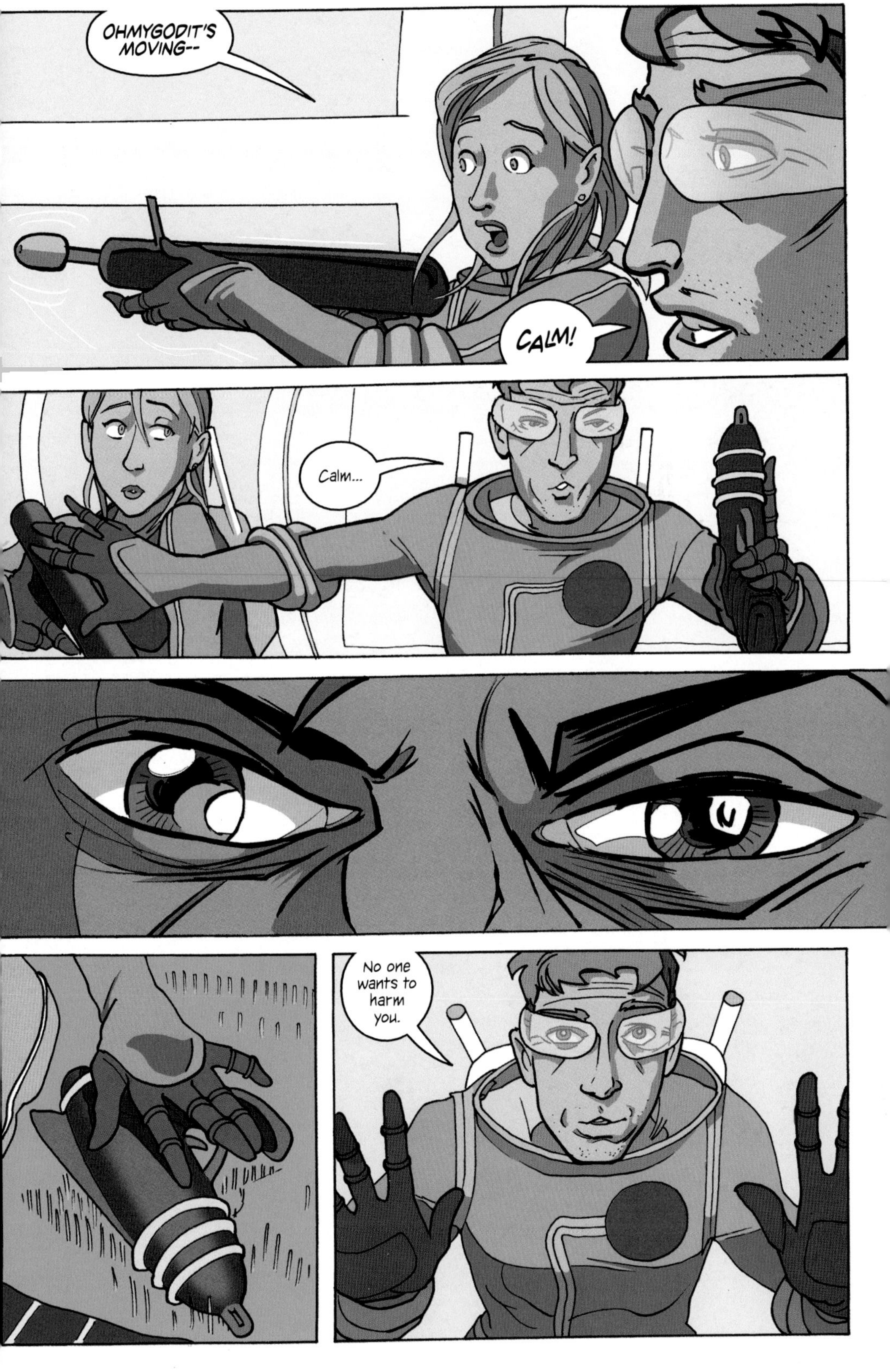
OHMYGODIT'S MOVING--
CALM!
Calm...
No one wants to harm you.

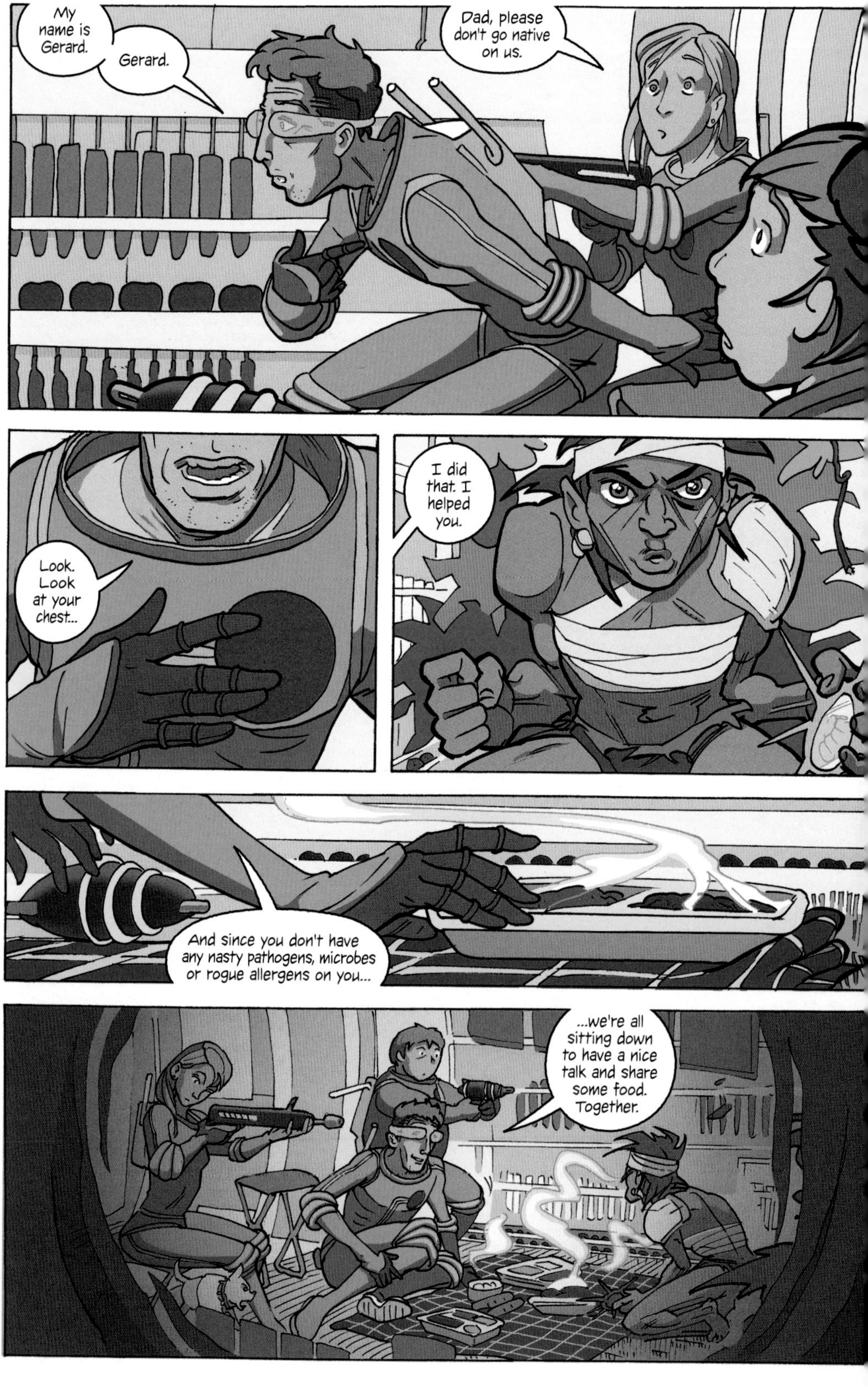
My name is Gerard.
Gerard.
Dad, please don't go native on us.
Look. Look at your chest...
I did that. I helped you.
And since you don't have any nasty pathogens, microbes or rogue allergens on you...
...we're all sitting down to have a nice talk and share some food. Together.

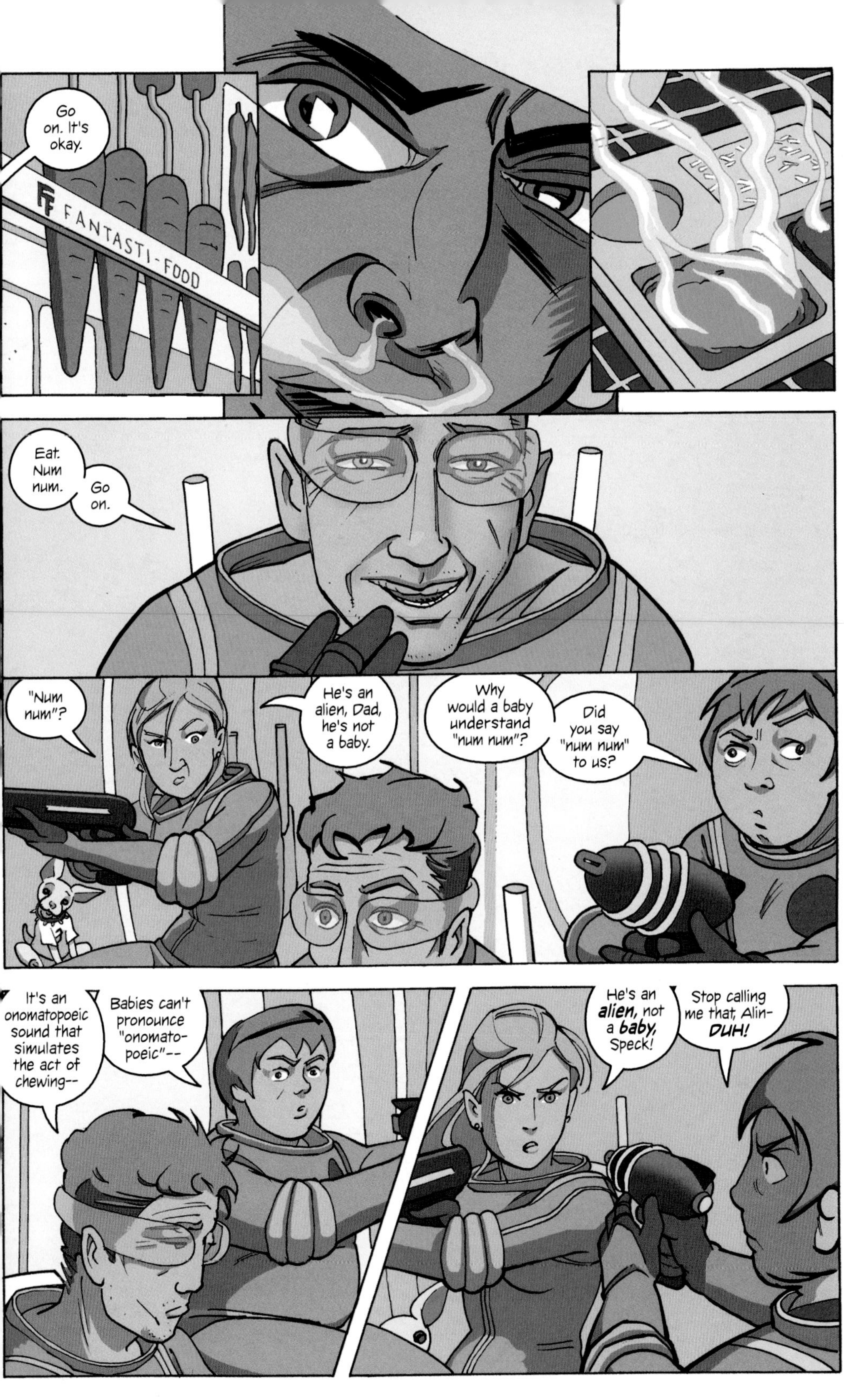
Go on. It's okay.
FF FANTASTI-FOOD
Eat. Num num.
Go on.
"Num num"?
He's an alien, Dad, he's not a baby.
Why would a baby understand "num num"?
Did you say "num num" to us?
It's an onomatopoeic sound that simulates the act of chewing--
Babies can't pronounce "onomato-poeic"--
He's an *alien,* not a *baby,* Speck!
Stop calling me that, Alin-*DUH!*

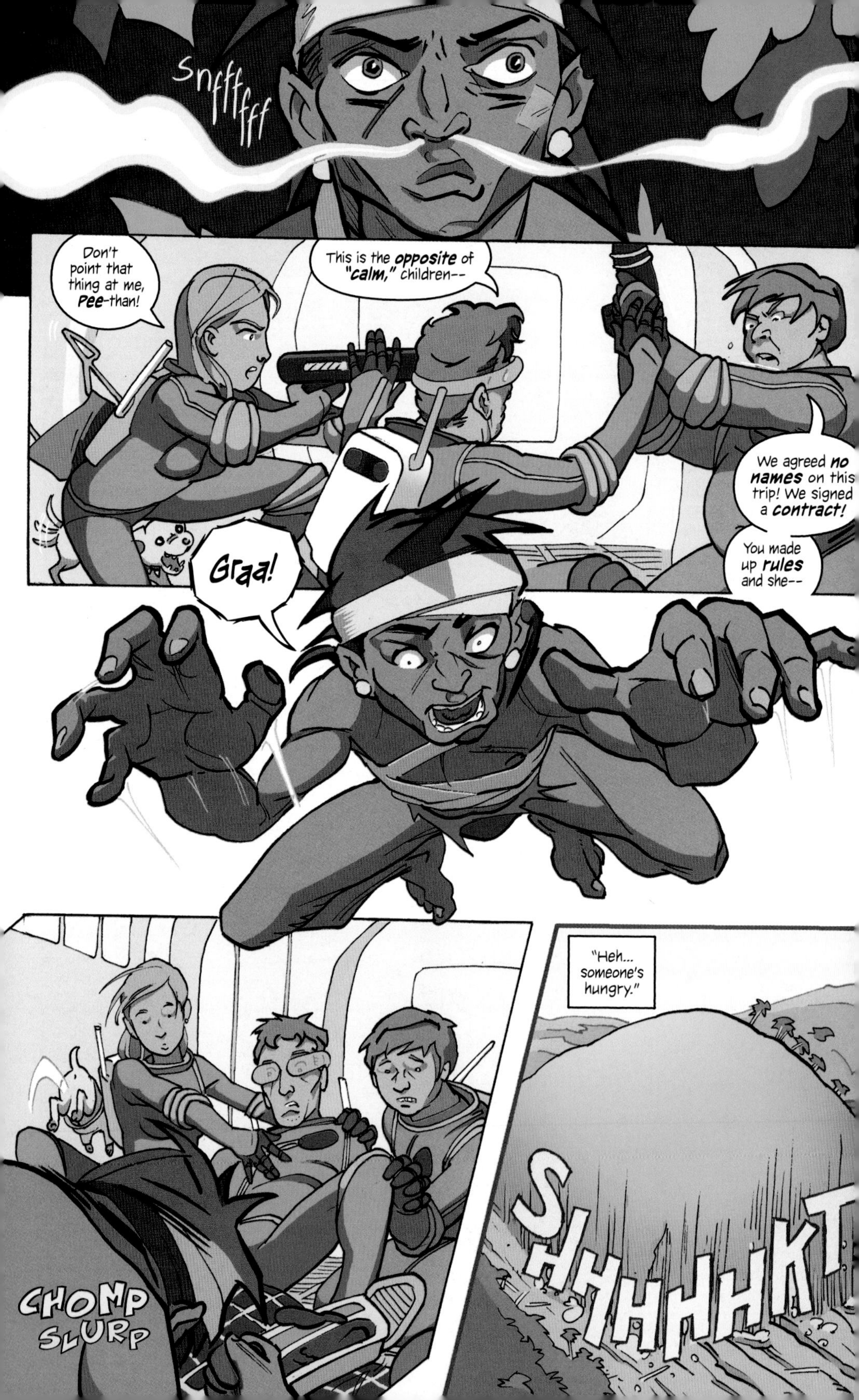
Snffffff
Don't point that thing at me, Pee-than!
This is the opposite of "calm," children--
We agreed no names on this trip! We signed a contract!
You made up rules and she--
Graa!
CHOMP SLURP
"Heh... someone's hungry."
SHHHHHKT

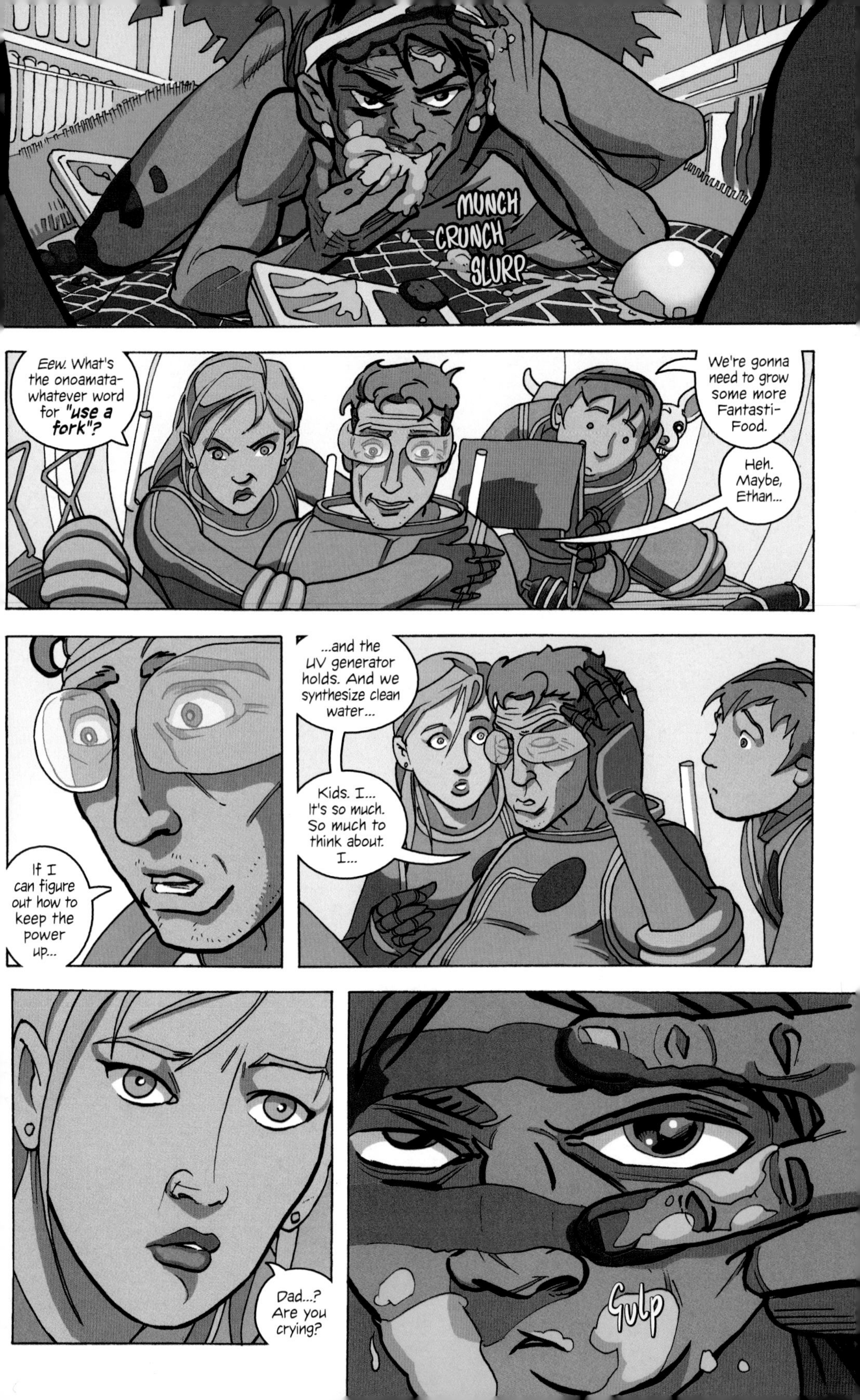
MUNCH
CRUNCH
SLURP
Eew. What's the onoamata-whatever word for "use a fork"?
We're gonna need to grow some more Fantasti-Food.
Heh. Maybe, Ethan...
If I can figure out how to keep the power up...
...and the UV generator holds. And we synthesize clean water...
Kids. I... It's so much. So much to think about. I...
Dad...? Are you crying?
Gulp

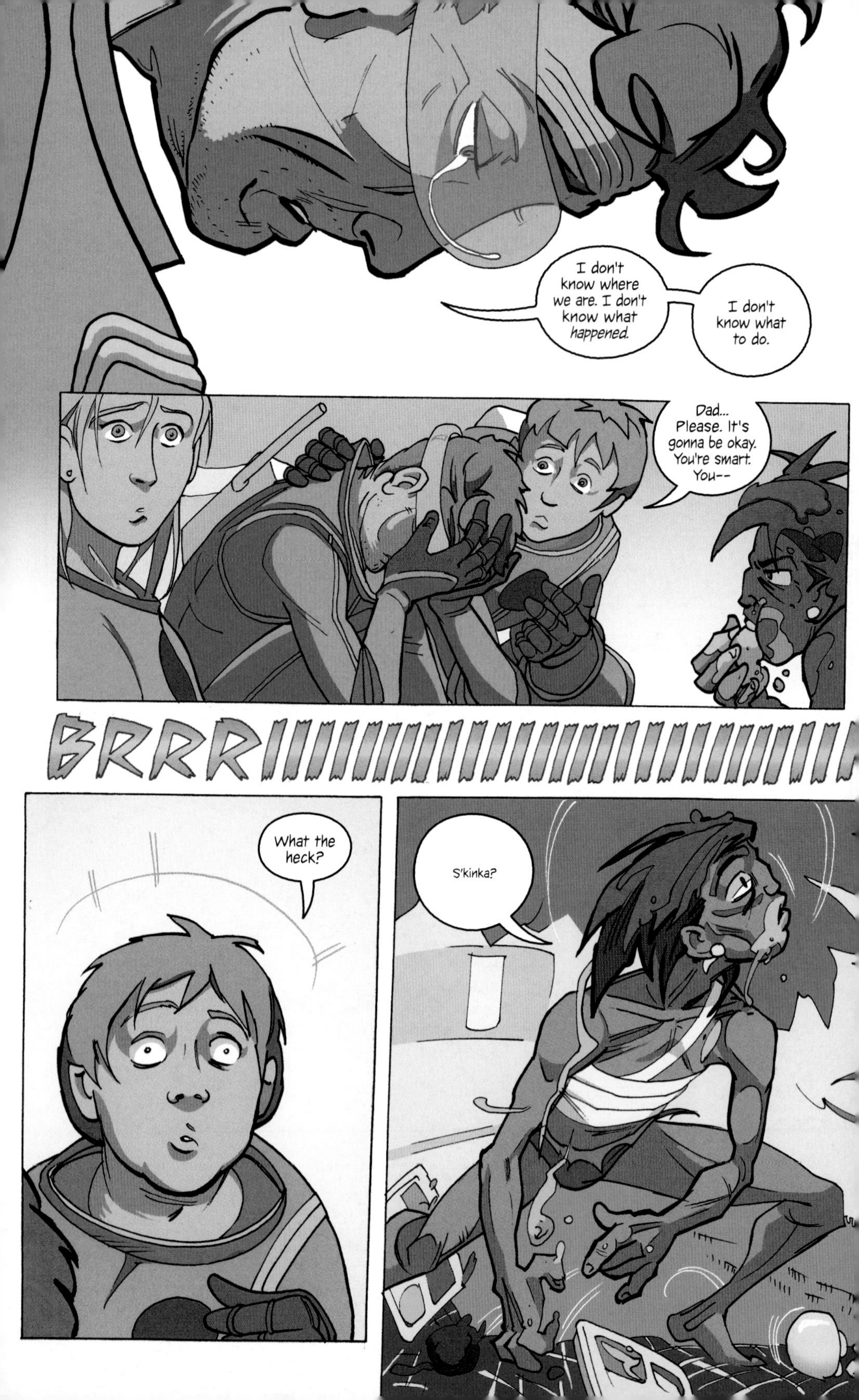
I don't know where we are. I don't know what *happened.*
I don't know what to do.
Dad... Please. It's gonna be okay. You're smart. You--
BRRRIIIIIIIIIIIIIIIIIIIIIIIIIIIIIIII
What the heck?
S'kinka?

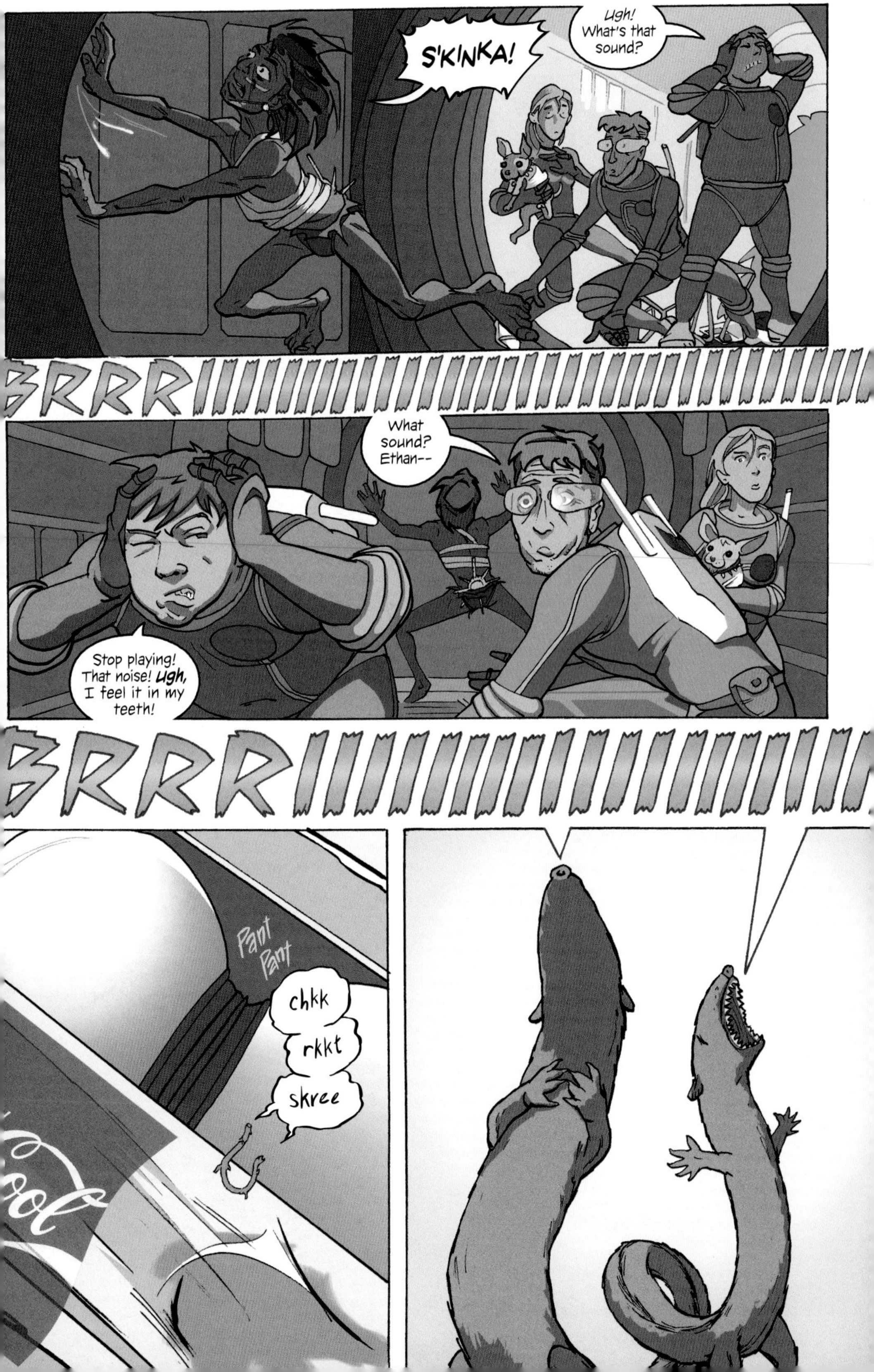
S'KINKA!
Ugh! What's that sound?
BRRRIIIIIIIIIIIIIIIIIIIIIIIIIIII
What sound? Ethan--
Stop playing! That noise! Ugh, I feel it in my teeth!
BRRRIIIIIIIIIIIIIIIIIIIIIIIIIII
Pant Pant
chkk
rkkt
skree

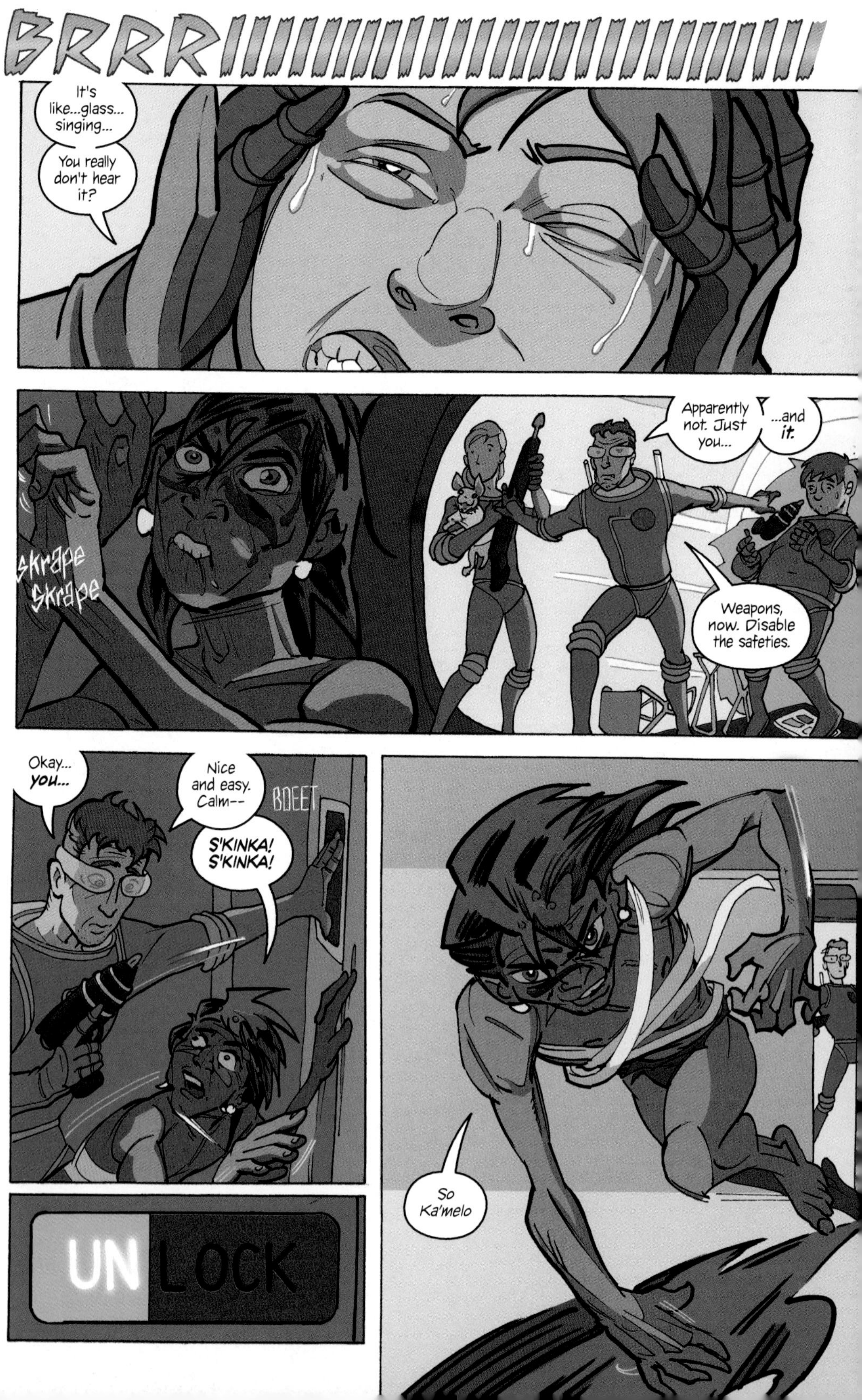
BRRRIIIIIIIIIIIIIIIIIIIIIIIIIII
It's like...glass... singing...
You really don't hear it?
Skrape Skrape
Apparently not. Just you...
...and *it.*
Weapons, now. Disable the safeties.
Okay... *you...*
Nice and easy. Calm--
BDEET
S'KINKA! S'KINKA!
UNLOCK
So Ka'melo

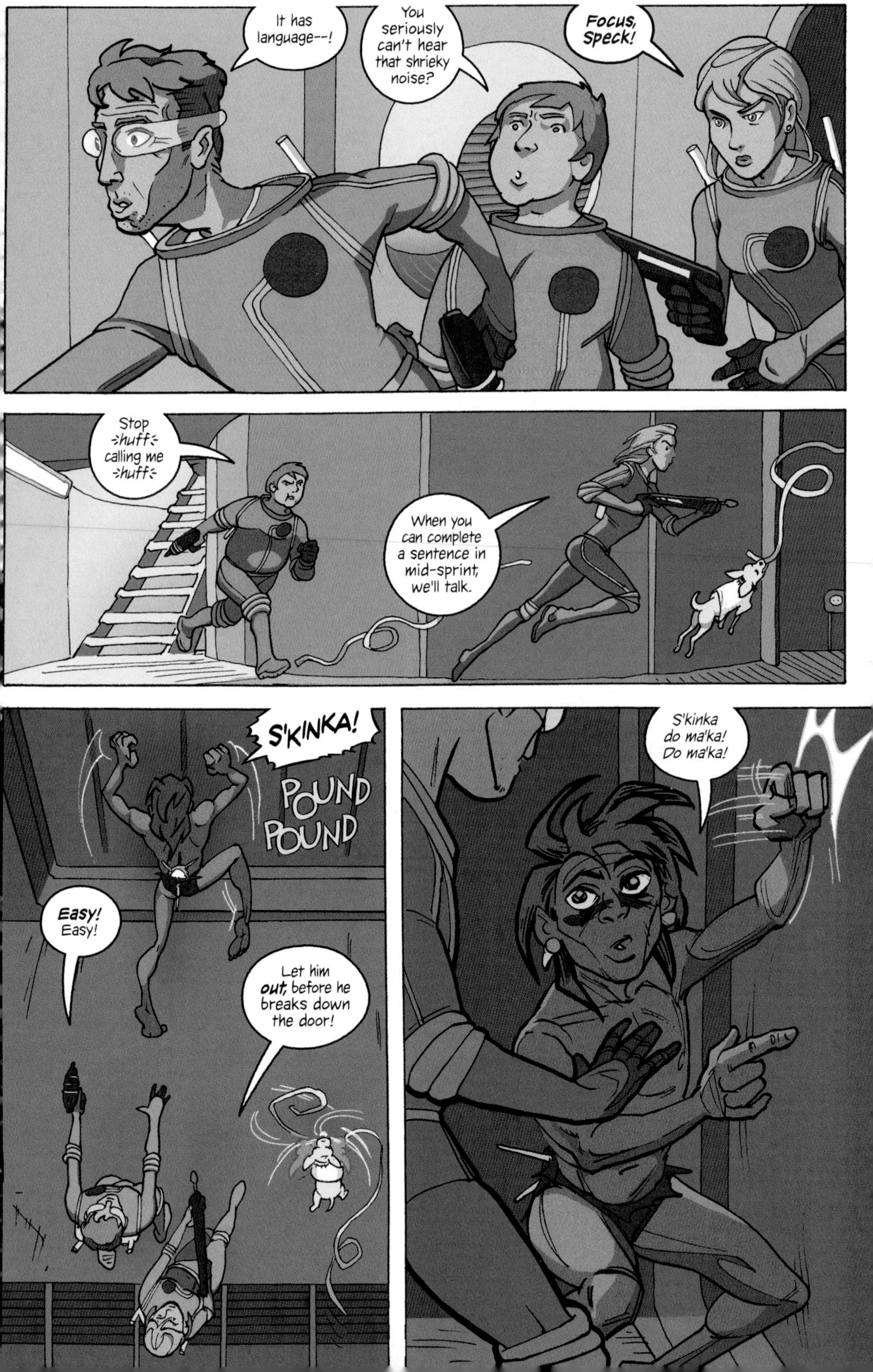

It has language--!
You seriously can't hear that shrieky noise?
Focus, Speck!
Stop -huff- calling me -huff-
When you can complete a sentence in mid-sprint, we'll talk.
S'KINKA!
POUND POUND
Easy! Easy!
Let him *out,* before he breaks down the door!
S'kinka do ma'ka! Do ma'ka!

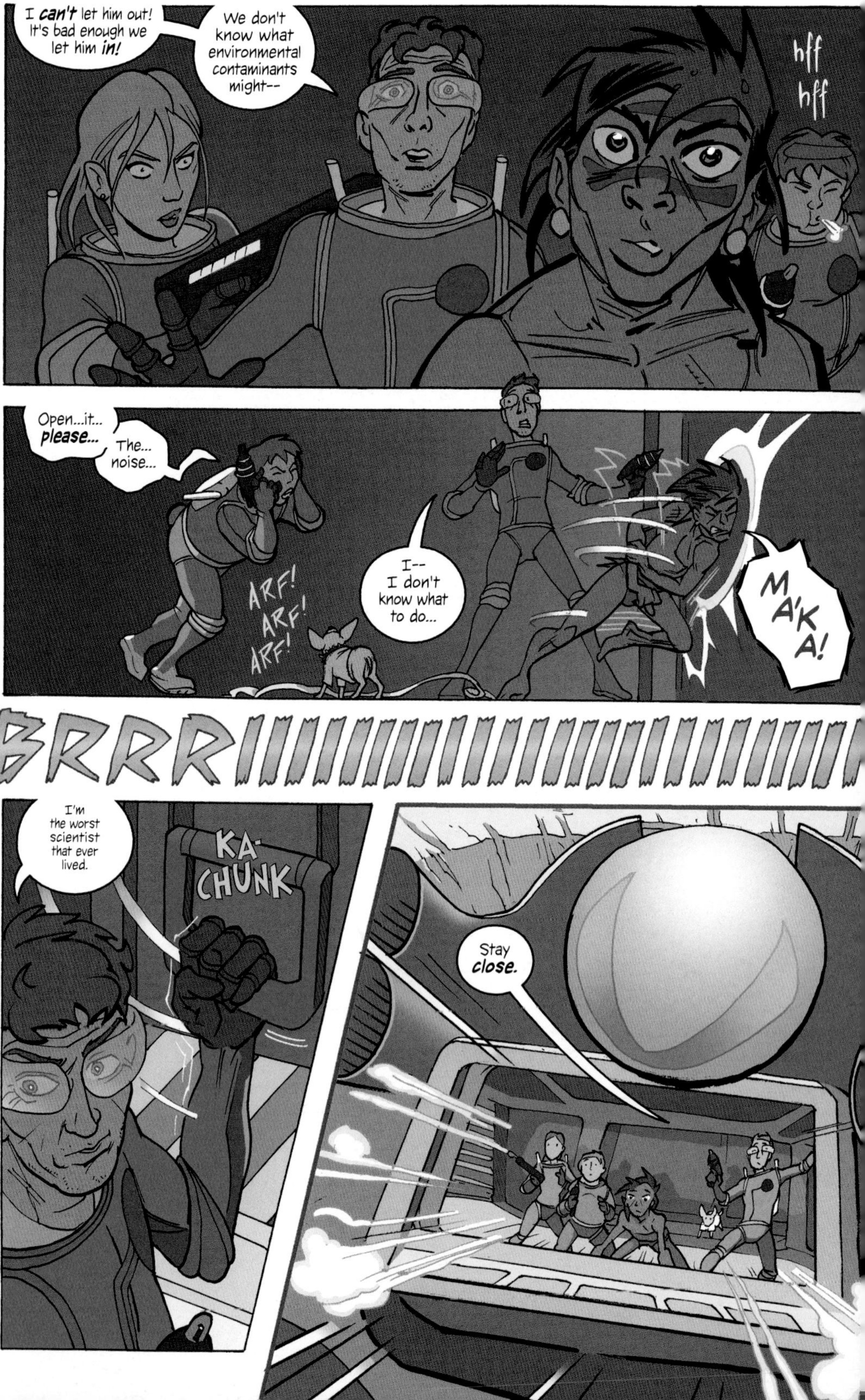
I can't let him out! It's bad enough we let him in!
We don't know what environmental contaminants might--
hff hff
Open...it... please...
The... noise...
I-- I don't know what to do...
ARF! ARF! ARF!
MA'KA!
BRRRIIIIIIIIIIIIIIIIIIIIIIIIIIIII
I'm the worst scientist that ever lived.
KA-CHUNK
Stay close.

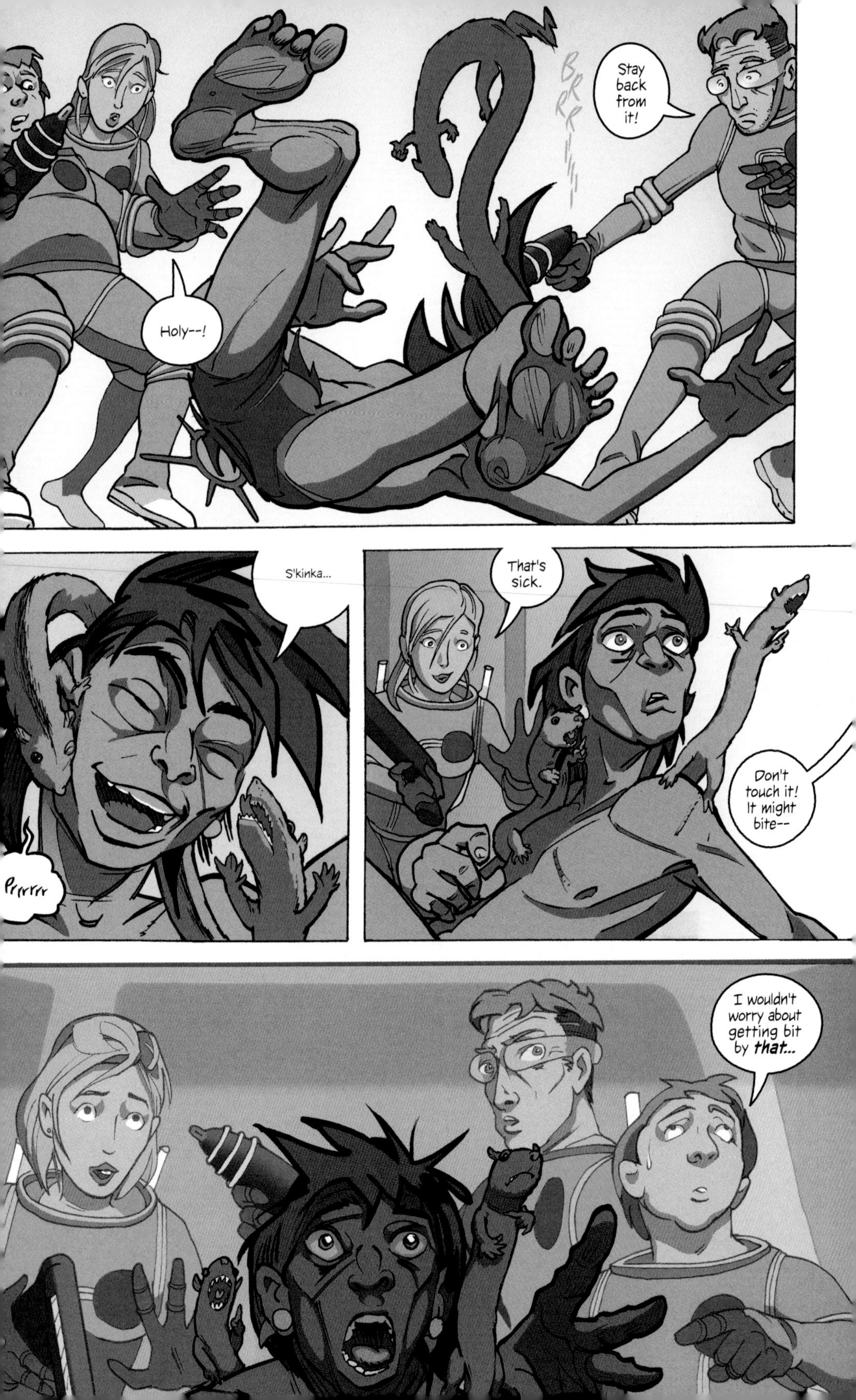
BRRRIIII
Stay back from it!
Holy--!
S'kinka...
Prrrrr
That's sick.
Don't touch it! It might bite--
I wouldn't worry about getting bit by *that...*

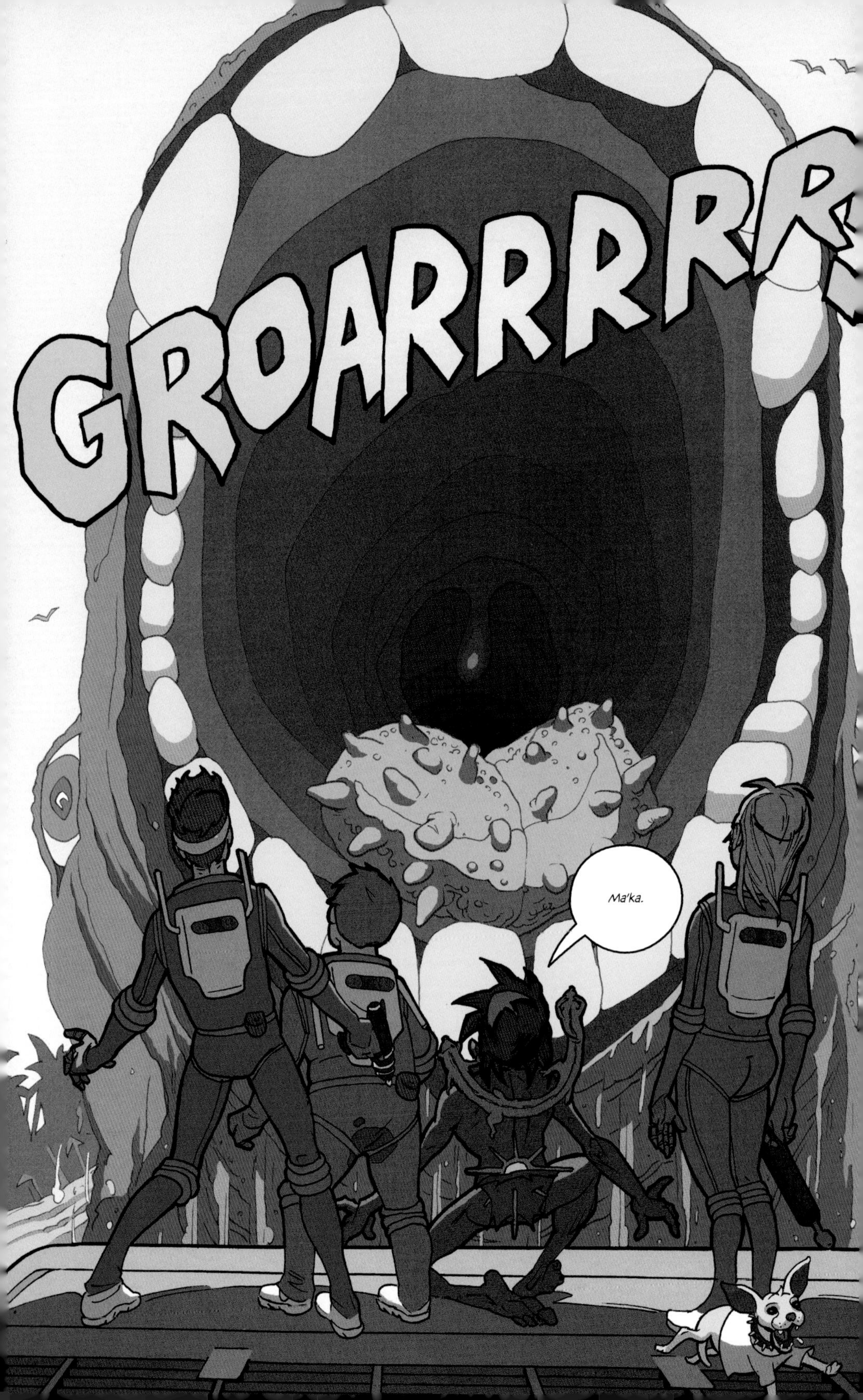
GROARRRRRR
Ma'ka.

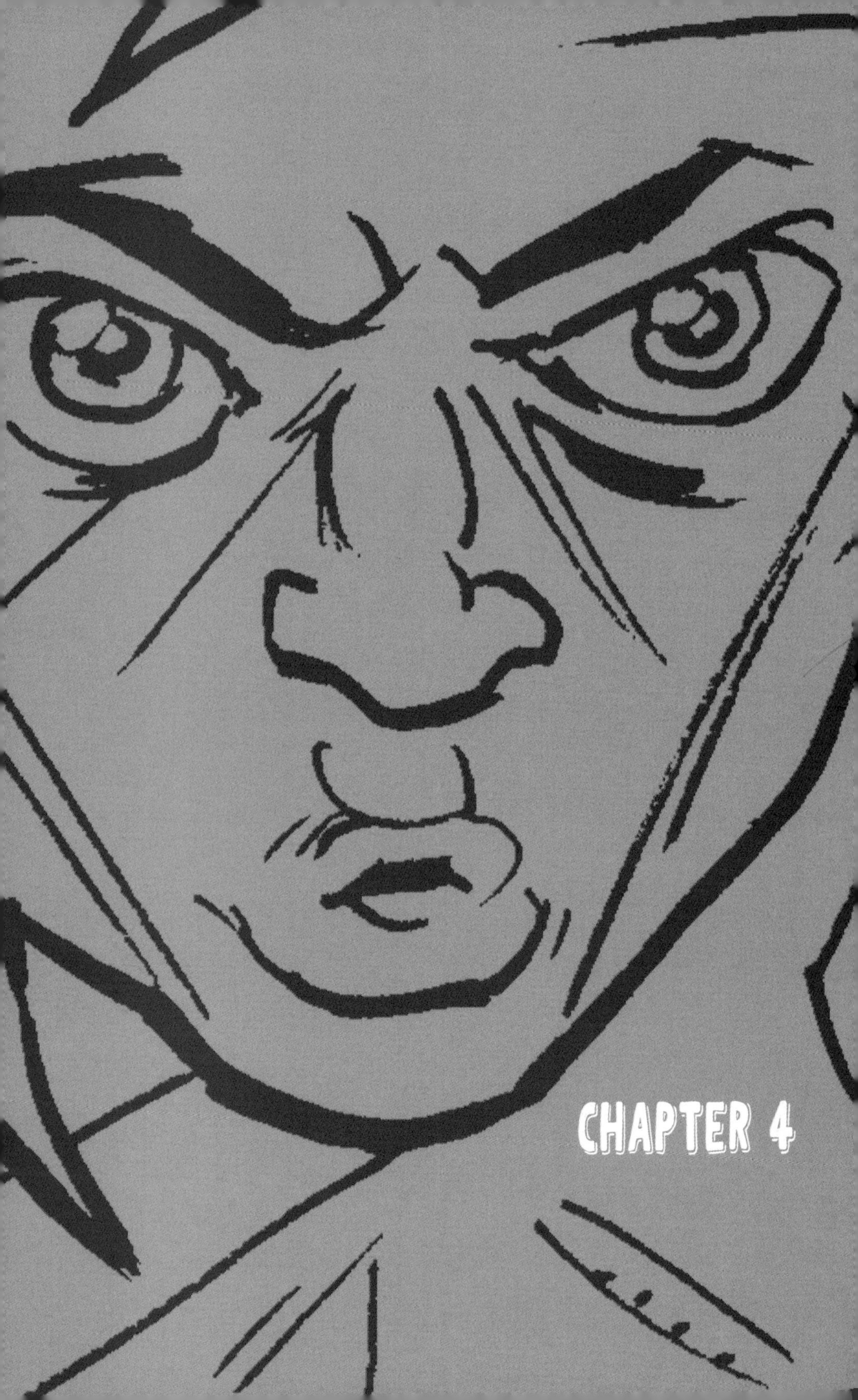
CHAPTER 4

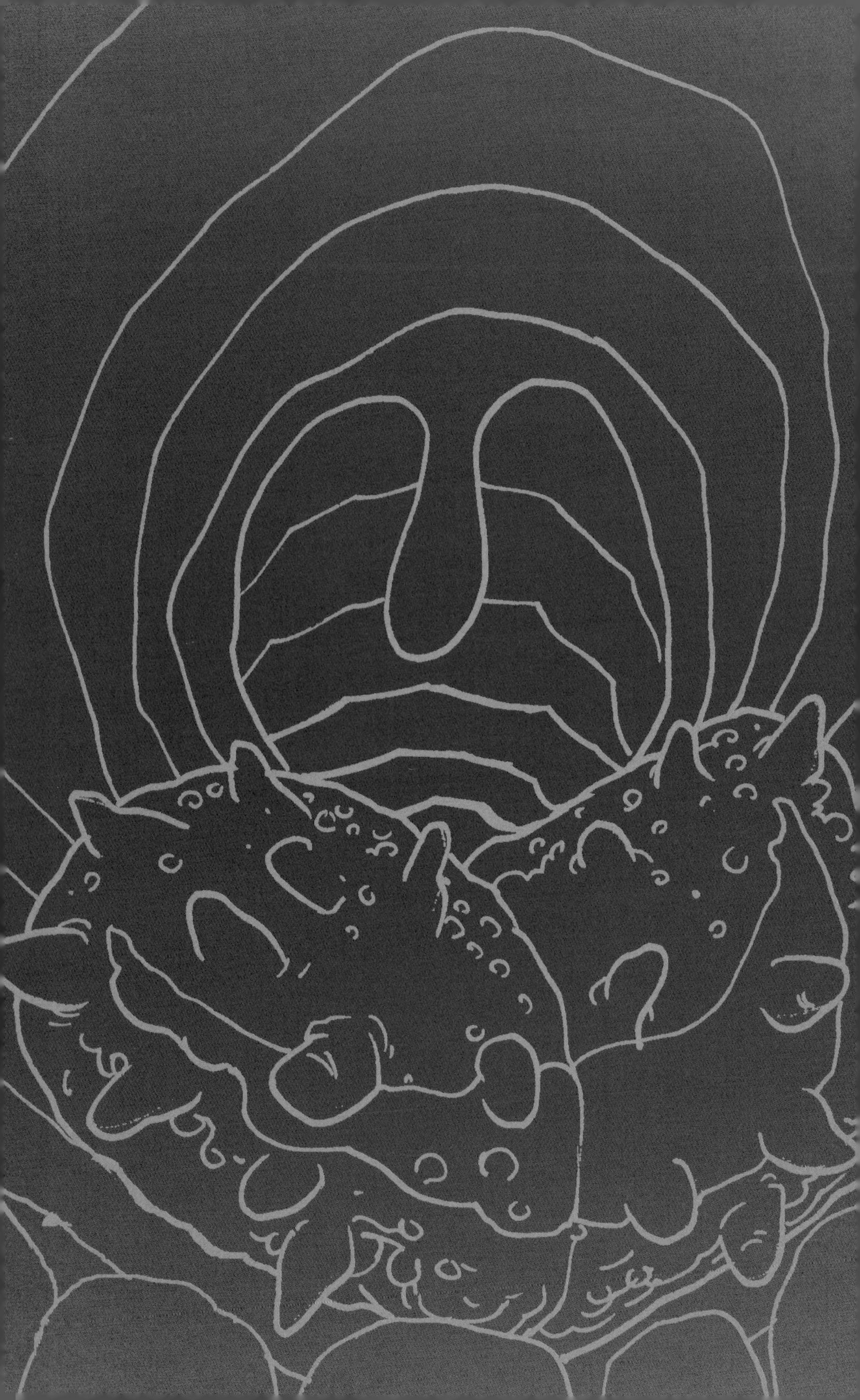

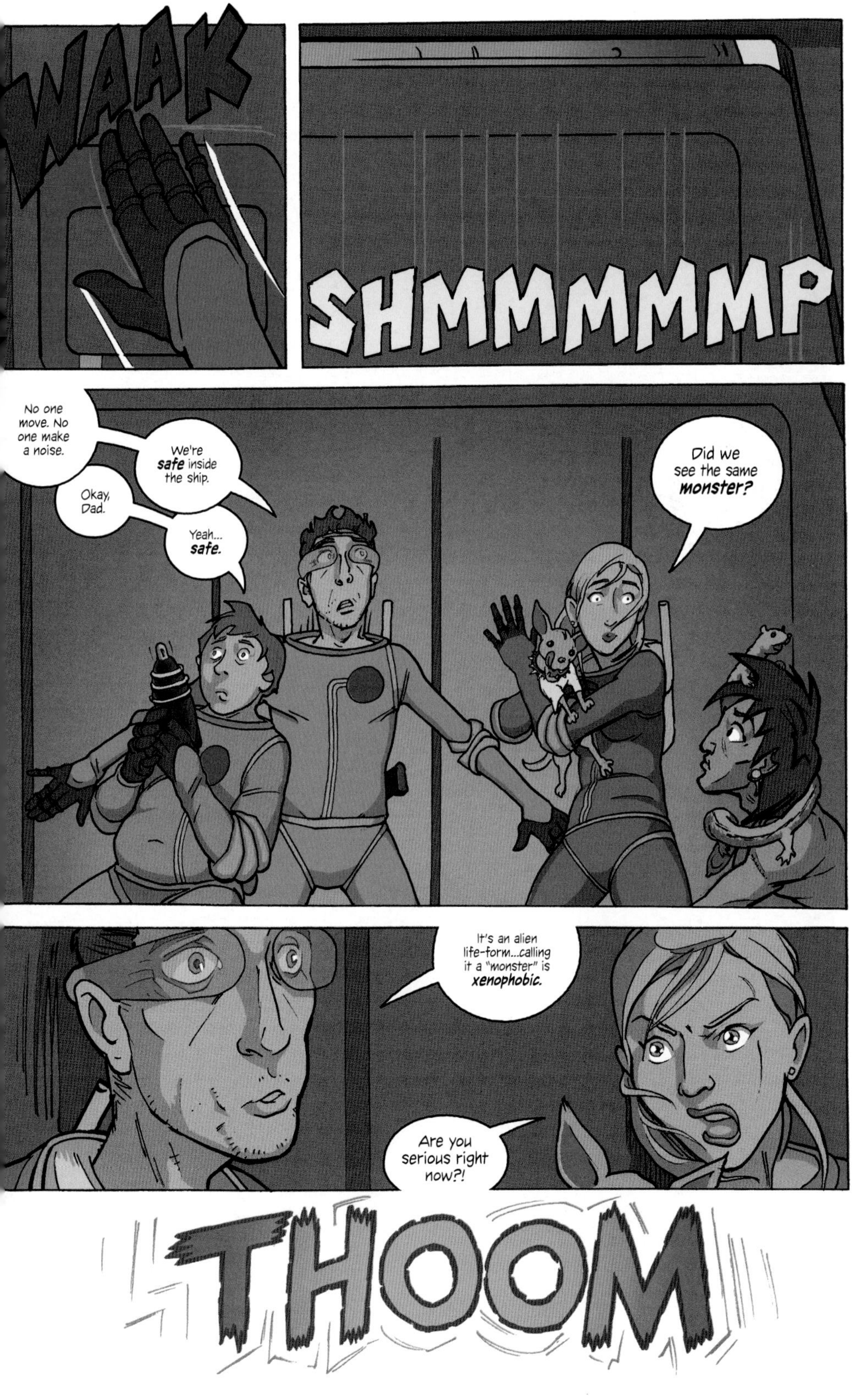
WAAK
SHMMMMMP
No one move. No one make a noise.
We're safe inside the ship.
Okay, Dad.
Yeah... safe.
Did we see the same monster?
It's an alien life-form...calling it a "monster" is xenophobic.
Are you serious right now?!
THOOM

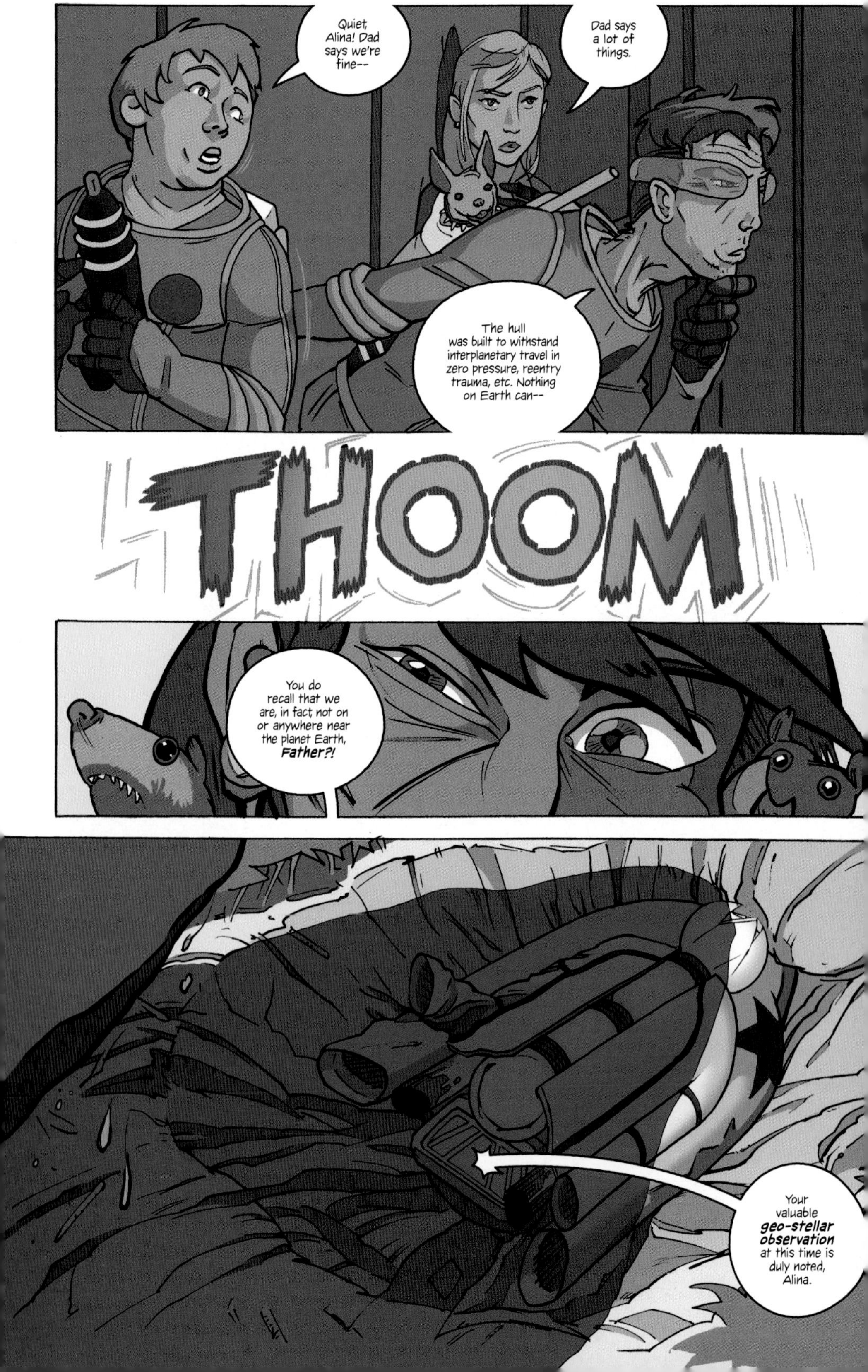
Quiet, Alina! Dad says we're fine--
Dad says a lot of things.
The hull was built to withstand interplanetary travel in zero pressure, reentry trauma, etc. Nothing on Earth can--
THOOM
You do recall that we are, in fact, not on or anywhere near the planet Earth, **Father?!**
Your valuable ***geo-stellar observation*** at this time is duly noted, Alina.

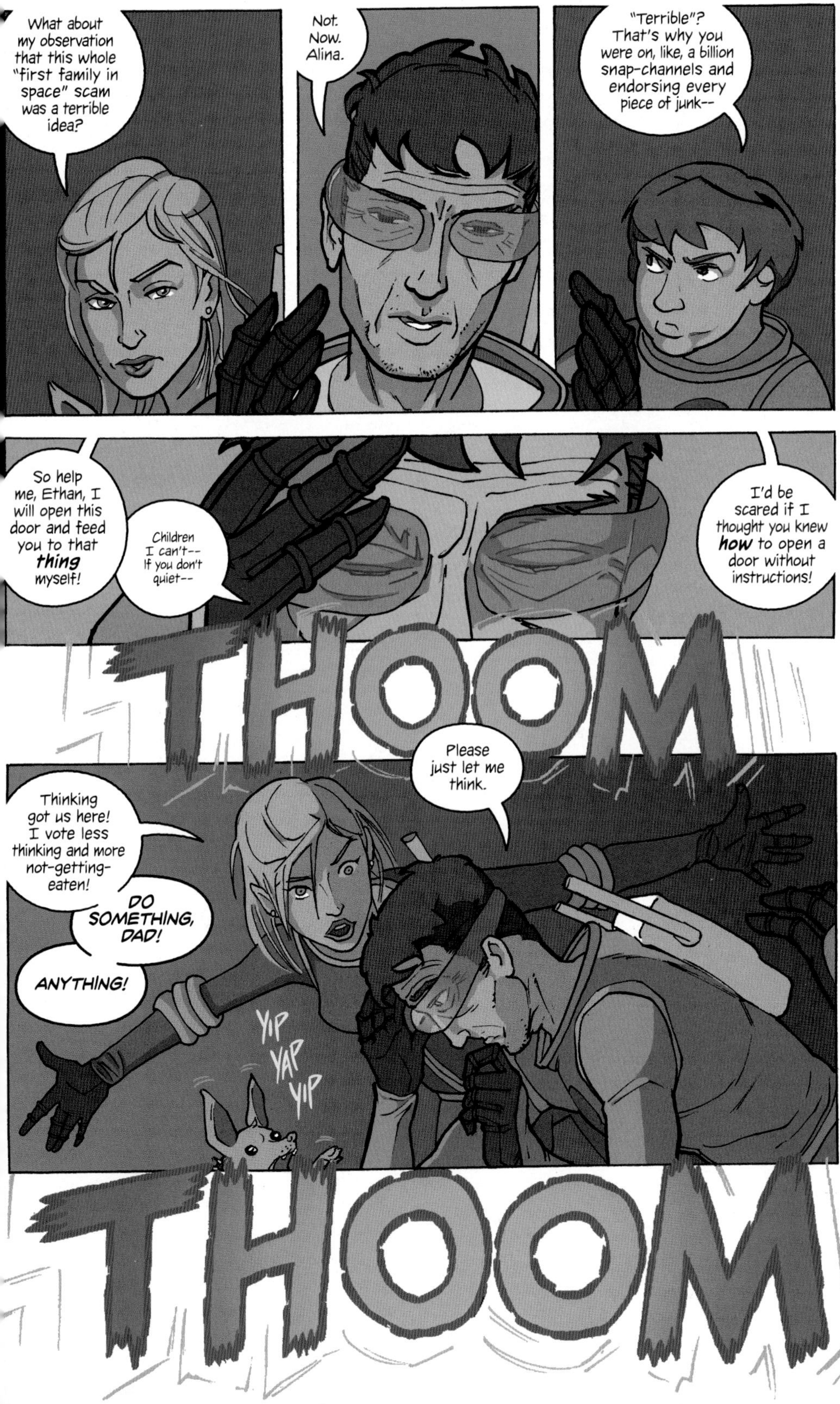
What about my observation that this whole "first family in space" scam was a terrible idea?
Not. Now. Alina.
"Terrible"? That's why you were on, like, a billion snap-channels and endorsing every piece of junk--
So help me, Ethan, I will open this door and feed you to that *thing* myself!
Children I can't-- If you don't quiet--
I'd be scared if I thought you knew *how* to open a door without instructions!
THOOM
Please just let me think.
Thinking got us here! I vote less thinking and more not-getting-eaten!
DO SOMETHING, DAD!
ANYTHING!
YIP YAP YIP
THOOM

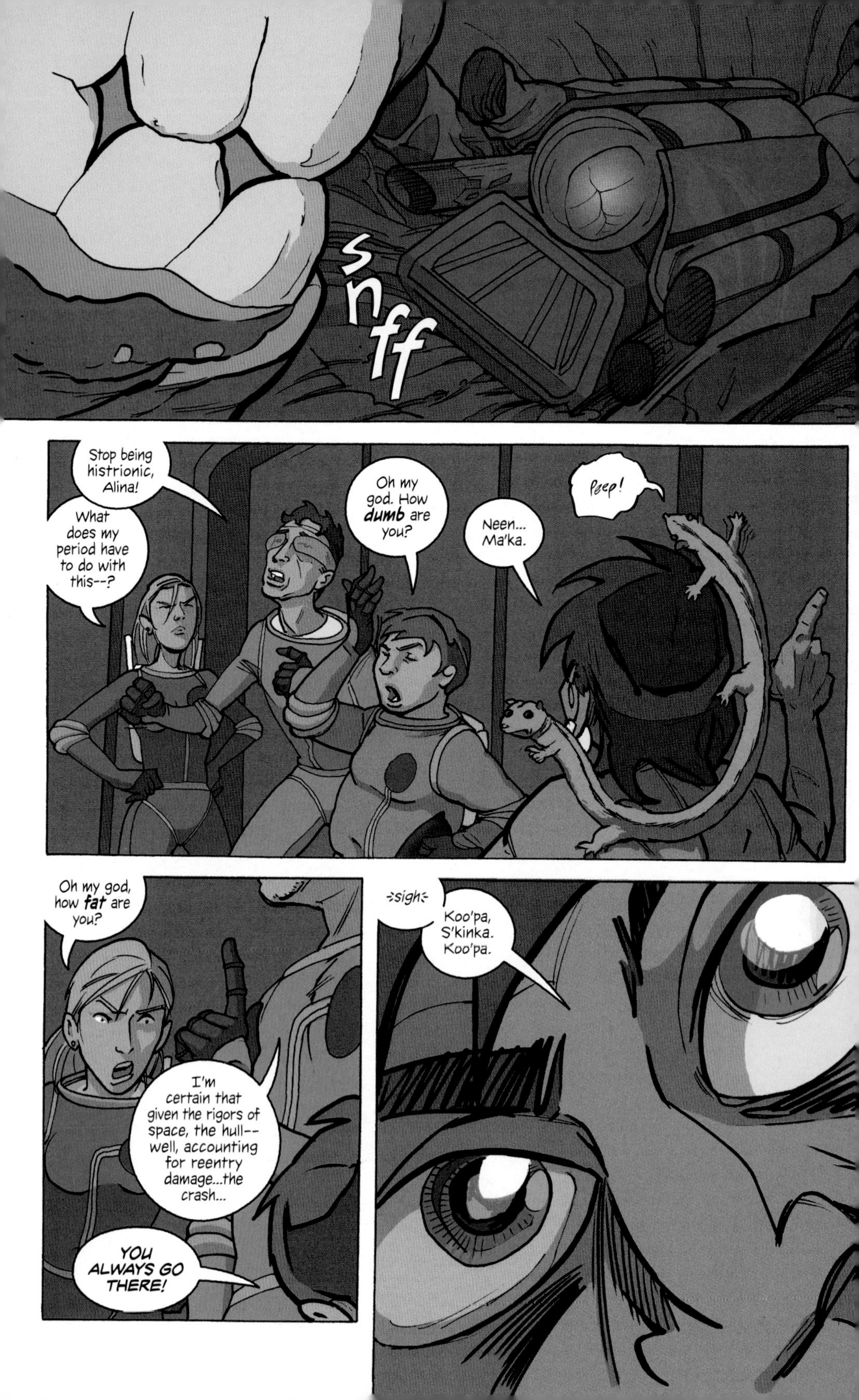
snff
Stop being histrionic, Alina!
What does my period have to do with this--?
Oh my god. How dumb are you?
Neen... Ma'ka.
Peep!
Oh my god, how fat are you?
I'm certain that given the rigors of space, the hull--well, accounting for reentry damage...the crash...
YOU ALWAYS GO THERE!
sigh
Koo'pa, S'kinka. Koo'pa.

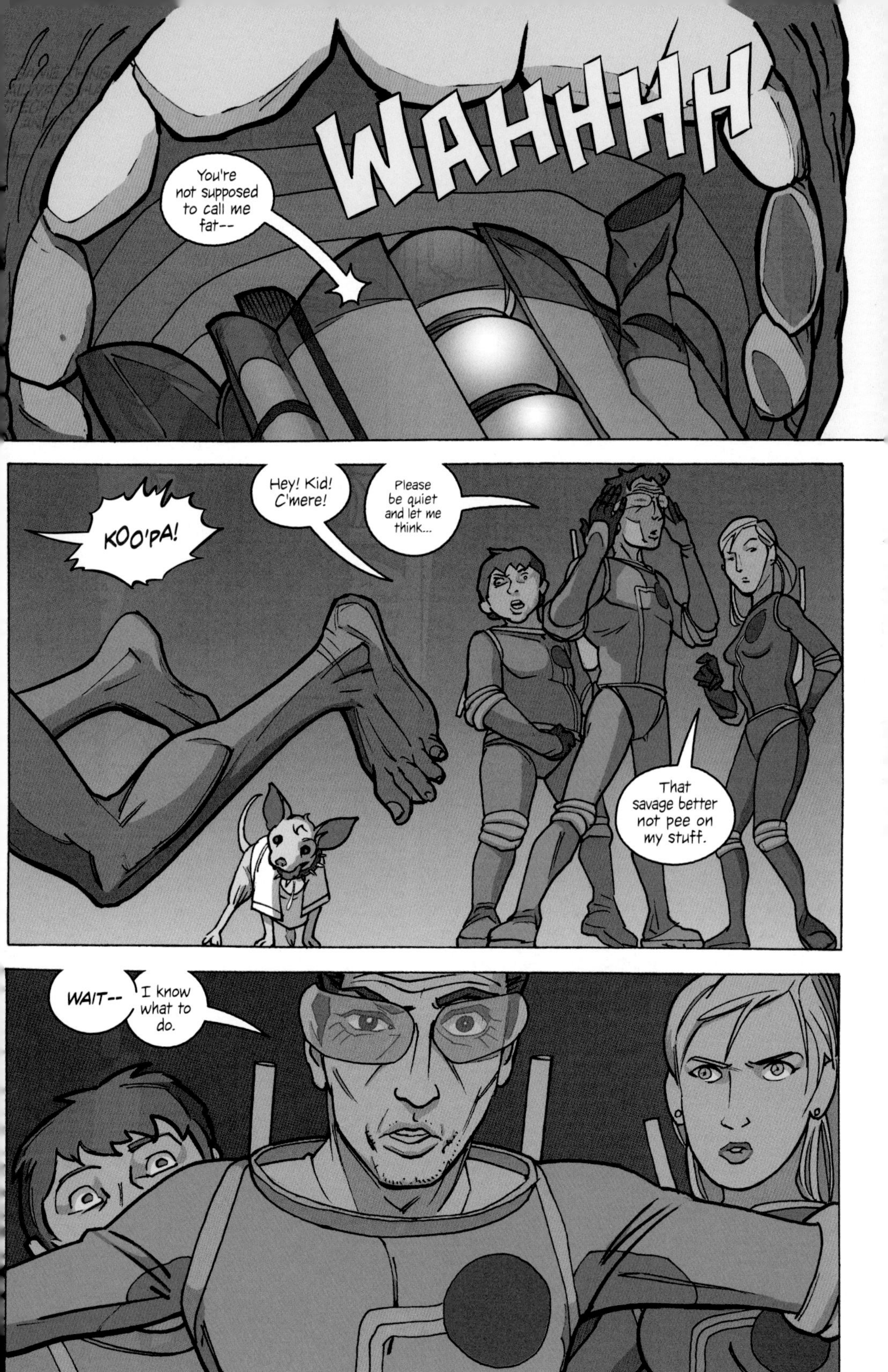
WAHHHH
You're not supposed to call me fat--
KOO'PA!
Hey! Kid! C'mere!
Please be quiet and let me think...
That savage better not pee on my stuff.
WAIT--
I know what to do.

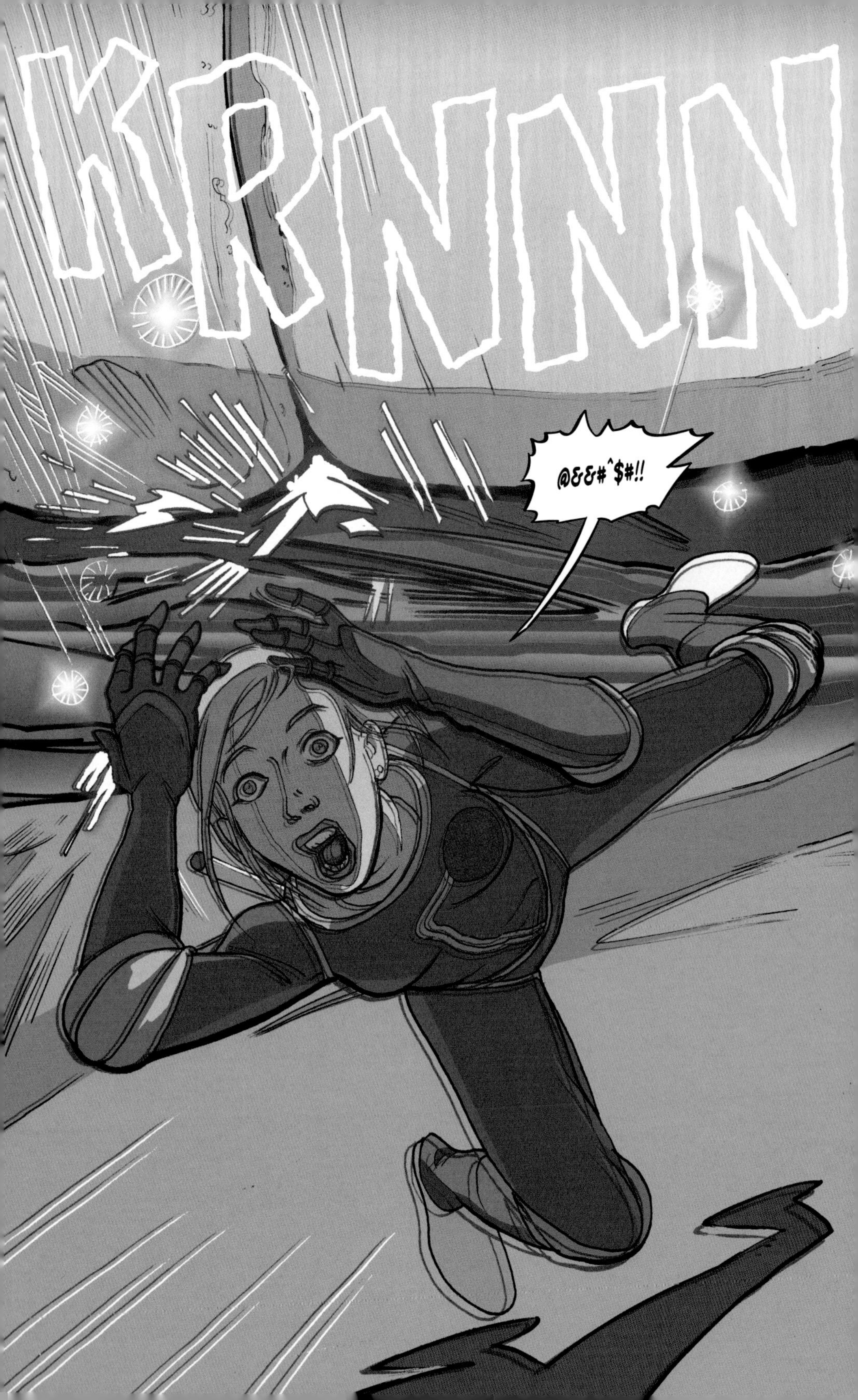
KRNNN
@&&#^$#!!

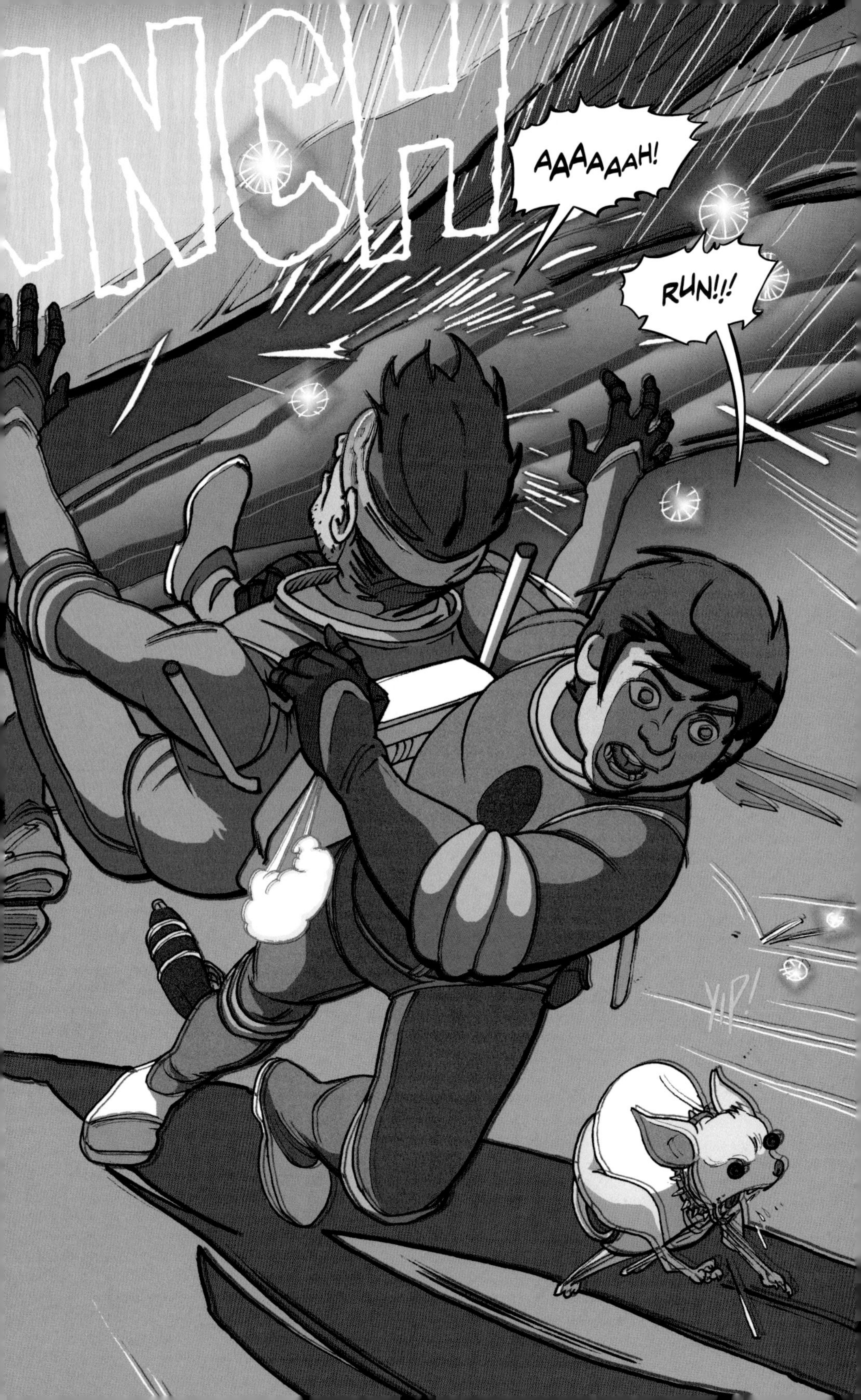

NCH
AAAAAAH!
RUN!!!
YIP!

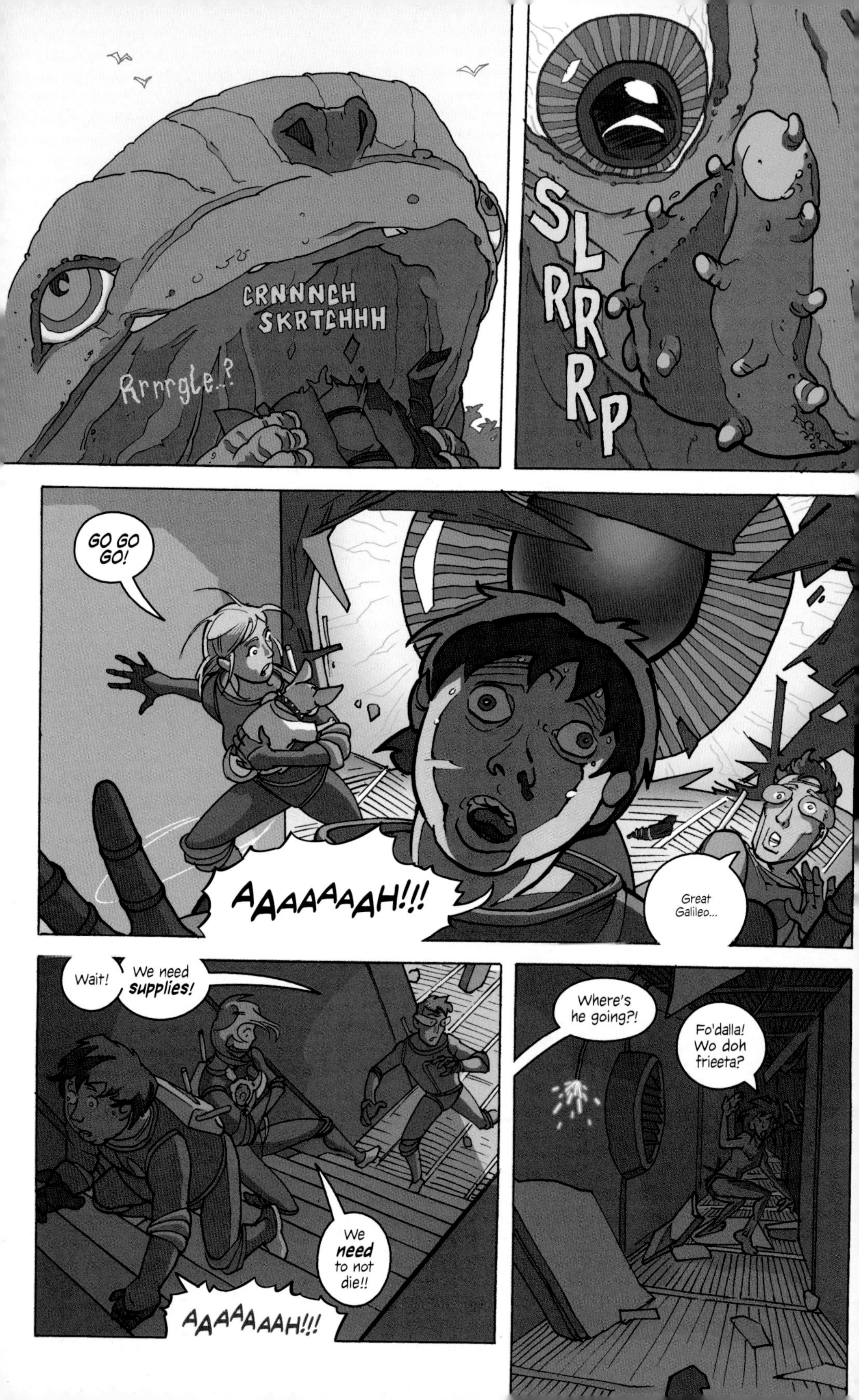
CRNNNCH
SKRTCHHH
Rrrrgle..?
SLRRRP
GO GO GO!
AAAAAAAH!!!
Great Galileo...
Wait!
We need supplies!
We need to not die!!
AAAAAAAH!!!
Where's he going?!
Fo'dalla! Wo doh frieeta?

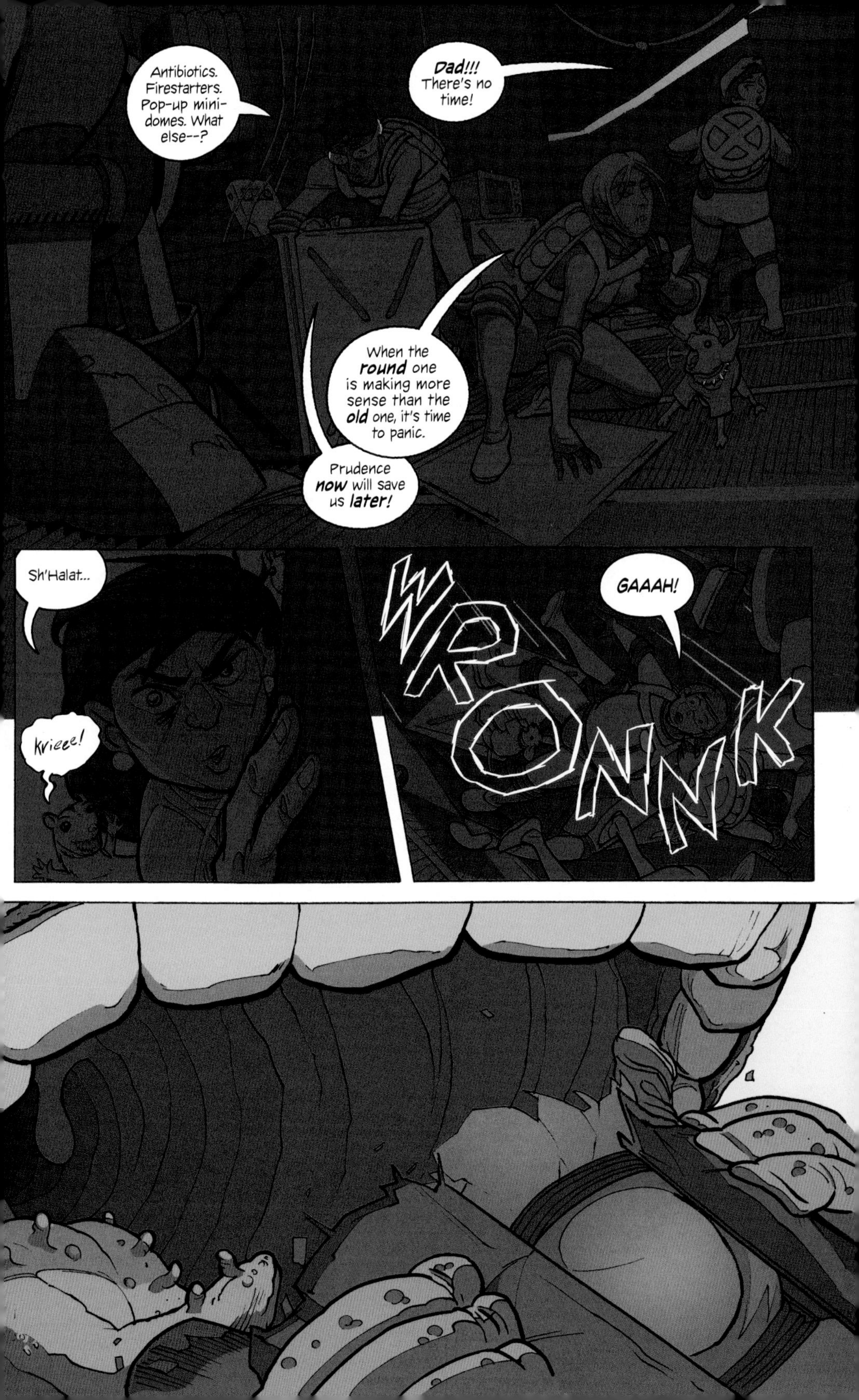
Antibiotics. Firestarters. Pop-up mini-domes. What else--?
Dad!!! There's no time!
When the round one is making more sense than the old one, it's time to panic.
Prudence now will save us later!
Sh'Halat...
krieee!
WRONNK
GAAAH!

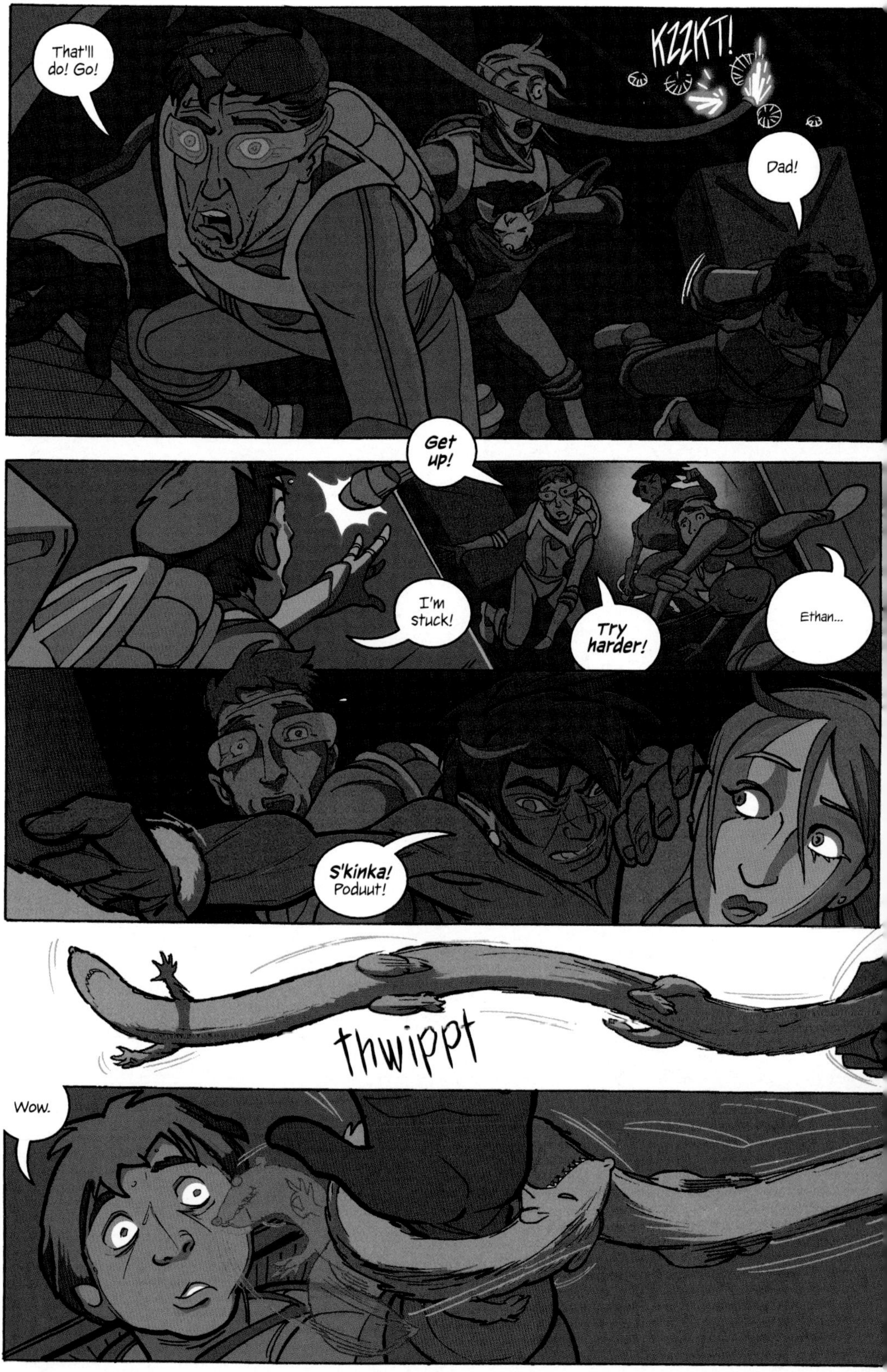
That'll do! Go!
KZZKT!
Dad!
Get up!
I'm stuck!
Try harder!
Ethan...
S'kinka! Poduut!
thwippt
Wow.

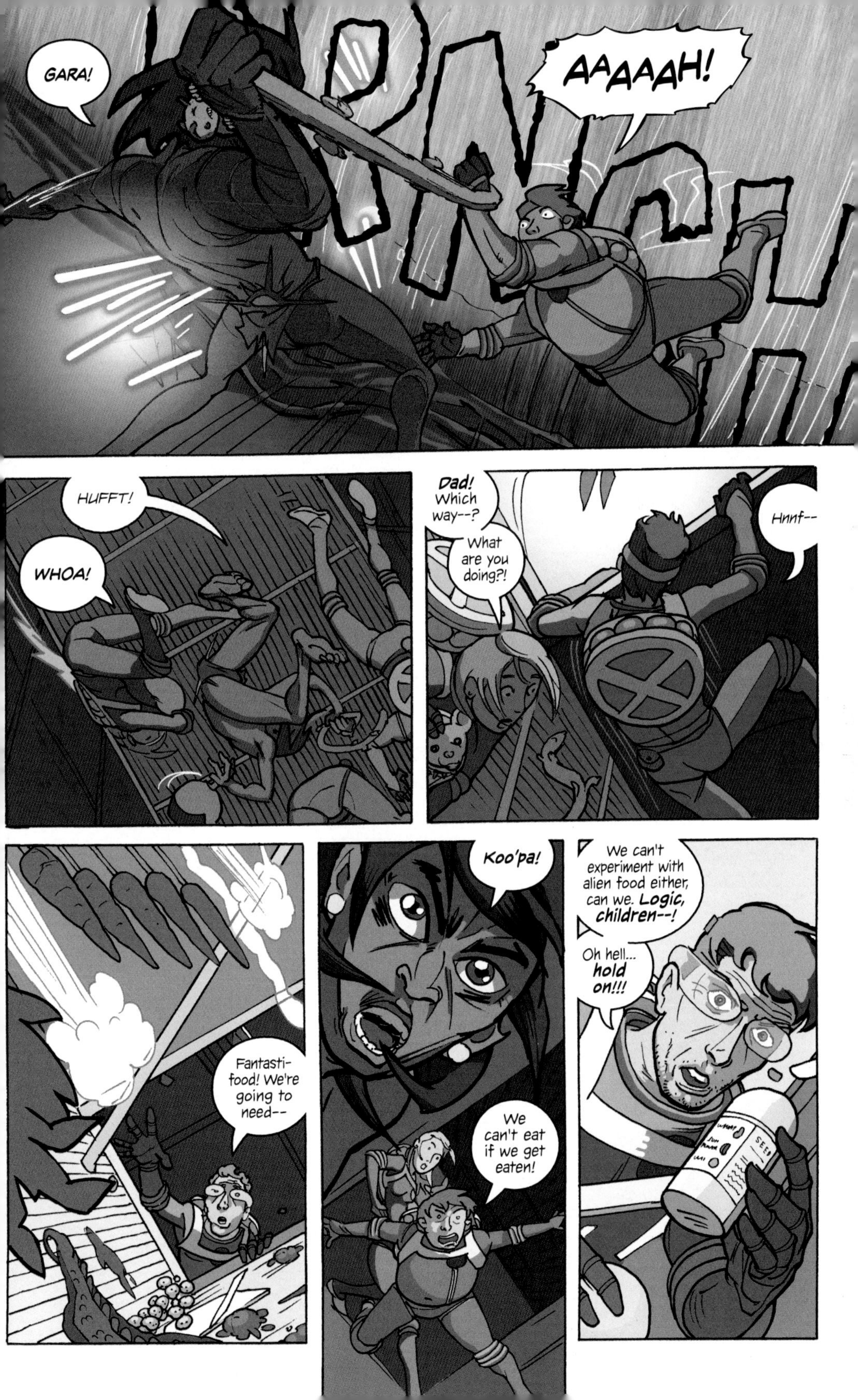

GARA!
AAAAAH!
HUFFT!
WHOA!
Dad! Which way--?
What are you doing?!
Hnnf--
Fantasti-food! We're going to need--
Koo'pa!
We can't eat if we get eaten!
We can't experiment with alien food either, can we. Logic, children--!
Oh hell... hold on!!!

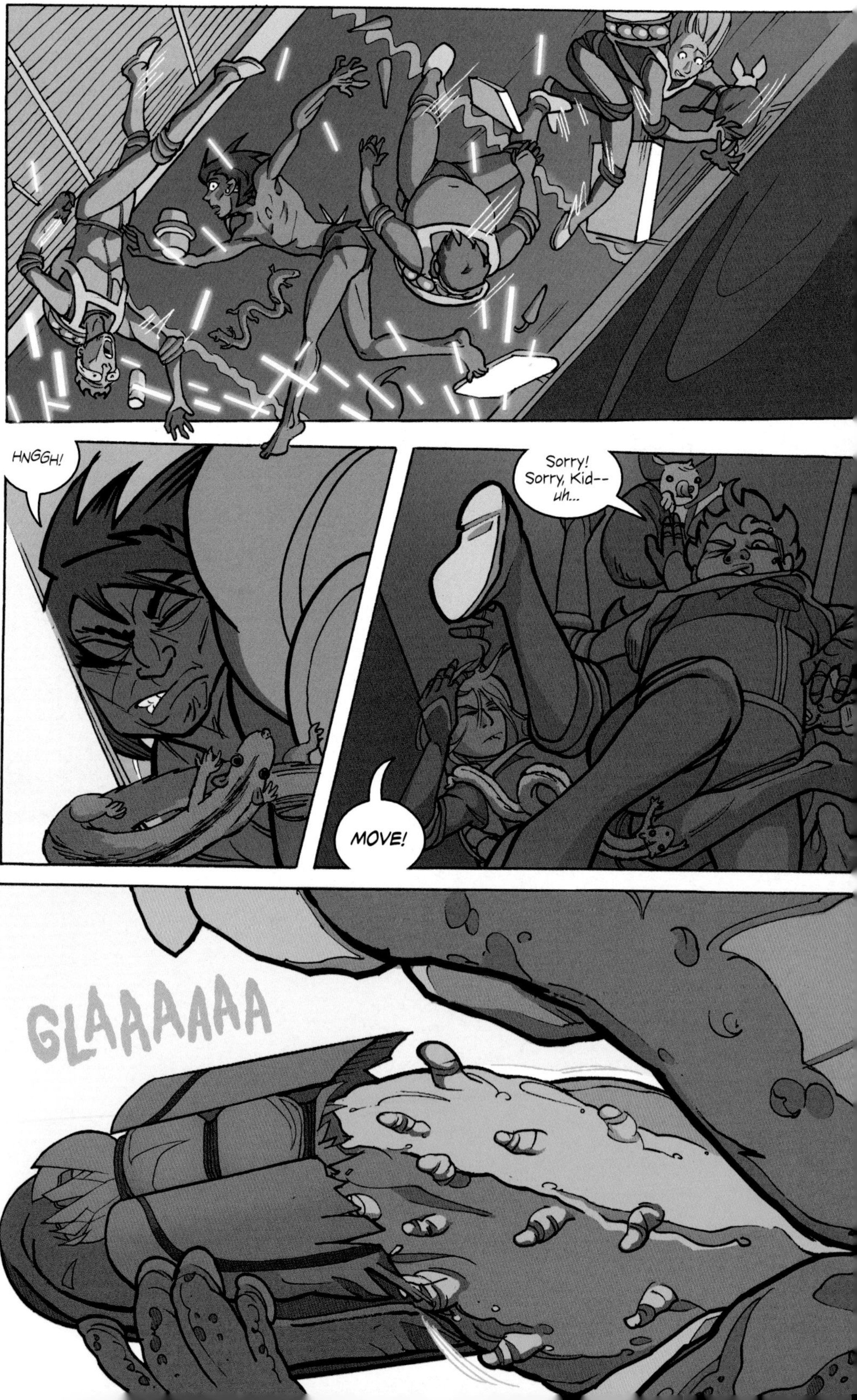
HNGGH!
Sorry! Sorry, Kid-- uh...
MOVE!
GLAAAAAA

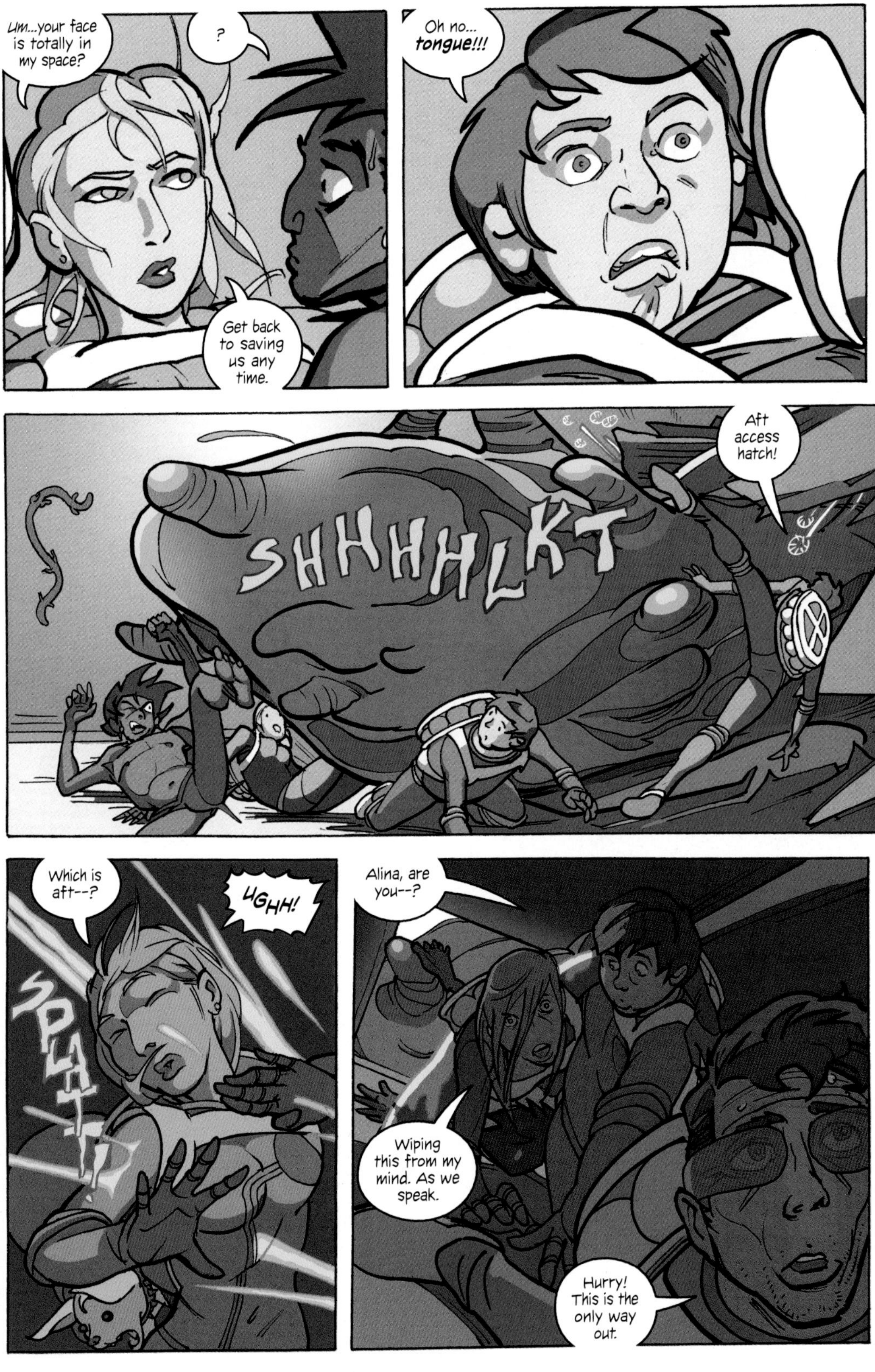
Um...your face is totally in my space?
?
Get back to saving us any time.
Oh no... **tongue!!!**
SHHHHLKT
Aft access hatch!
Which is aft--?
UGHH!
SPLATT!
Alina, are you--?
Wiping this from my mind. As we speak.
Hurry! This is the only way out.

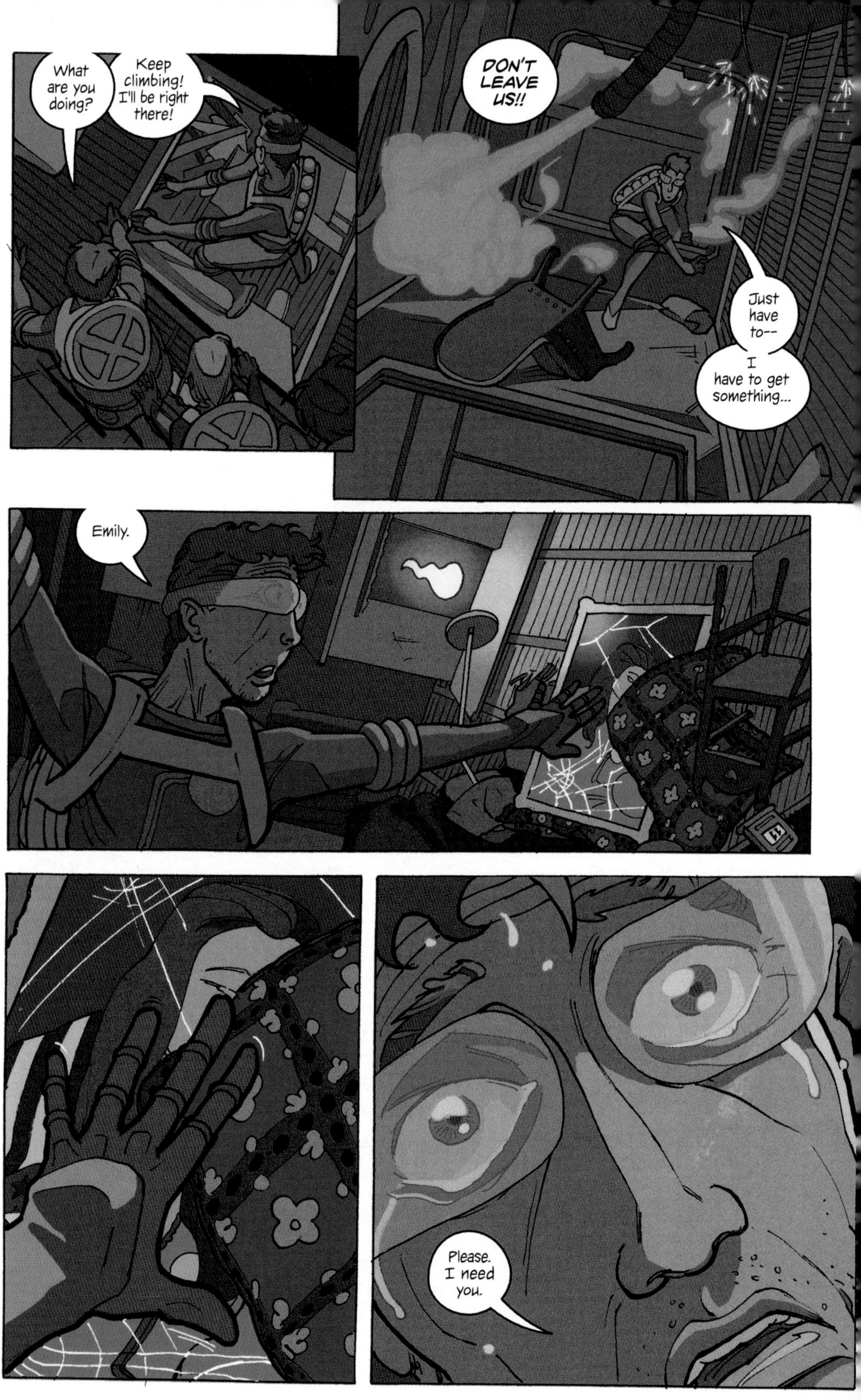
What are you doing?
Keep climbing! I'll be right there!
DON'T LEAVE US!!
Just have to--
I have to get something...
Emily.
Please. I need you.

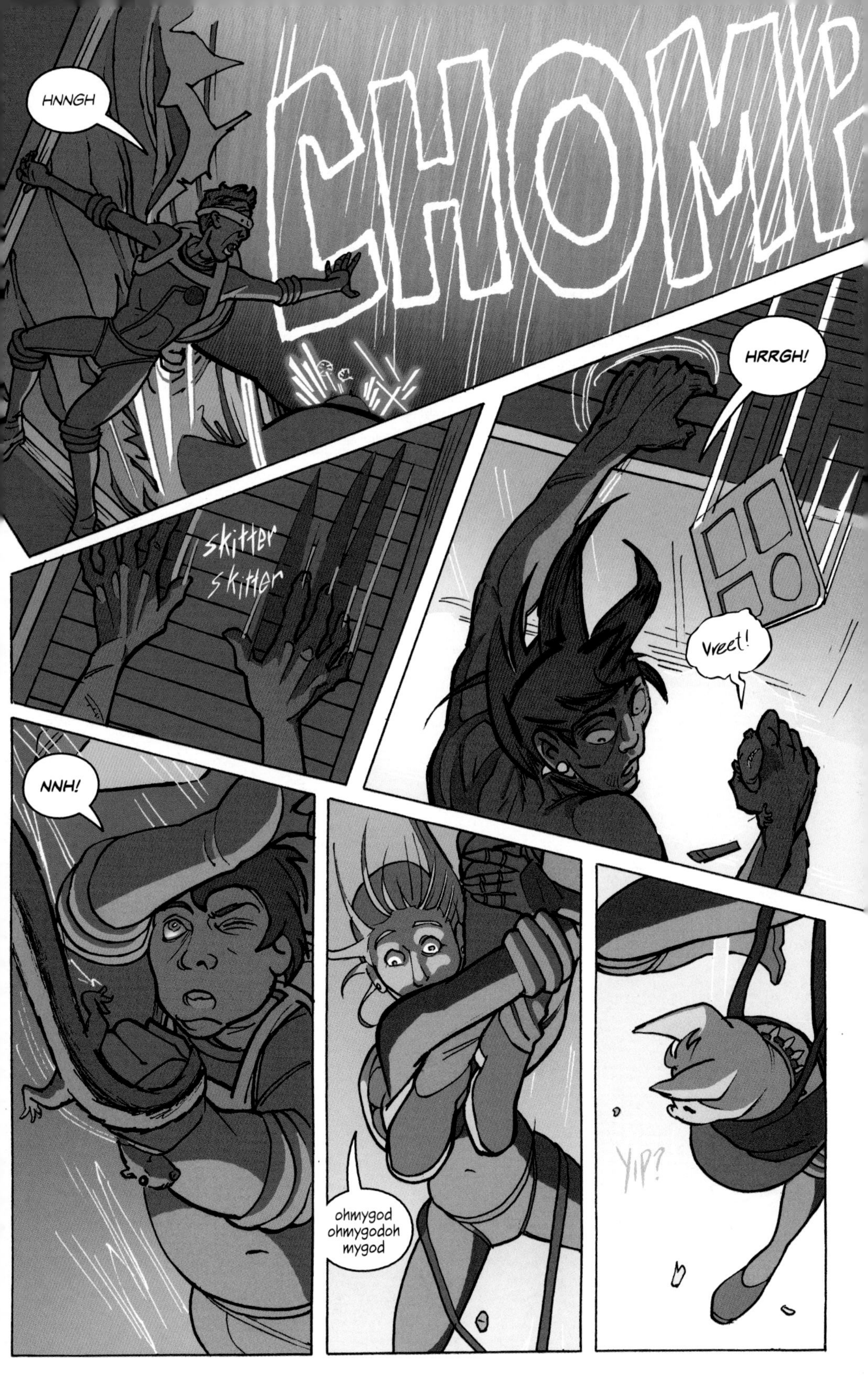
HNNGH
CHOMP
HRRGH!
skitter
skitter
Vreet!
NNH!
ohmygod
ohmygodoh
mygod
YIP?

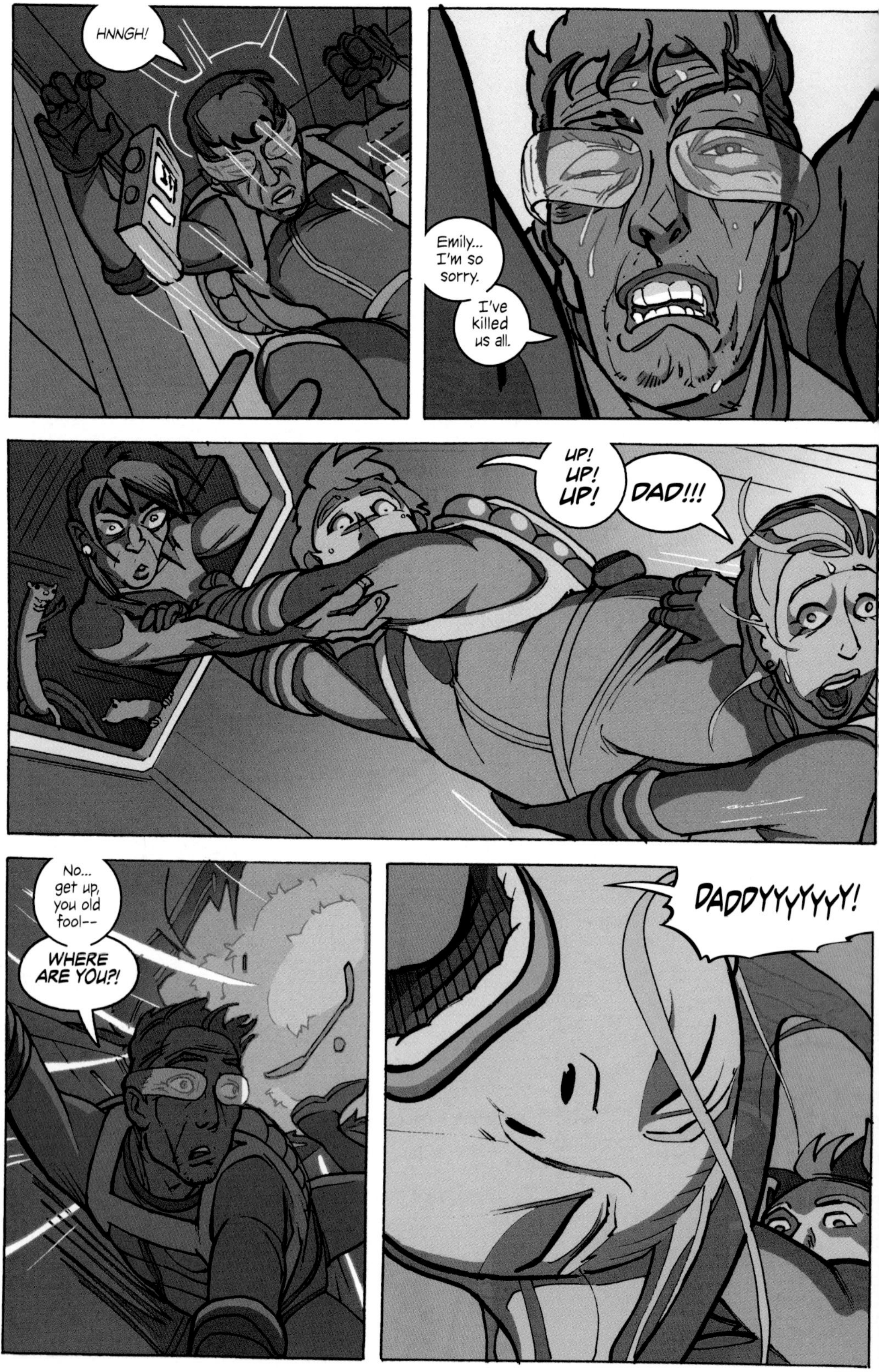
HNNGH!
Emily... I'm so sorry.
I've killed us all.
UP! UP! UP!
DAD!!!
No... get up, you old fool--
WHERE ARE YOU?!
DADDYYYYYYY!

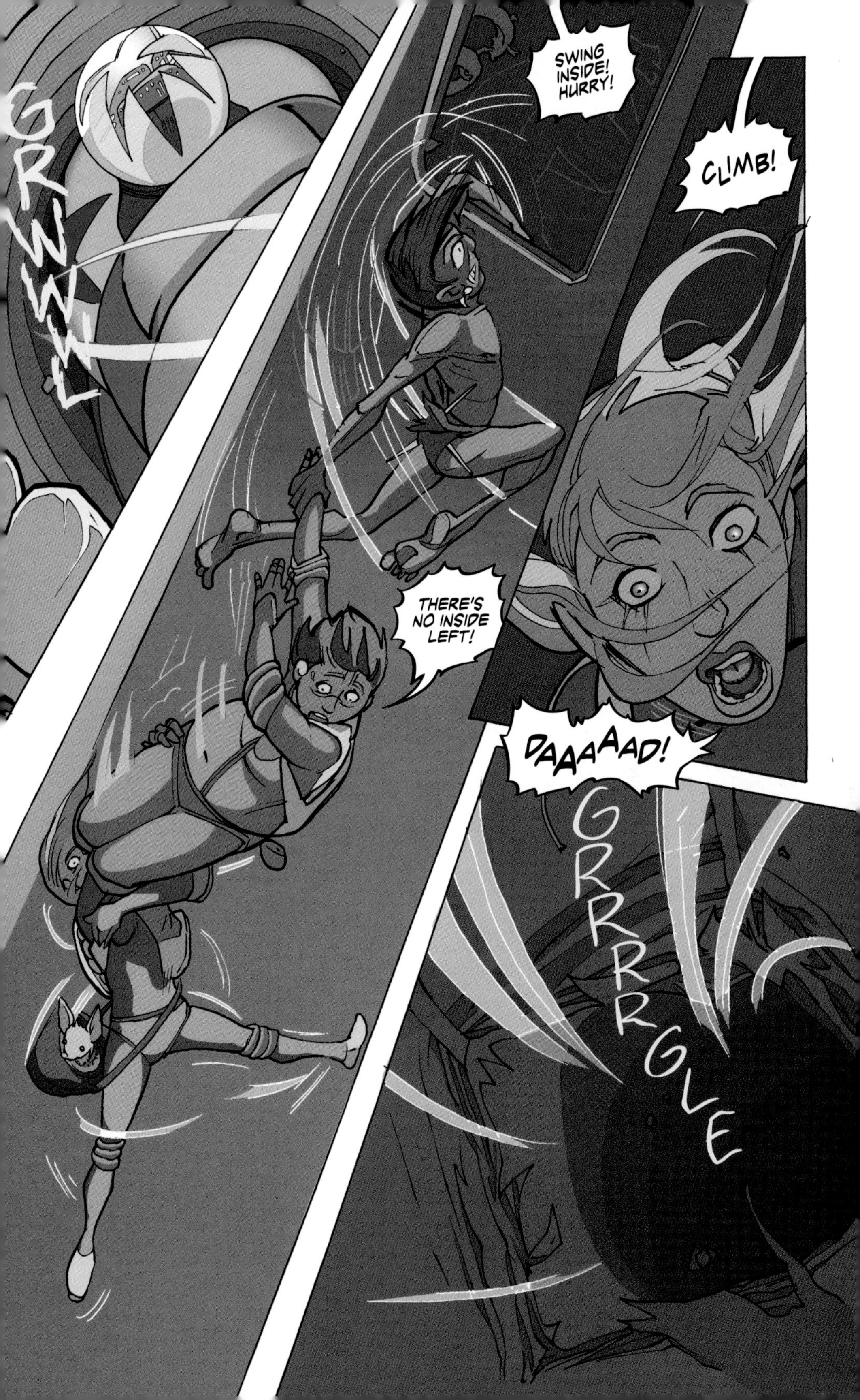
GRWWWL
SWING INSIDE! HURRY!
CLIMB!
THERE'S NO INSIDE LEFT!
DAAAAAD!
GRRRRGLE

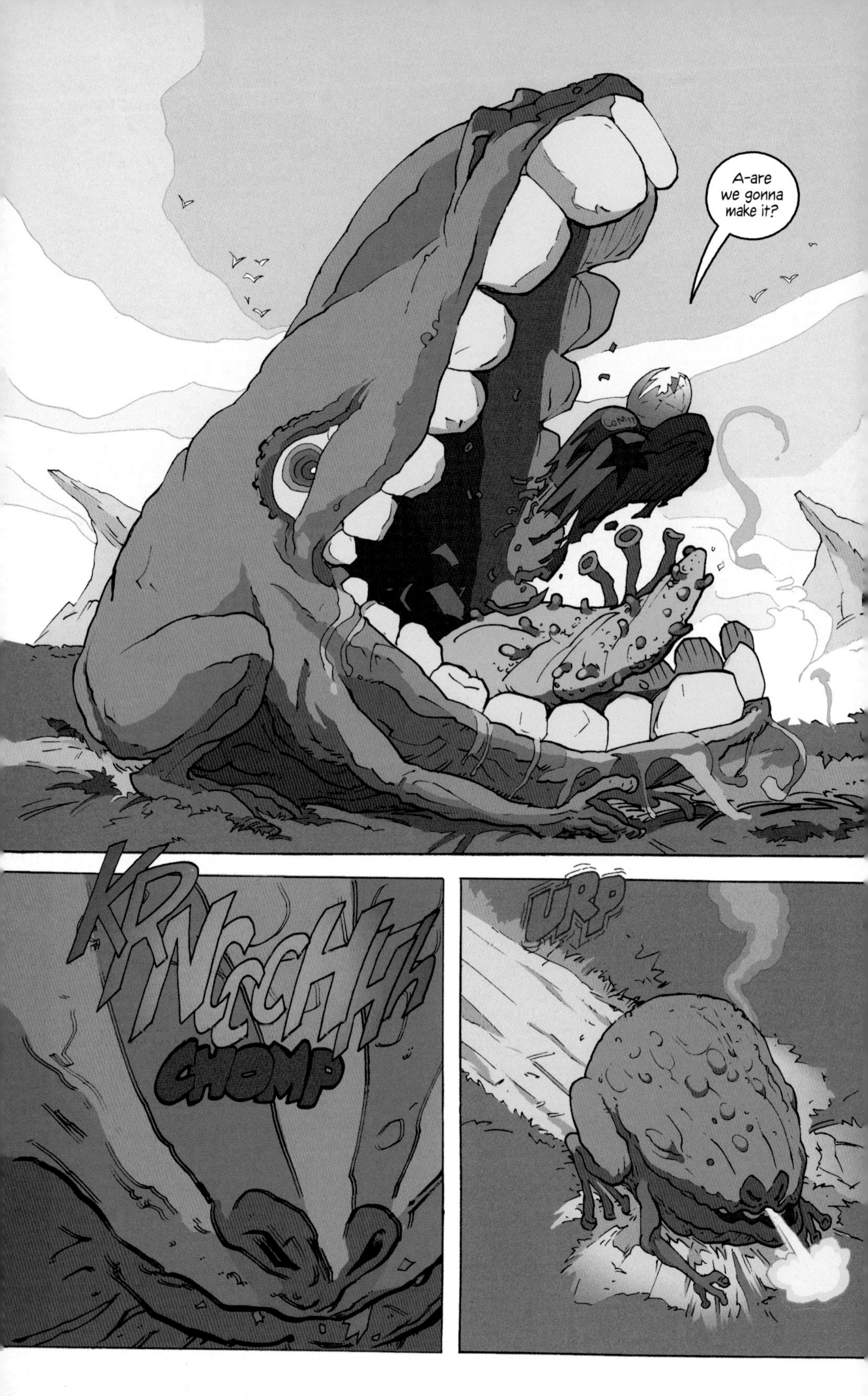
A-are we gonna make it?
KRNCCCHHK
CHOMP
URP

CHAPTER 5

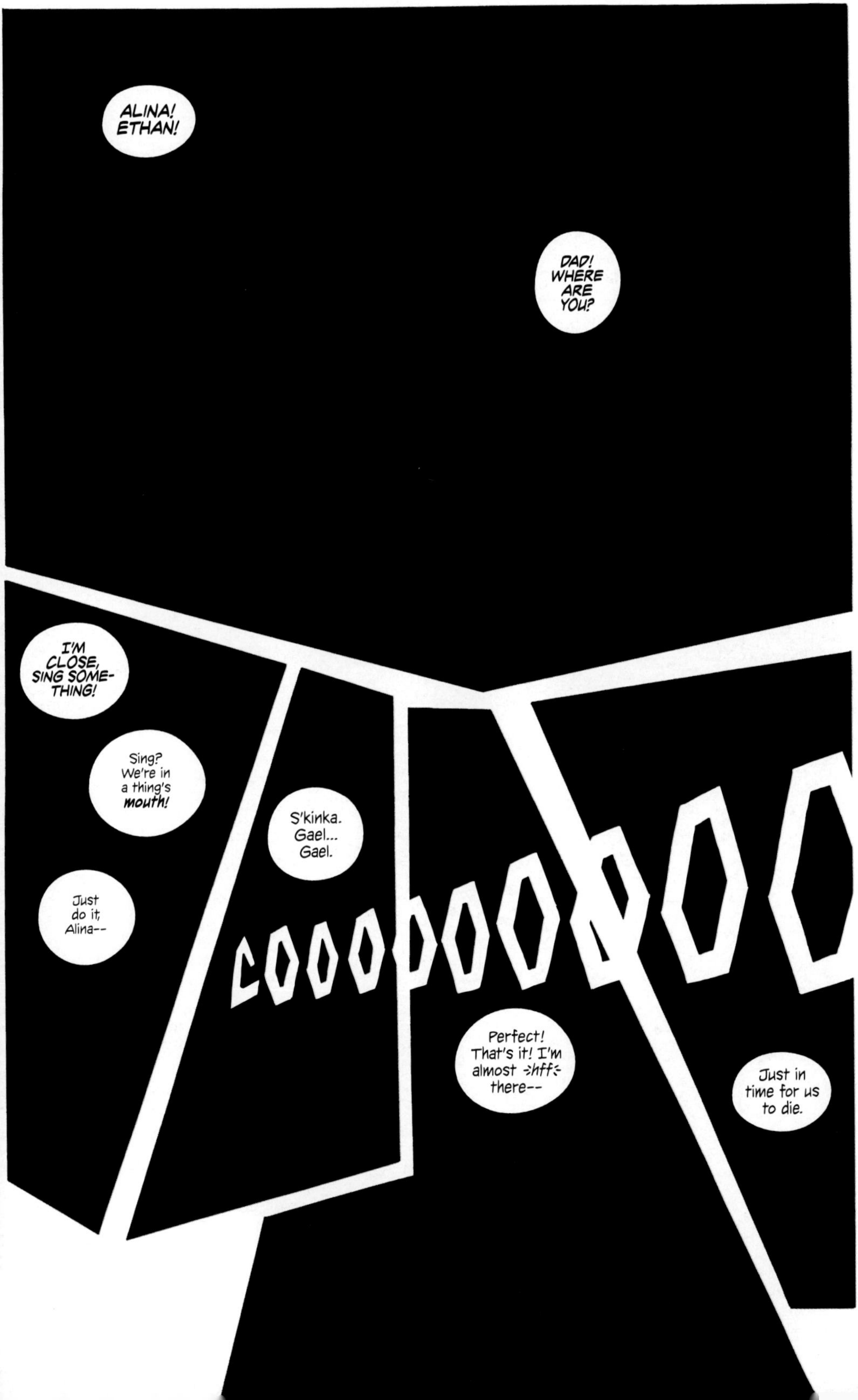
ALINA! ETHAN!
DAD! WHERE ARE YOU?
I'M CLOSE, SING SOME-THING!
Sing? We're in a thing's mouth!
Just do it, Alina--
S'kinka. Gael... Gael.
LOOOOOOOOOO
Perfect! That's it! I'm almost ⪫hff⪪ there--
Just in time for us to die.

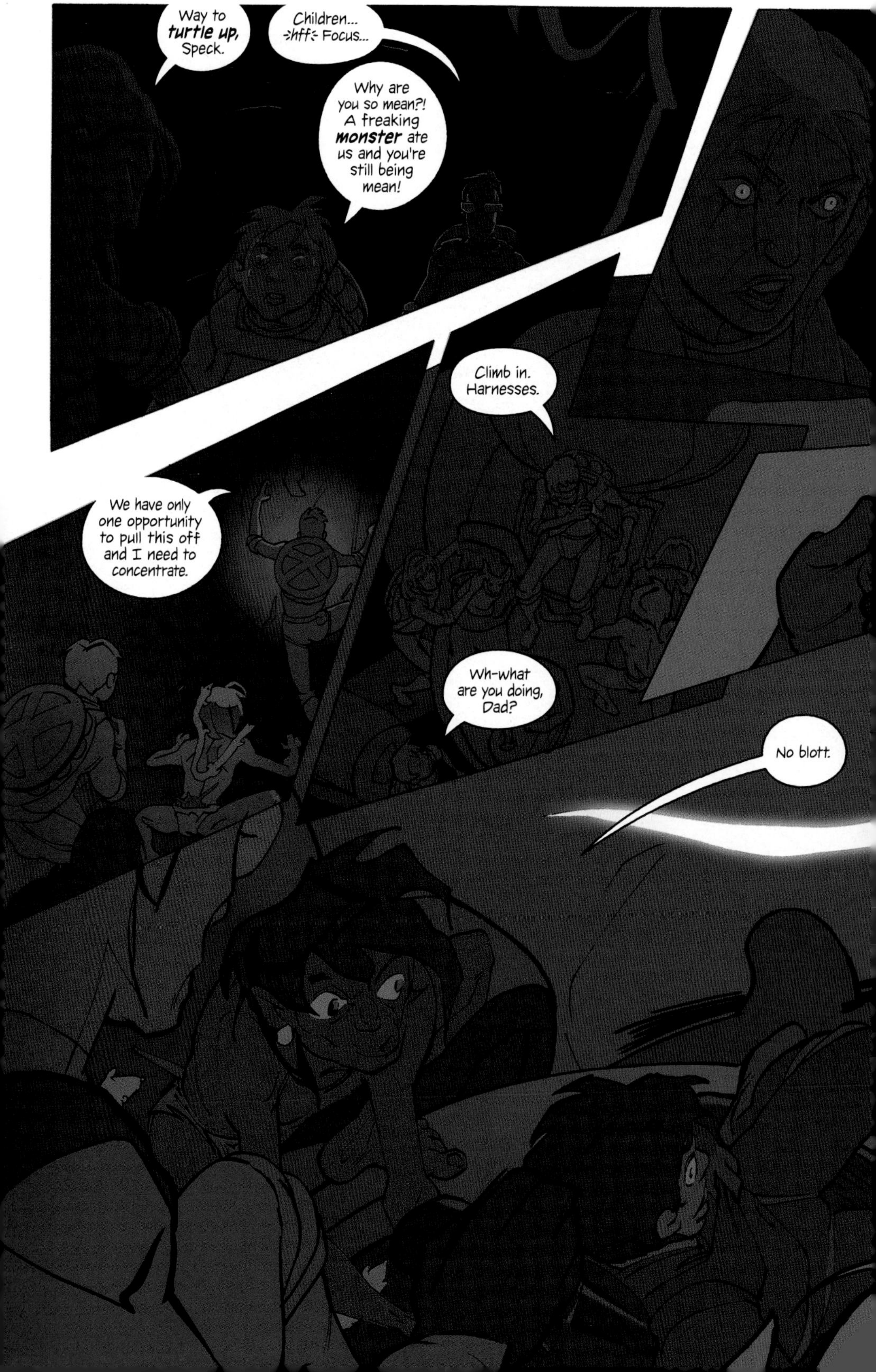
Way to turtle up, Speck.
Children... ⸗hff⸗ Focus...
Why are you so mean?! A freaking monster ate us and you're still being mean!
Climb in. Harnesses.
We have only one opportunity to pull this off and I need to concentrate.
Wh-what are you doing, Dad?
No blott.

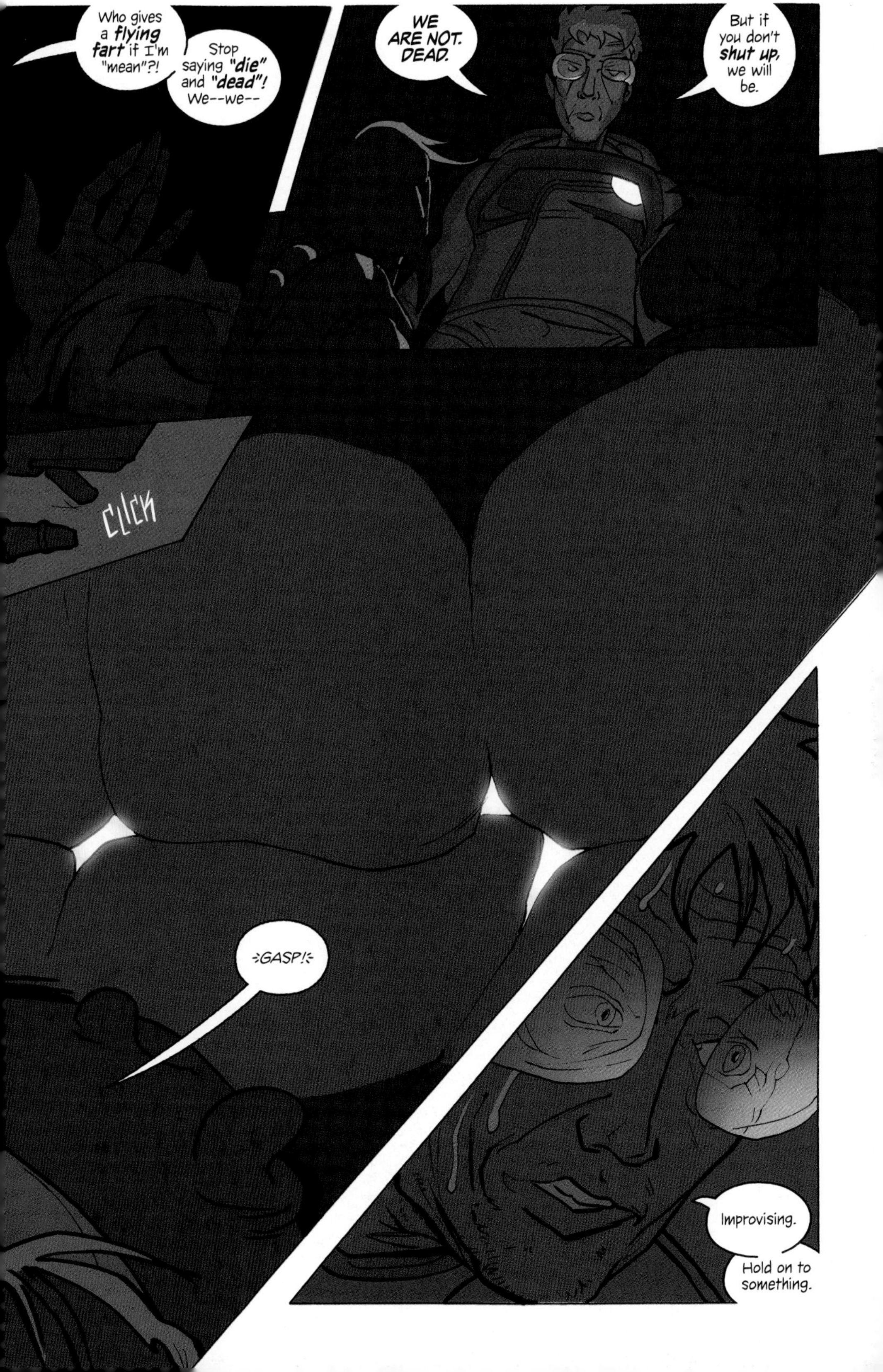

Who gives a **flying fart** if I'm "mean"?!
Stop saying **"die"** and **"dead"**! We--we--
WE ARE NOT. DEAD.
But if you don't **shut up,** we will be.
CLICK
GASP!
Improvising.
Hold on to something.

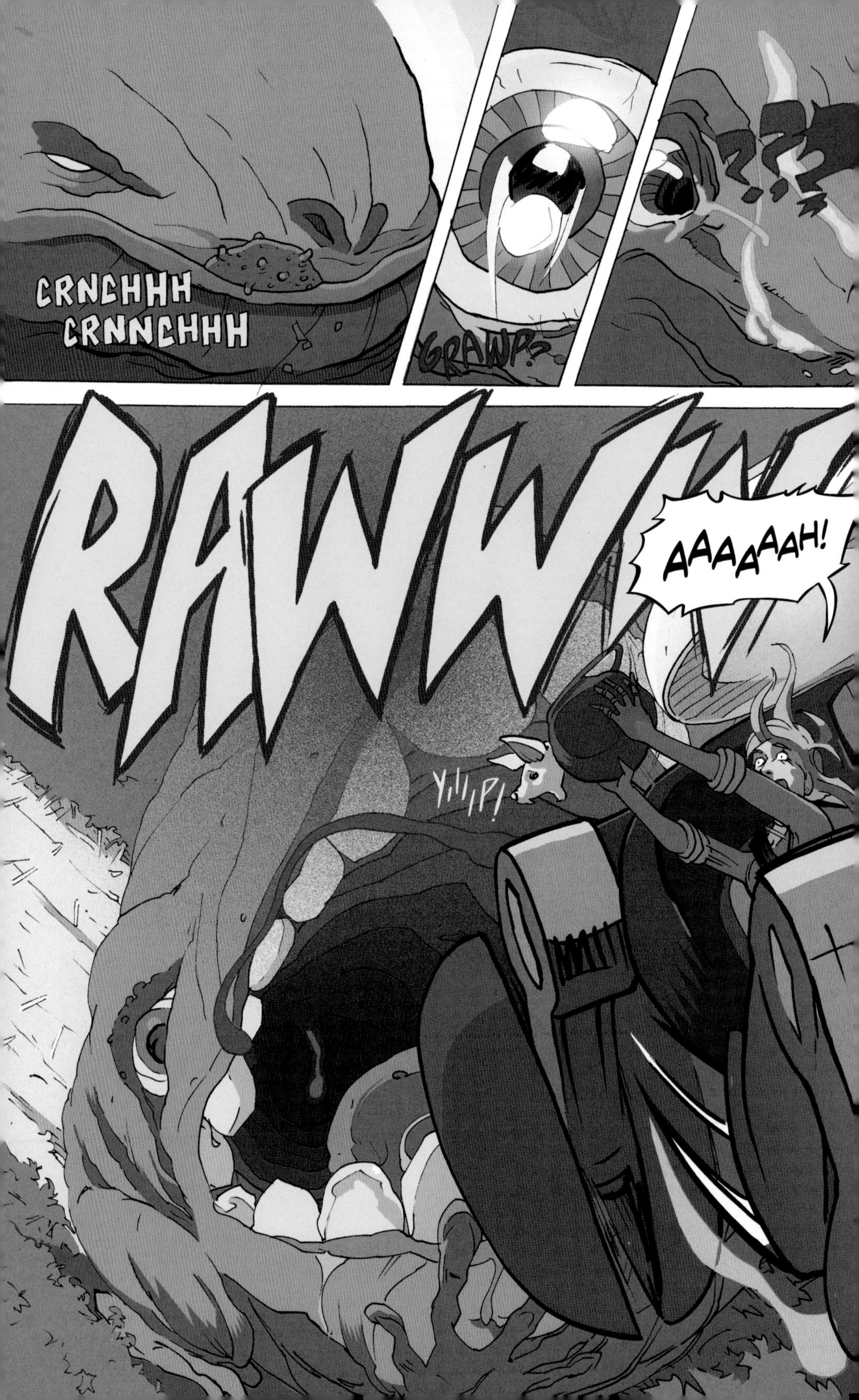
CRNCHHH
CRNNCHHH
GRAWP?
???
RAWW
AAAAAAH!
YIIIP!

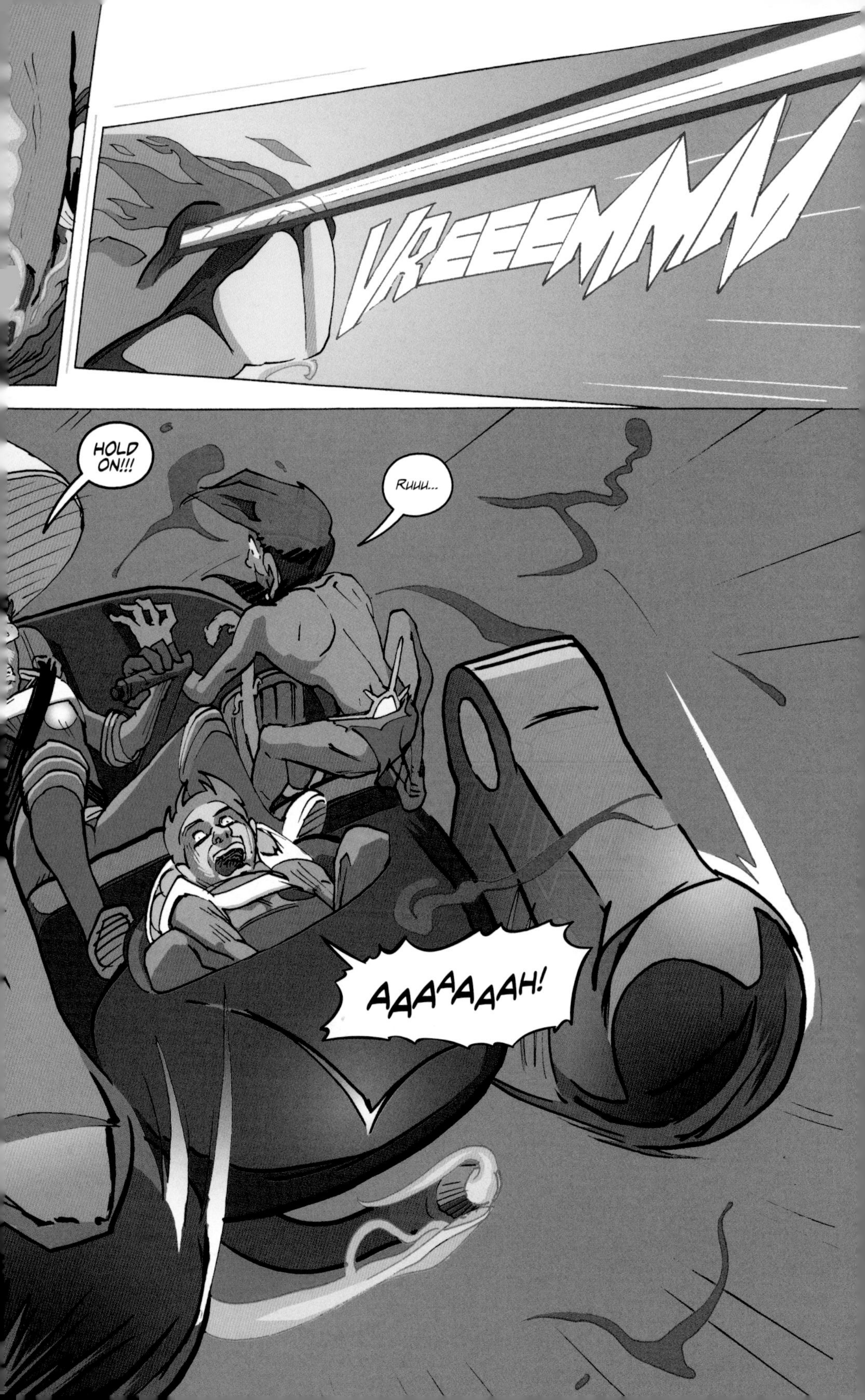
VREEEMMM
HOLD ON!!!
Ruuu...
AAAAAAAH!

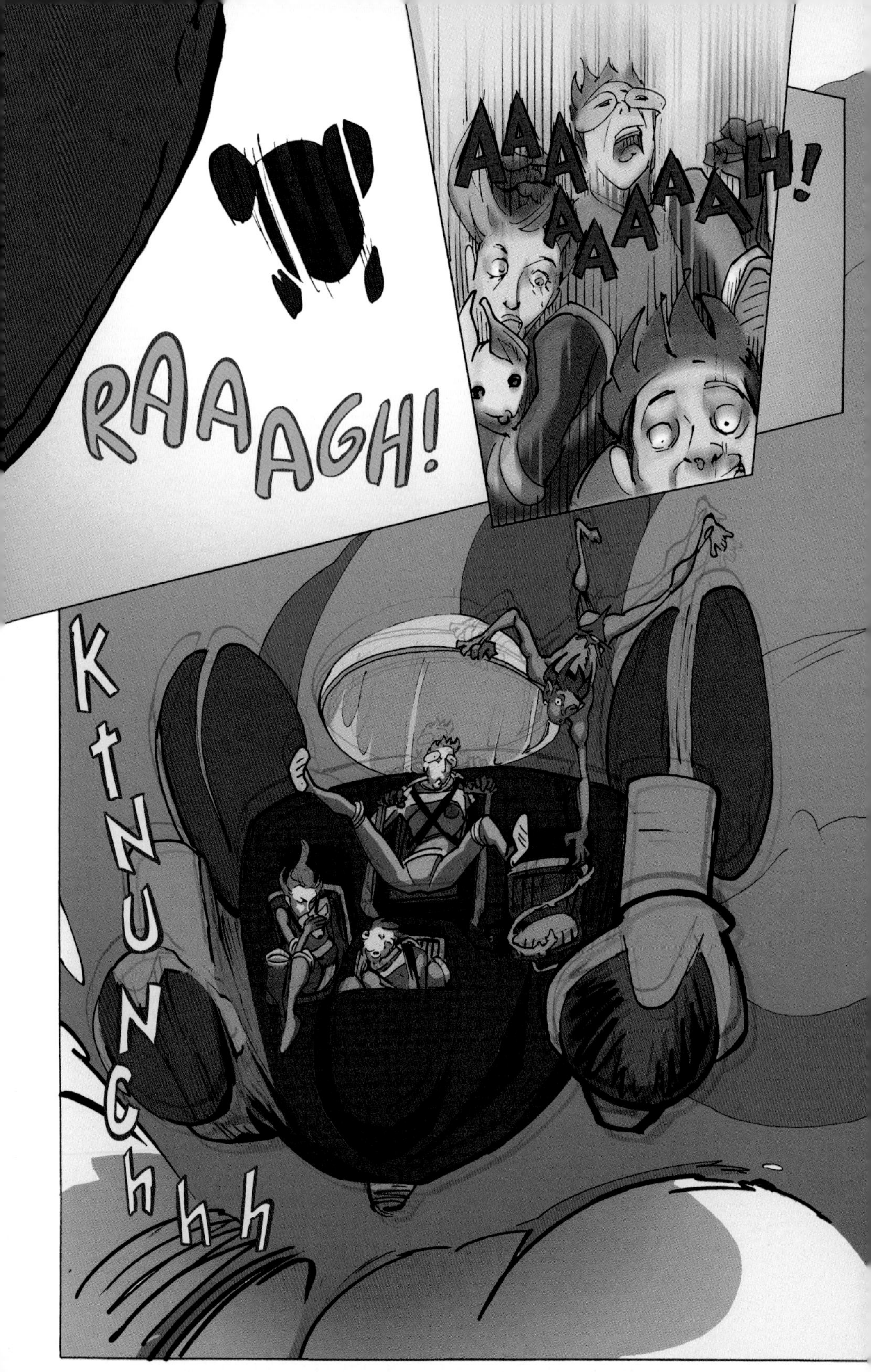

RAAAGH!
AAAAAAAAH!
KtNUNChhh

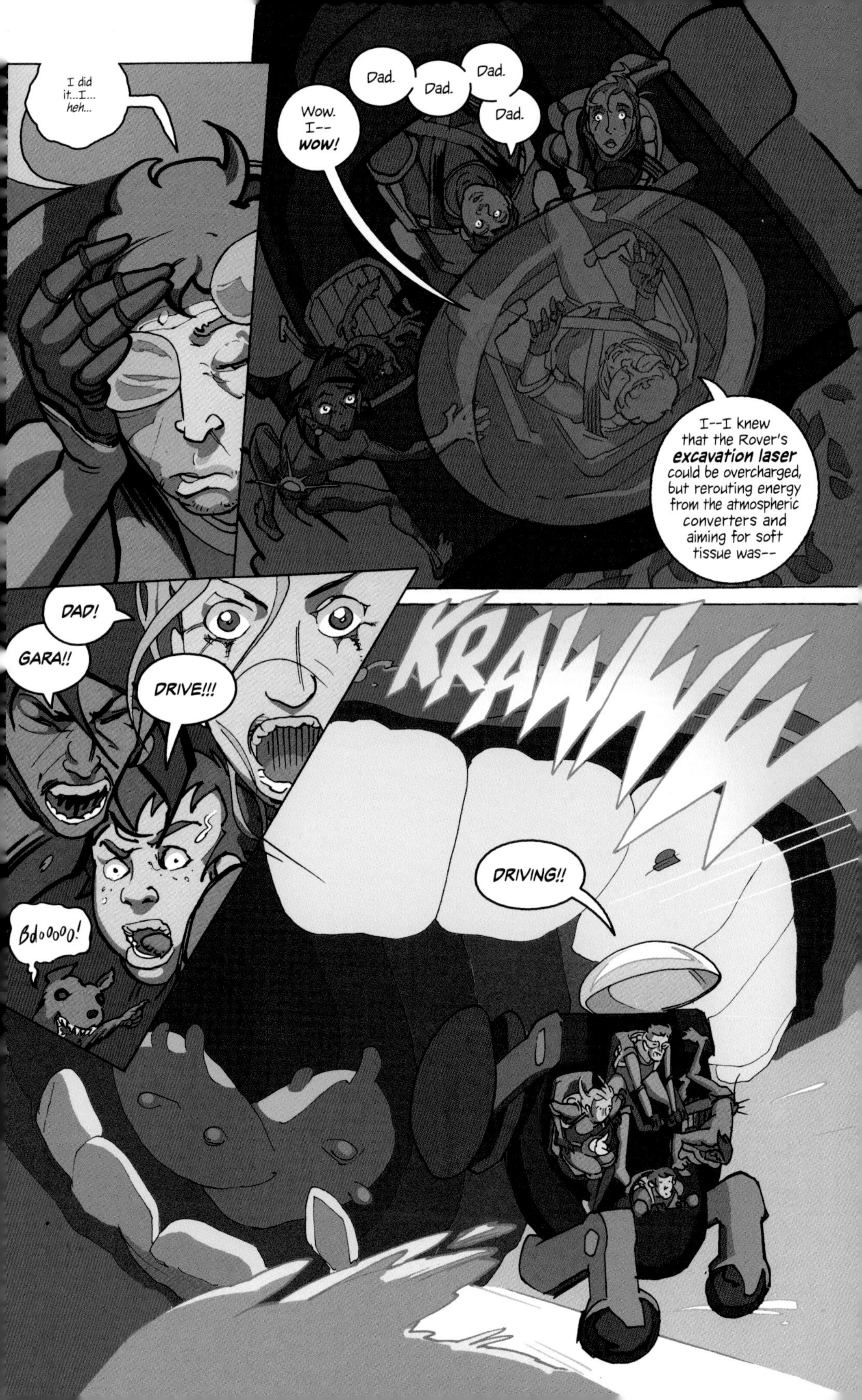
I did it...I... heh...
Wow. I-- WOW!
Dad.
Dad.
Dad.
Dad.
I--I knew that the Rover's **excavation laser** could be overcharged, but rerouting energy from the atmospheric converters and aiming for soft tissue was--
DAD!
GARA!!
DRIVE!!!
Bdooooo!
KRAWWW
DRIVING!!

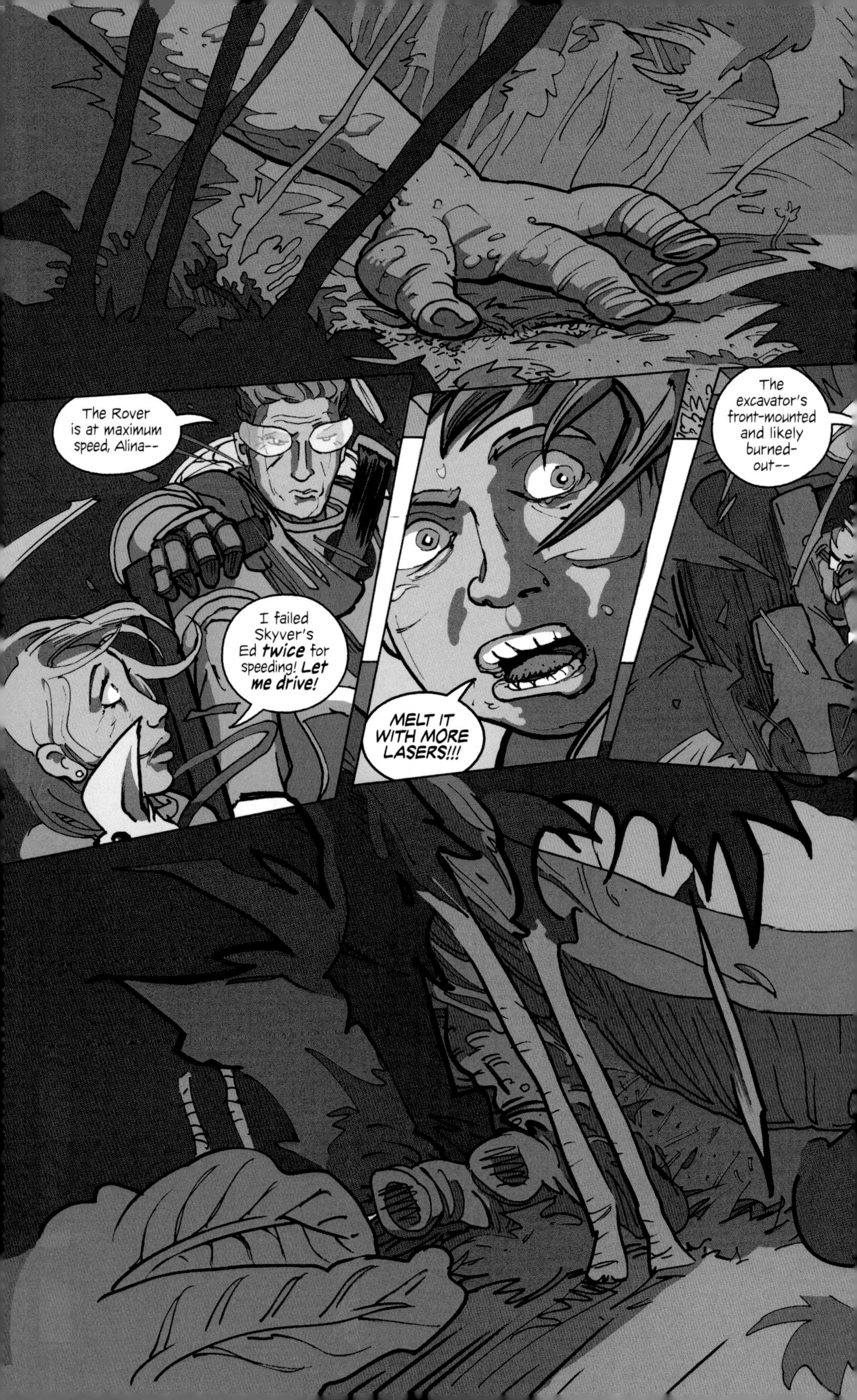
The Rover is at maximum speed, Alina--
I failed Skyver's Ed twice for speeding! Let me drive!
MELT IT WITH MORE LASERS!!!
The excavator's front-mounted and likely burned-out--

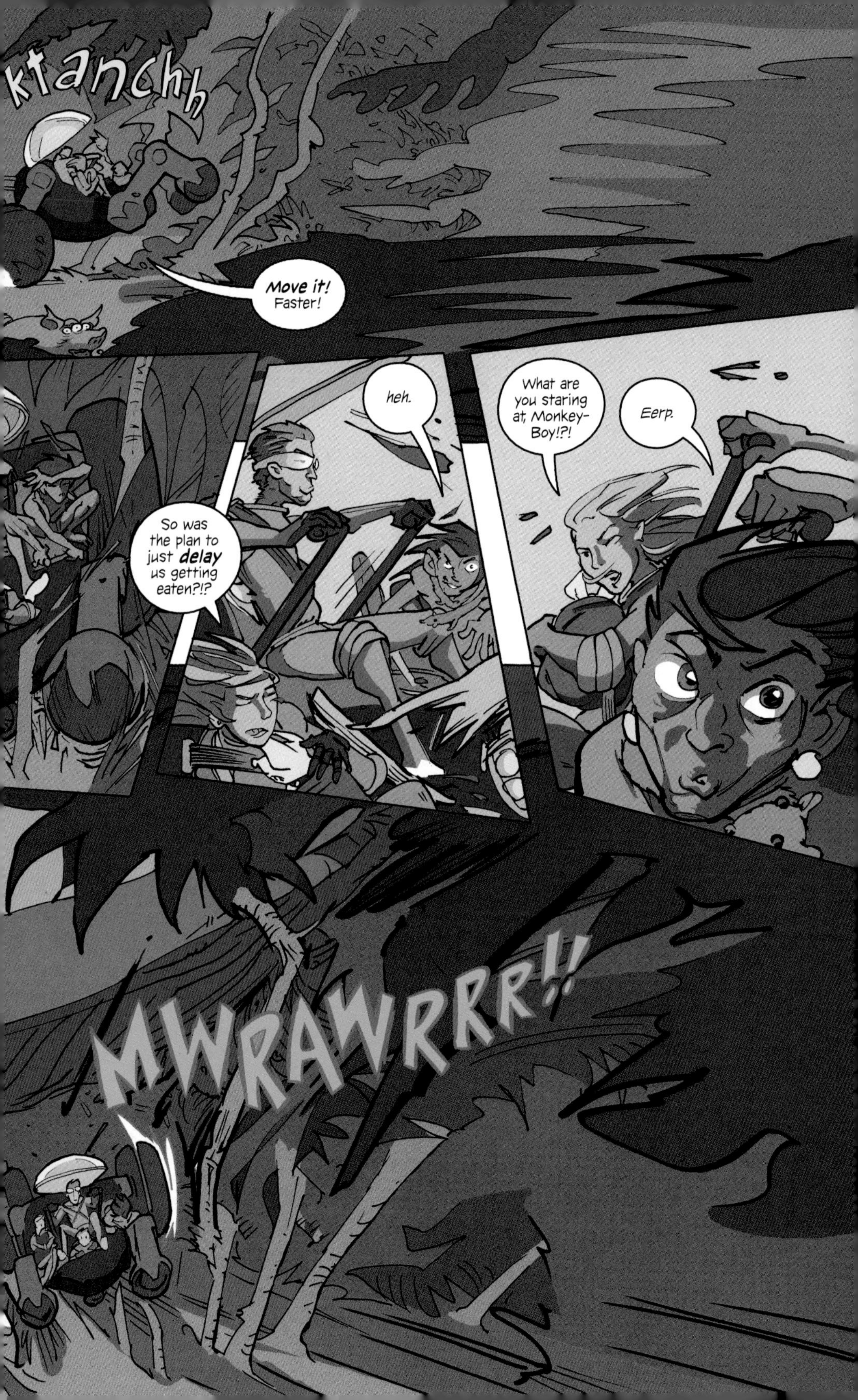

ktanchh
Move it! Faster!
So was the plan to just delay us getting eaten?!?
heh.
What are you staring at, Monkey-Boy!?!
Eerp.
MWRAWRRR!!

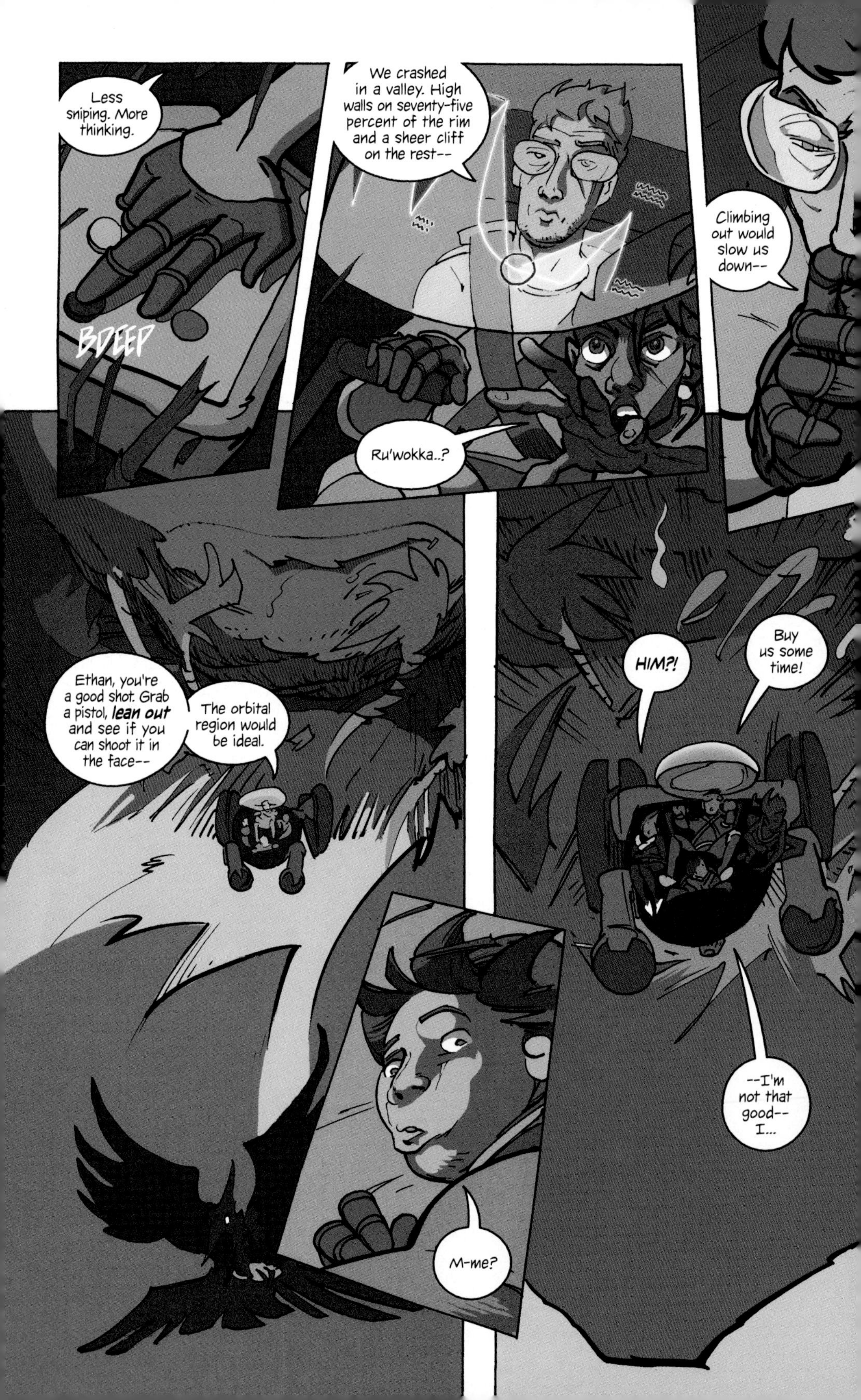
Less sniping. More thinking.
BDEEP
We crashed in a valley. High walls on seventy-five percent of the rim and a sheer cliff on the rest--
Ru'wokka..?
Climbing out would slow us down--
Ethan, you're a good shot. Grab a pistol, ***lean out*** and see if you can shoot it in the face--
The orbital region would be ideal.
HIM?!
Buy us some time!
M-me?
--I'm not that good-- I...

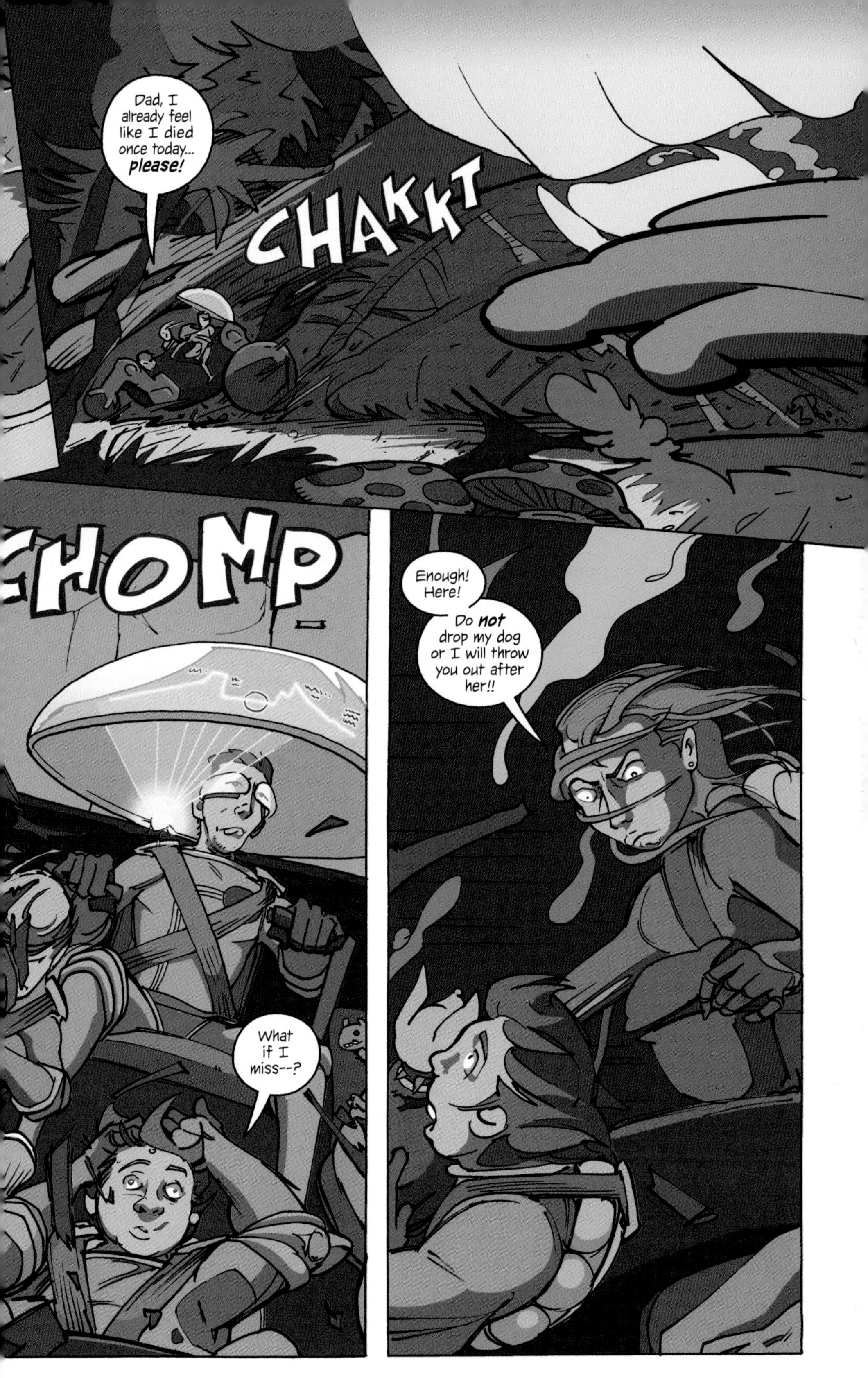
Dad, I already feel like I died once today... **please!**
CHAKKT
CHOMP
What if I miss--?
Enough! Here!
Do **not** drop my dog or I will throw you out after her!!

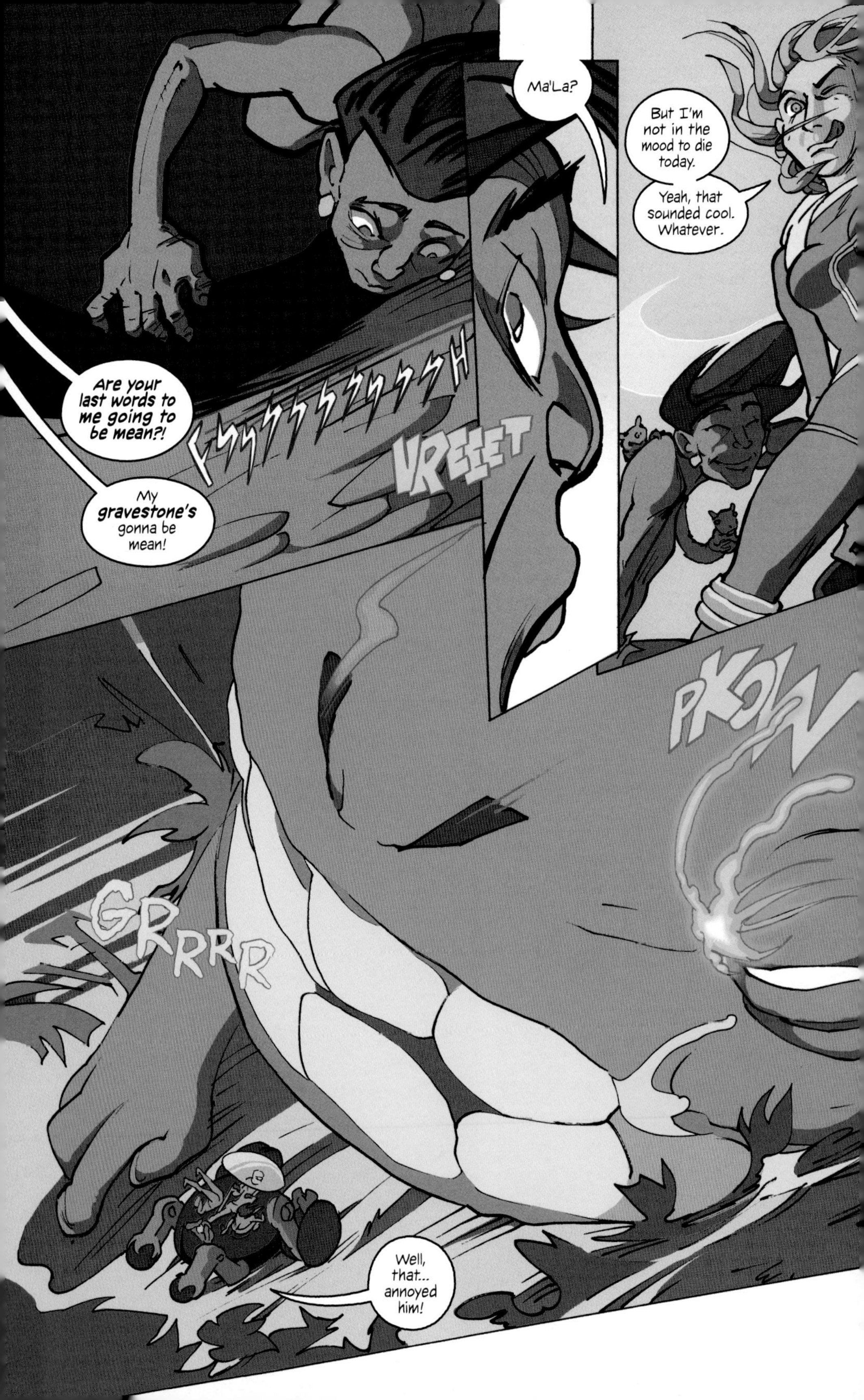
Are your last words to me going to be mean?!
My gravestone's gonna be mean!
Ma'La?
But I'm not in the mood to die today.
Yeah, that sounded cool. Whatever.
VREEET
PKOW
GRRRR
Well, that... annoyed him!

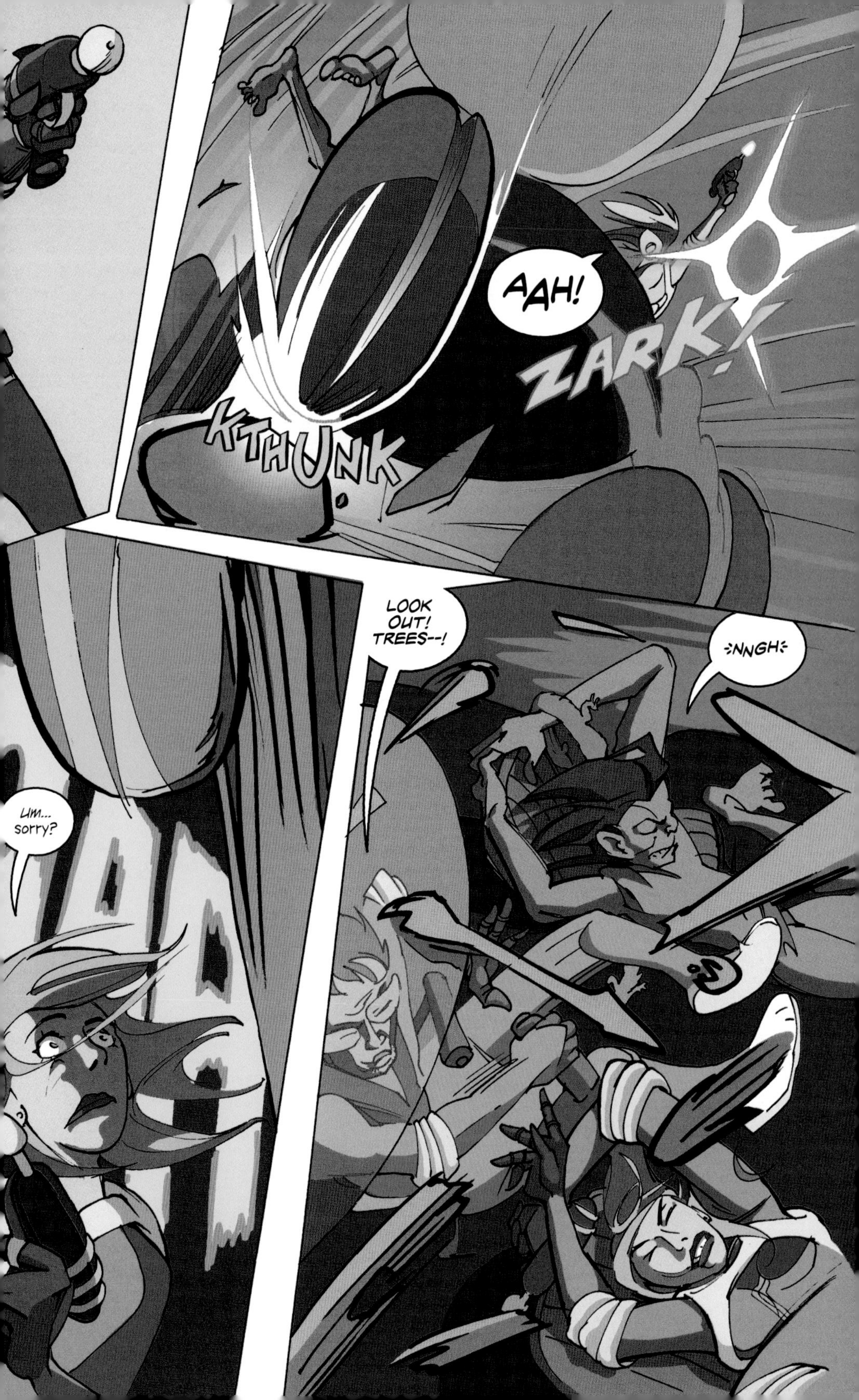
AAH!
ZARK!
KTHUNK
LOOK OUT! TREES--!
NNGH
Um... sorry?

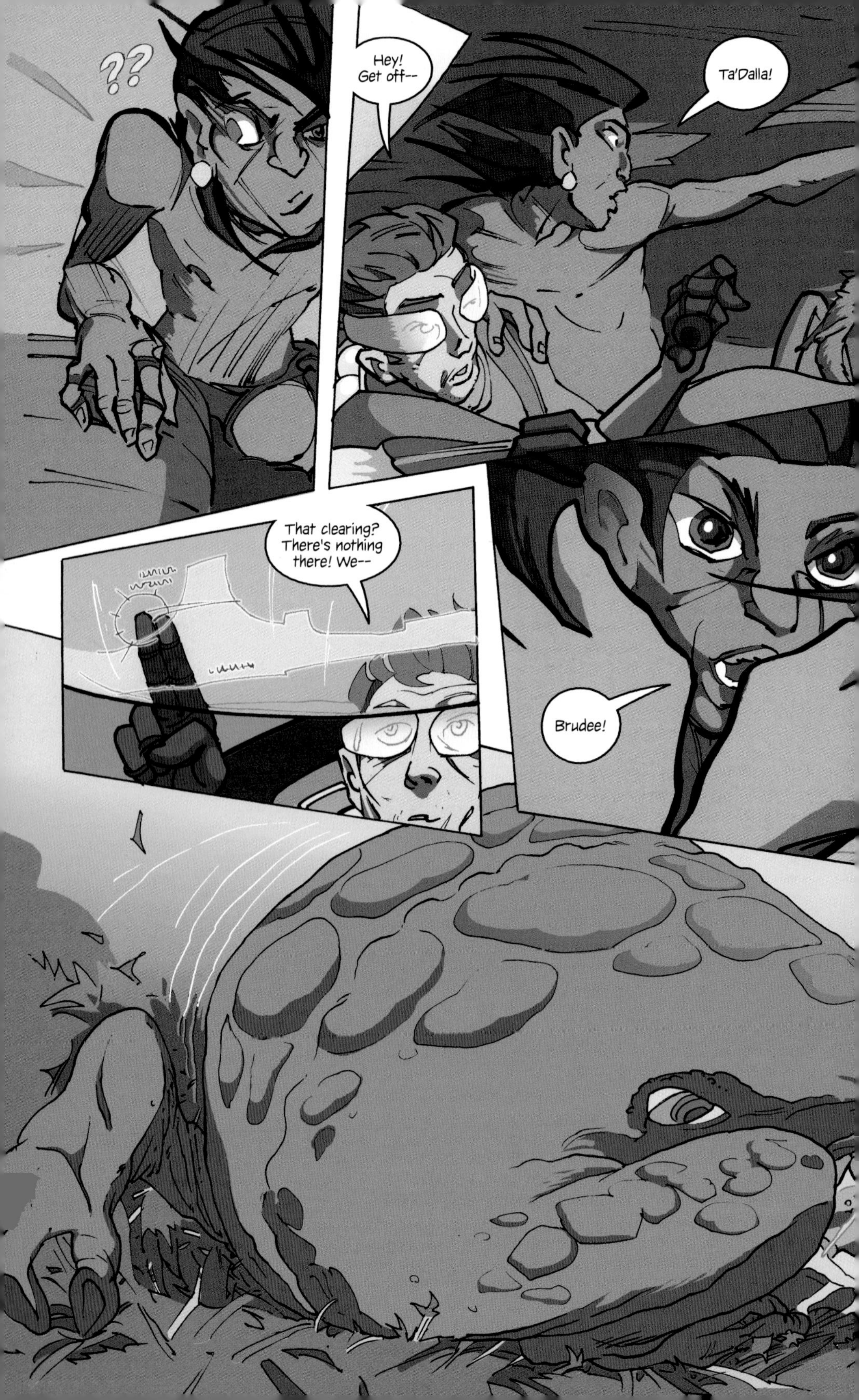
??
Hey! Get off--
Ta'Dalla!
That clearing? There's nothing there! We--
Brudee!

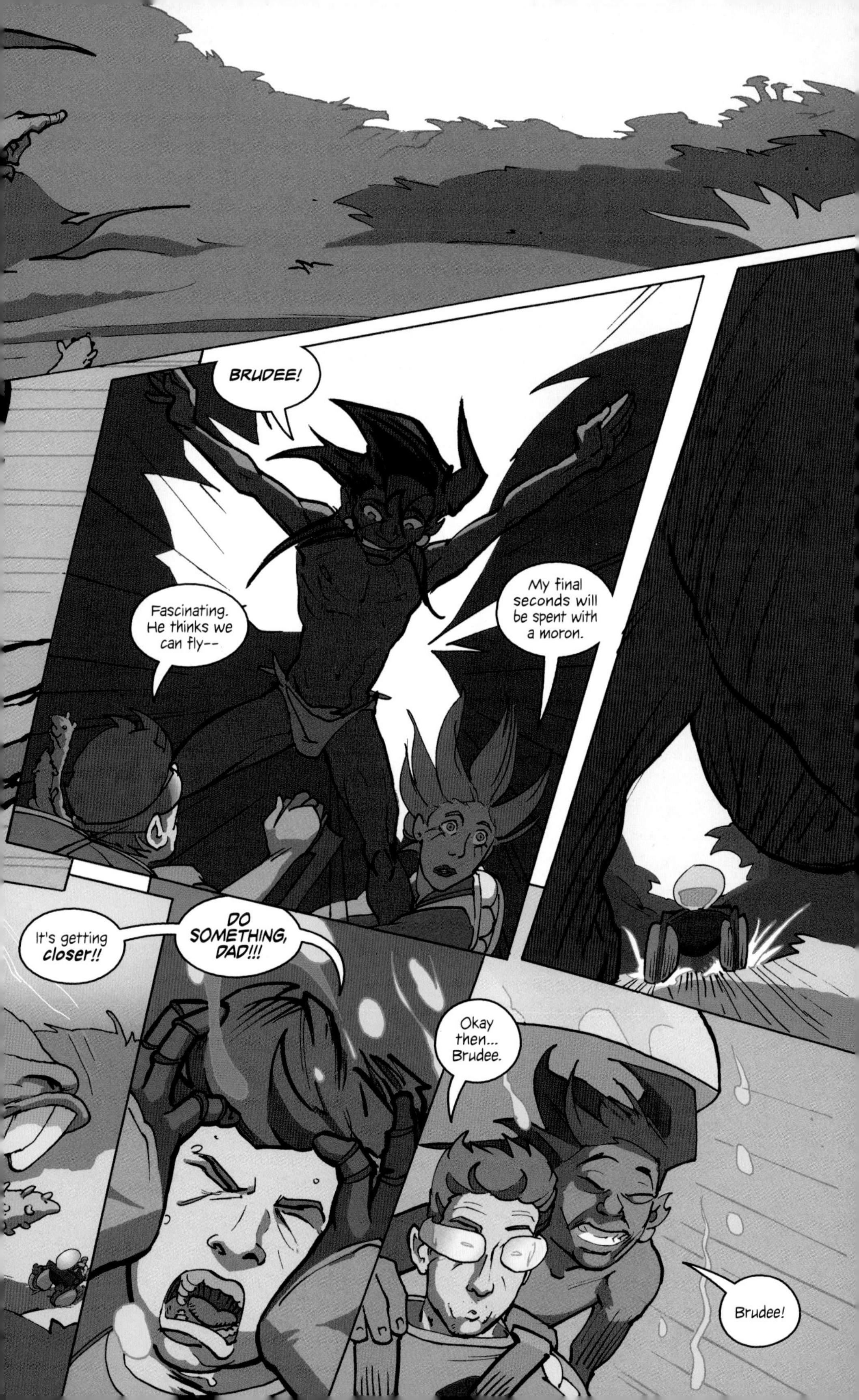
BRUDEE!
Fascinating. He thinks we can fly--
My final seconds will be spent with a moron.
It's getting **closer!!**
DO SOMETHING, DAD!!!
Okay then... Brudee.
Brudee!

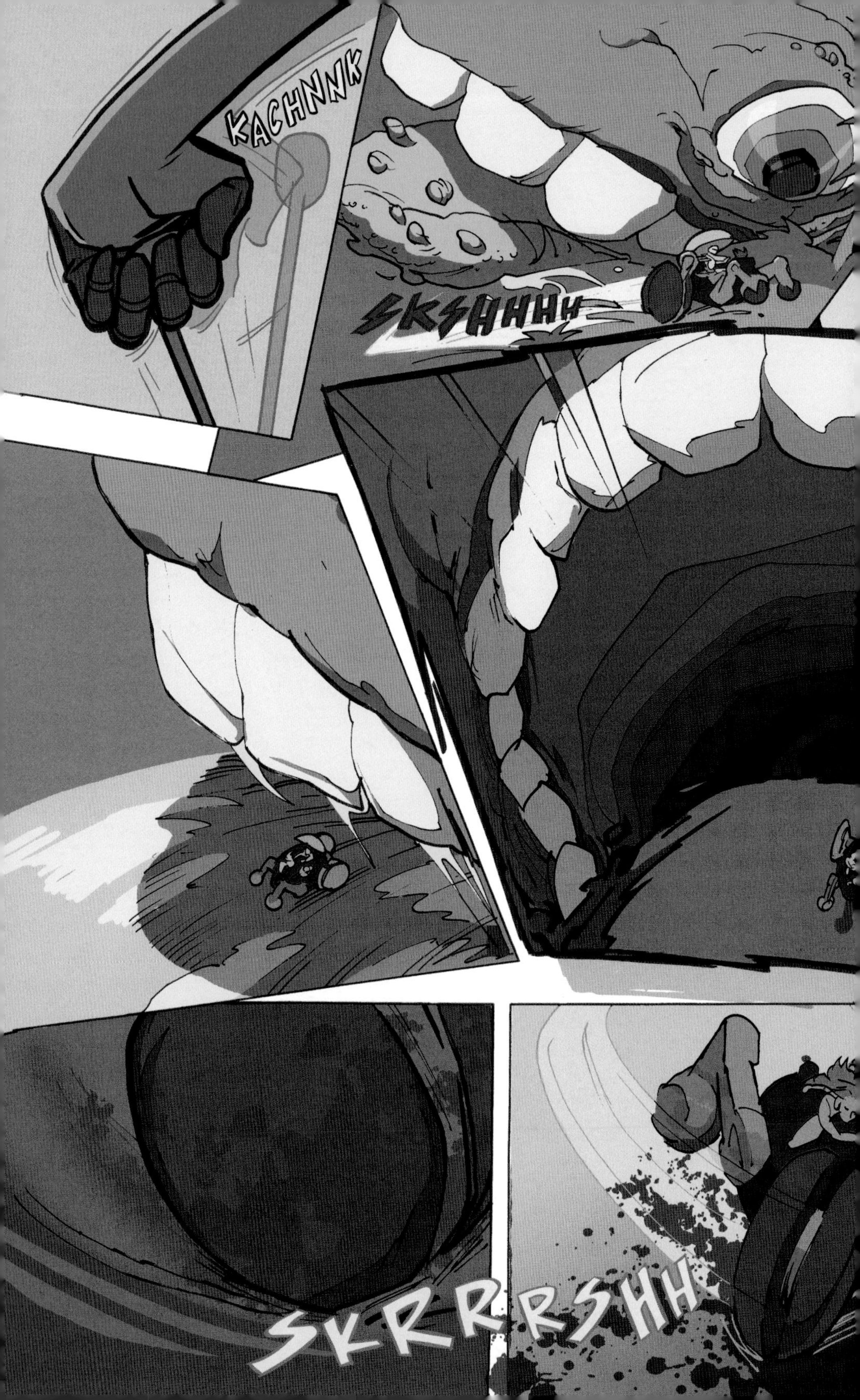
KACHNNNK
SKSHHHH
SKRRRSHH

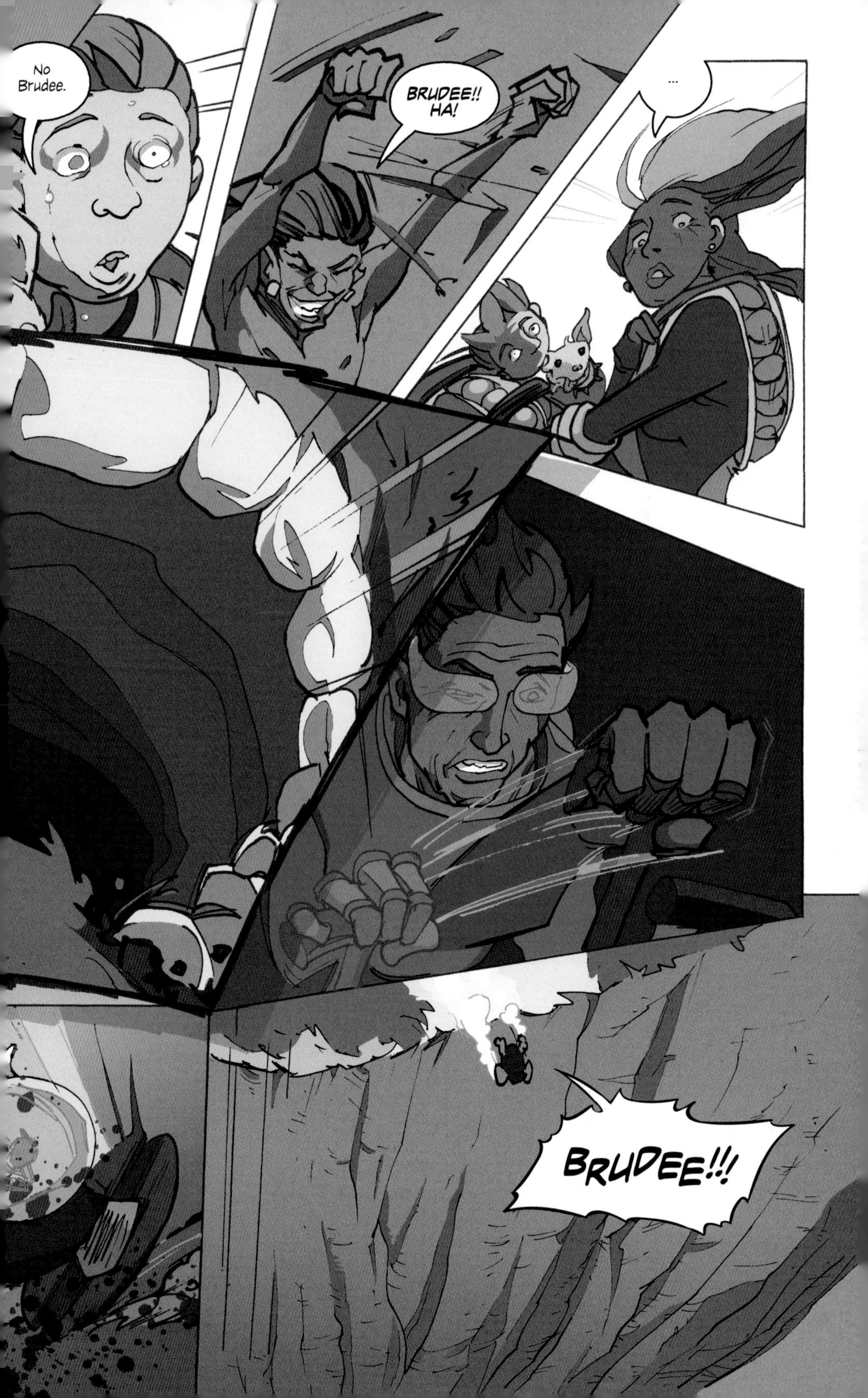
No Brudee.
BRUDEE!! HA!
...
BRUDEE!!!

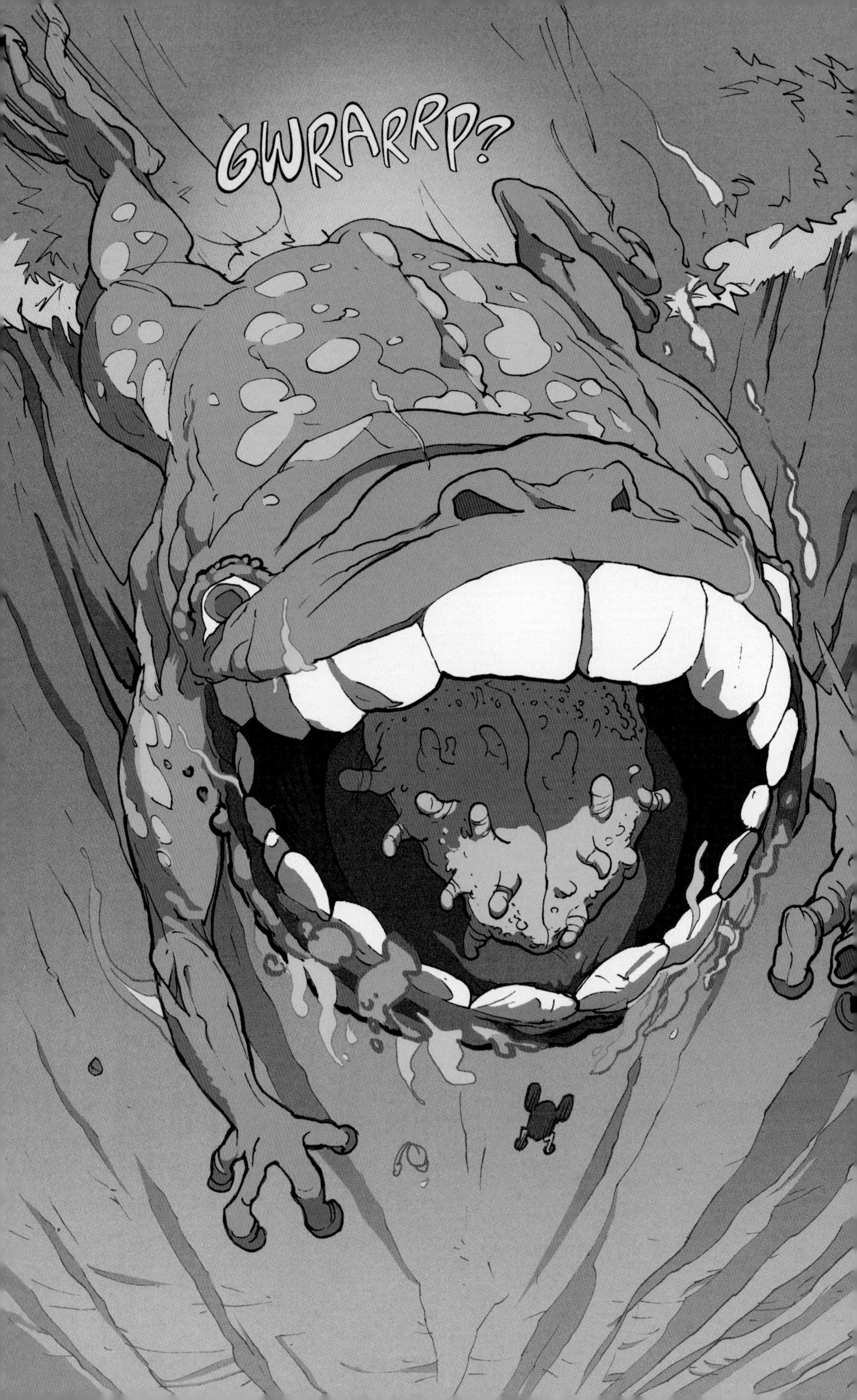
GWRARRP?

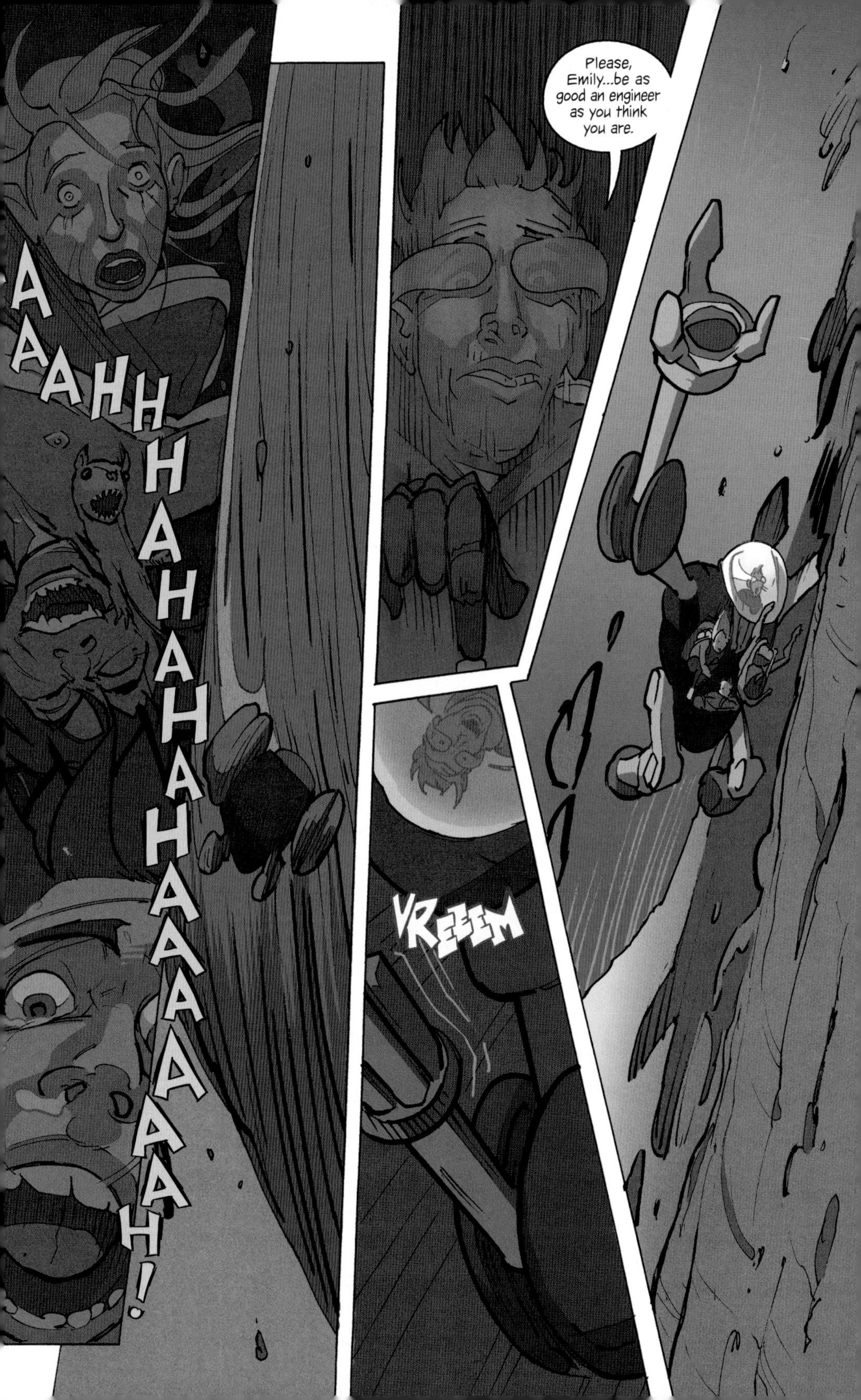
AAAHHHAHAHAHAHAHAAAAAAAH!
Please, Emily...be as good an engineer as you think you are.
VREEEM

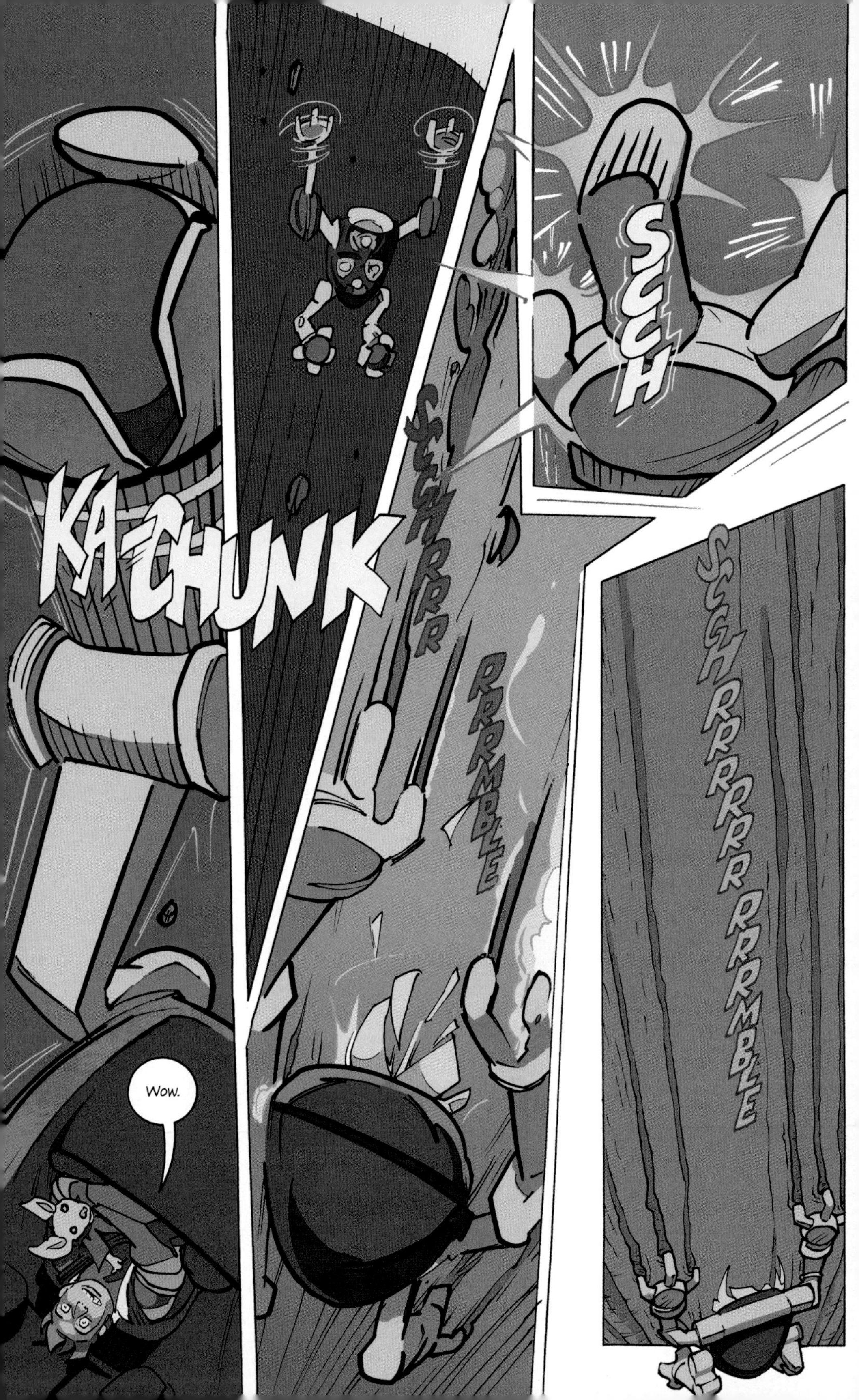
KA-CHUNK
SCCH
SCGHRRR
RRRMBLE
Wow.
SCGHRRRRRRRRRRMBLE

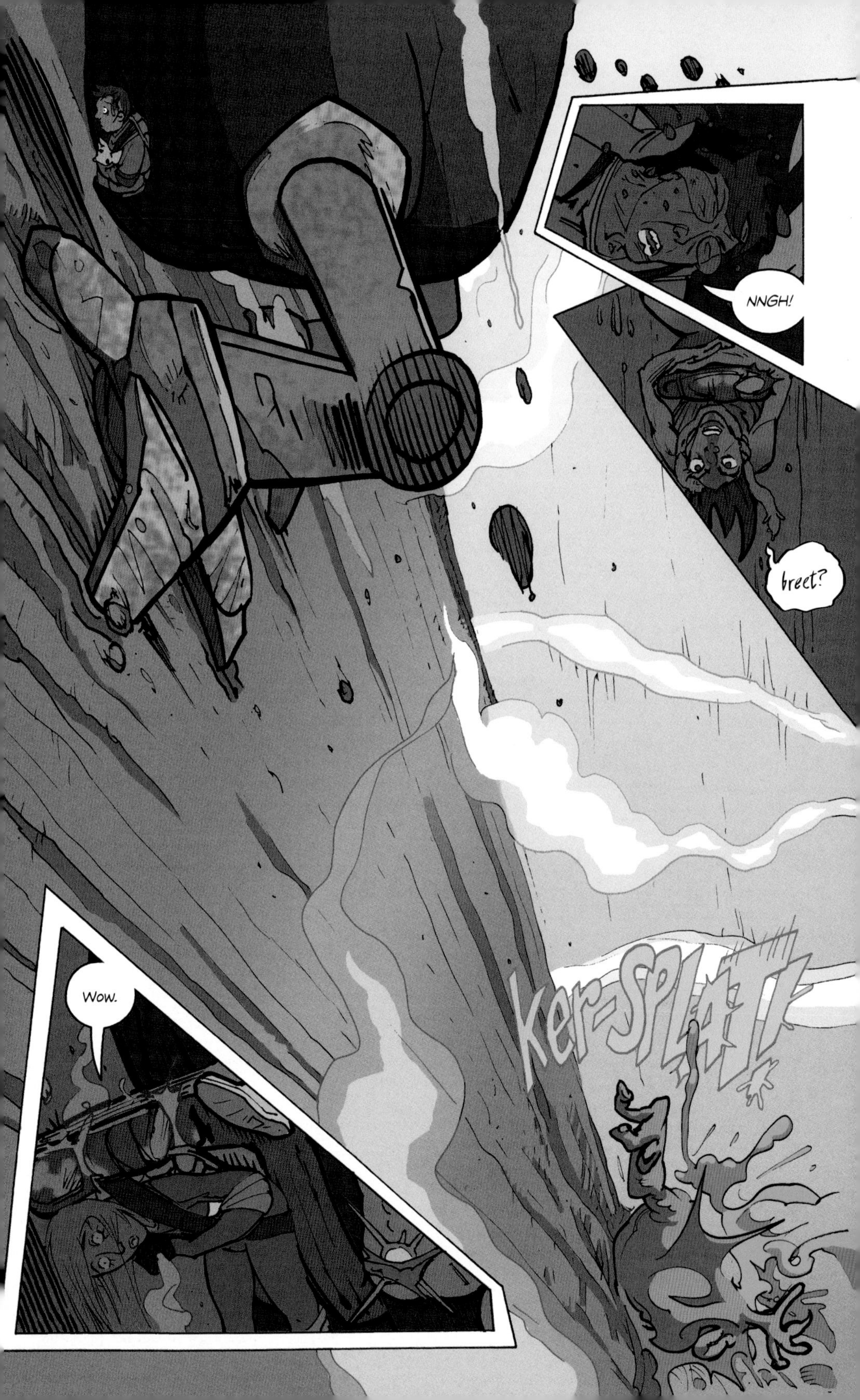
NNGH!
breet?
Wow.
KER-SPLATT

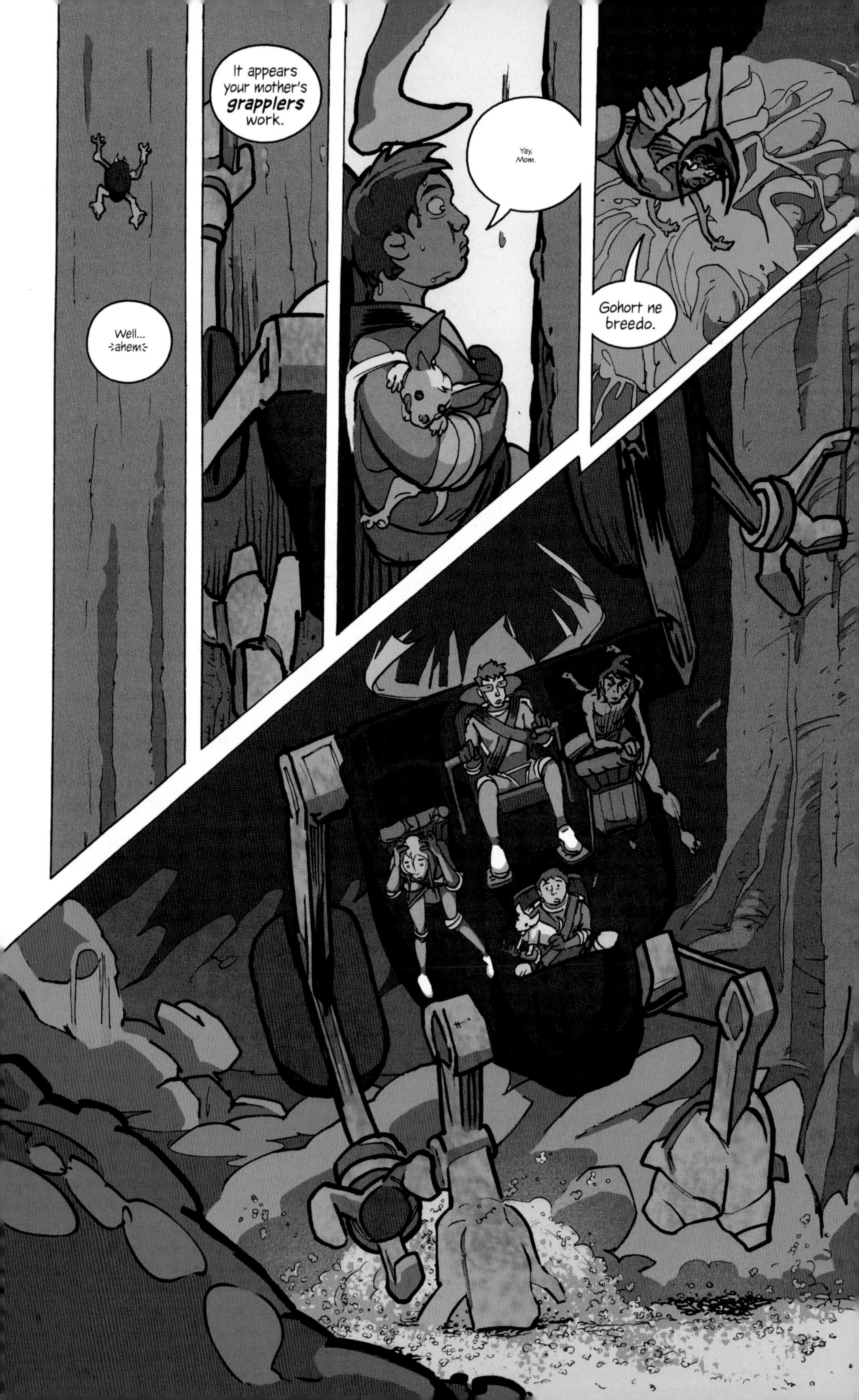

Well... ≈ahem≈
It appears your mother's **grapplers** work.
Yay, Mom.
Gohort ne breedo.

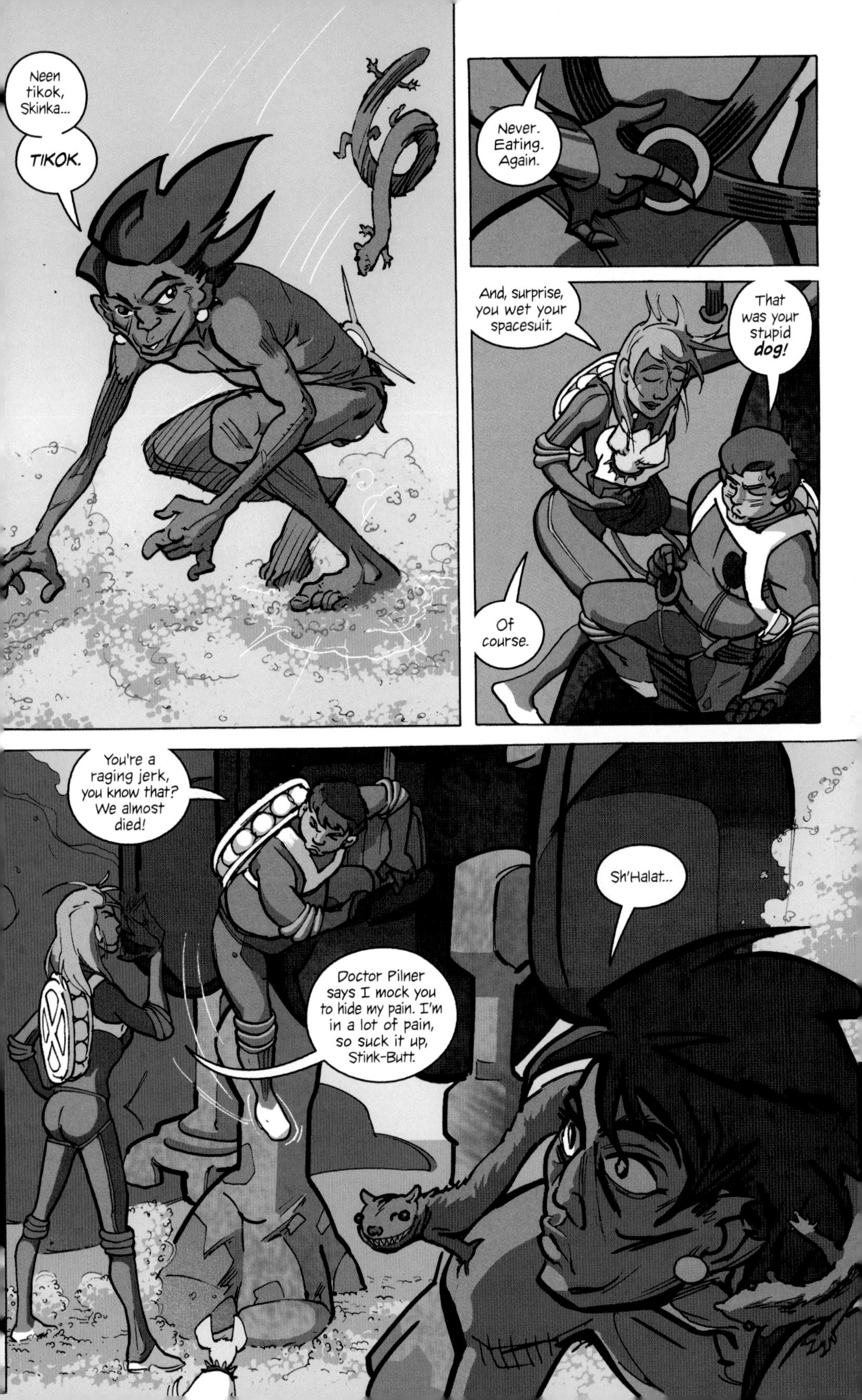
Neen tikok, Skinka...
TIKOK.
Never. Eating. Again.
And, surprise, you wet your spacesuit.
That was your stupid **dog!**
Of course.
You're a raging jerk, you know that? We almost died!
Sh'Halat...
Doctor Pilner says I mock you to hide my pain. I'm in a lot of pain, so suck it up, Stink-Butt.

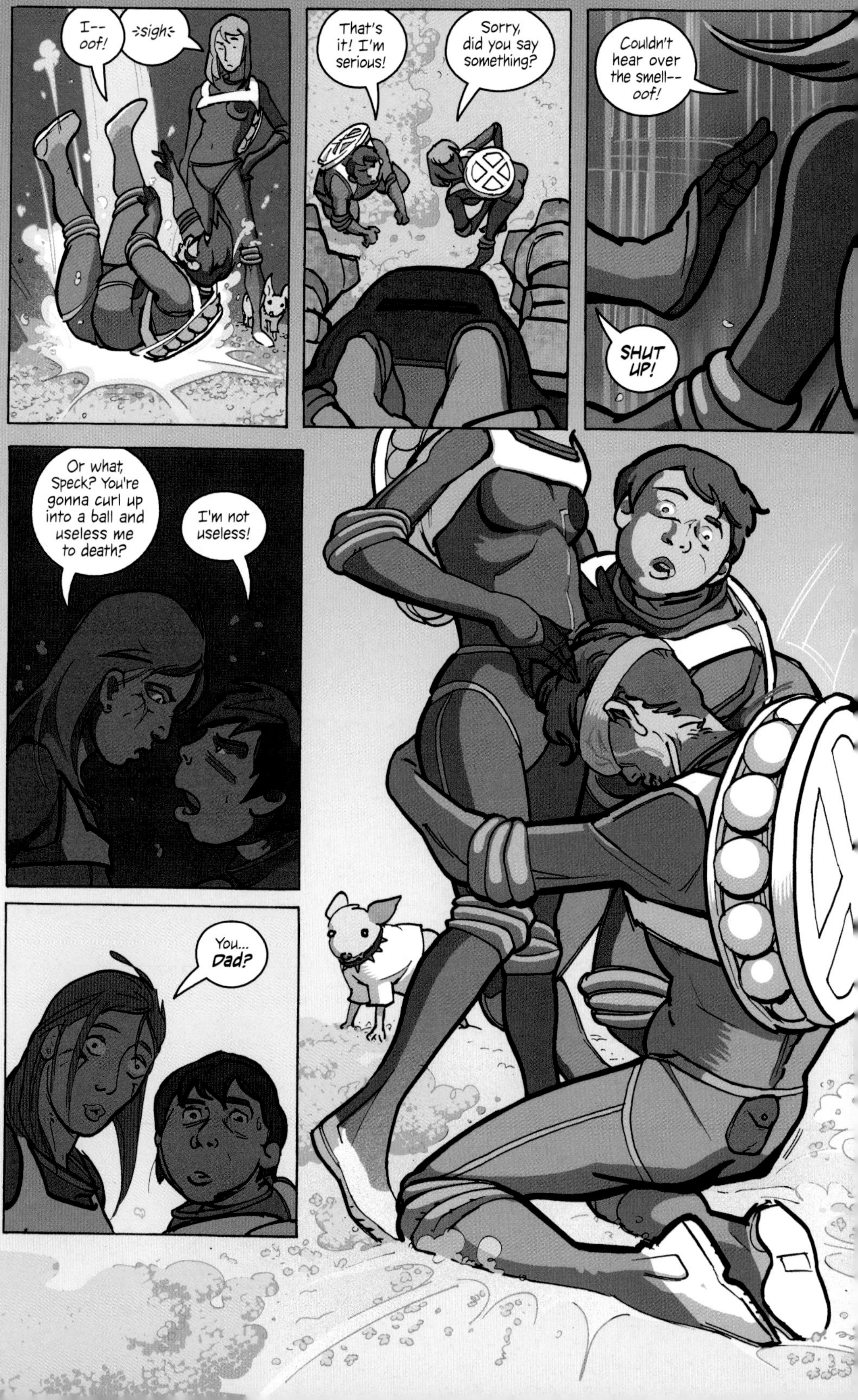
I-- oof!
sigh
That's it! I'm serious!
Sorry, did you say something?
Couldn't hear over the smell-- oof!
SHUT UP!
Or what, Speck? You're gonna curl up into a ball and useless me to death?
I'm not useless!
You... Dad?

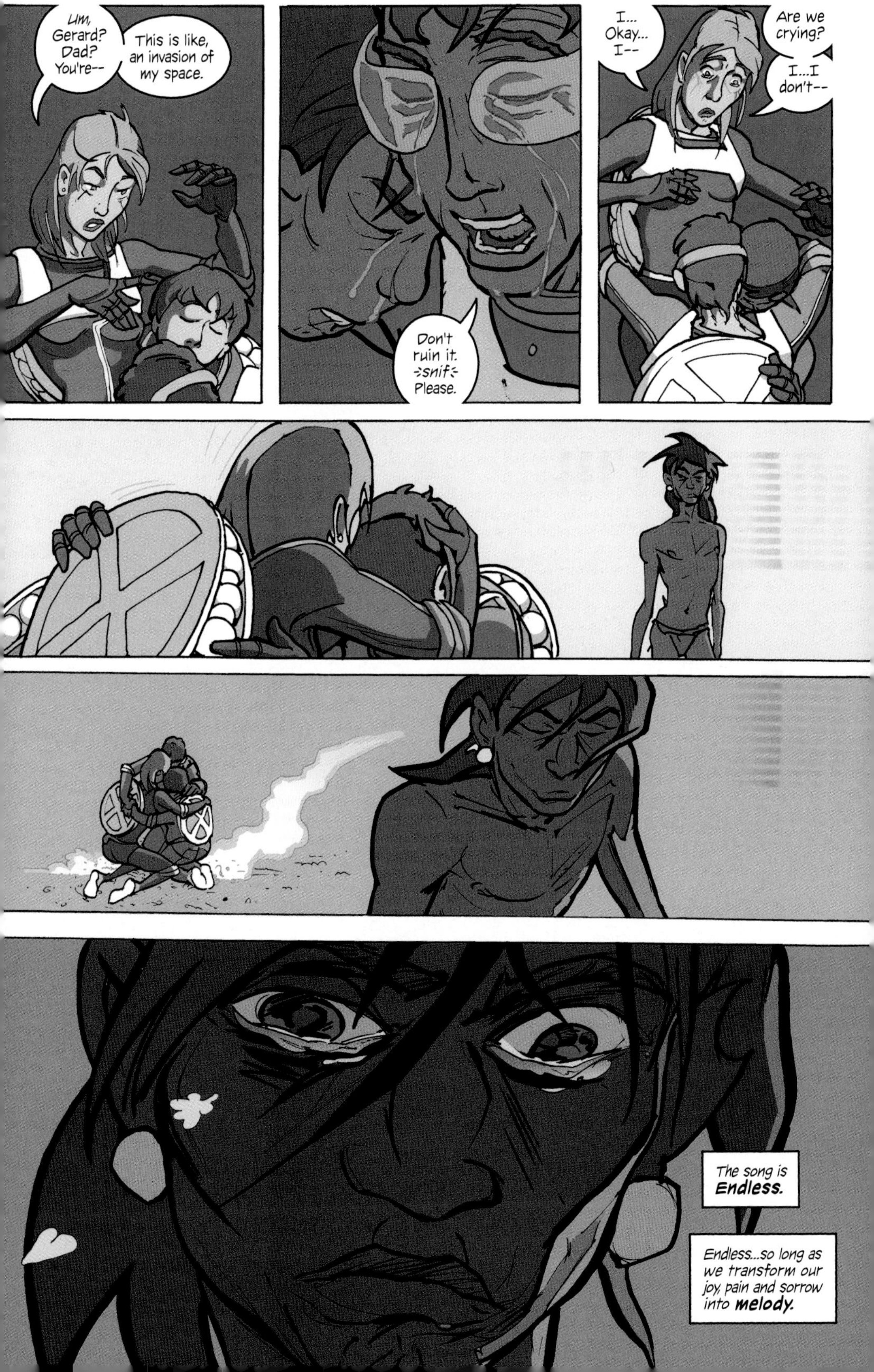
Um, Gerard? Dad? You're--
This is like, an invasion of my space.
Don't ruin it. ﾐsnifﾐ Please.
I... Okay... I--
Are we crying?
I...I don't--
The song is **Endless.**
Endless...so long as we transform our joy, pain and sorrow into **melody.**

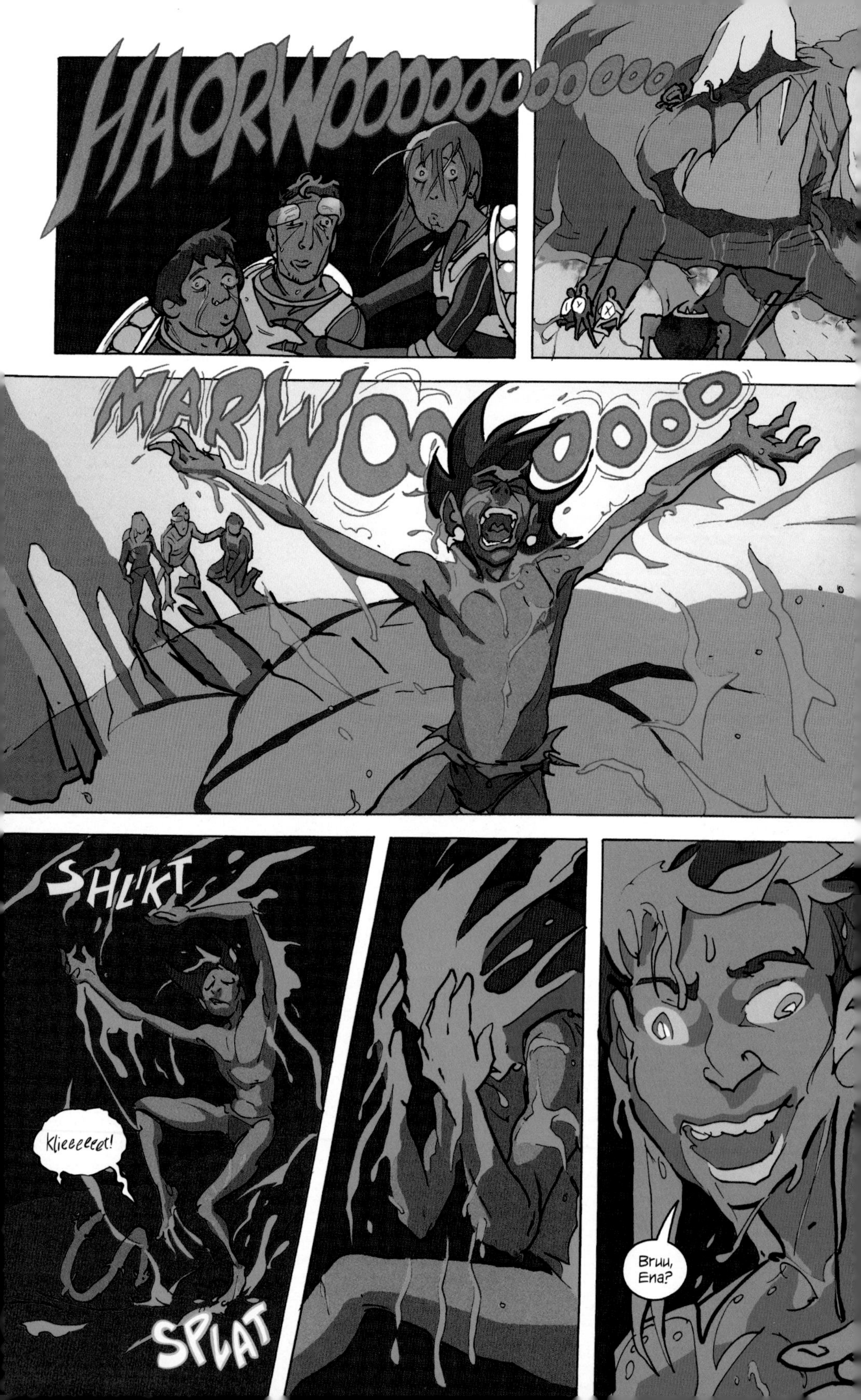
HAORWOOOOOOOOOOO
MARWOOOOOOD
SHLIKT
Klieeeeeet!
SPLAT
Bruu,
Ena?

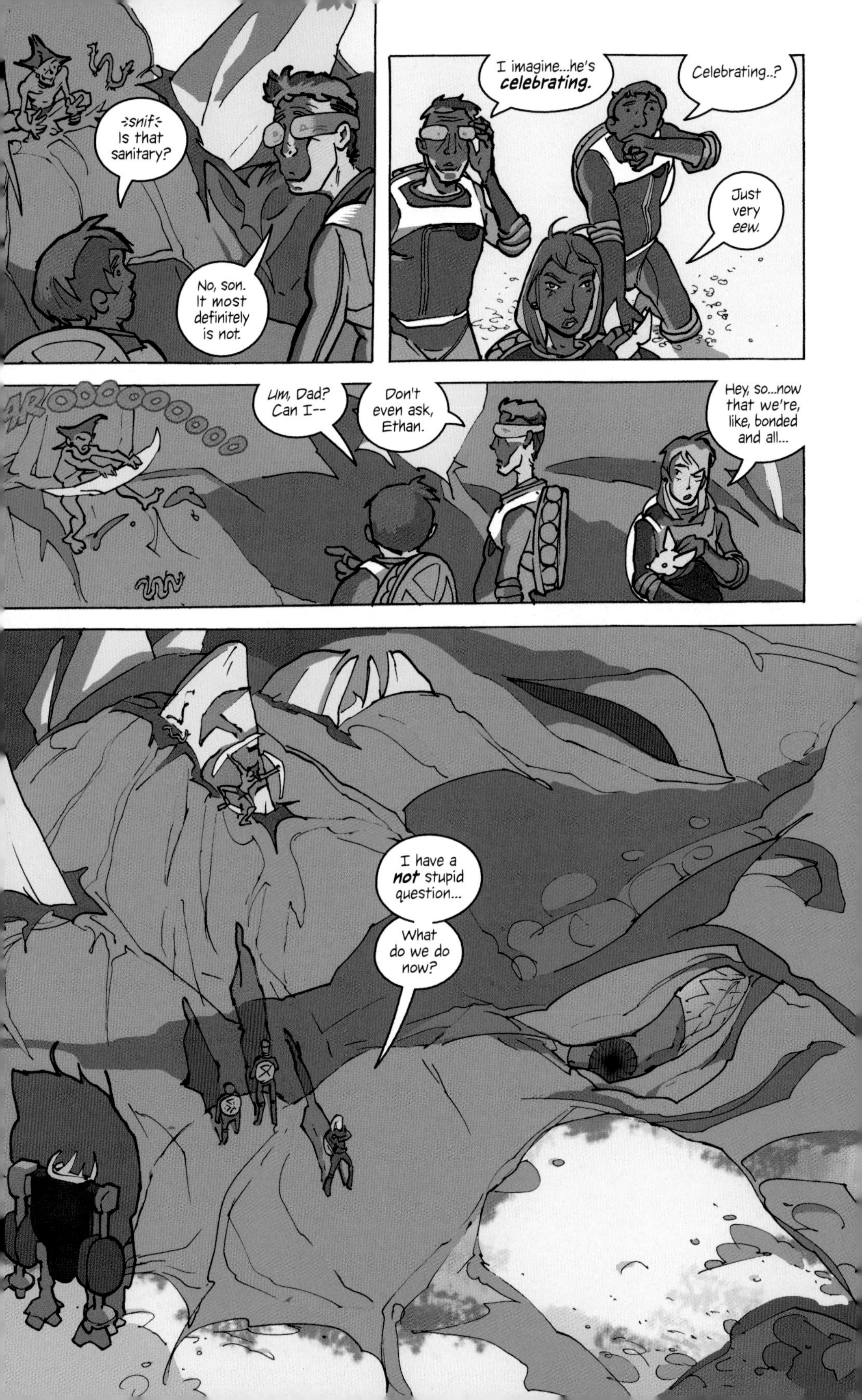

⇒snif⇐ Is that sanitary?
No, son. It most definitely is not.
I imagine...he's **celebrating.**
Celebrating..?
Just very eew.
AROOOOOOOOOOOO
Um, Dad? Can I--
Don't even ask, Ethan.
Hey, so...now that we're, like, bonded and all...
I have a **not** stupid question...
What do we do now?

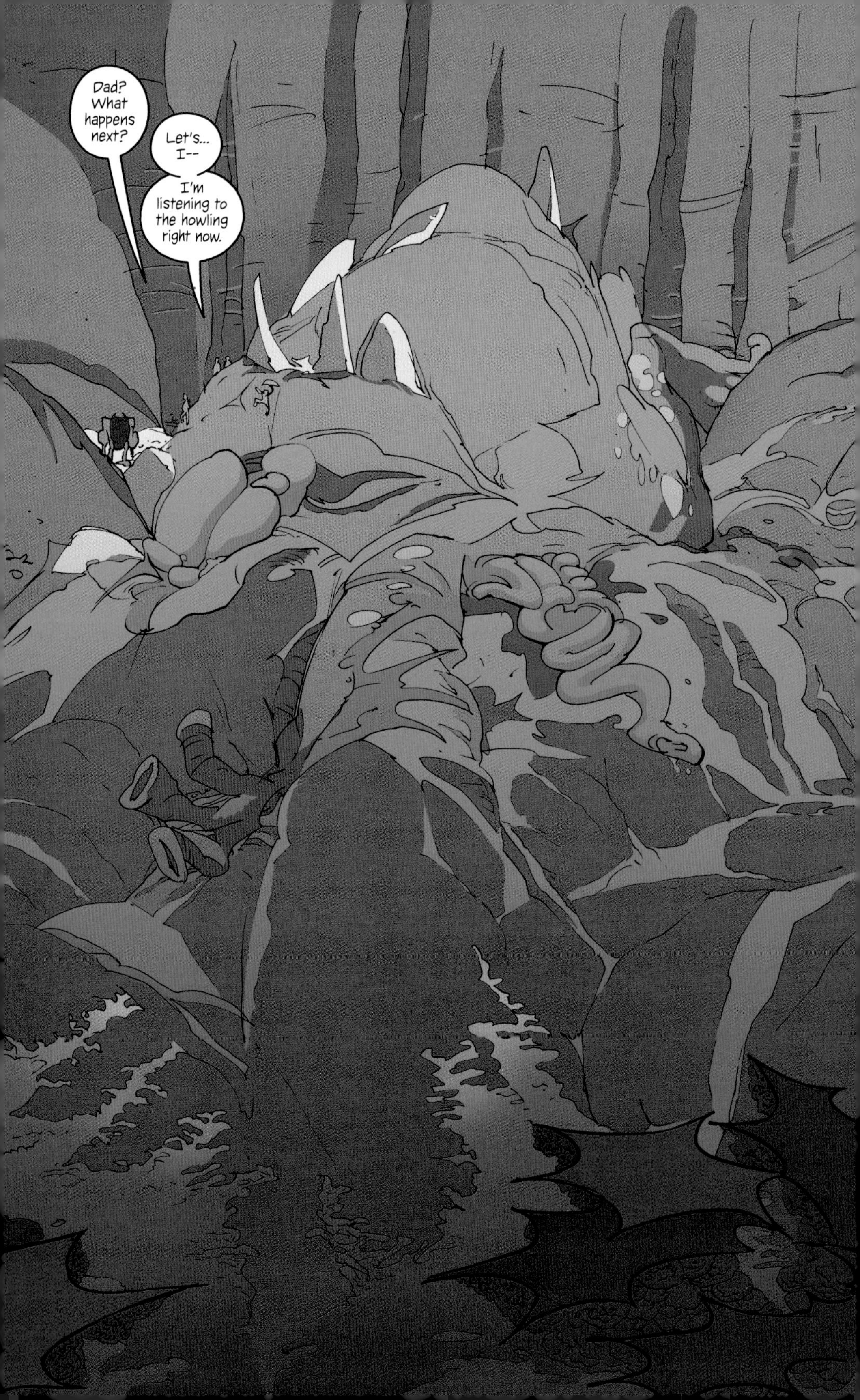
Dad? What happens next?
Let's... I--
I'm listening to the howling right now.

CHAPTER 6

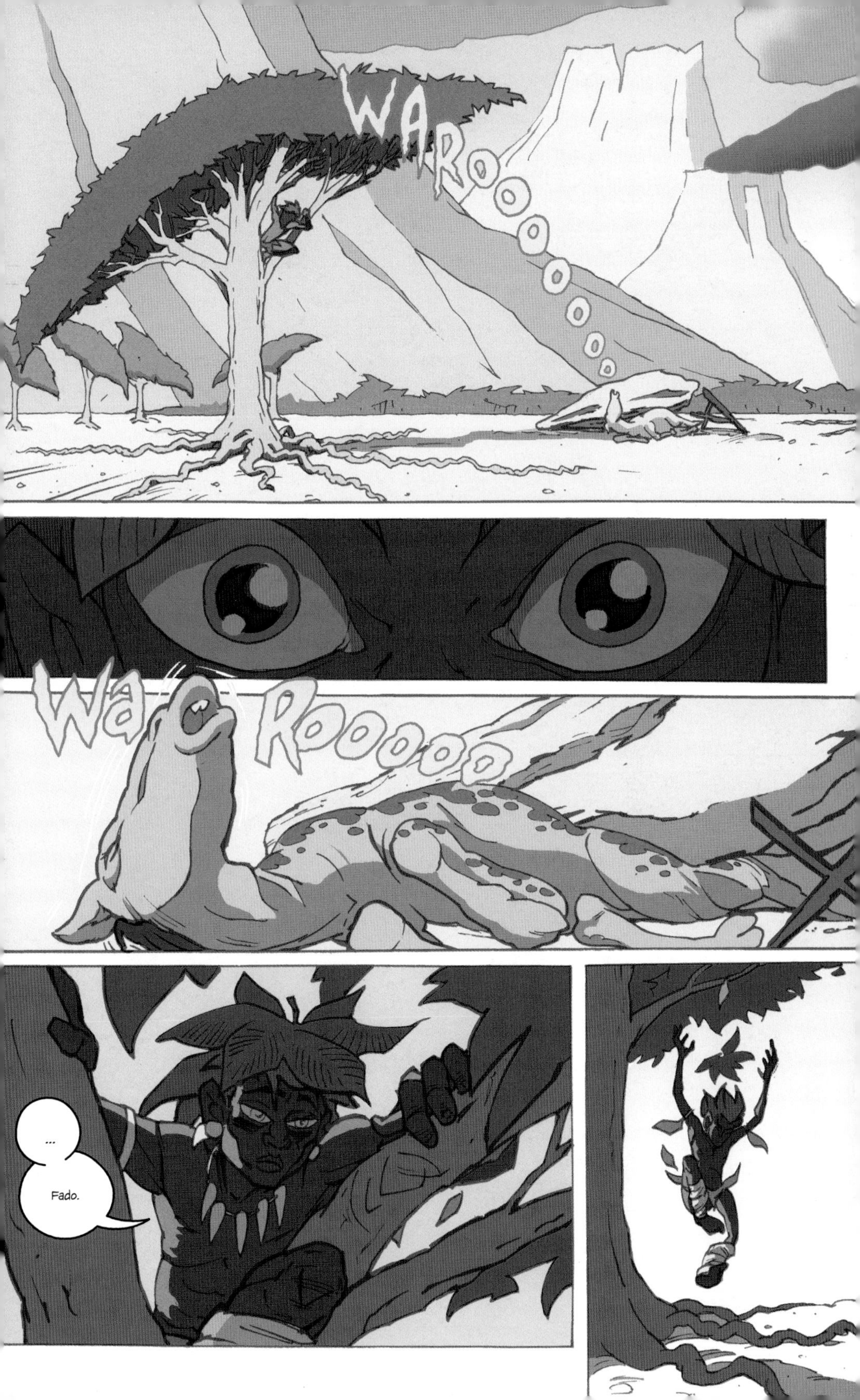
WAROOOOOOOOO
WaROOOOOO
...
Fado.

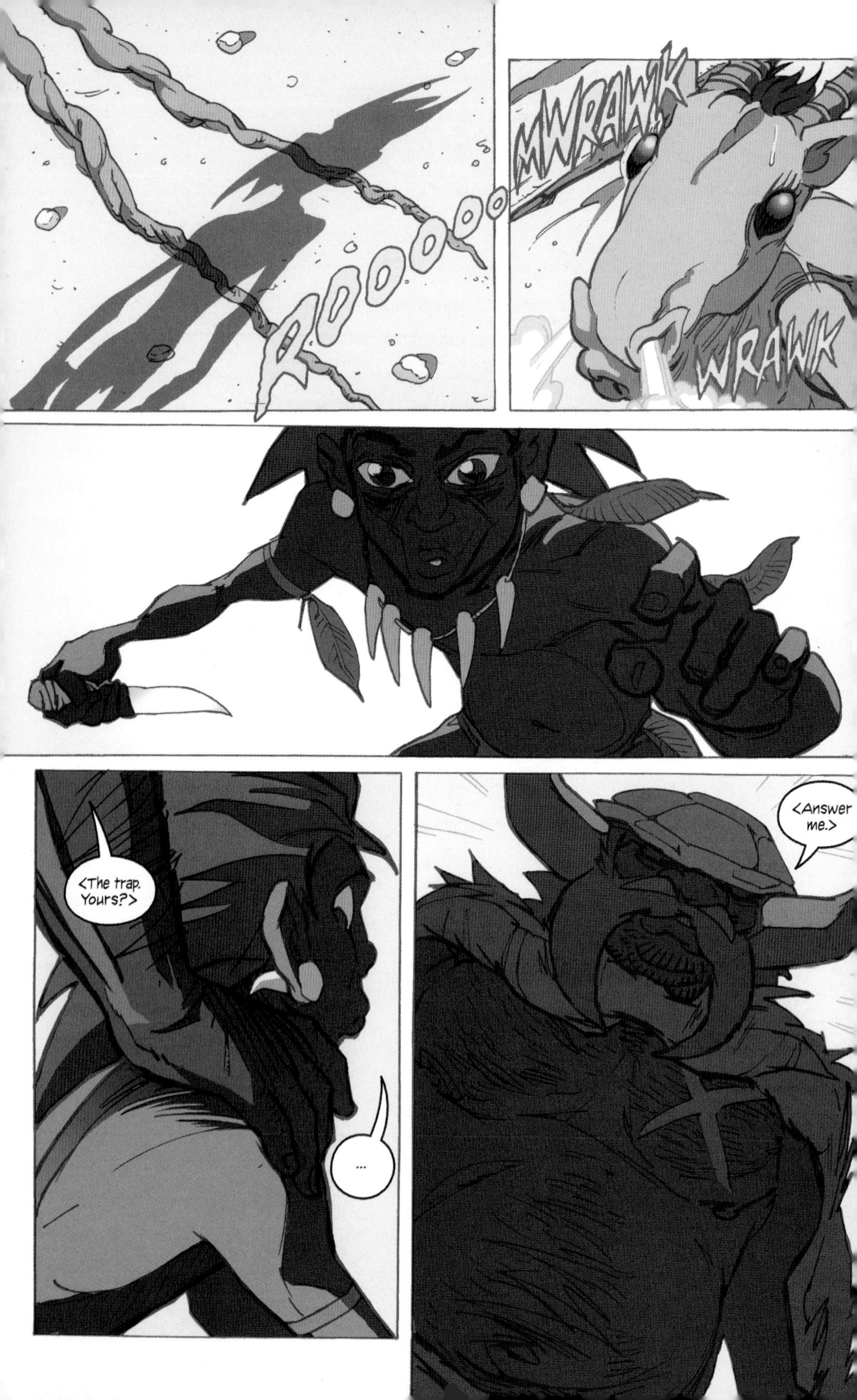
ROOOOOO
MWRAWK
WRAWK
<The trap. Yours?>
...
<Answer me.>

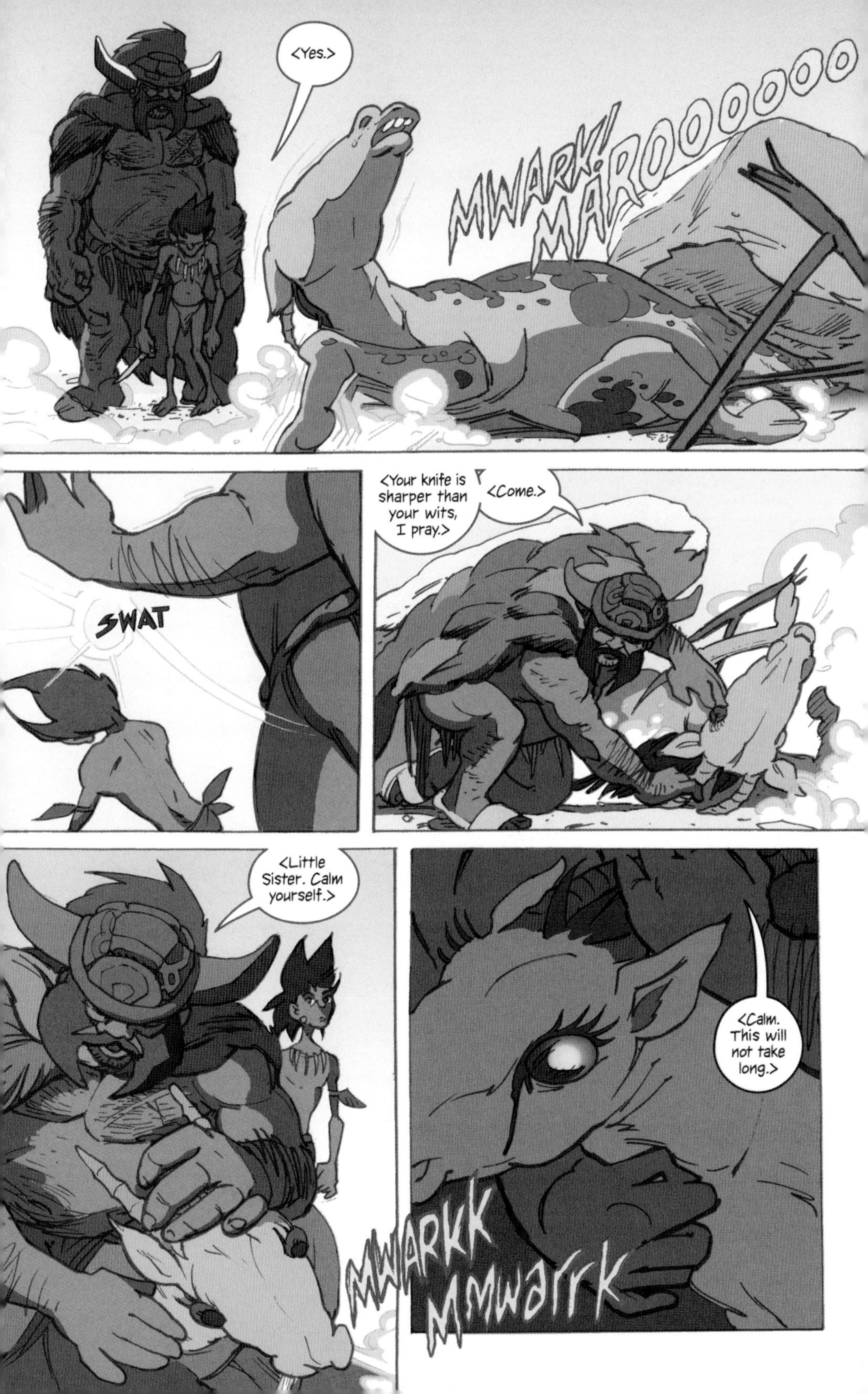

<Yes.>
MWARK! MAROOOOOOO
SWAT
<Your knife is sharper than your wits, I pray.>
<Come.>
<Little Sister. Calm yourself.>
<Calm. This will not take long.>
MWARKK Mmwarrk

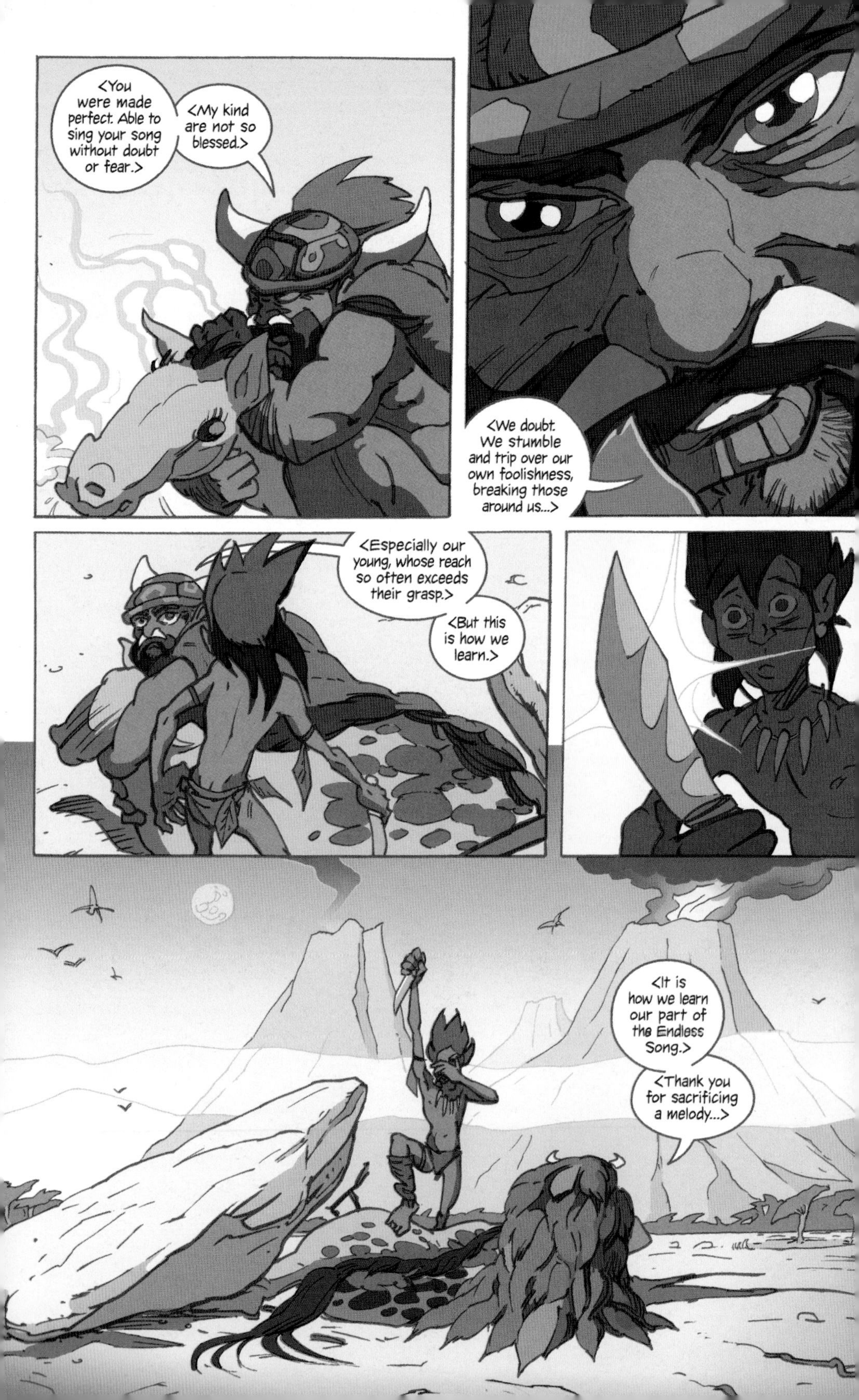
<You were made perfect. Able to sing your song without doubt or fear.>
<My kind are not so blessed.>
<We doubt. We stumble and trip over our own foolishness, breaking those around us...>
<Especially our young, whose reach so often exceeds their grasp.>
<But this is how we learn.>
<It is how we learn our part of the Endless Song.>
<Thank you for sacrificing a melody...>

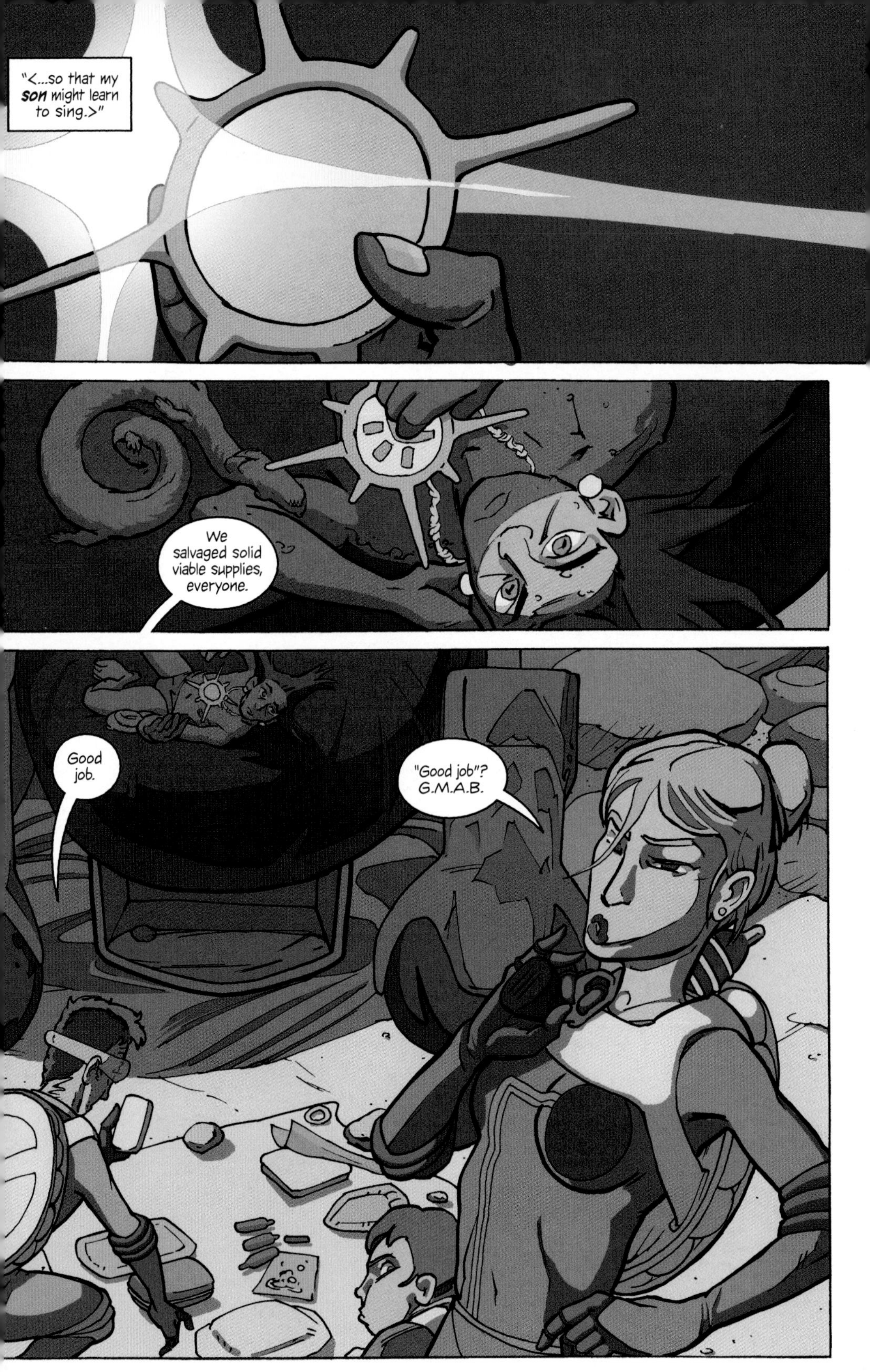
"<...so that my **son** might learn to sing.>"
We salvaged solid viable supplies, everyone.
Good job.
"Good job"? G.M.A.B.

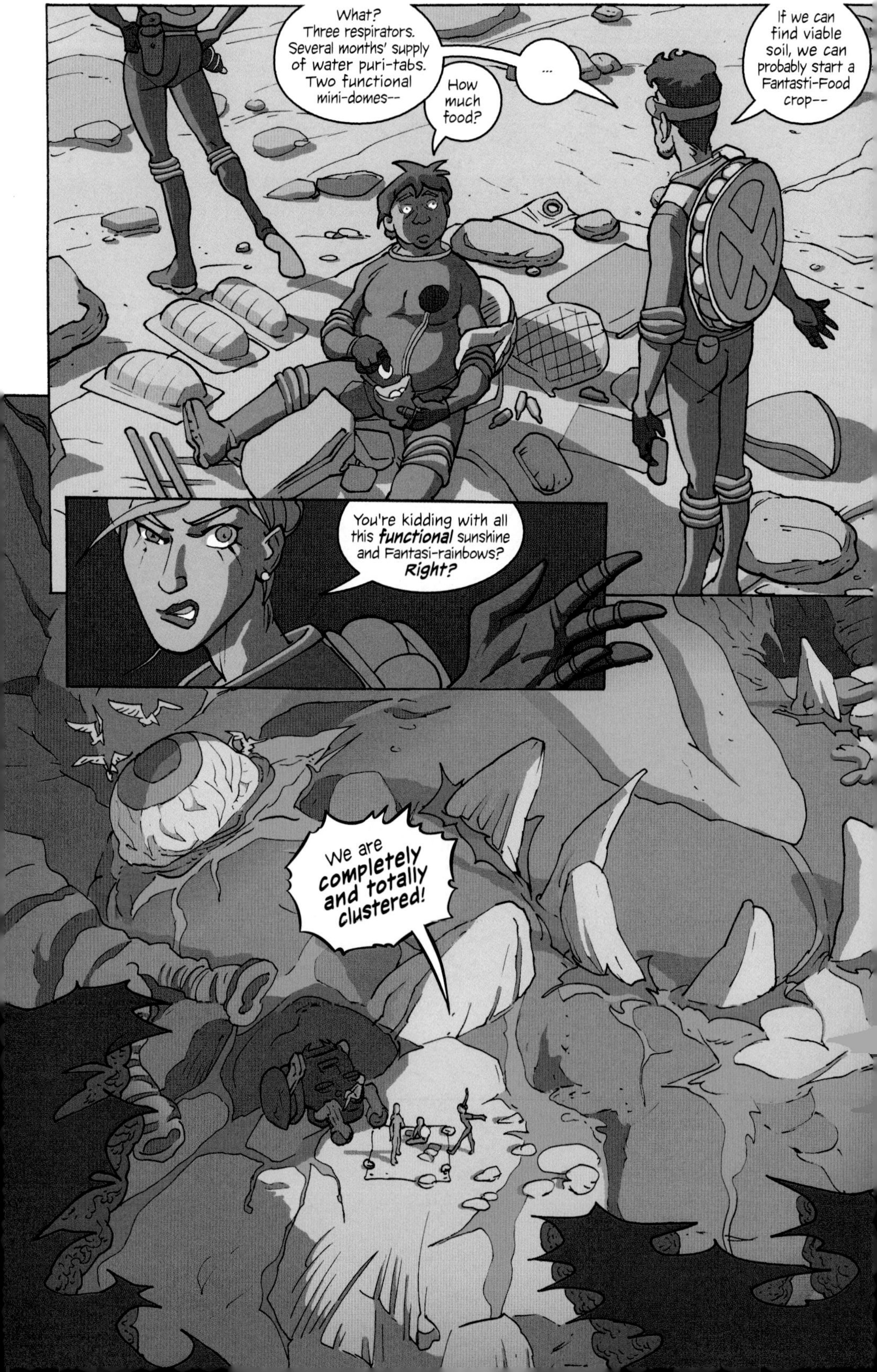
What? Three respirators. Several months' supply of water puri-tabs. Two functional mini-domes--
How much food?
...
If we can find viable soil, we can probably start a Fantasti-Food crop--
You're kidding with all this **functional** sunshine and Fantasi-rainbows? **Right?**
We are **completely and totally clustered!**

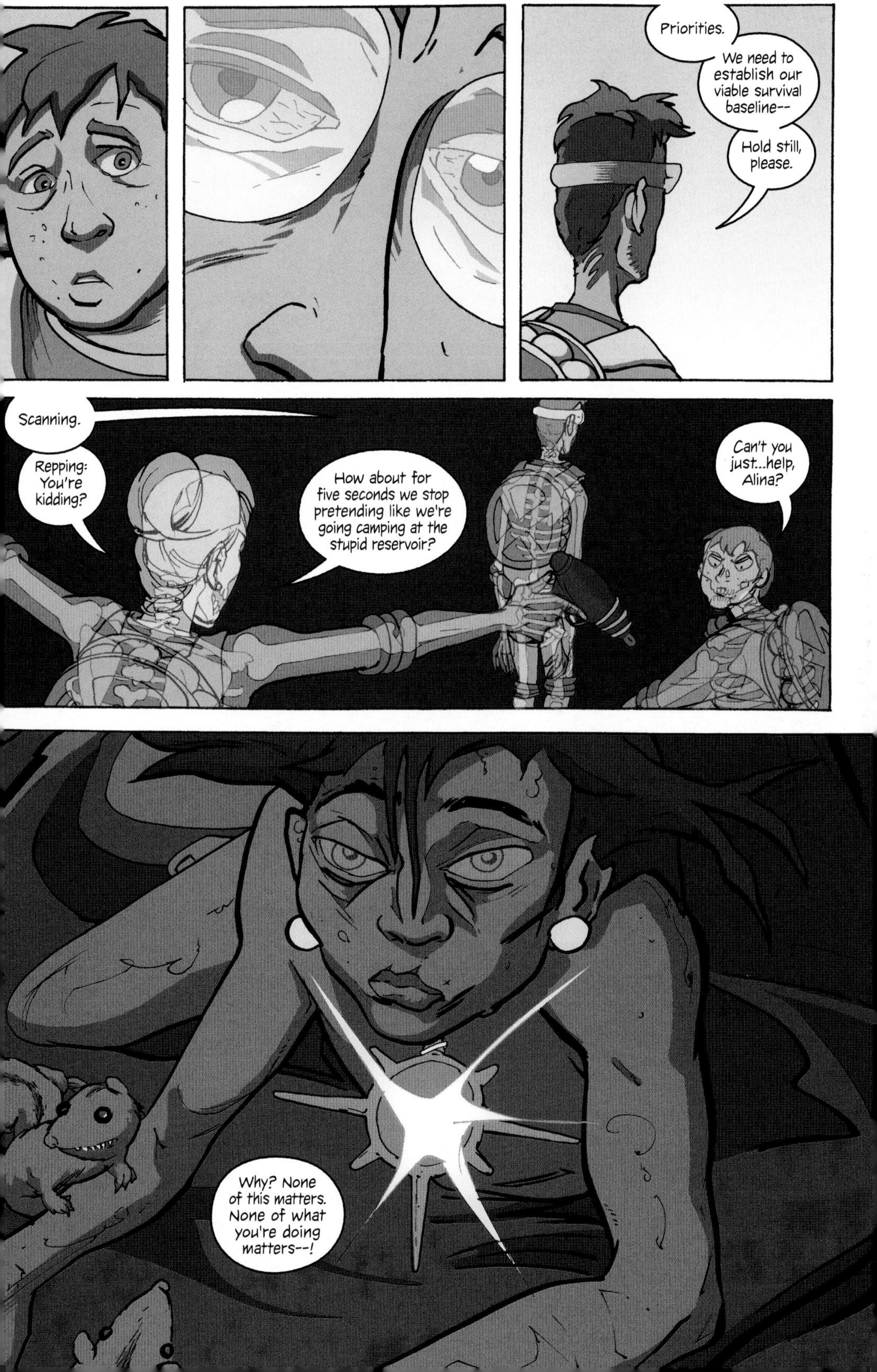
Priorities.
We need to establish our viable survival baseline--
Hold still, please.
Scanning.
Repping: You're kidding?
How about for five seconds we stop pretending like we're going camping at the stupid reservoir?
Can't you just...help, Alina?
Why? None of this matters. None of what you're doing matters--!

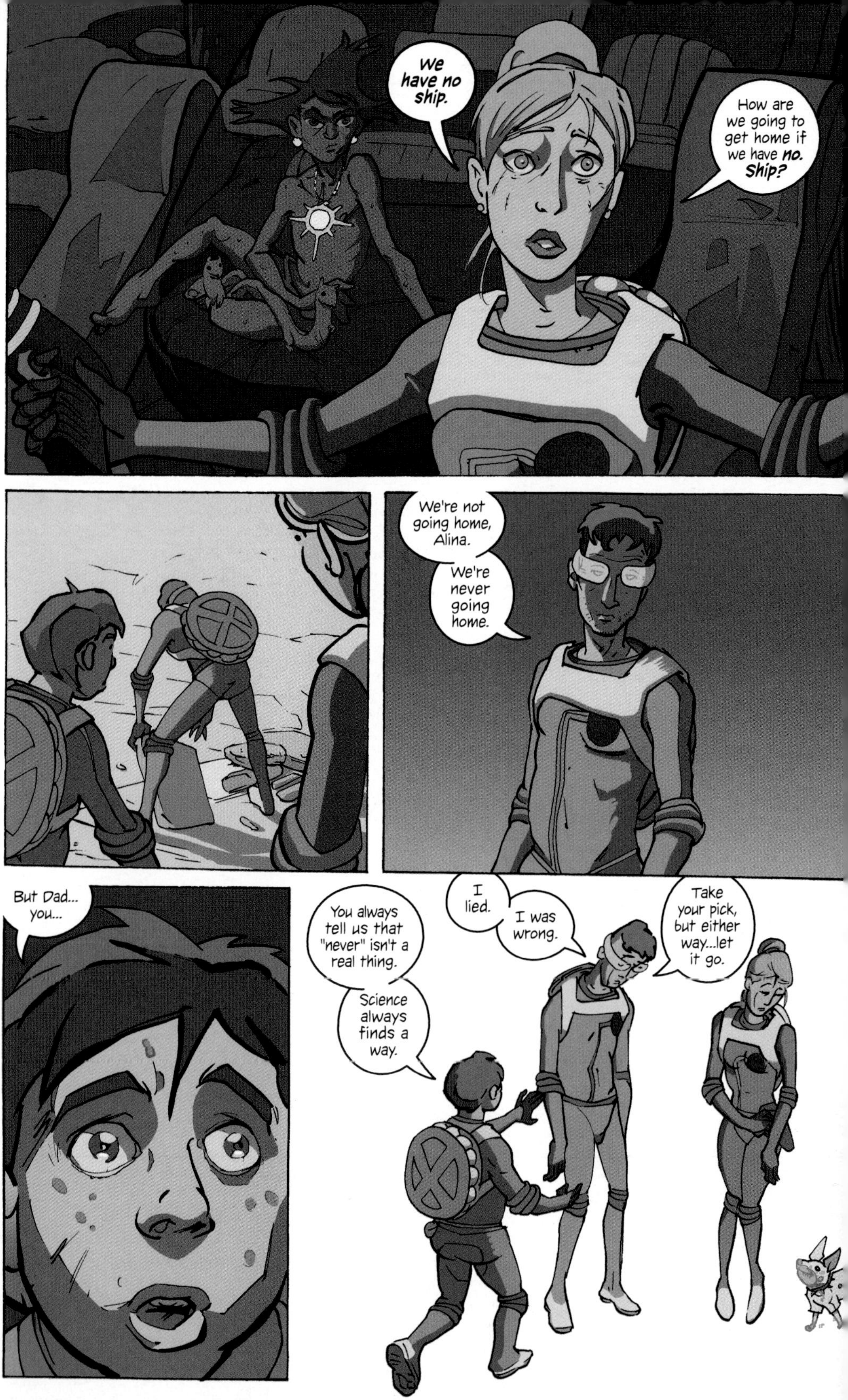
We have no ship.
How are we going to get home if we have no. Ship?
We're not going home, Alina.
We're never going home.
But Dad... you...
You always tell us that "never" isn't a real thing.
Science always finds a way.
I lied.
I was wrong.
Take your pick, but either way...let it go.

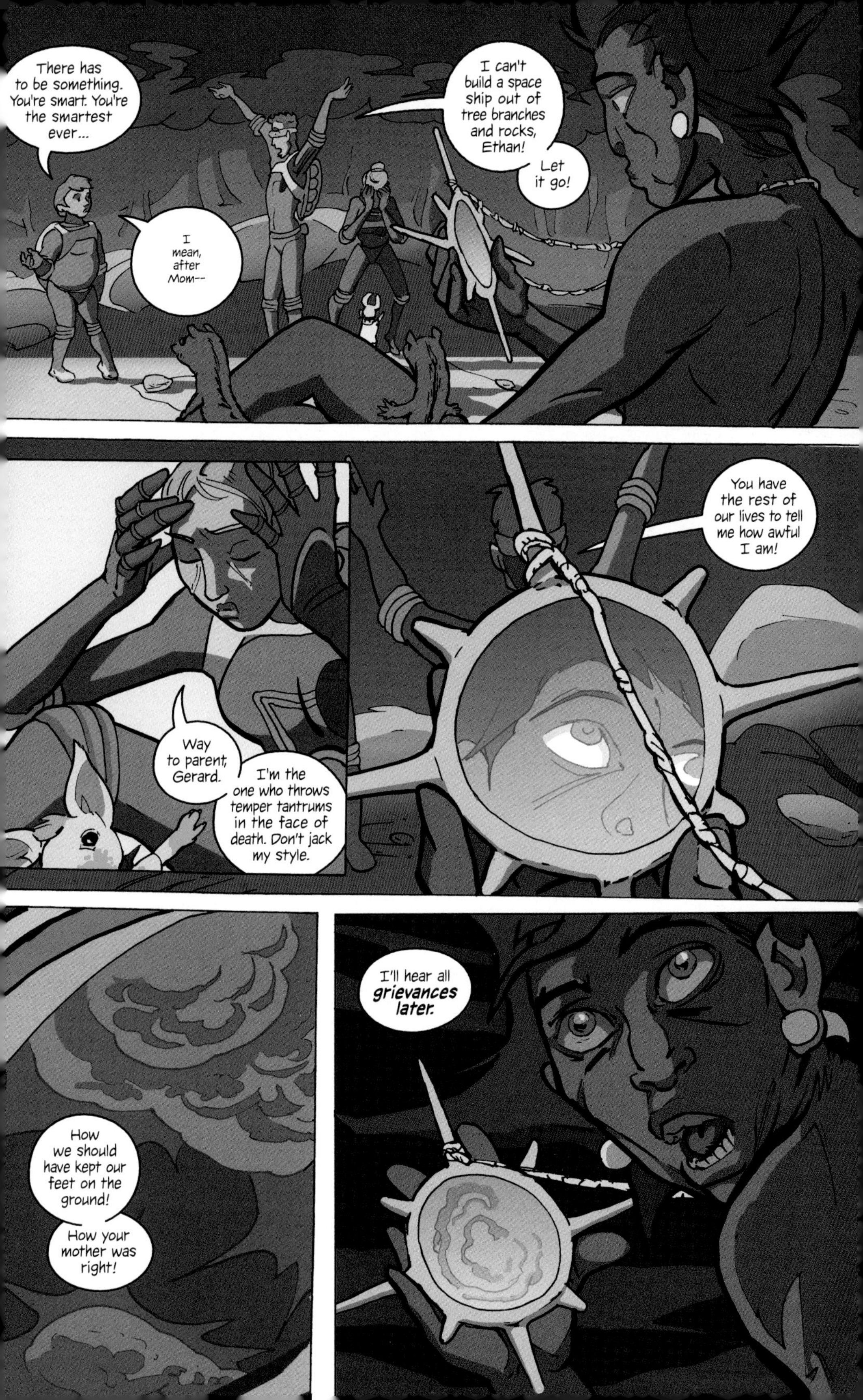

There has to be something. You're smart. You're the smartest ever...
I mean, after Mom--
I can't build a space ship out of tree branches and rocks, Ethan!
Let it go!
Way to parent, Gerard.
I'm the one who throws temper tantrums in the face of death. Don't jack my style.
You have the rest of our lives to tell me how awful I am!
How we should have kept our feet on the ground!
How your mother was right!
I'll hear all **grievances later.**

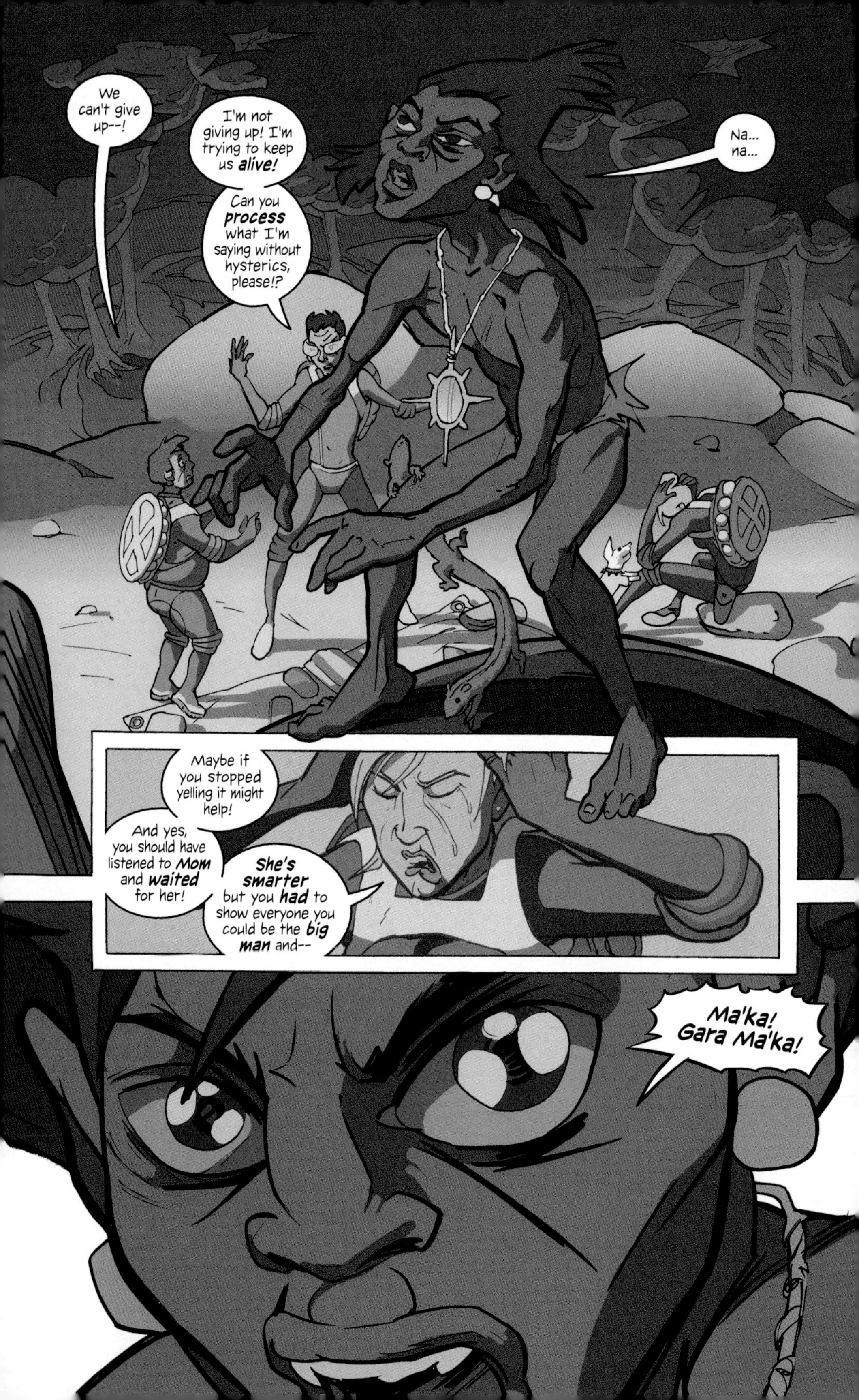
We can't give up--!
I'm not giving up! I'm trying to keep us **alive!**
Can you **process** what I'm saying without hysterics, please!?
Na... na...
Maybe if you stopped yelling it might help!
And yes, you should have listened to **Mom** and **waited** for her!
She's smarter but you **had** to show everyone you could be the **big man** and--
Ma'ka! Gara Ma'ka!

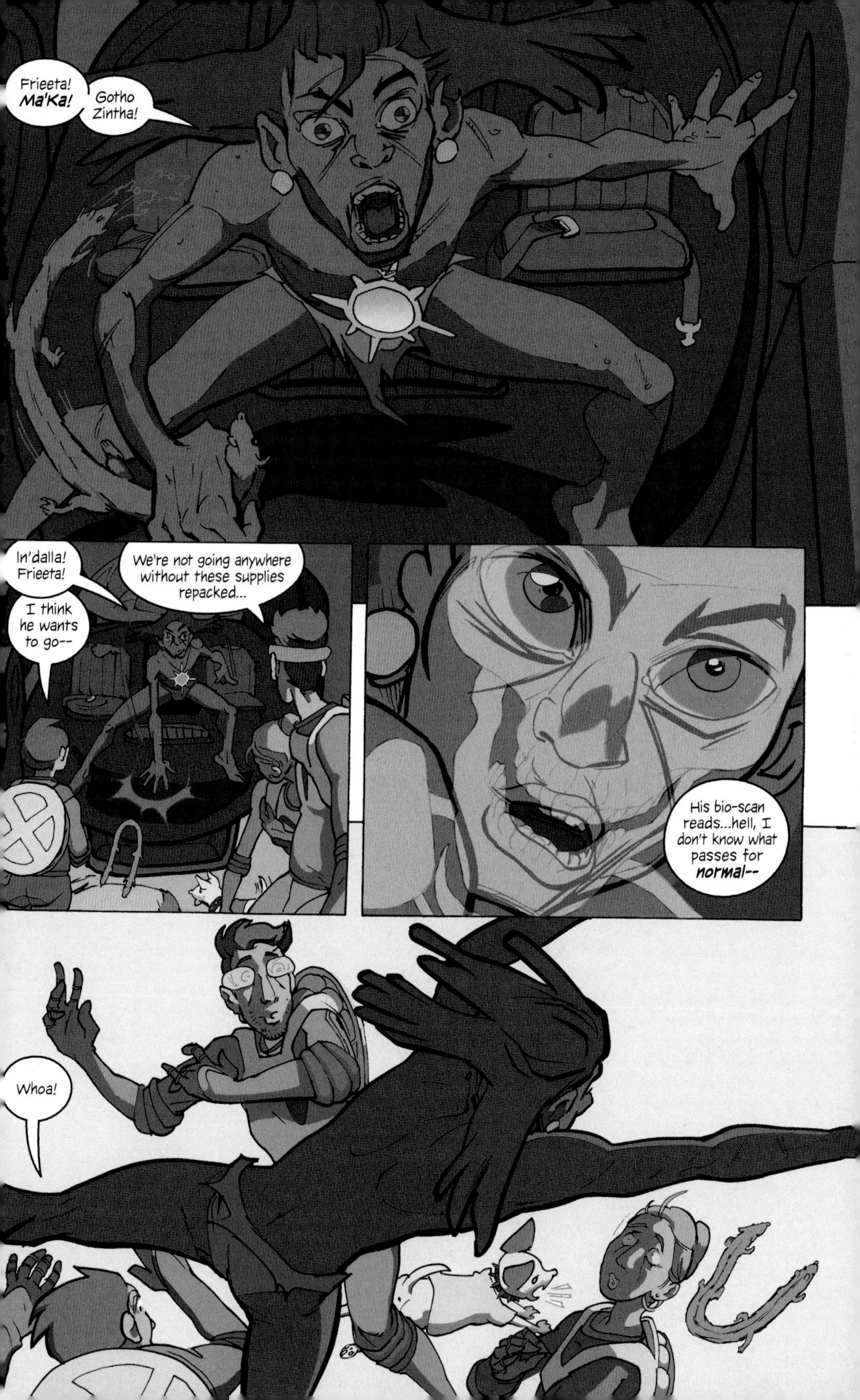

Frieeta! **Ma'Ka!**
Gotho Zintha!
In'dalla! Frieeta!
I think he wants to go--
We're not going anywhere without these supplies repacked...
His bio-scan reads...hell, I don't know what passes for **normal--**
Whoa!

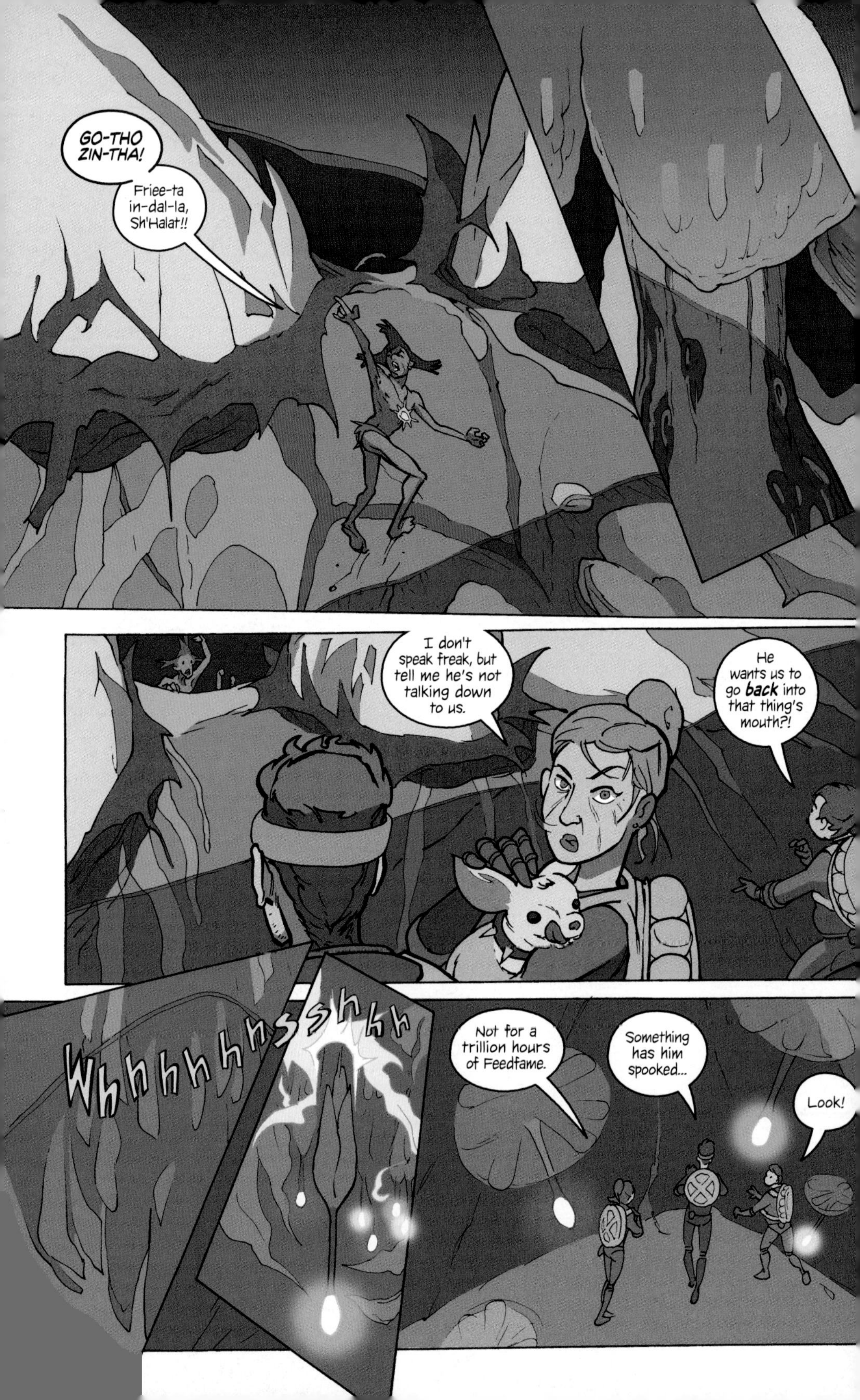
GO-THO ZIN-THA!
Friee-ta in-dal-la, Sh'Halat!!
I don't speak freak, but tell me he's not talking down to us.
He wants us to go back into that thing's mouth?!
Whhhhhhssshhh
Not for a trillion hours of Feedfame.
Something has him spooked...
Look!

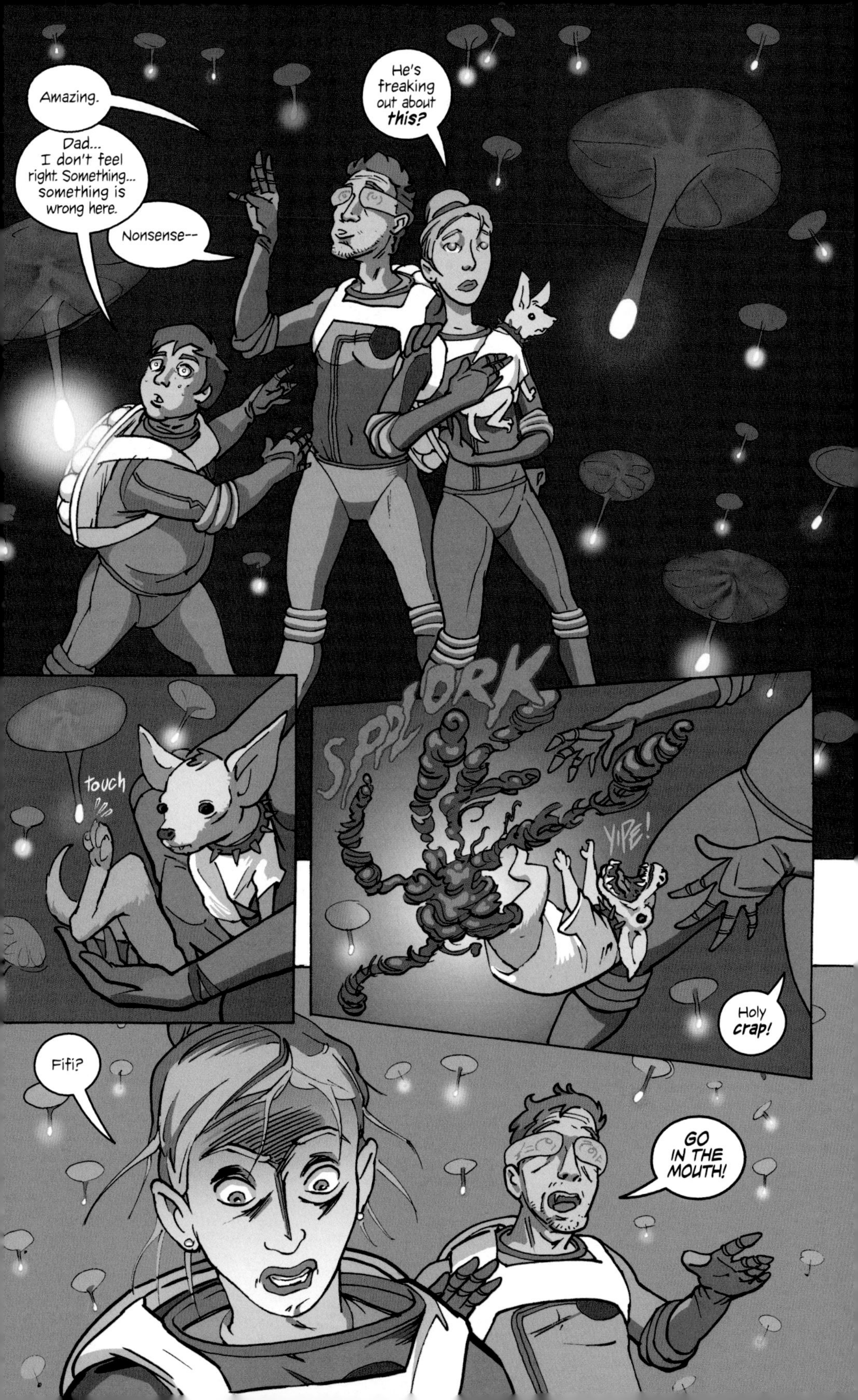
Amazing.
He's freaking out about this?
Dad... I don't feel right. Something... something is wrong here.
Nonsense--
touch
SPPLORK
YIPE!
Holy crap!
Fifi?
GO IN THE MOUTH!

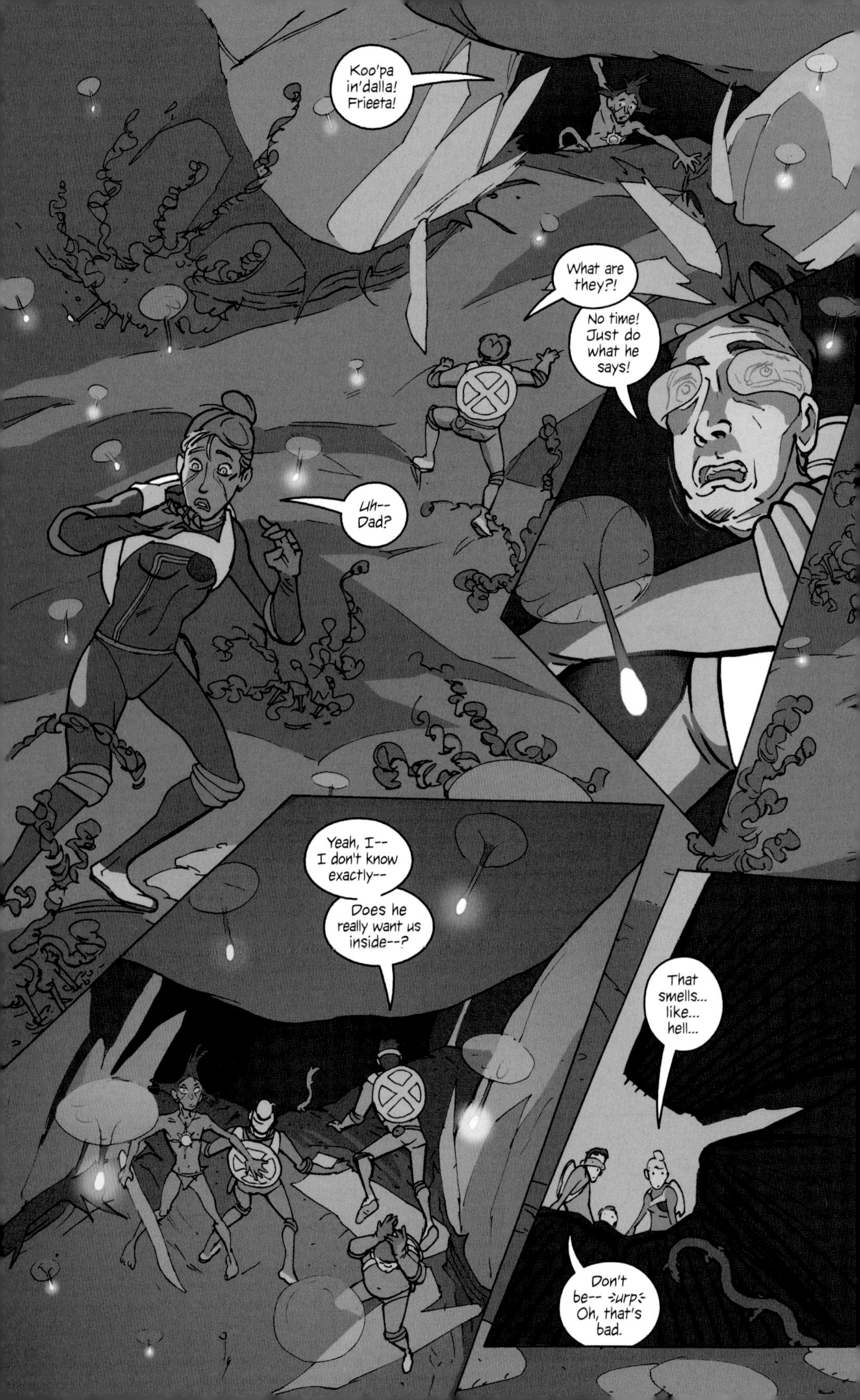
Koo'pa in'dalla! Frieeta!
What are they?!
No time! Just do what he says!
Uh-- Dad?
Yeah, I-- I don't know exactly--
Does he really want us inside--?
That smells... like... hell...
Don't be-- ⁒urp⁒ Oh, that's bad.

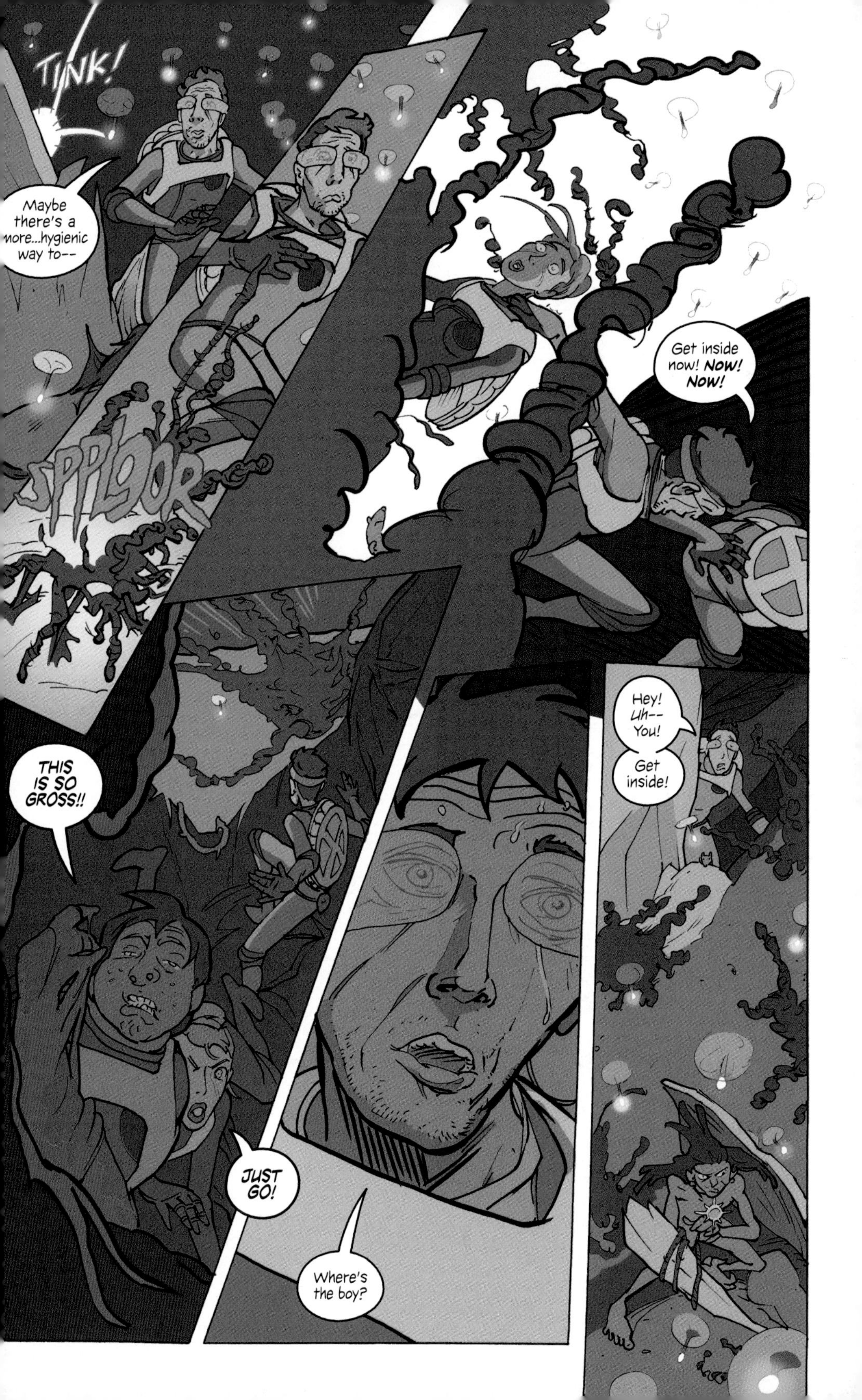
TINK!
Maybe there's a more...hygienic way to--
SPPLOOR
Get inside now! **NOW! NOW!**
THIS IS SO GROSS!!
JUST GO!
Where's the boy?
Hey! Uh-- You!
Get inside!

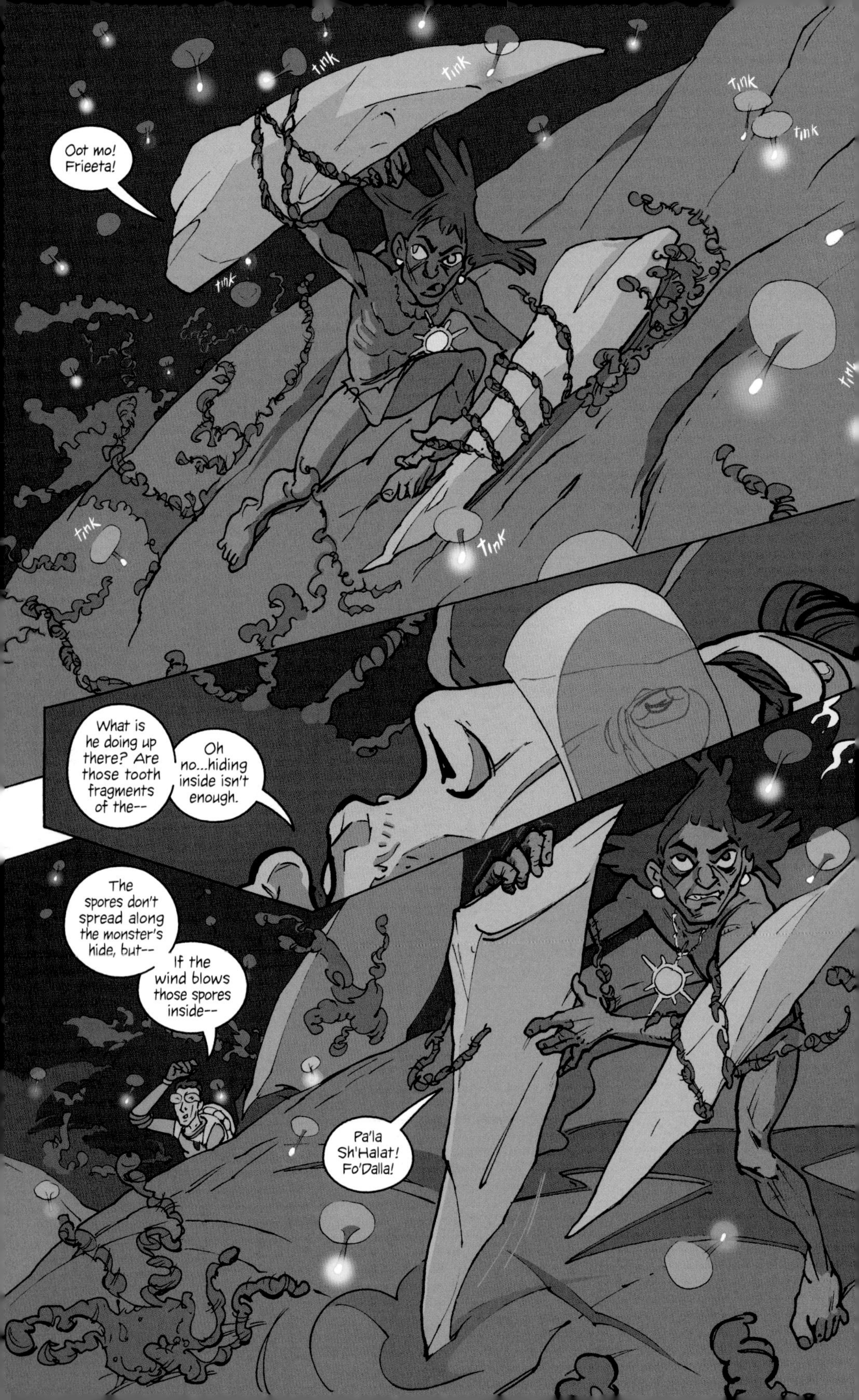
tink
tink
tink
tink
Oot mo! Frieeta!
tink
tink
tink
What is he doing up there? Are those tooth fragments of the--
Oh no...hiding inside isn't enough.
The spores don't spread along the monster's hide, but--
If the wind blows those spores inside--
Pa'la Sh'Halat! Fo'Dalla!

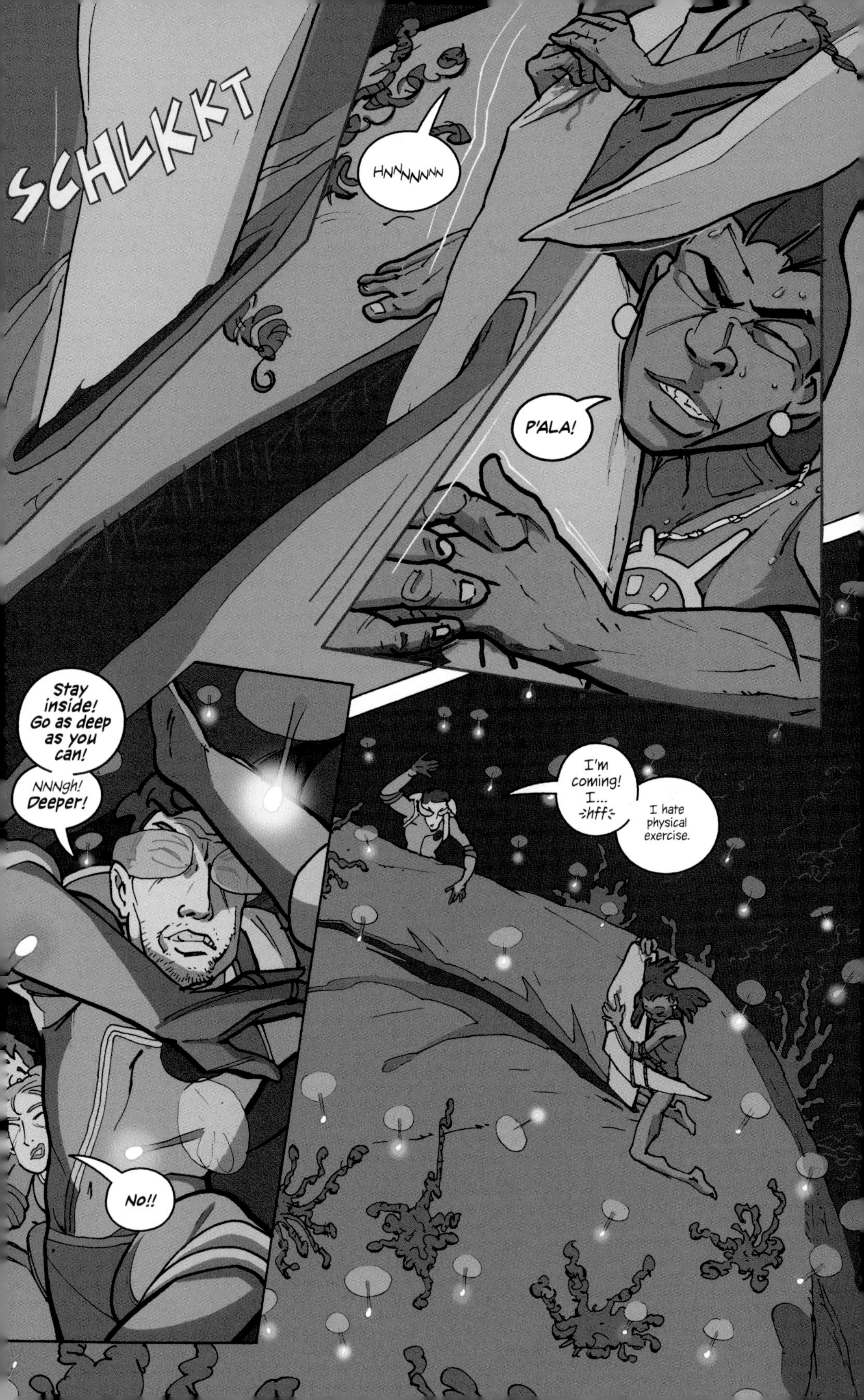
SCHLKKT
HNNNNNNN
P'ALA!
Stay inside! Go as deep as you can!
NNNgh! Deeper!
I'm coming! I... hff
I hate physical exercise.
No!!

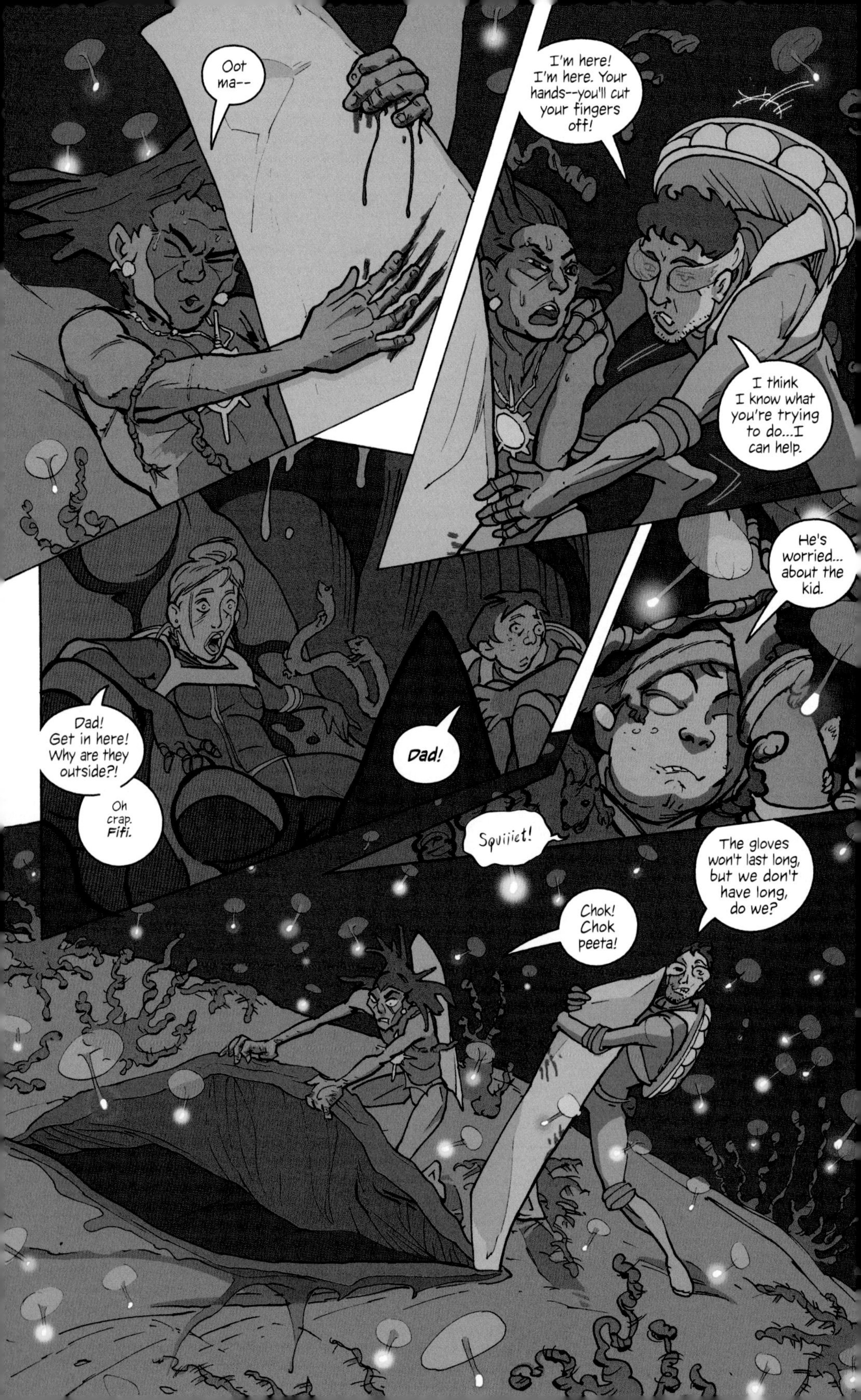
Oot ma--
I'm here! I'm here. Your hands--you'll cut your fingers off!
I think I know what you're trying to do...I can help.
He's worried... about the kid.
Dad! Get in here! Why are they outside?!
Oh crap. **Fifi.**
Dad!
Squiiiet!
The gloves won't last long, but we don't have long, do we?
Chok! Chok peeta!

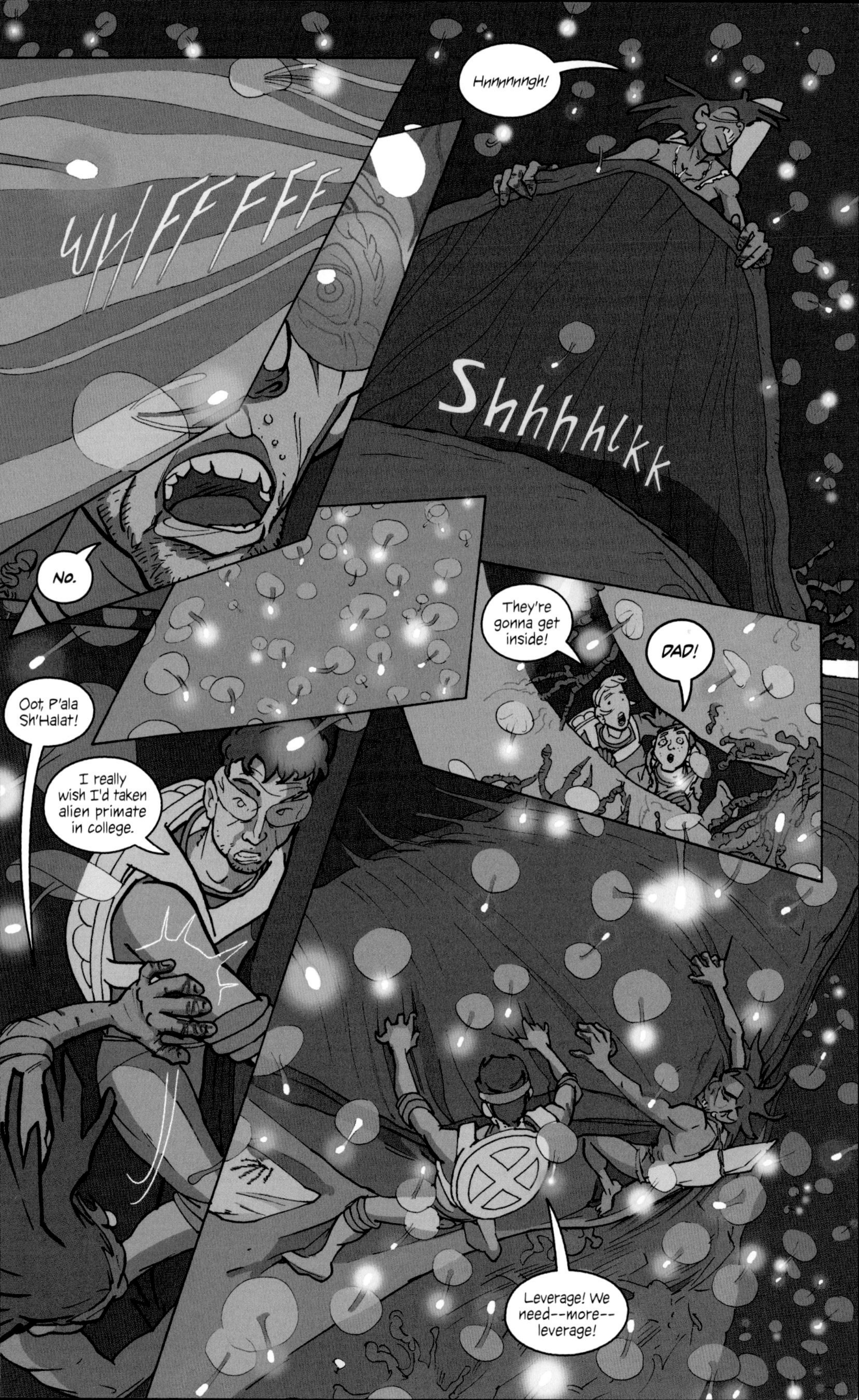
WHFFFFF
Hnnnnnngh!
Shhhhlkk
No.
They're gonna get inside!
DAD!
Oot, P'ala Sh'Halat!
I really wish I'd taken alien primate in college.
Leverage! We need--more--leverage!

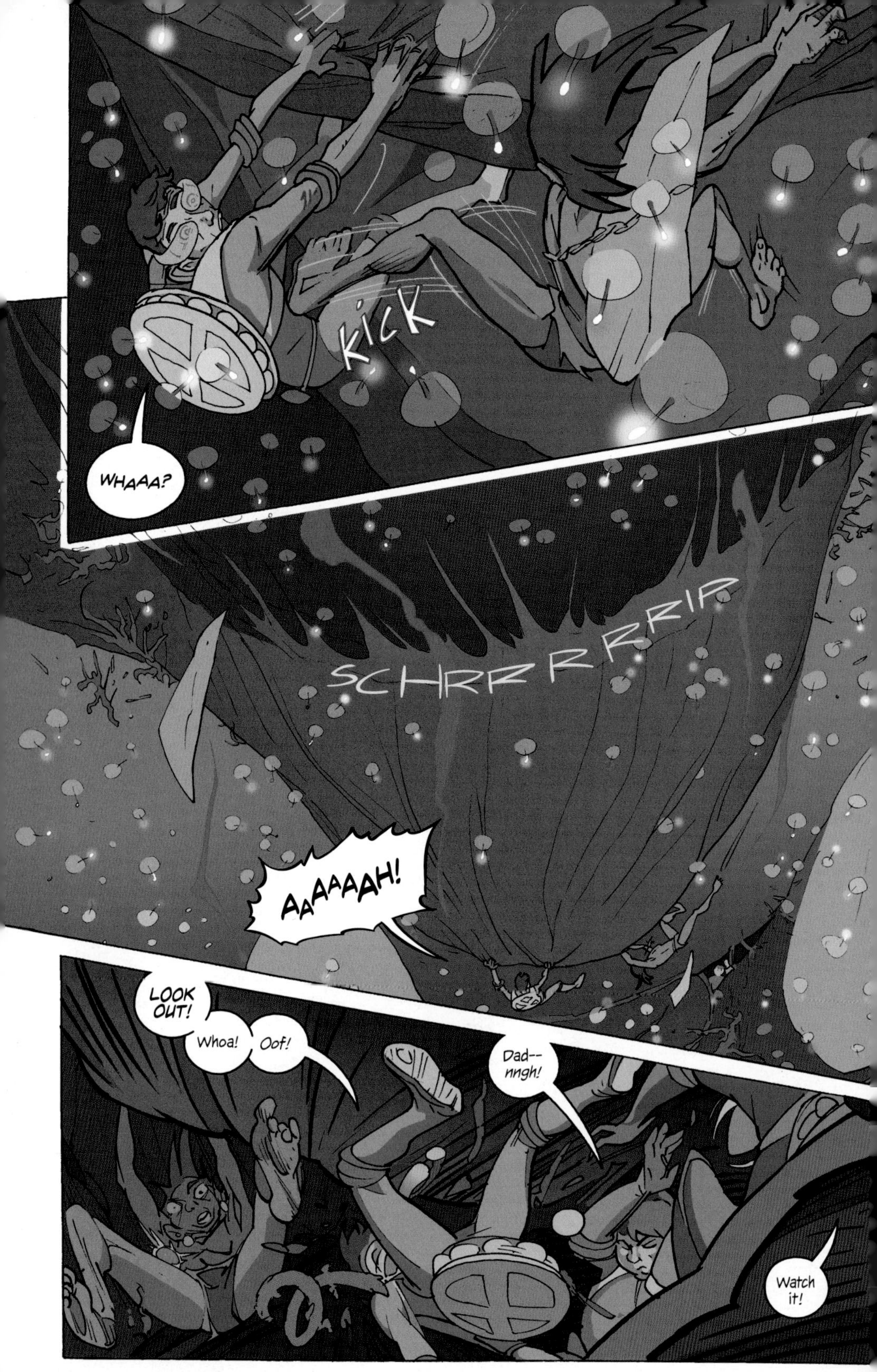
KICK
WHAAA?
SCHRRRRRIP
AAAAAAH!
LOOK OUT!
Whoa!
Oof!
Dad--nngh!
Watch it!

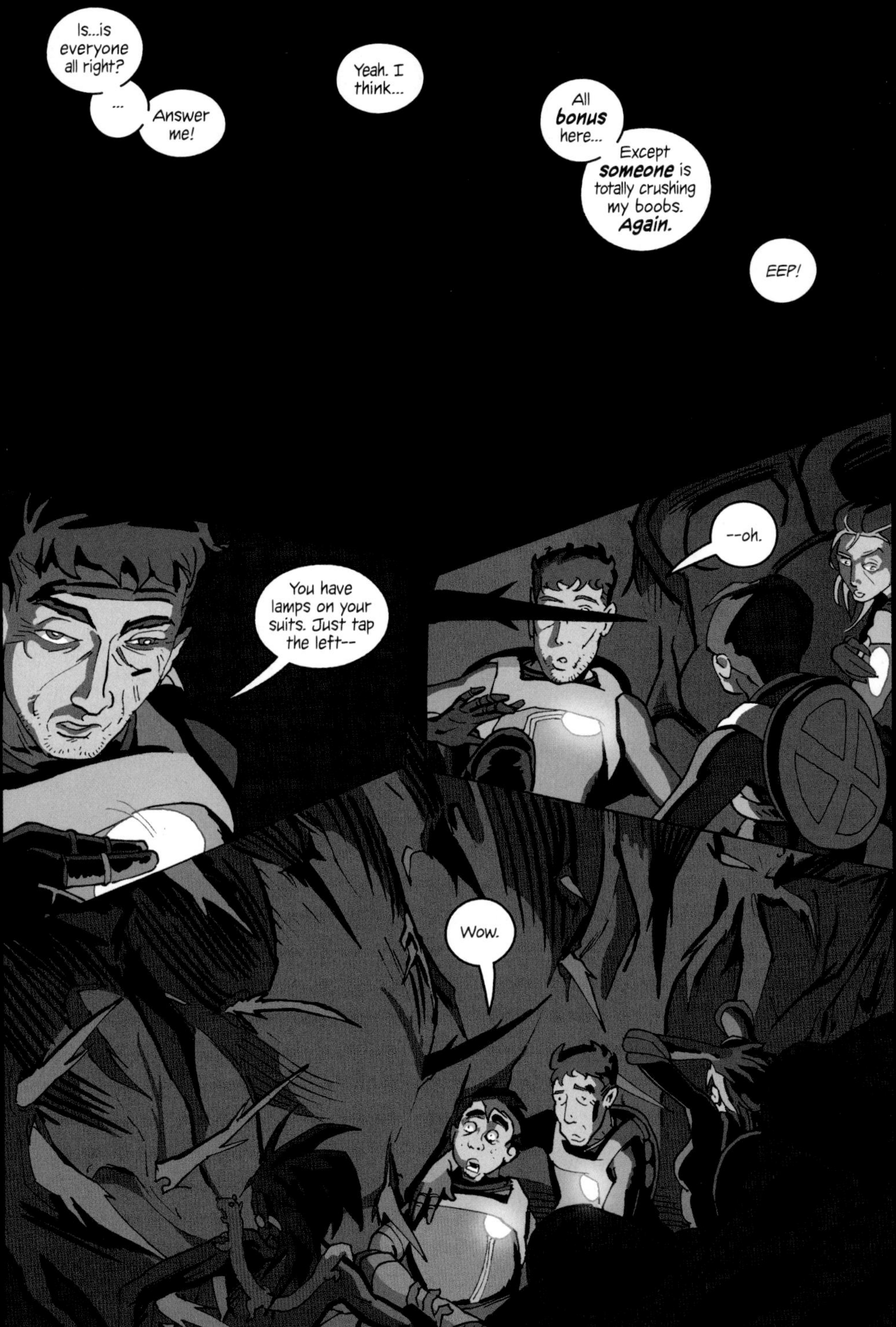
Is...is everyone all right?
...
Answer me!
Yeah. I think...
All bonus here...
Except someone is totally crushing my boobs. Again.
EEP!
You have lamps on your suits. Just tap the left--
--oh.
Wow.

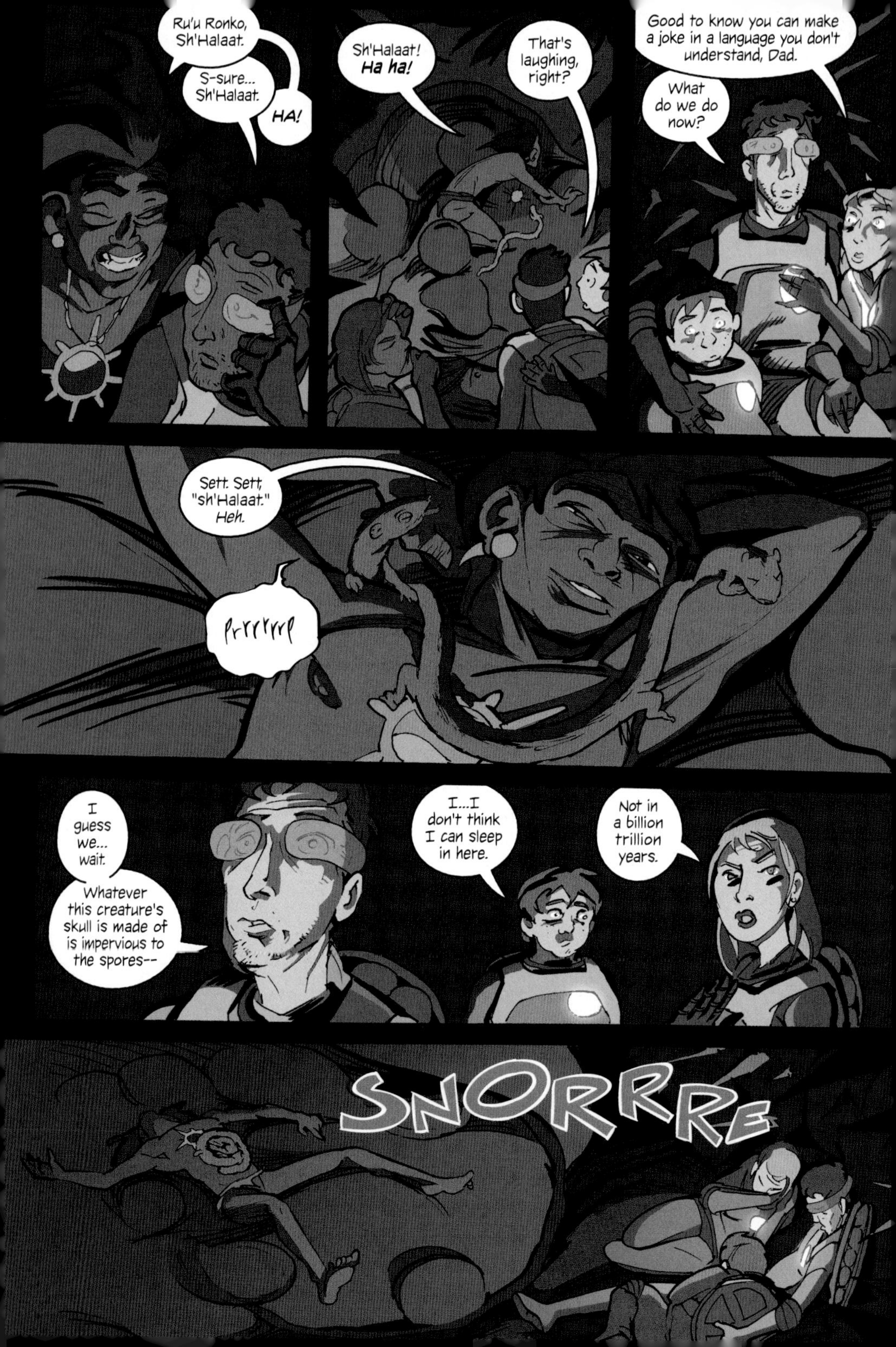

Ru'u Ronko, Sh'Halaat.
S-sure... Sh'Halaat.
HA!
Sh'Halaat! **Ha ha!**
That's laughing, right?
Good to know you can make a joke in a language you don't understand, Dad.
What do we do now?
Sett. Sett, "sh'Halaat." Heh.
Prrrrrrp
I guess we... wait.
Whatever this creature's skull is made of is impervious to the spores--
I...I don't think I can sleep in here.
Not in a billion trillion years.
SNORRRE

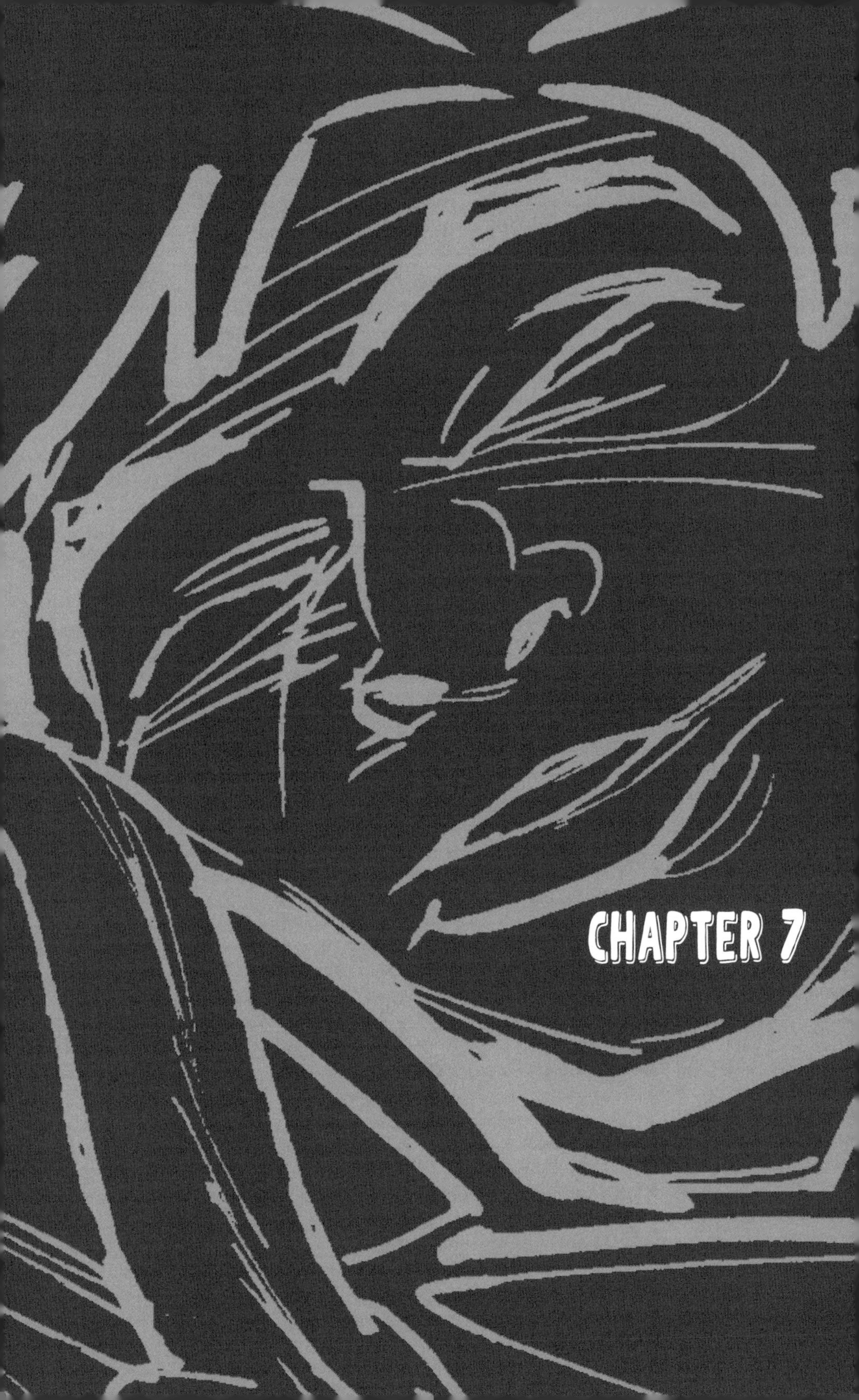
CHAPTER 7

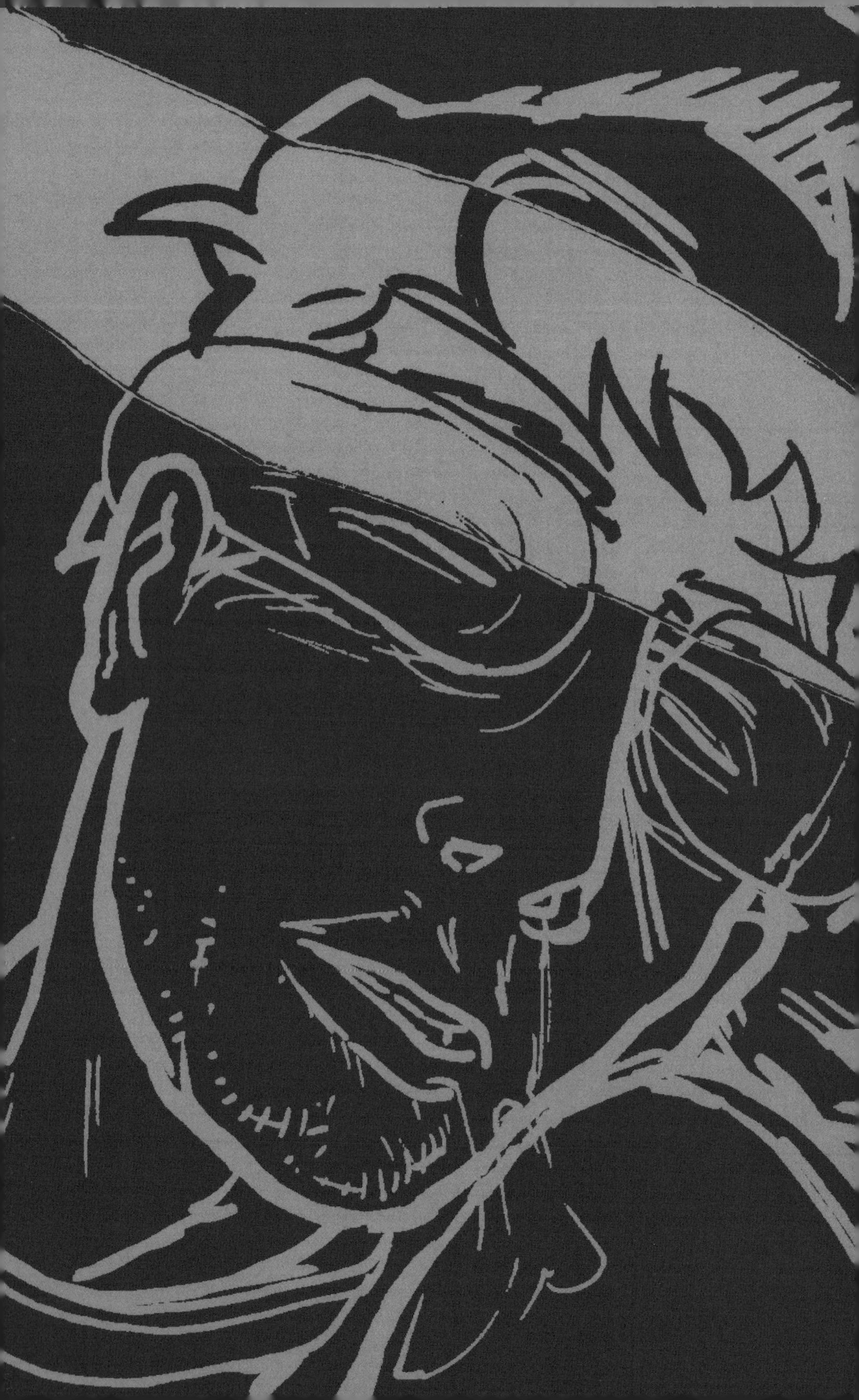

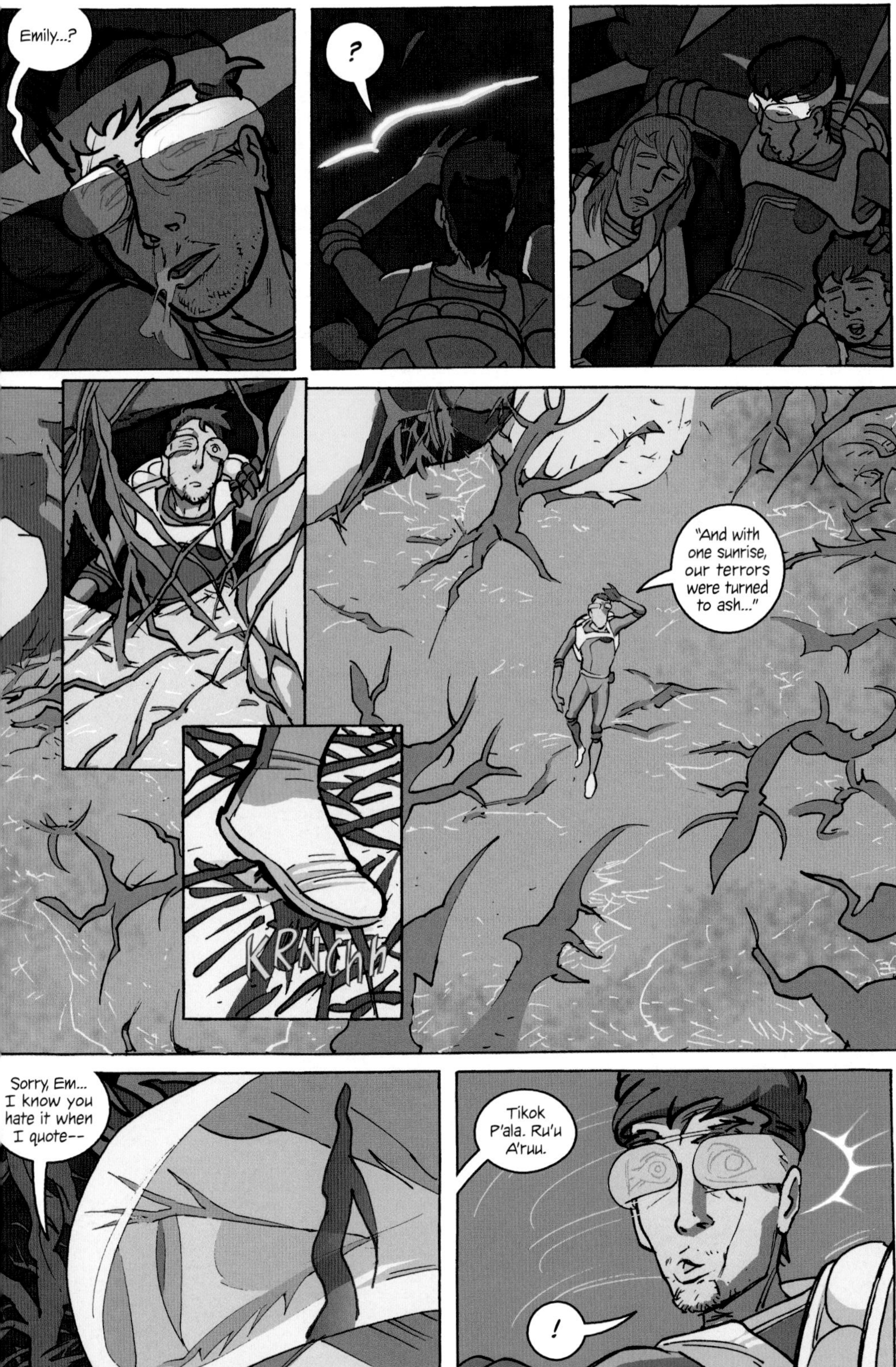
Emily...?
?
"And with one sunrise, our terrors were turned to ash..."
KRNCHH
Sorry, Em... I know you hate it when I quote--
Tikok P'ala. Ru'u A'ruu.
!

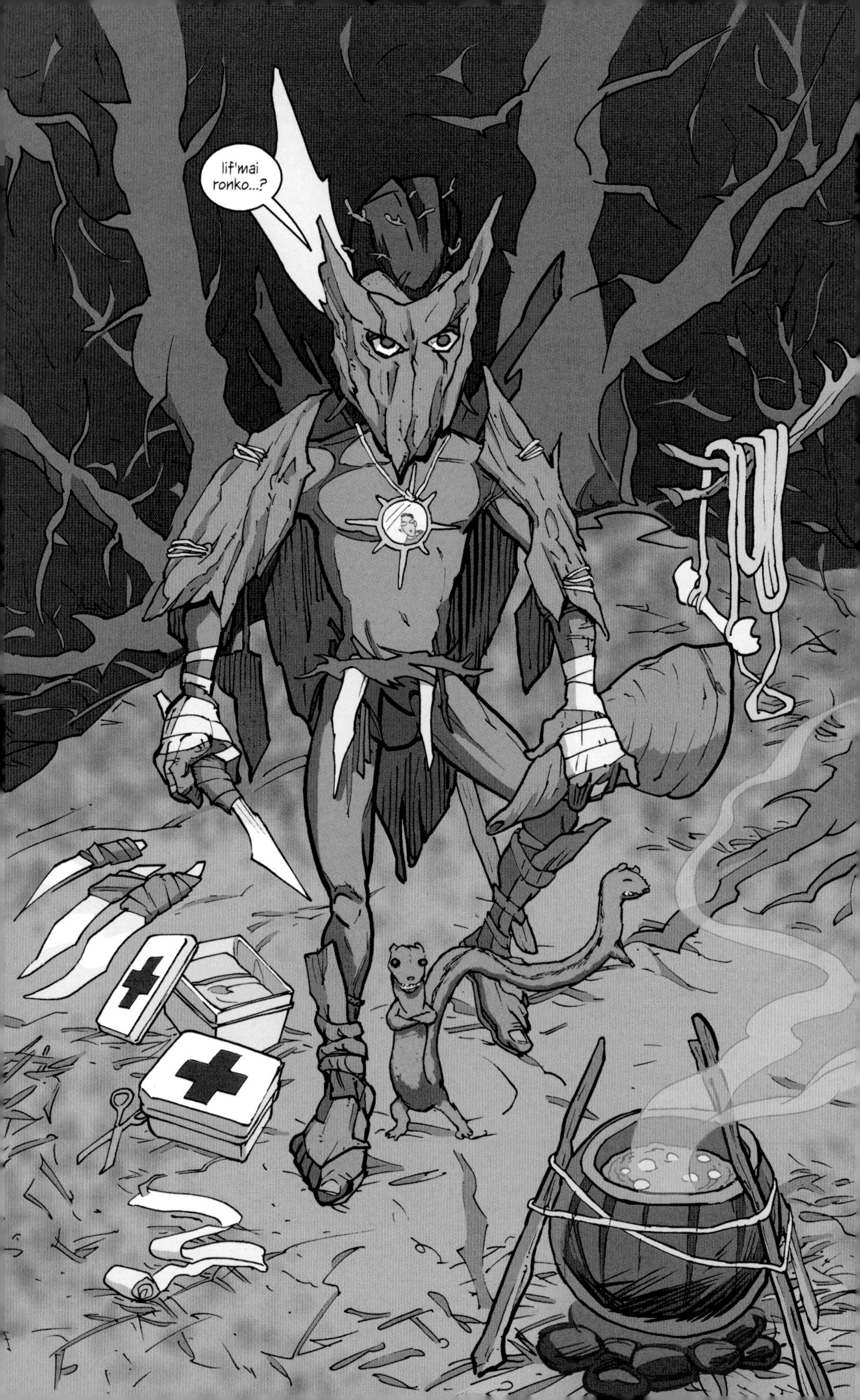
lif'mai ronko...?

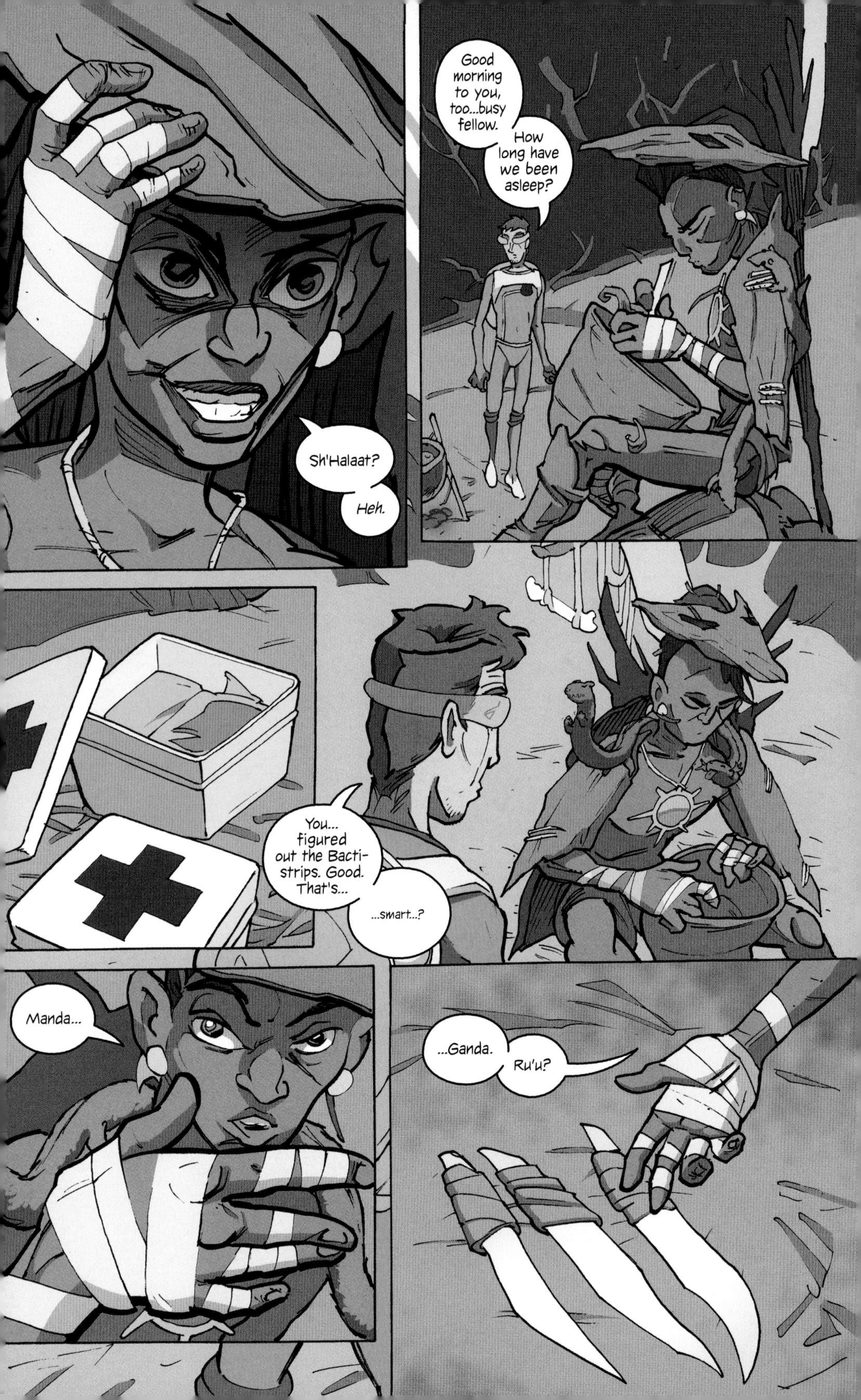
Sh'Halaat?
Heh.
Good morning to you, too...busy fellow.
How long have we been asleep?
You... figured out the Bacti-strips. Good. That's...
...smart...?
Manda...
...Ganda.
Ru'u?

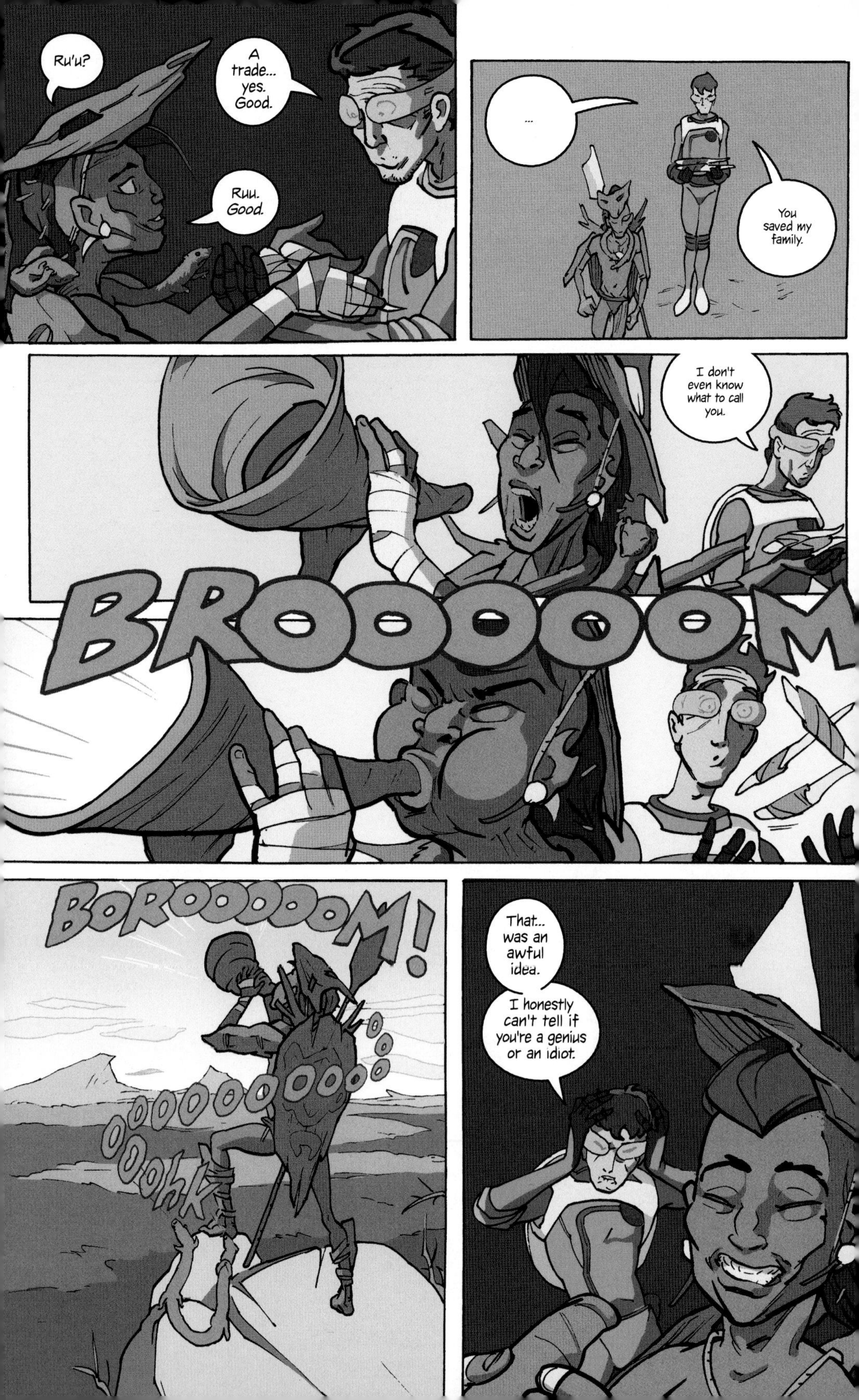
Ru'u?
A trade... yes. Good.
Ruu. Good.
...
You saved my family.
I don't even know what to call you.
BROOOOOOM
BOROOOOOOM!
OOOOOOOOOOOOOOOOhk
That... was an awful idea.
I honestly can't tell if you're a genius or an idiot.

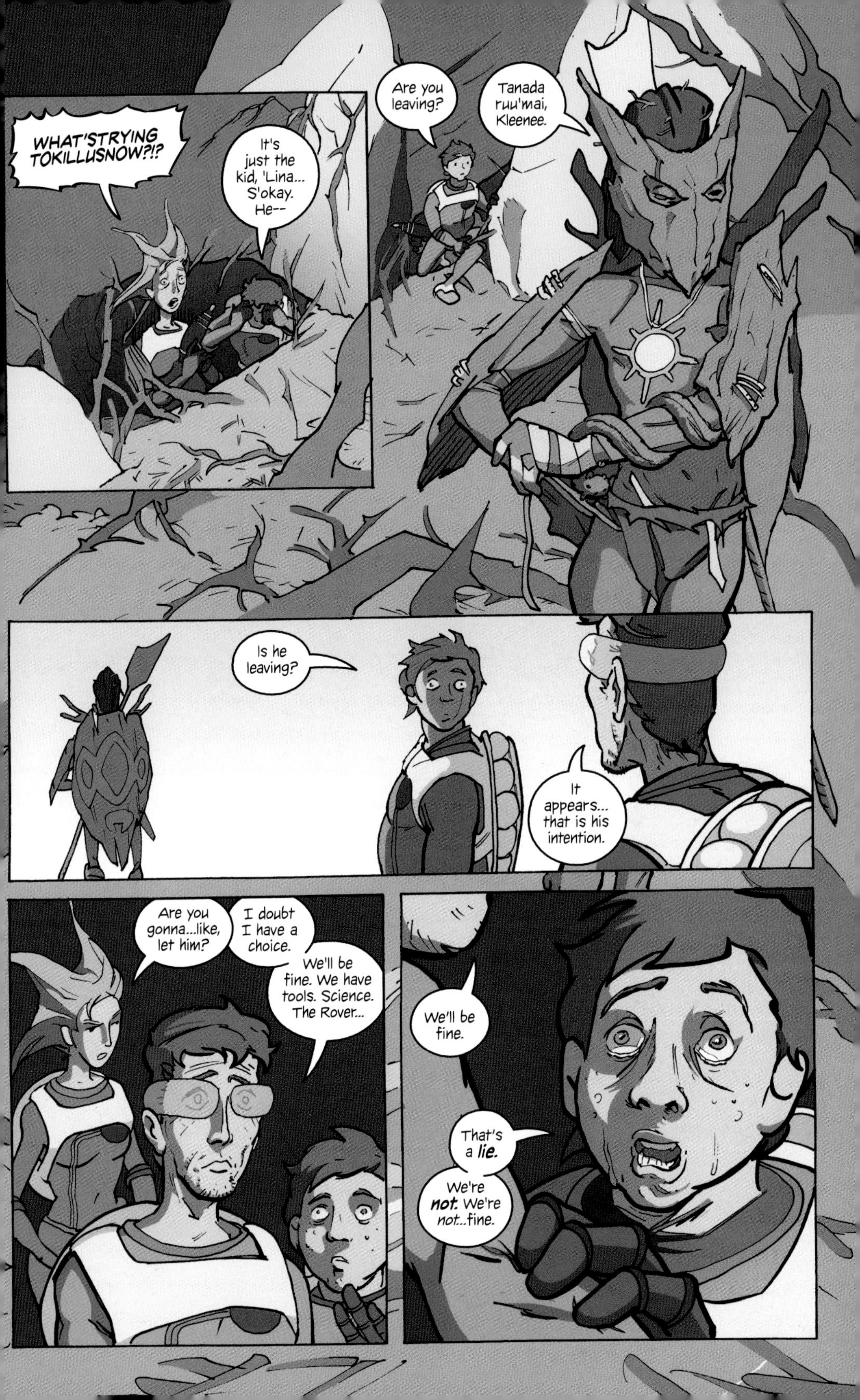
WHAT'STRYING TOKILLUSNOW?!?
It's just the kid, 'Lina... S'okay. He--
Are you leaving?
Tanada ruu'mai, Kleenee.
Is he leaving?
It appears... that is his intention.
Are you gonna...like, let him?
I doubt I have a choice.
We'll be fine. We have tools. Science. The Rover...
We'll be fine.
That's a ***lie.***
We're ***not.*** We're *not*...fine.

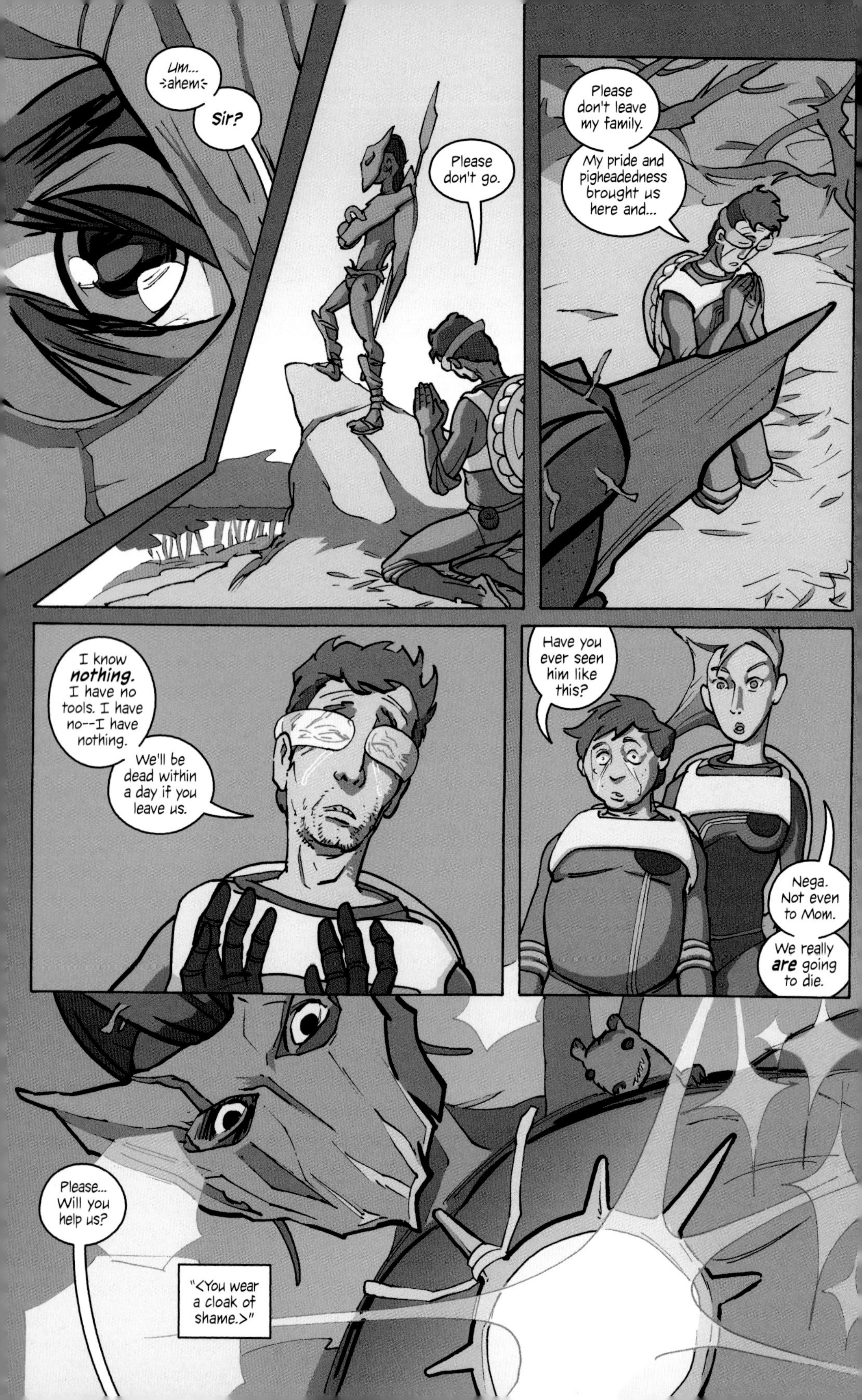
Um... ahem Sir?
Please don't go.
Please don't leave my family.
My pride and pigheadedness brought us here and...
I know **nothing.** I have no tools. I have no--I have nothing.
We'll be dead within a day if you leave us.
Have you ever seen him like this?
Nega. Not even to Mom.
We really **are** going to die.
Please... Will you help us?
"<You wear a cloak of shame.>"

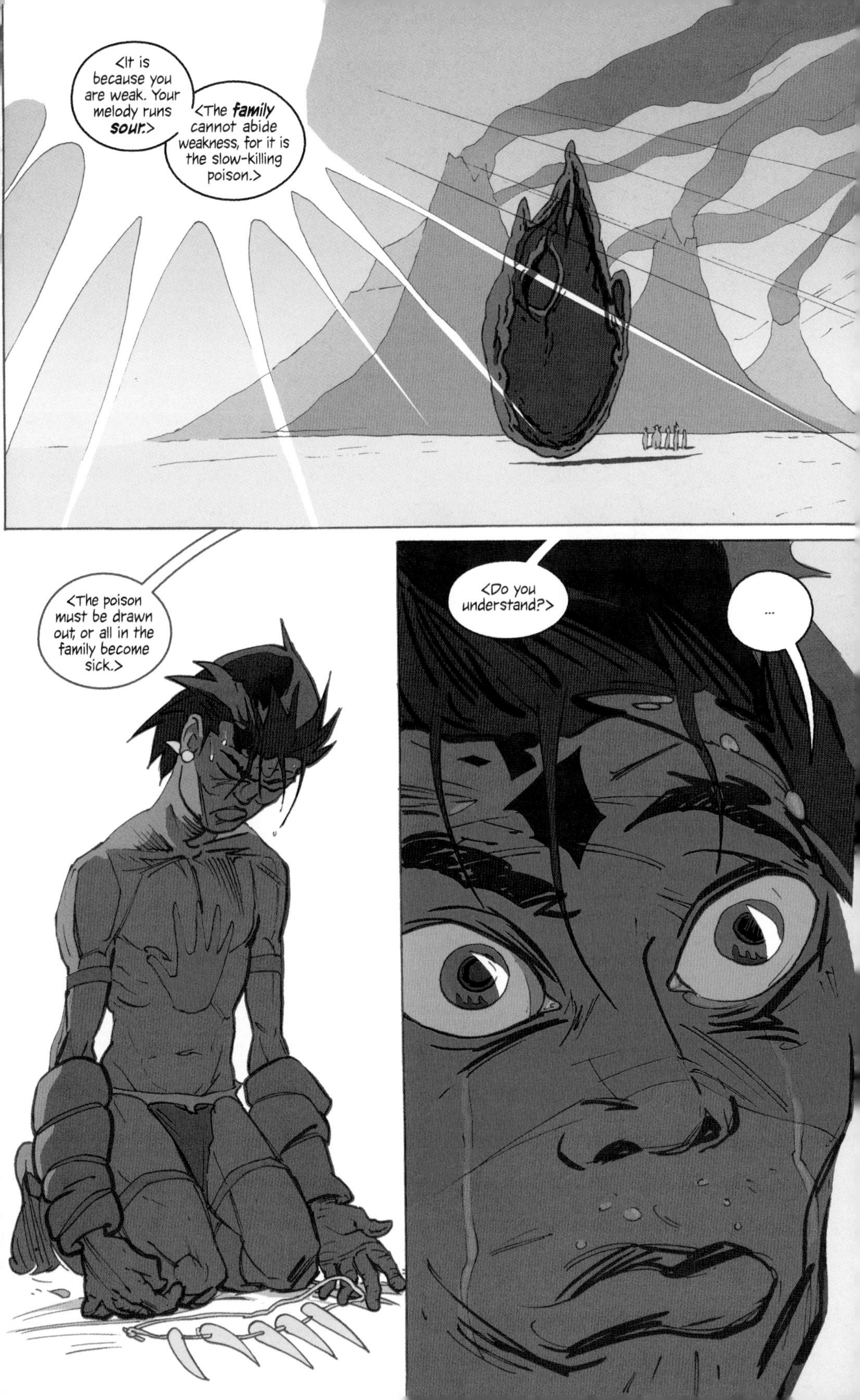

<It is because you are weak. Your melody runs **sour.**>
<The **family** cannot abide weakness, for it is the slow-killing poison.>
<The poison must be drawn out, or all in the family become sick.>
<Do you understand?>
...

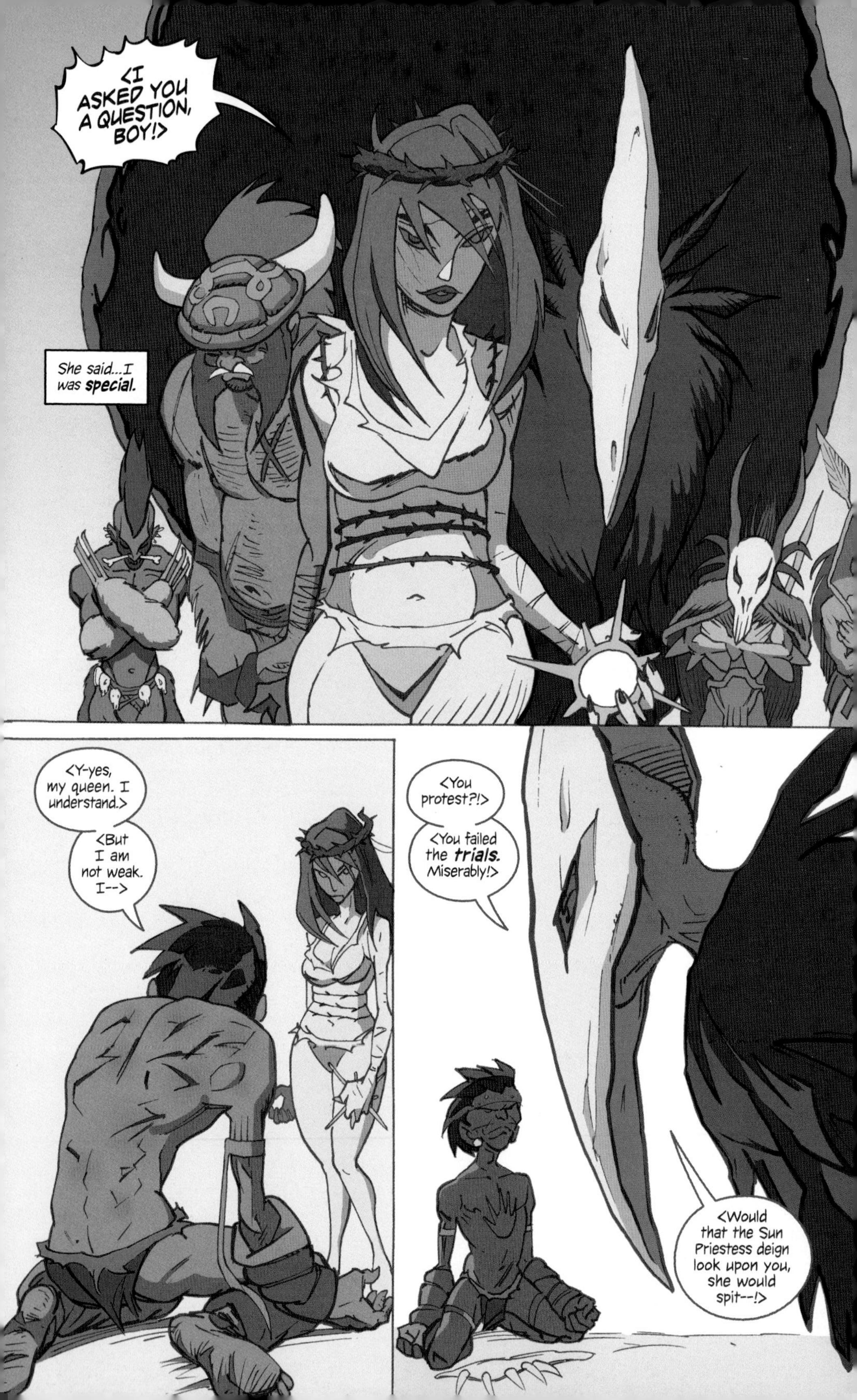
<I ASKED YOU A QUESTION, BOY!>
She said...I was **special.**
<Y-yes, my queen. I understand.>
<But I am not weak. I-->
<You protest?!>
<You failed the ***trials.*** Miserably!>
<Would that the Sun Priestess deign look upon you, she would spit--!>

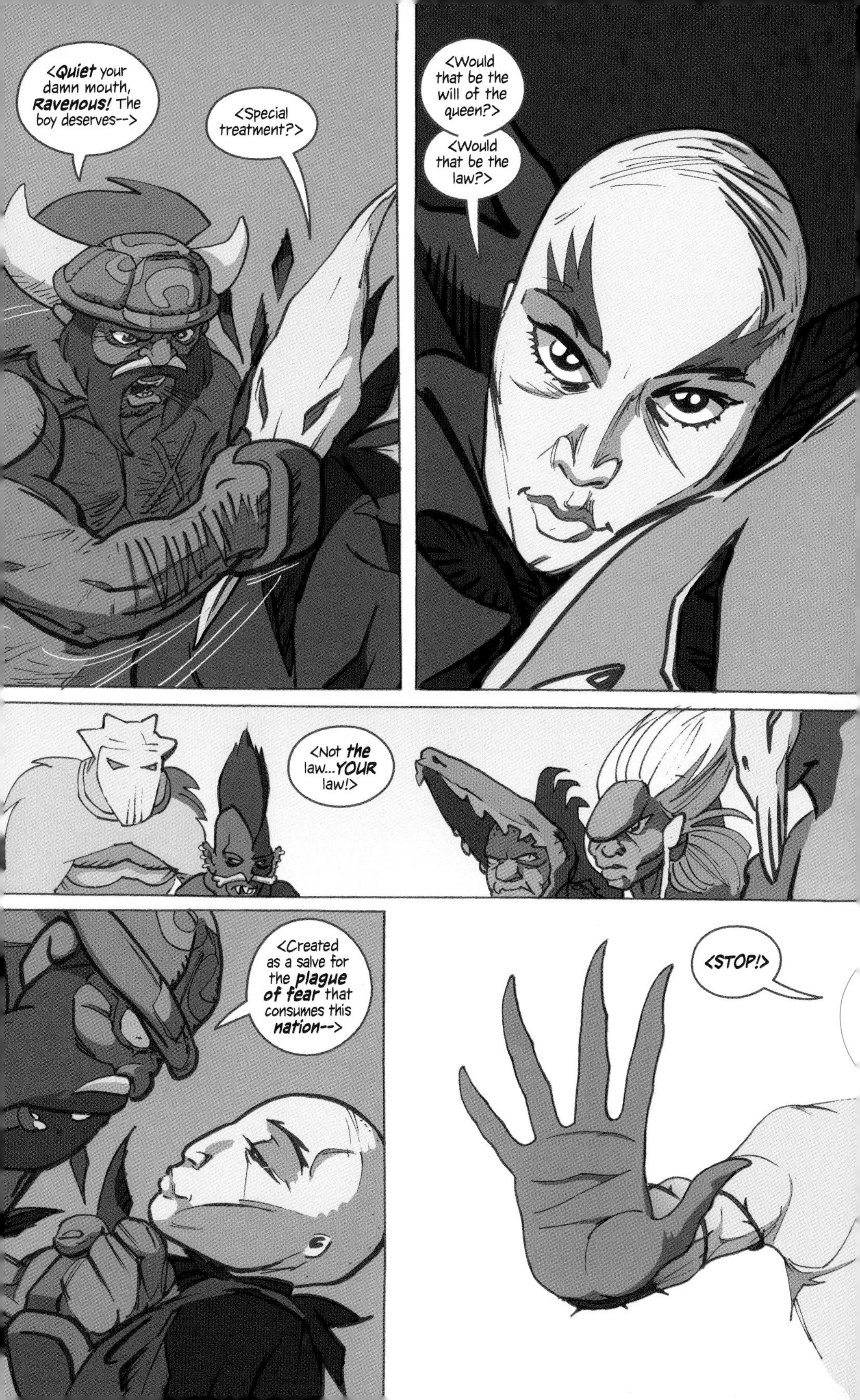
<Quiet your damn mouth, Ravenous! The boy deserves-->
<Special treatment?>
<Would that be the will of the queen?>
<Would that be the law?>
<Not the law...YOUR law!>
<Created as a salve for the plague of fear that consumes this nation-->
<STOP!>

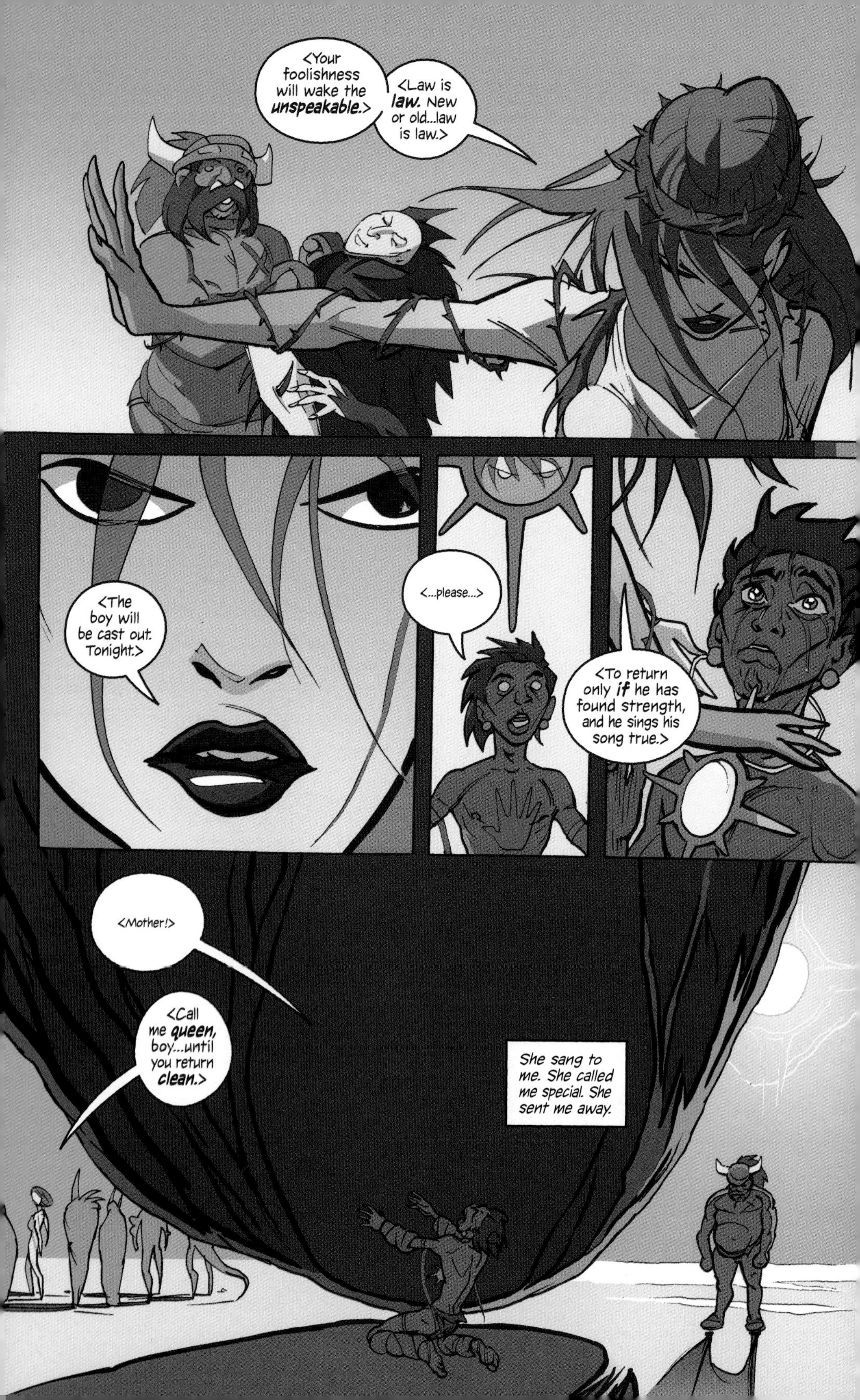
<Your foolishness will wake the unspeakable.>
<Law is law. New or old...law is law.>
<The boy will be cast out. Tonight.>
<...please...>
<To return only if he has found strength, and he sings his song true.>
<Mother!>
<Call me queen, boy...until you return clean.>
She sang to me. She called me special. She sent me away.

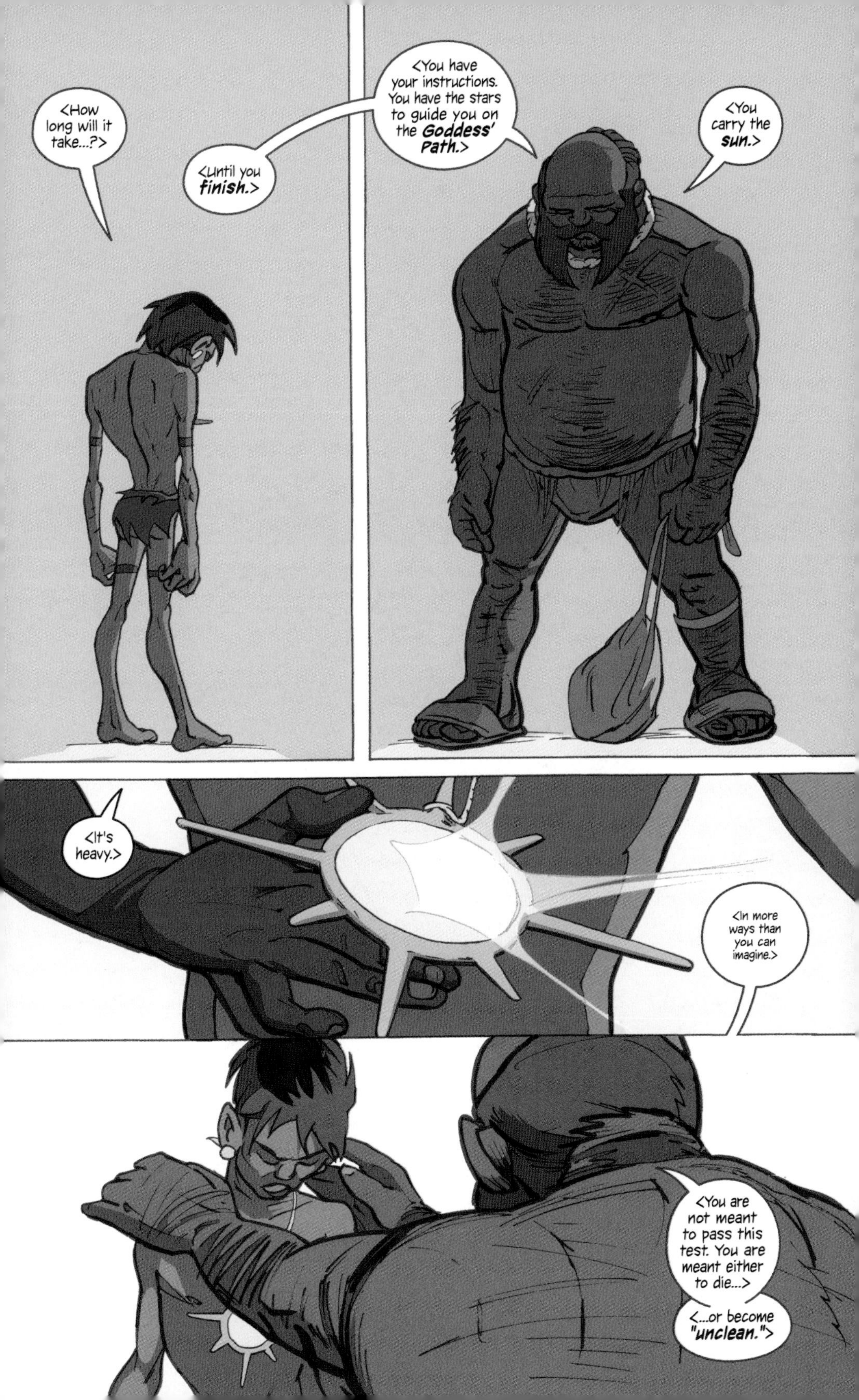

<How long will it take...?>
<Until you finish.>
<You have your instructions. You have the stars to guide you on the Goddess' Path.>
<You carry the sun.>
<It's heavy.>
<In more ways than you can imagine.>
<You are not meant to pass this test. You are meant either to die...>
<...or become "unclean.">

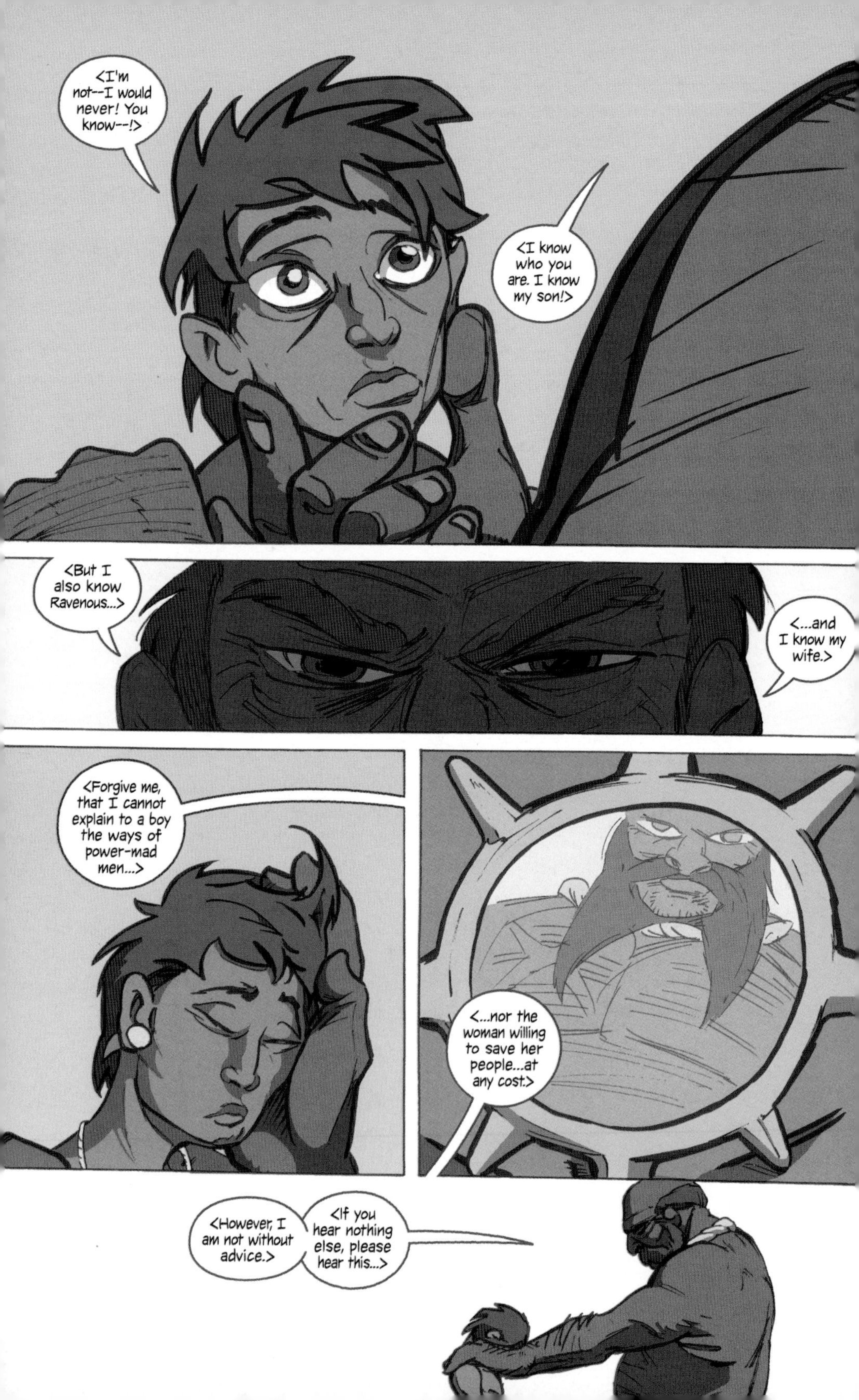
<I'm not--I would never! You know--!>
<I know who you are. I know my son!>
<But I also know Ravenous...>
<...and I know my wife.>
<Forgive me, that I cannot explain to a boy the ways of power-mad men...>
<...nor the woman willing to save her people...at any cost.>
<However, I am not without advice.>
<If you hear nothing else, please hear this...>

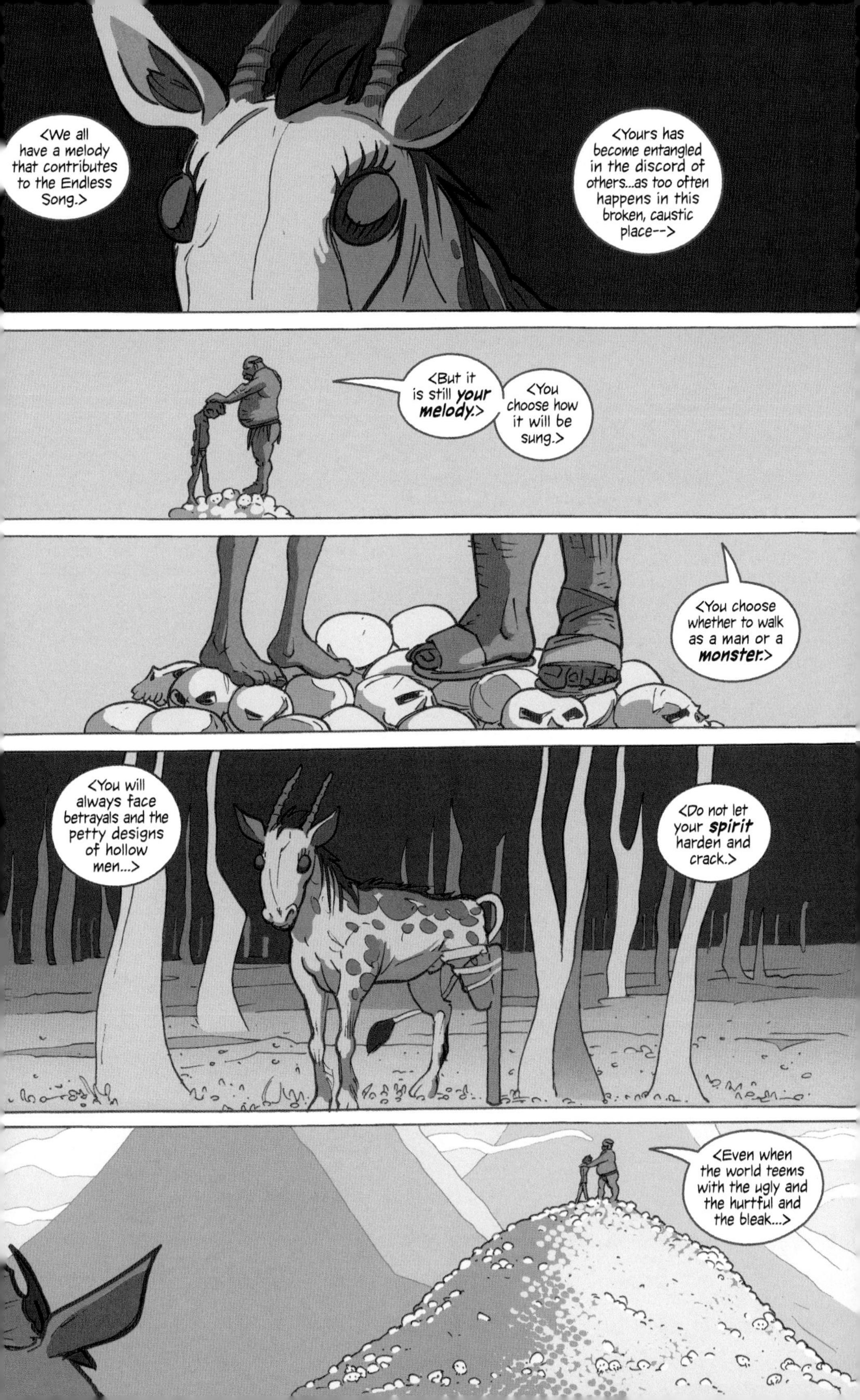
<We all have a melody that contributes to the Endless Song.>
<Yours has become entangled in the discord of others...as too often happens in this broken, caustic place-->
<But it is still **your melody.**>
<You choose how it will be sung.>
<You choose whether to walk as a man or a **monster.**>
<You will always face betrayals and the petty designs of hollow men...>
<Do not let your **spirit** harden and crack.>
<Even when the world teems with the ugly and the hurtful and the bleak...>

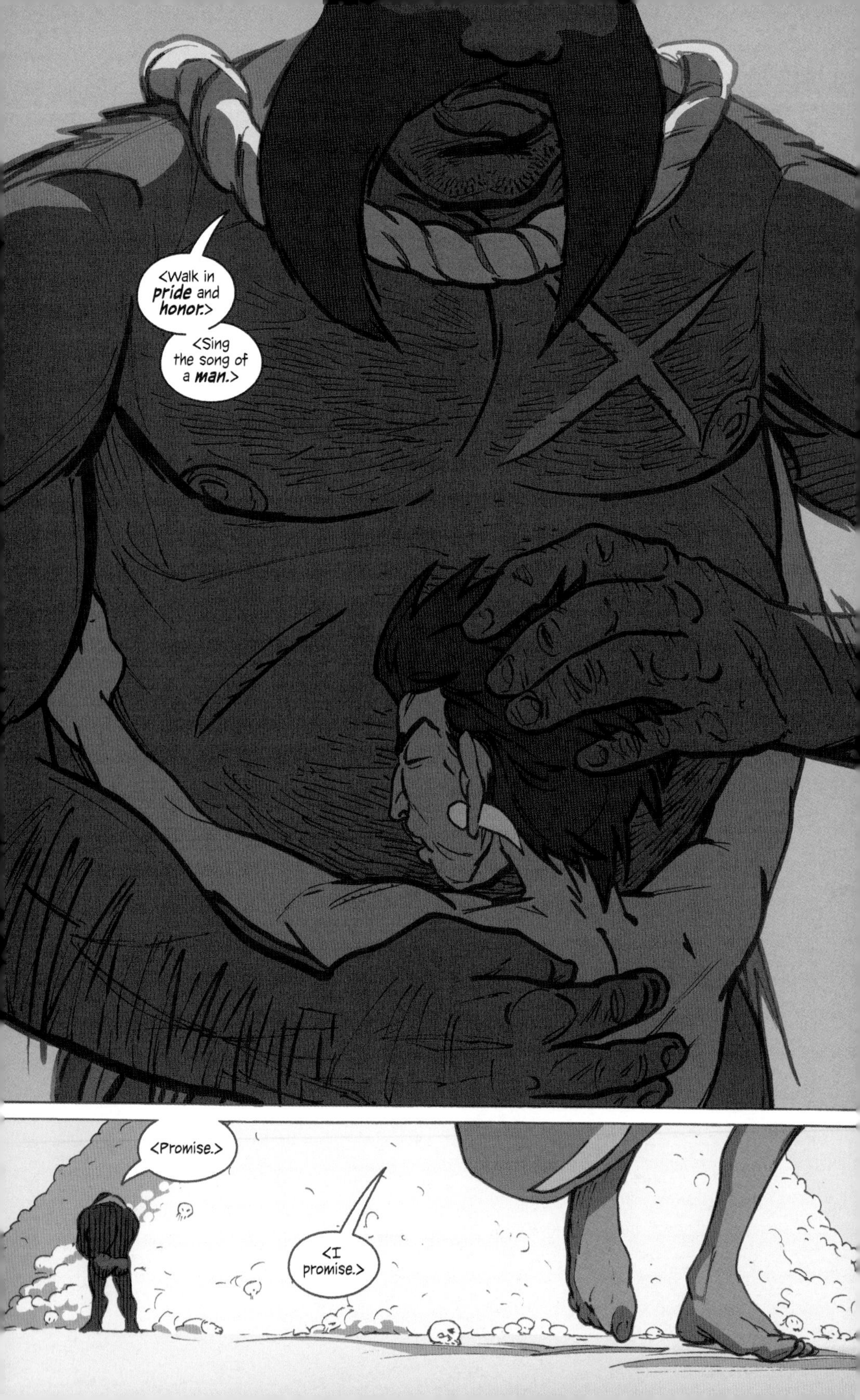
<Walk in **pride** and **honor.**>
<Sing the song of a **man.**>
<Promise.>
<I promise.>

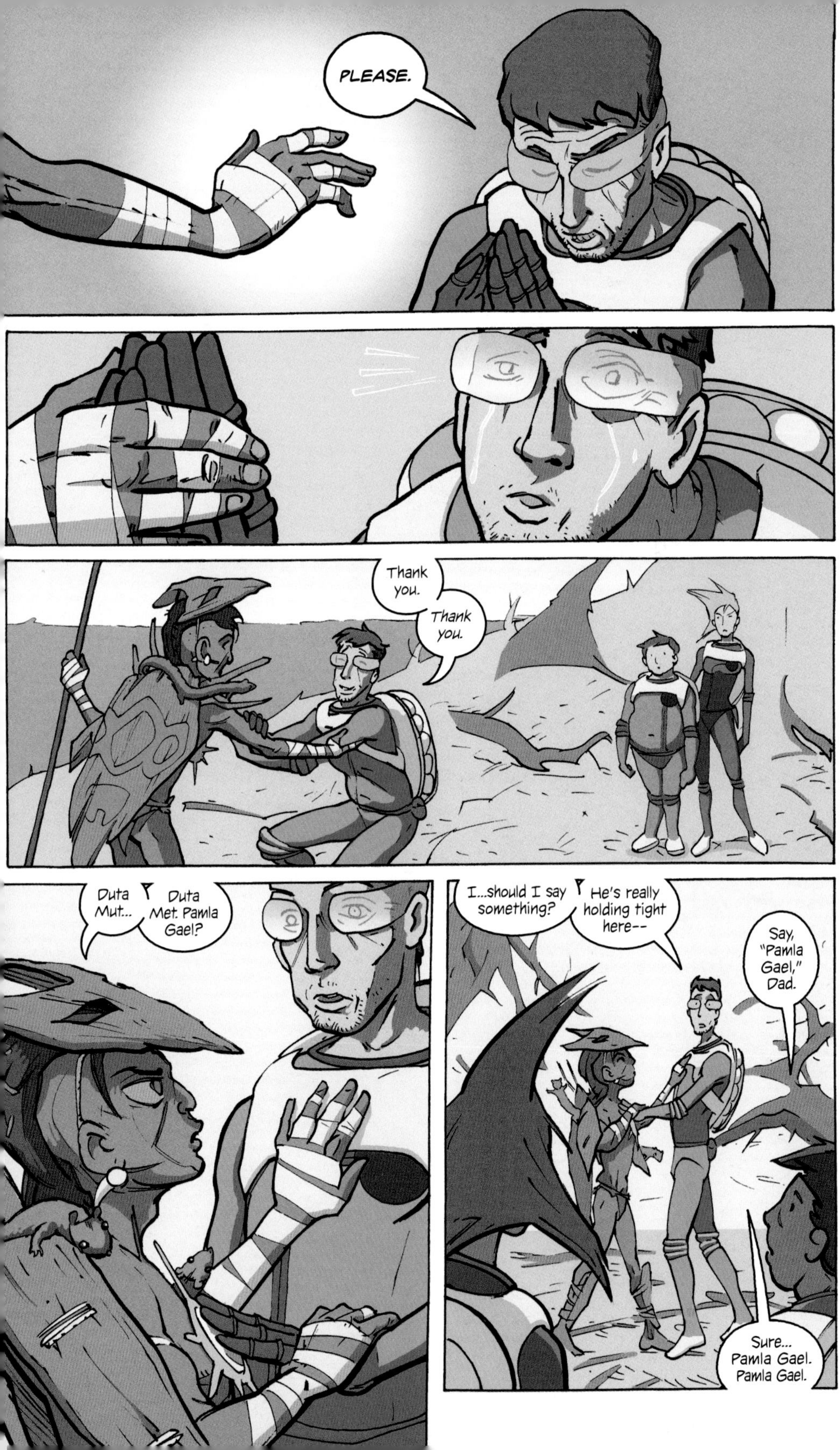
PLEASE.
Thank you.
Thank you.
Duta Mut...
Duta Met. Pamla Gael?
I...should I say something?
He's really holding tight here--
Say, "Pamla Gael," Dad.
Sure... Pamla Gael. Pamla Gael.

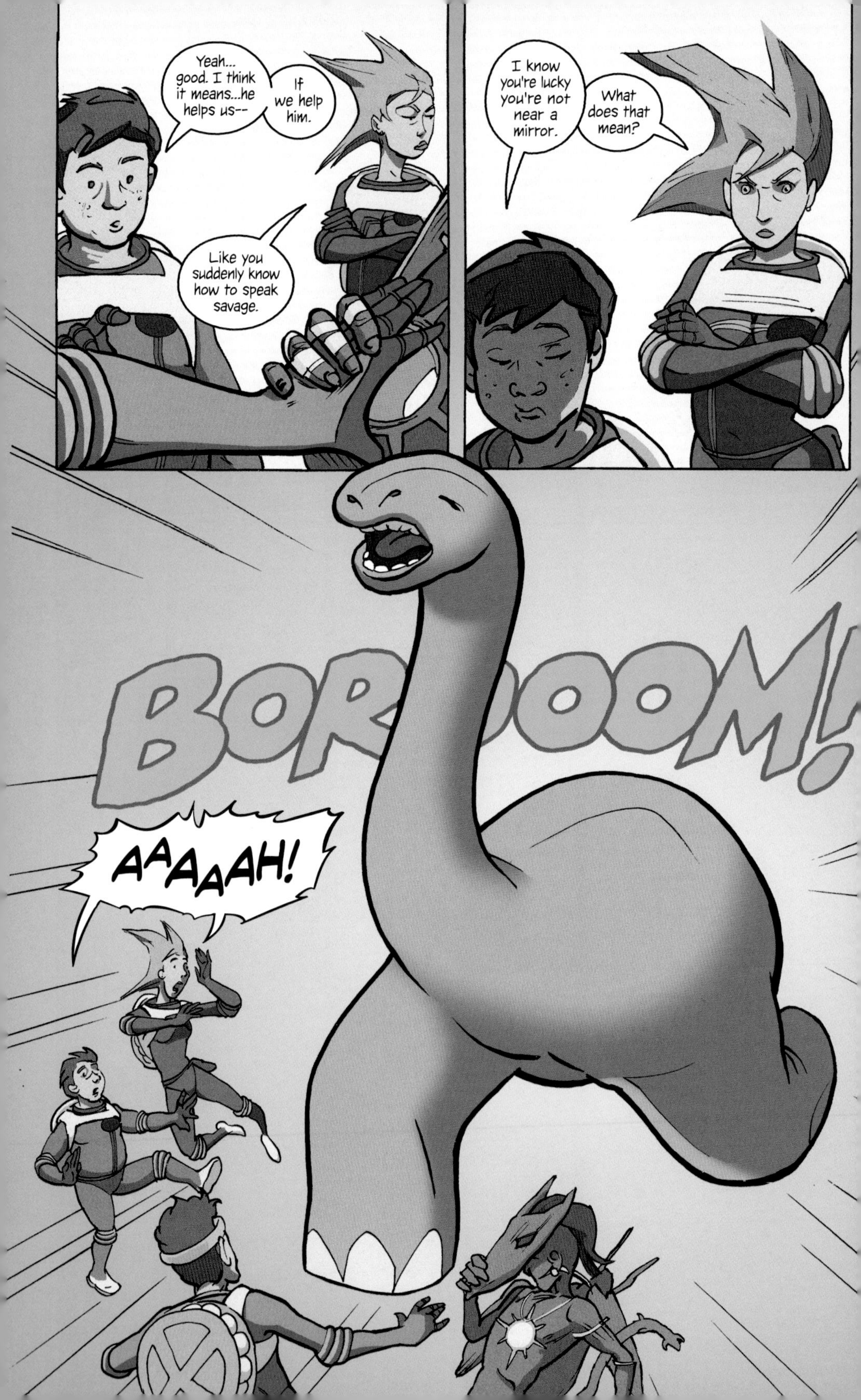
Yeah... good. I think it means...he helps us--
If we help him.
Like you suddenly know how to speak savage.
I know you're lucky you're not near a mirror.
What does that mean?
BOROOOM!
AAAAAH!

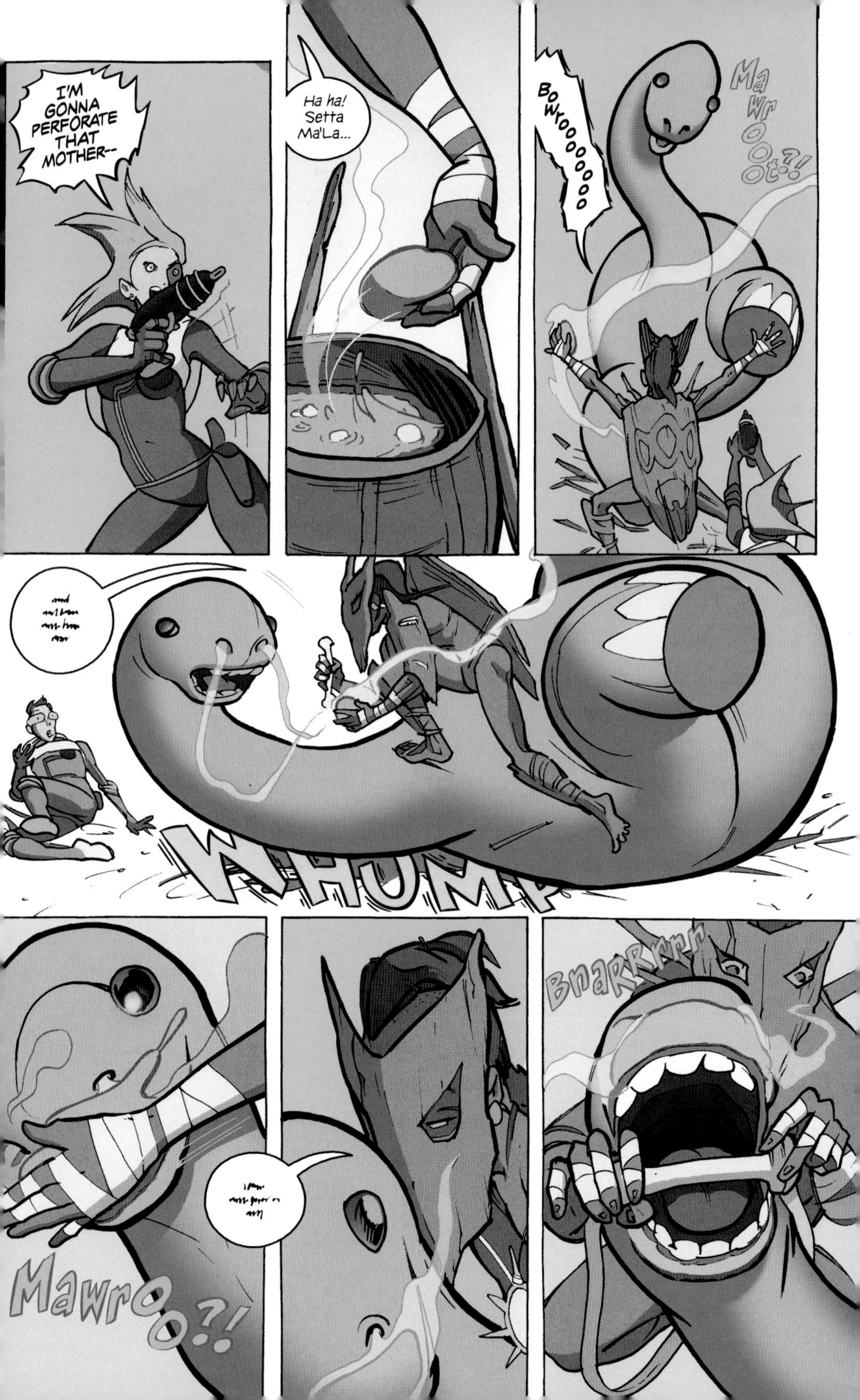

I'M GONNA PERFORATE THAT MOTHER--
Ha ha! Setta Ma'La...
Bowrooooooooo
Mawrooot?!
WHUMP
Mawroo?!
BnaRRrrrr

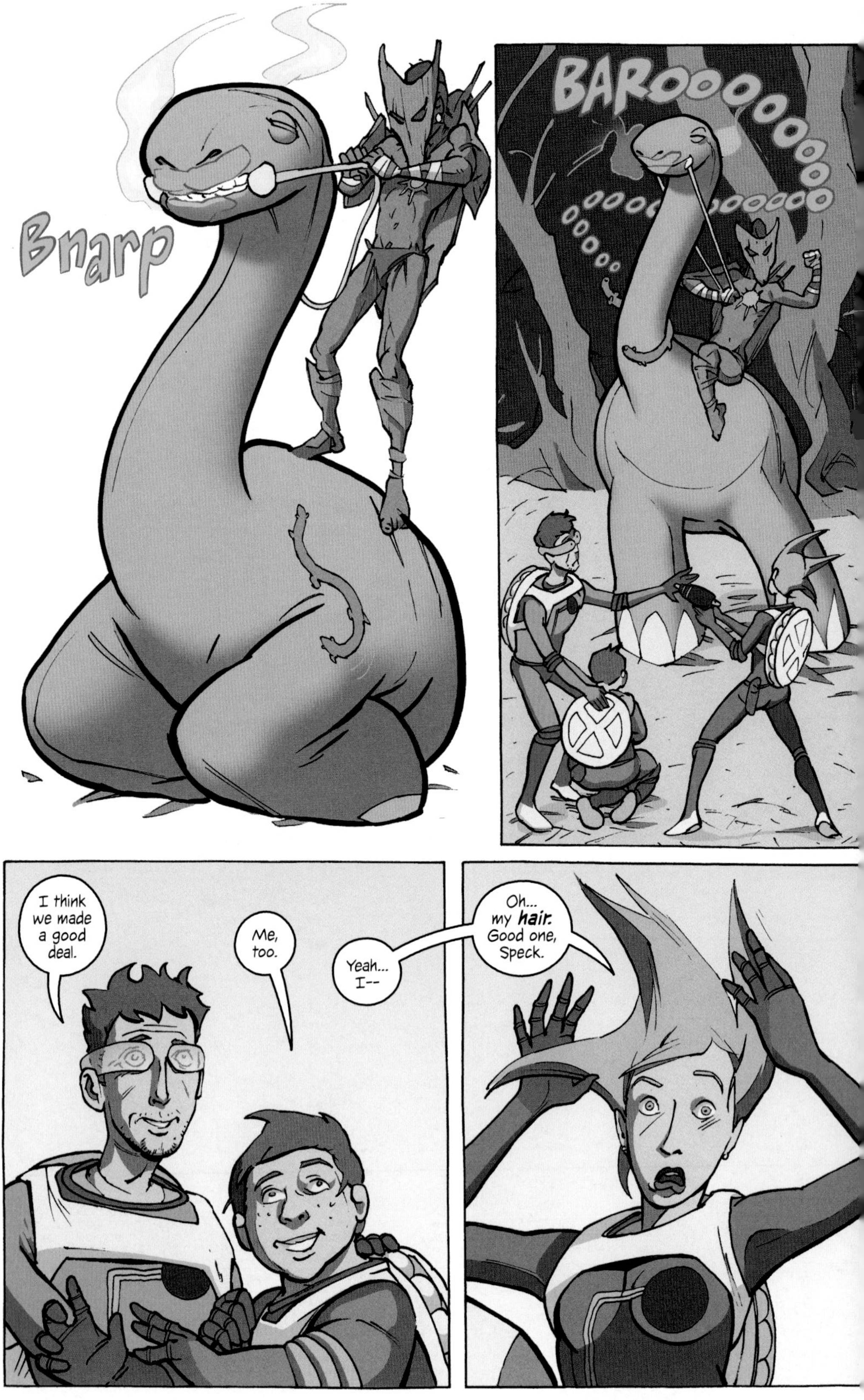
Bnarp
BAROOOOOOOOOOOOOOOOOOO
I think we made a good deal.
Me, too.
Yeah... I--
Oh... my **hair.** Good one, Speck.

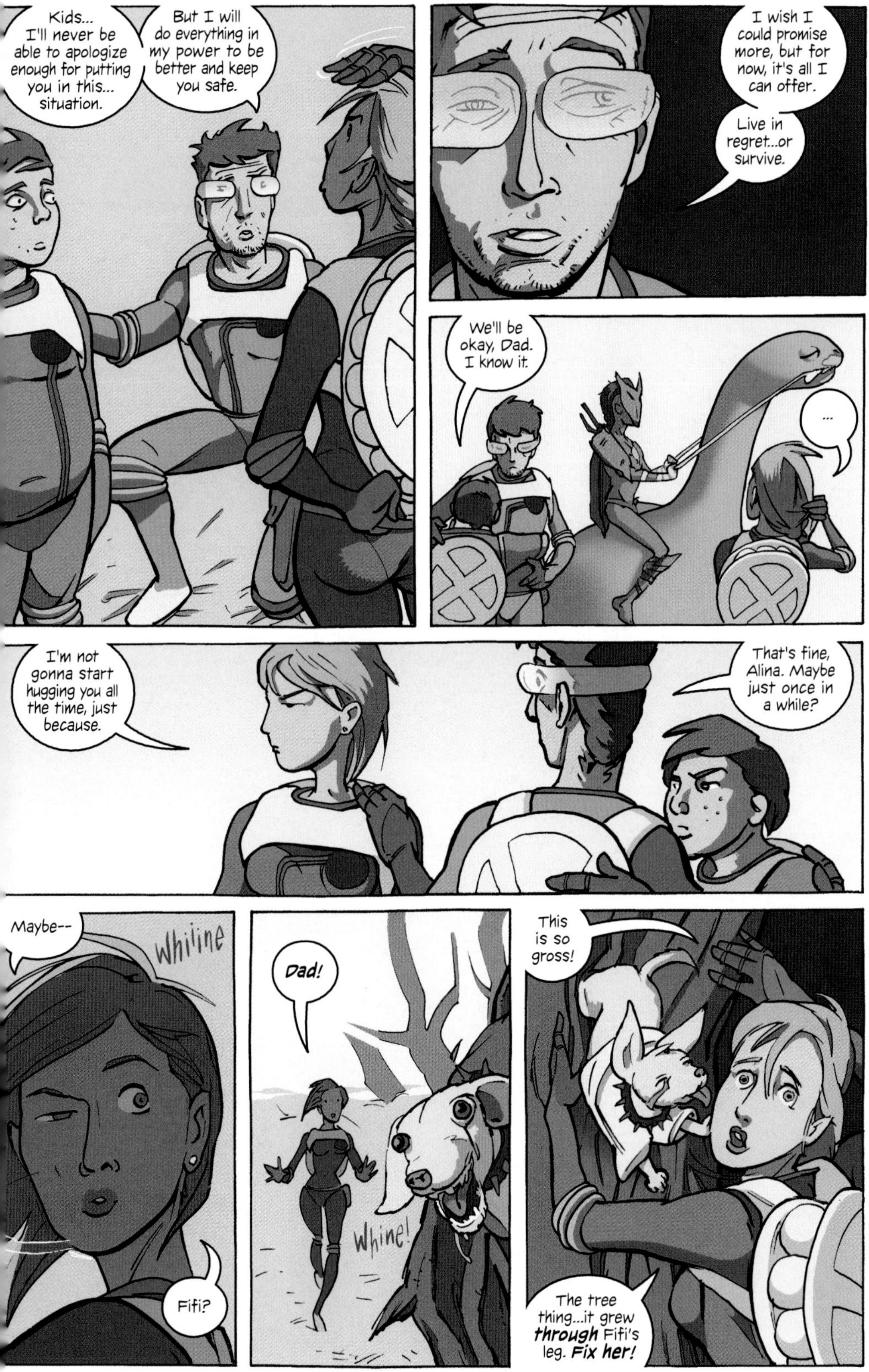
Kids... I'll never be able to apologize enough for putting you in this... situation.
But I will do everything in my power to be better and keep you safe.
I wish I could promise more, but for now, it's all I can offer.
Live in regret...or survive.
We'll be okay, Dad. I know it.
...
I'm not gonna start hugging you all the time, just because.
That's fine, Alina. Maybe just once in a while?
Maybe--
Whiiine
Fifi?
Dad!
Whine!
This is so gross!
The tree thing...it grew **through** Fifi's leg. **Fix her!**

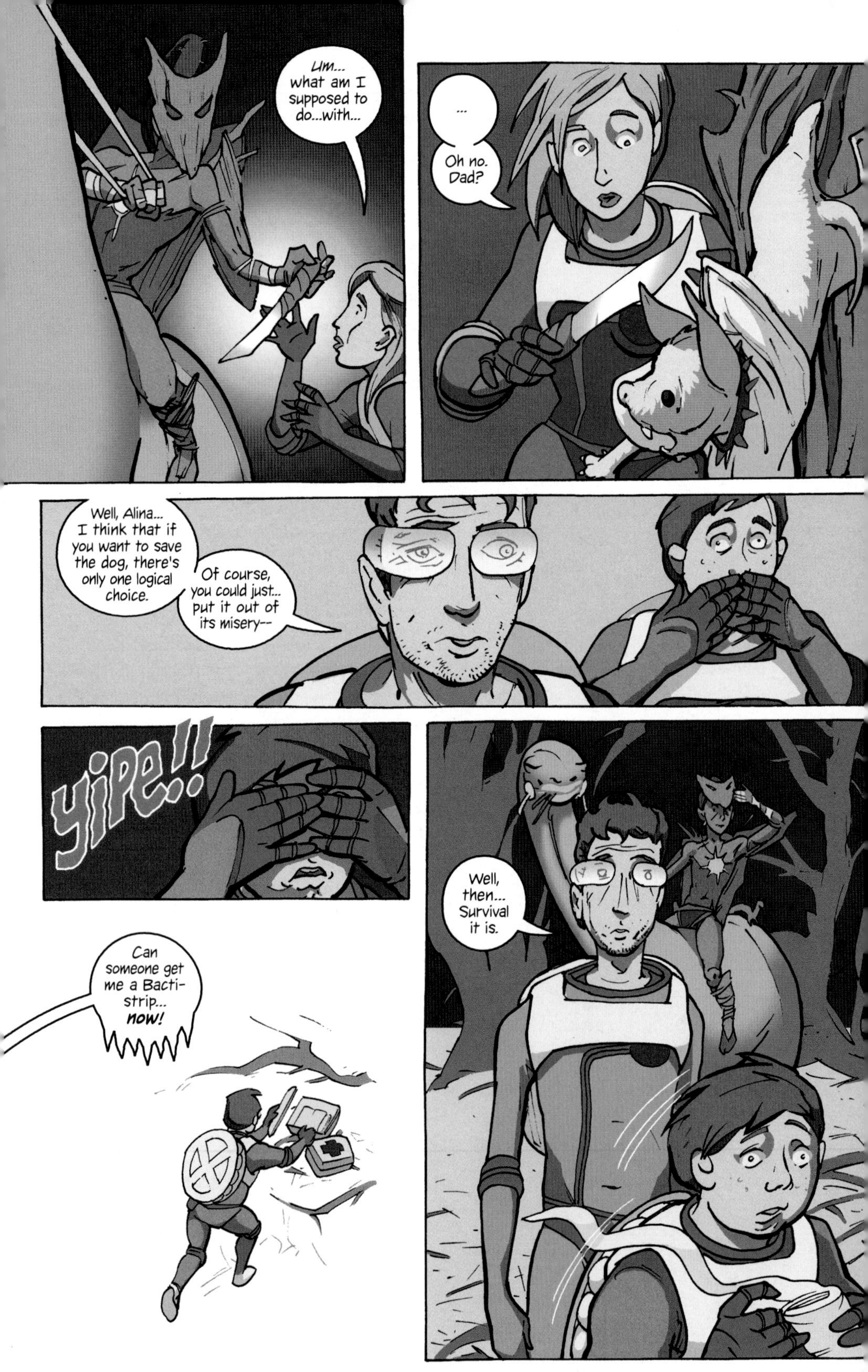

Um... what am I supposed to do...with...
...
Oh no. Dad?
Well, Alina... I think that if you want to save the dog, there's only one logical choice.
Of course, you could just... put it out of its misery--
yiPe!!
Well, then... Survival it is.
Can someone get me a Bacti-strip... now!

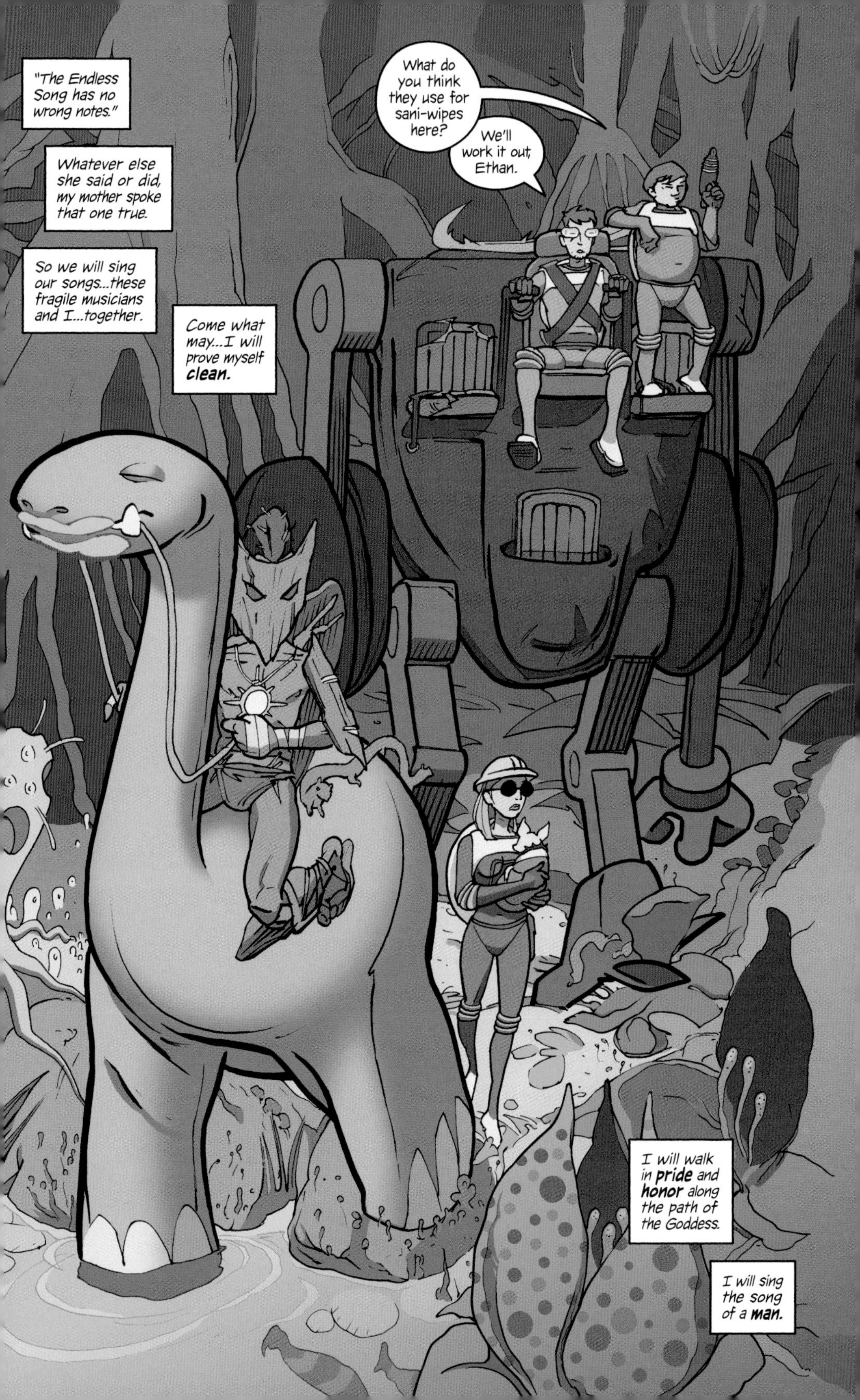
"The Endless Song has no wrong notes."
Whatever else she said or did, my mother spoke that one true.
So we will sing our songs...these fragile musicians and I...together.
Come what may...I will prove myself **clean.**
What do you think they use for sani-wipes here?
We'll work it out, Ethan.
I will walk in **pride** and **honor** along the path of the Goddess.
I will sing the song of a **man.**

For better or worse... This alien world is home.

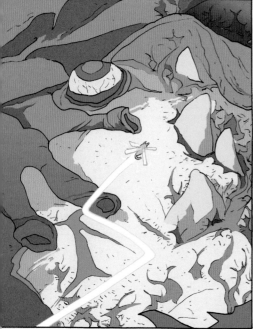

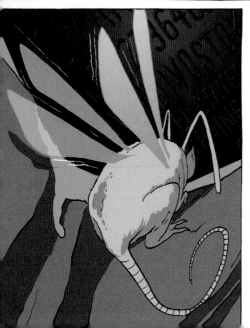

END OF BOOK 1

CERTIFIED ORGANIC
SMARTSTEEL ™
LOT 27364637O596
VLADIVOSTOKTON
UNITED STATES
OF UKRAINE PATENT

IED ORGANIC

ARTSTEEL™

2736463705990

ADIVOSTOKTON

NITED STATES

OF UKRAINE PATENT

C978

IFIED ORGANIC
ARTSTEEL™
T 27364637059
VLADIVOSTOKTO
UNITED STATES
OF UKRAINE PATENT
C978

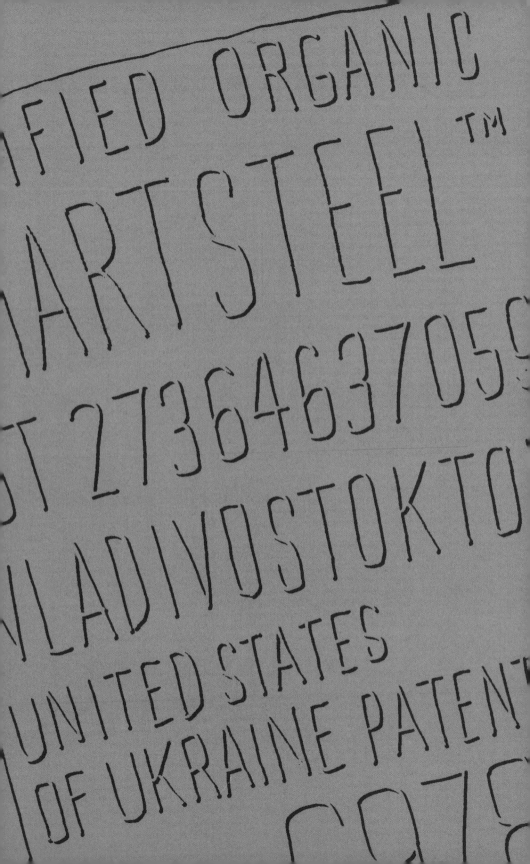

BEHIND THE SCENES

The following is taken from Joe and ILYA's initial discussion about building the world of KID SAVAGE.

Joe's emails are orange text on blue background.

ILYA's replies are blue on orange.

JK- JOE KELLY

MY INFLUENCES FOR KID SAVAGE ARE [OLD ANIMATION SERIES] HERCULOIDS AND THUNDARR, BUT WITH [ANCIENT TV DRAMAS] LAND OF THE LOST/LOST IN SPACE THROWN INTO THE MIX. HANNA-BARBERA PULP WITH MODERN TRAPPINGS —THE COMBO OF MAGIC AND TECH AND A SAVAGE WORLD. I THOUGHT OF YOU BECAUSE YOU LOVE KAMANDI* (SP?). RIGHT OFF THE BAT I WANT TO SAY—I KNOW NOTHING ABOUT KAMANDI. NEVER READ IT, DON'T KNOW THE STATUS QUO, NOTHING. (I KNOW, SHAME ON ME!)

* KAMANDI was "The Last Boy on Earth", created by Jack "King" Kirby for DC Comics back in 1972. Artist ILYA was then 9 years old and it blew his tiny mind. Writer Joe was probably pulling at his toes or something.

I- ILYA

OK. INTERESTING. YOU'VE NEVER READ KAMANDI, I'VE NEVER SEEN ANY OF THOSE OTHERS THAT YOU MENTION APART FROM LOST IN SPACE, SO I GUESS WE'RE EVEN! I HAVE ONLY VAGUE IDEAS OR IMPRESSIONS OF THEM, JUST AS YOU PROBABLY DO WITH KAMANDI, PERHAPS THAT'S THE BEST WAY FOR US TO PROCEED—BLISSFULLY IGNORANT! THAT WAY, WE CAN COME UP WITH SOMETHING THAT IS TRULY ORIGINAL.

TO ME, THE ALLEGORY IS THIS: A MODERN DYSFUNCTIONAL FAMILY WHO RELY ON TECHNOLOGY AND DO NOT COMMUNICATE WELL WITH ONE ANOTHER (TEXTS INSTEAD OF TALK) ARE FORCED INTO A SITUATION WHERE TECHNOLOGY IS ESSENTIALLY USELESS AND THEY HAVE TO PULL TOGETHER AS A FAMILY UNIT IN ORDER TO SURVIVE. THE WORLD THEY FIND IS MORE MAGIC/NATURE THAN TECH.

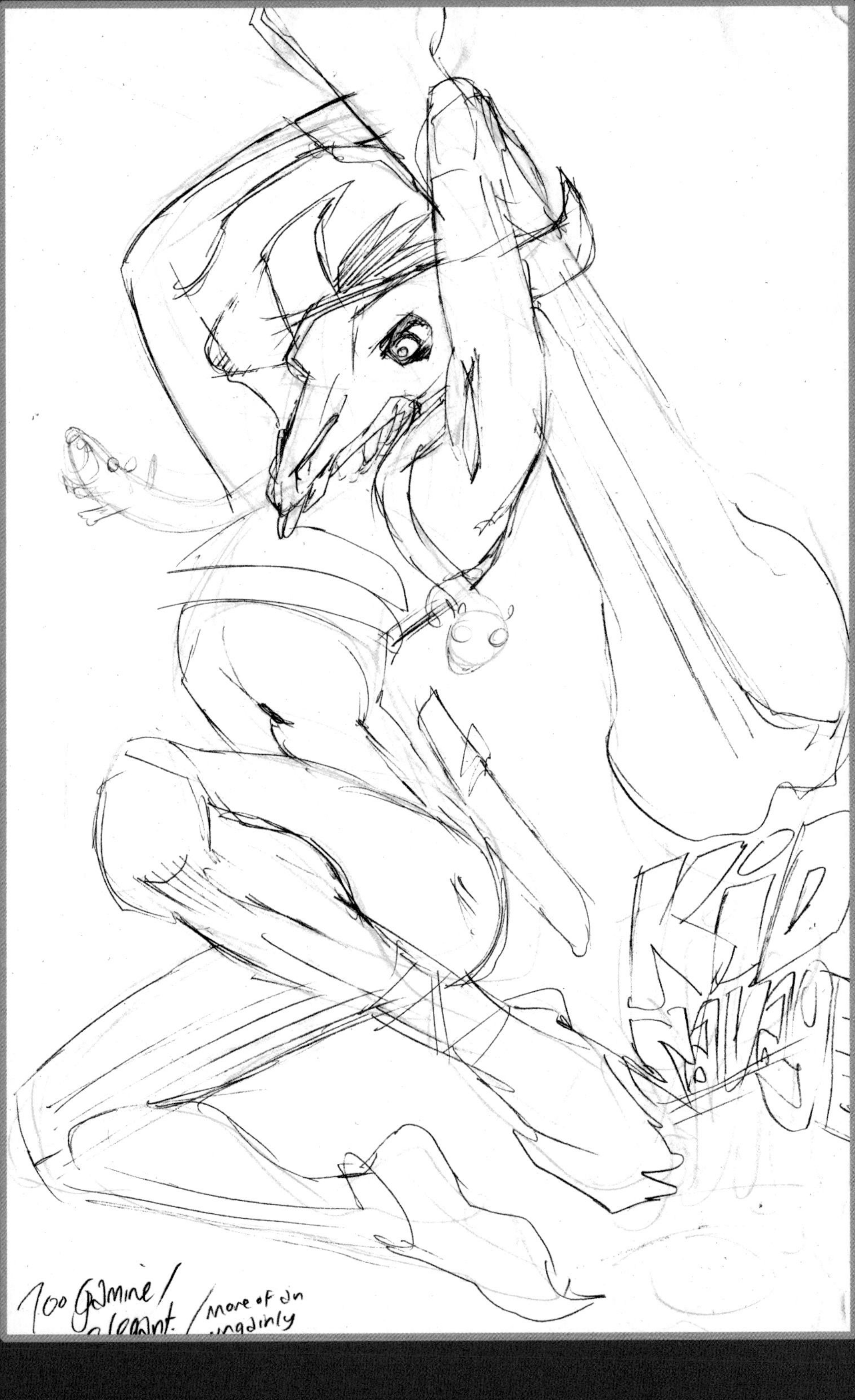
Too Gamine / elegant.
More of an ungainly

A LITTLE **AVATAR**-Y* IN THAT DESCRIPTION, BUT THERE WOULD DEFINITELY BE MACHINES, TOO.

> * The animated series, AVATAR—THE LEGEND OF AANG, not the James Cameron movies with blue fauns, etc.

AANG'S STORIES ARE WAR STORIES, HEAVY ON RESPONSIBILITY, ETC., BUT ALWAYS MANAGE TO FIND THE FUN AND HUMOR OF BIG ADVENTURE. THAT'S MY GOAL WITHOUT A DOUBT. THERE WILL BE MANY, MANY MONSTERS. MANY UN-HUMANS. (YET) IT'S MORE ABOUT LANDSCAPE AND LESS ABOUT THEME, OKAY?

I LIKE THE SOUND OF THAT A LOT. IT IS ESSENTIALLY HOW I PREFER TO LIVE WITHIN THE MODERN MODEM WORLD AS IT IS (LITTLE INTERNET, NO MOBILE, TWITTER, ETC.) I AM THE ORIGINAL **FERAL KID!** SO I FEEL TUNED IN, BY VIRTUE OF BEING TUNED OUT. THERE'S A LOT OF POTENTIAL FUN TO BE HAD WITH THAT DYNAMIC AND DICHOTOMY.

...THE SULLEN SHUT-IN TEEN, COMBINED WITH THE EFFERVESCENT AND OUTGOING MUCH YOUNGER ONE. BOY/GIRL EITHER WAY...

FRIENDS OF MINE WHO ARE QUITE WELL OFF AND ALL X-BOX AND WII'ED UP TOOK THEIR KIDS TO THE MIDDLE OF NOWHERE IN THE SCOTTISH HIGHLANDS FOR A HOLIDAY ABOUT A YEAR AGO, AND AT THE END, THE KIDS, DEPRIVED OF ALL MOD-CONS FOR TWO WEEKS AND LEFT WITH WINDSWEPT HEATHLAND AND LONG HIKES, SAID HOW IT HAD BEEN THEIR BEST HOLIDAY EVER. WE ARE THE SAME OLD MONKEYS ON THE INSIDE, IS MY FIRM BELIEF. IF WE CAN GET AWAY FROM IT ALL AND TAKE AN AUDIENCE WITH US, I'M UP FOR THAT.

MAD, AND EXCITING. I'M FEELING ALL ABOUT THE NU-PRIMITIVE!

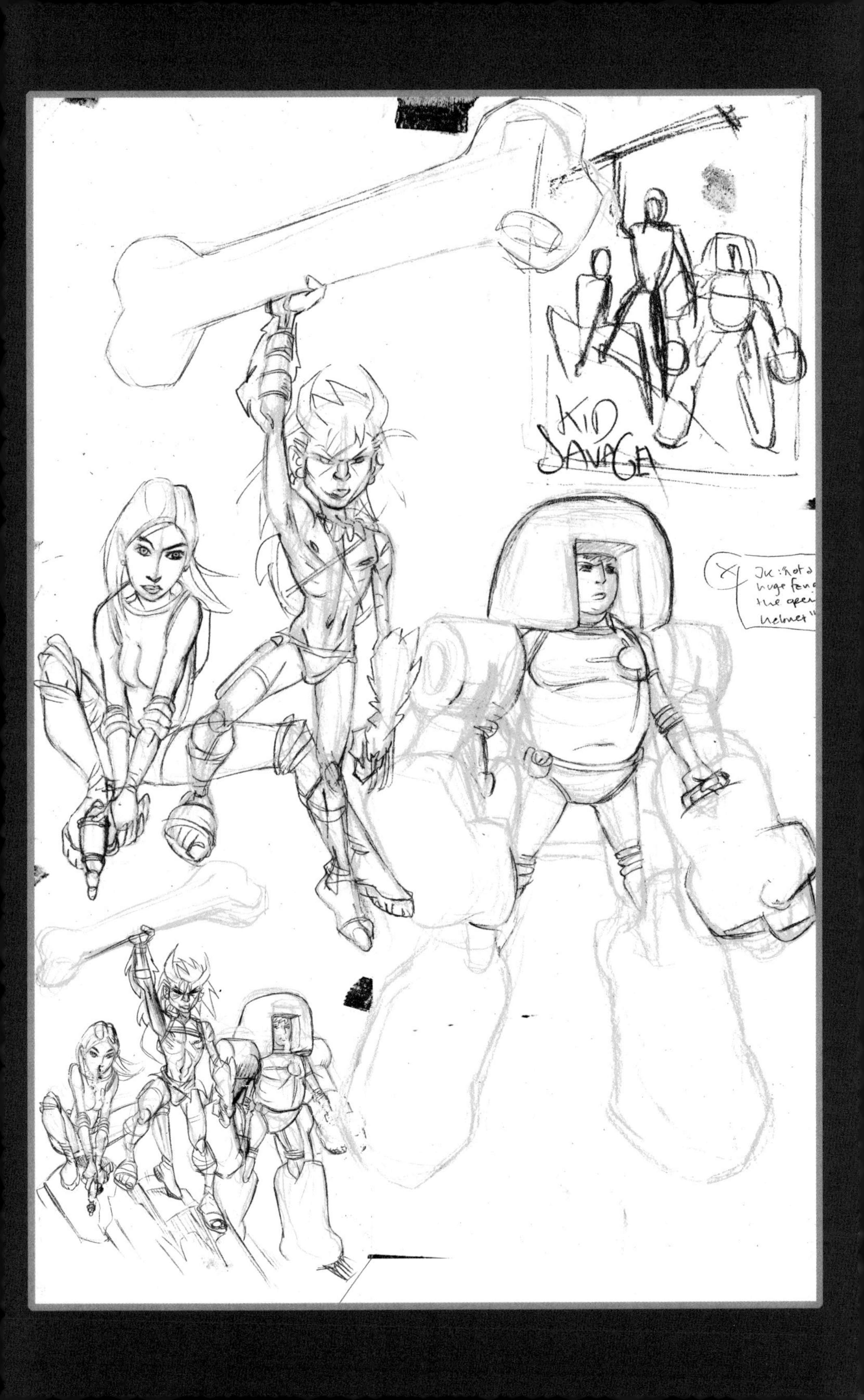
KID SAVAGE
X
JK: "not a
huge fan
the ope
helmet"

THE LOOK—I THINK WE HAVE TO STAY AWAY FROM AVATAR (BOTH OF THEM) AND KAMANDI, BUT FIND THE NEW POST-MODERN "PALEO". ACCIDENTALLY CAME ACROSS A "MODERN PRIMITIVE/PALEO WEBSITE" THE OTHER DAY, WAS COOL TO SEE THIS RETROGRADE SURVIVALIST MOVEMENT BUBBLING.* MAYBE [WE CAN ALLOW] A LITTLE MONONOKE.** I LOVE THAT SHE WORE A SKULL AS A HELMET/MASK. ALSO NEED TO STAY AWAY FROM TARZAN (DISNEYFIED).

* http://www.marksdailyapple.com/ — not at all what ILYA was expecting. Sigh.
** PRINCESS MONONOKE, Studio Ghibli animated film...see it!

WHAT WOULD HE WEAR?
EVERY PIECE IS MORE IMPORTANT FOR ITS SPIRITUAL/EMOTIONAL SIGNIFICANCE THAN SHEER FUNCTIONALITY.

WEAPONS - MOSTLY HOME MADE FROM THE STUFF AROUND, BUT FOR EXAMPLE, ARROWS TIPPED WITH FOLDED "ALBATROSS FEATHERS" WOULD EXPLODE ON IMPACT. LIKE BATTLE GLOVES THAT GIVE HIM CLAWS. JUST SOME SMALL STICKS FOR THE FIRE... SORRY TO BE FRACTURED. PASSING OUT. :-)

STARTED OFF BY EASING INTO IT WITH THE DESIGN OF SOME ACCESSORIES.

BIG BONE AS A WEAPON OF CHOICE. THAT IMPROVISATORY THING, PROBABLY NOT BONE AS WE KNOW IT, BUT TAKEN FROM A CREATURE WITH HARD METAL BONES, SO DARK GUNMETAL GREY IN COLOUR.***

BEARCLAW FIGHTING GLOVES (+ MATCHING FEET SOCKS?)

POCKET MONSTERS I SEE A PAIR OF STOAT WEASEL THINGS, EXCEPT THEIR MAMMALIAN DNA IS CROSSED WITH SERPENTINE.

*** This idea cropped up somewhere else...in the end.

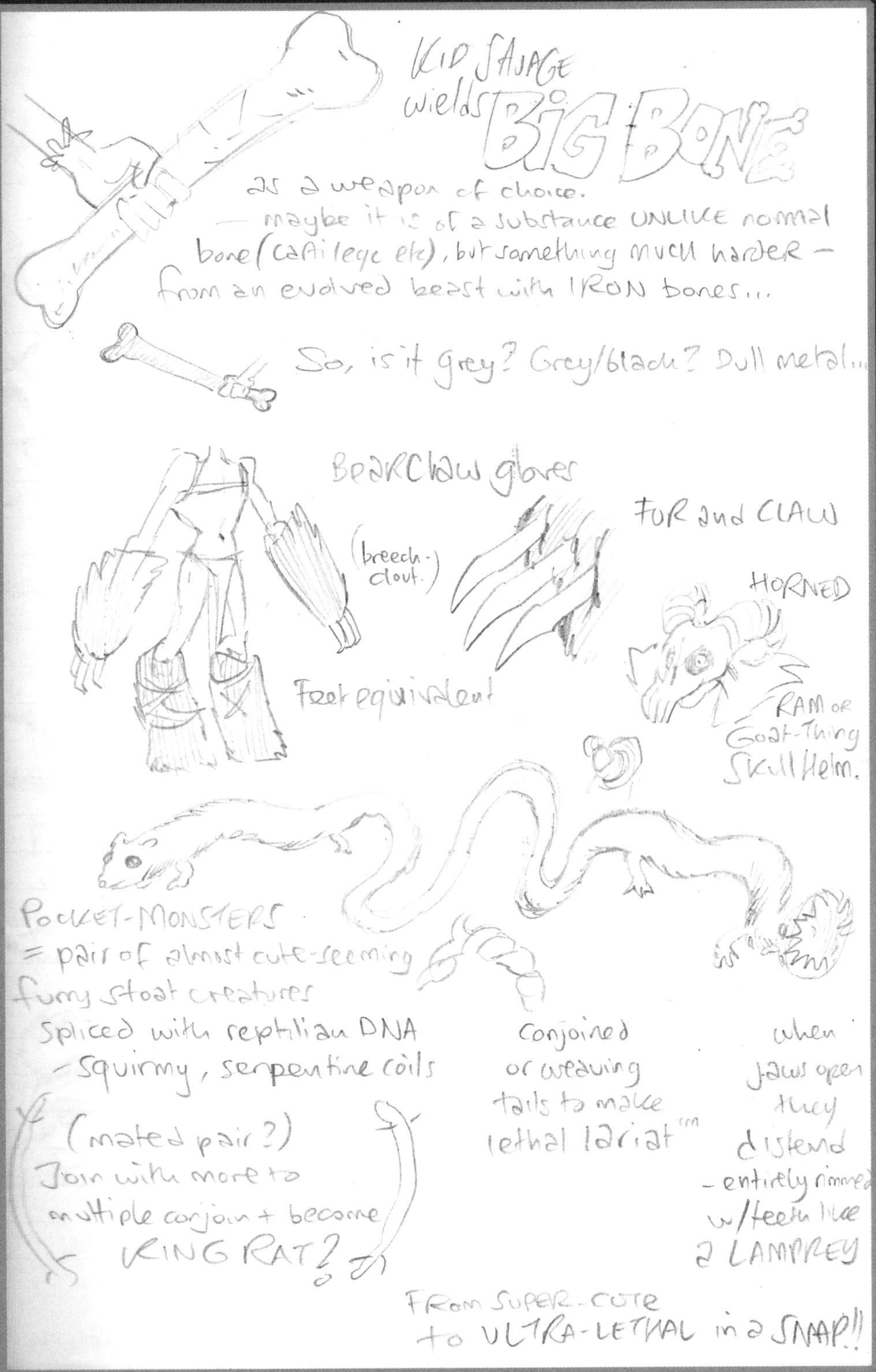
KID SAVAGE wields BIG BONE
as a weapon of choice.
— maybe it is of a substance UNLIKE normal bone (cartilege etc), but something MUCH harder — from an evolved beast with IRON bones...
So, is it grey? Grey/black? Dull metal...
BearClaw gloves
(breech-clout.)
FUR and CLAW
HORNED
Feet equivalent
RAM or Goat-Thing Skull Helm.
POCKET-MONSTERS
= pair of almost cute-seeming furry stoat creatures spliced with reptilian DNA
- squirmy, serpentine coils
Conjoined or weaving tails to make lethal lariat™
when jaws open they distend - entirely rimmed w/teeth like a LAMPREY
(mated pair?) Join with more to multiple conjoin + become KING RAT?
FROM SUPER-CUTE to ULTRA-LETHAL in a SNAP!!

KID HOLDS NO LIFE FORM SUPERIOR TO ANOTHER, THOUGH HE UNDERSTANDS THAT SOME EXIST TO FULFILL A PURPOSE THAT ENDS IN THEIR DEATH.

KID HAS "PETS" (ENTER THE HERCULOIDS!) WHICH ARE ANIMALS THAT RESPOND TO HIS COMMANDS. SOME STICK WITH HIM ALL THE TIME, SOME HE CALLS WHEN HE NEEDS THEM. EVENTUALLY, WE'LL LEARN HE CAN ████████████████████ ██ ████████████—BUT THAT'S FOR MUCH LATER.

POCKET CREATURES. HAVEN'T FULLY SHAKEN THAT OLD V-MOVIE BEASTMASTER (DEAR LORD!) BUT THOSE DARN FERRETS ARE USEFUL! ANY WAY TO GET A SLOAT/PLATYPUS GUY IN THERE?

UH, "SLOAT"? DO YOU MEAN STOAT?!
BUT BASICALLY, YEH, I'M READING THIS AS A PAIR OF FERRETS, OR SIMILAR. I'VE GOT A MONSTER IN MY POCKET!

NEVER SEEN BEASTMASTER. I HAVE A DVD I GOT SUPER-CHEAP, WHICH HAS NEVER WORKED. I STILL HANG ON TO IT, BECAUSE ONE DAY I'D QUITE LIKE TO SEE IT. I TRY THE TATTY OL' THING IN ANY MACHINES I COME ACROSS. NO JOY YET. SIGH.

DON'T BOTHER WATCHING IT UNLESS YOU WANT TO SEE A BAD MOVIE. HE HAD TWO TRAINED FERRETS. I THINK KIDS LOVE THE IDEA OF TINY ANIMALS THAT THEY CAN TRAIN—WE ALL DO. THINK SOMETHING CUTE WITH IMPOSSIBLY DANGEROUS MOUTHS LIKE THE CHESIRE CAT—CUTE AND SCARY. AND YEAH... "STOATS".

I DEBATED BUYING A COPY OF RED SONJA THE OTHER DAY, AND WISH I HAD. BRIGITTE NIELSEN IN THAT IS AN INSULT TO WOOD.

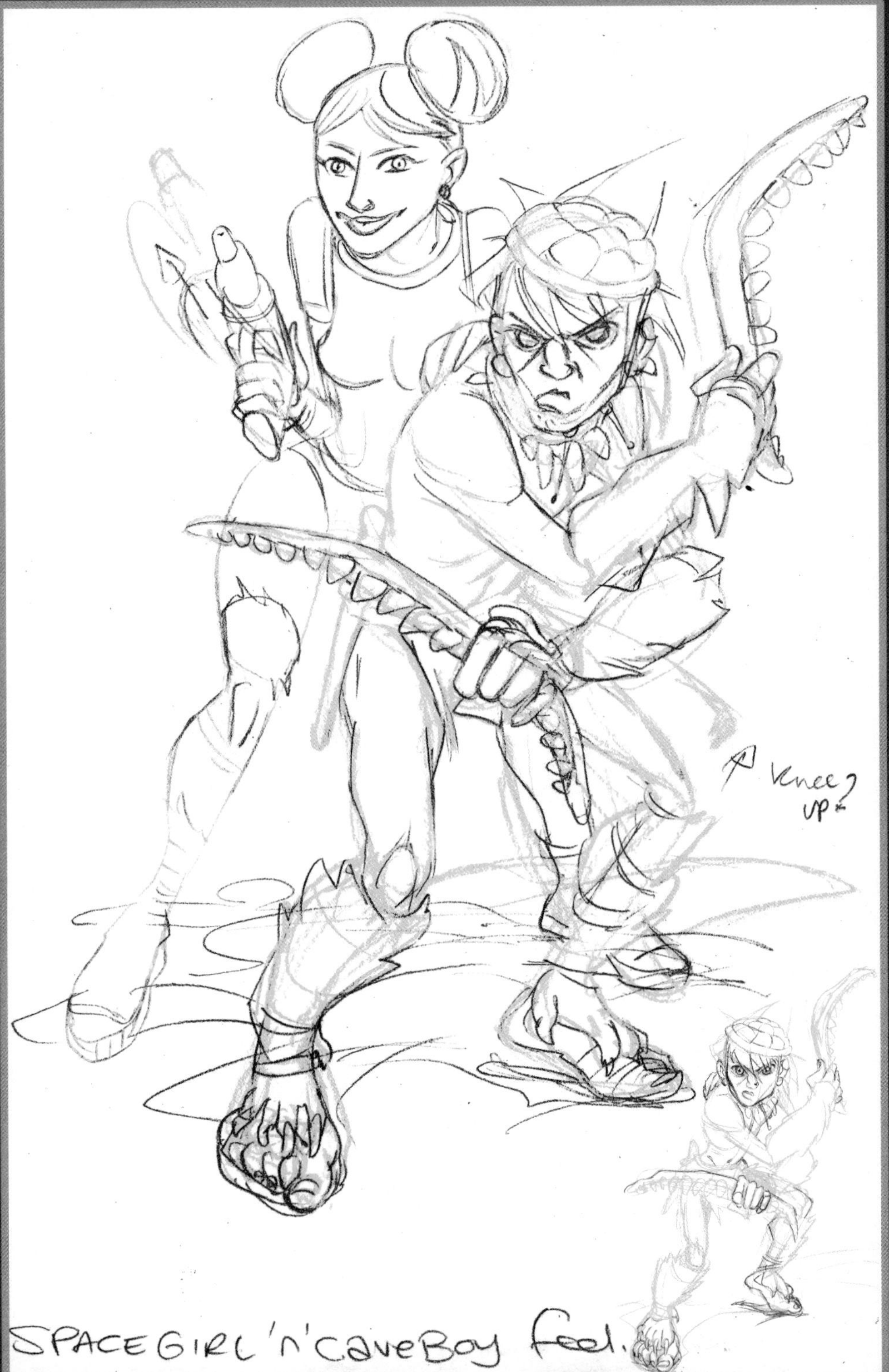
knee up?
SPACEGIRL 'n' caveBoy feel.

OUR FIRST IMPRESSION OF **KID SAVAGE** [KID, OR KS], THE
FIRST TIME WE SEE HIM, LIKE MONONOKE HERSELF, SHOULD
BE CONFRONTATIONAL AND ARRESTING—VERGING ON SCARY.
I PLAYED WITH VARIATIONS OF HIS HAIR AND FACIAL FEATURES
FOR A WHILE, WITH MIXED SUCCESS. THROUGH THESE ITERATIONS
I AM SETTLING ON THE FOLLOWING CHARACTERISTICS...

HOODED EYES, HARD TO READ, TO HIDE THE EMOTIONS (YOU CAN
ONLY SEE THEM WHEN YOU GET IN CLOSE, OR IN UNGUARDED
MOMENTS, OR INDEED ANY   ASHBACKS TO HIM WHEN HE WAS
YOUNGER—WHEN HIS PUPILS WERE BIG AND DARK/INNOCENT).

THE BIG EYEBROWS SHOULD GO, I THINK, BUT HIS STRONG
BROWS ARE ALWAYS KNOTTED AND CASTING HIS EYE AREA IN
SHADOW—AND I MIGHT KEEP THE MONOBROW BRIDGE OF HAIR
AT THE TOP OF THE NOSE, BETWEEN THEM.

WHEN HIS EYES GET TOO SLIM THEY MAKE HIM LOOK LIKE A
TEENAGER (16-17). TOO OLD. I LIKE A LITTLE "SQUASH AND
STRETCH" FOR HIM—SO THE IDEA THAT HE COULD GO FROM A
DEFAULT WHEN HE'S RELAXED TO THE CLINT EASTWOOD SQUINT
WHEN HE'S ANNOYED MAKES SENSE TO ME.

CLINT QUINT NOT THE DEFAULT BUT THE "GOT A FACE ON"
LOOK—GOTCHA. ≈ THE OPEN HEART HE'S HIDING.

WIDE FACE (BIG CHEEKBONES, STRONG BUT SMALL JAW,
TAUTLY LINKED).

BUTTON NOSE—IF HE WASN'T SNARLING ALL TH ETIME, HE'D
HAVE CLASSIC ALL-AMERICAN COLLEGE-BOY GOOD LOOKS.
IN LIGHT OF THAT...WE SHOULD GIVE HIM SOME FLAWS.
THESE FEEL IMPORTANT, AND HUMANISING.

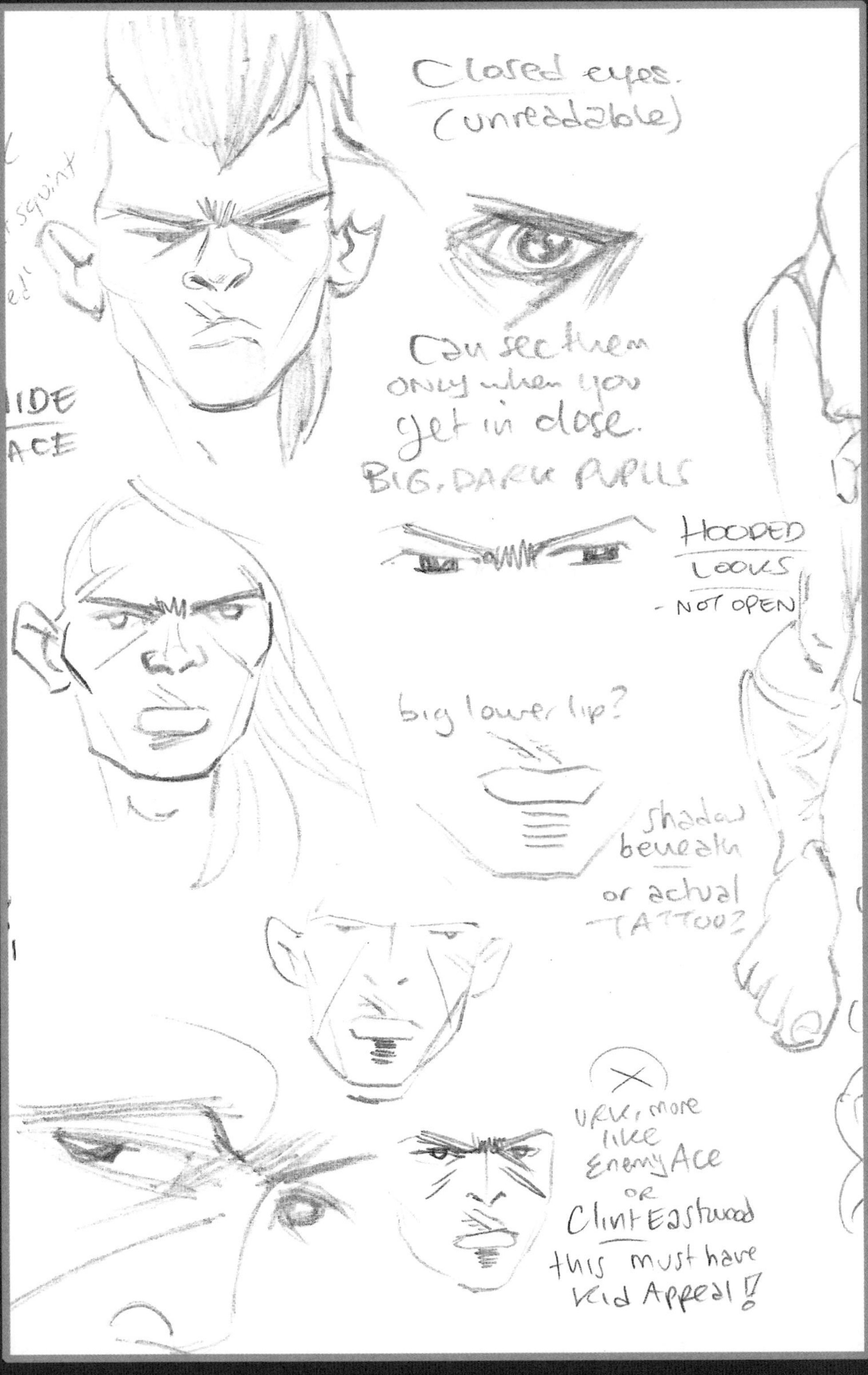
Closed eyes.
(unreadable)
squint
Can see them
ONLY when you
get in close.
BIG, DARK PUPILS
HOODED
LOOKS
- NOT OPEN
big lower lip?
shadow
beneath
or actual
TATTOO?
UKK, more
like
Enemy Ace
OR
Clint Eastwood
this must have
Kid Appeal!!

I'D LIKE TO GIVE HIM A BIRTH DEFECT (A "HARE LIP", OR CLEFT
PALATE), AND ALSO SOME WOUNDS THAT TELL OF A LIFE OF
SURVIVAL AND CLOSE SHAVES—ONE OF HIS HEARS HALF-MISSING,
LIKE A FIGHTING DOG; A COUPLE OF PROMINENT AND PERMANENT
SCARS, ASIDE FROM SOME CUSTOMARY BATTLE-DAMAGE
("RAVAGED" AS THE TOY PACKS SEEM TO LIKE TO CALL IT).
WE MAY EVEN GET **BACKSTORY** FOR THESE AT SOME STAGE?

I REALLY LIKE HIS POUTY LIP—JUST WONDERING IF IT'S EASY
TO CONVEY A CLEFT PALATE. THE EAR MAY BE THE BETTER WAY
TO GO—ALSO SYMBOLIC BECAUSE HE DOESN'T ALWAYS LISTEN
TO HIS ADOPTED FAMILY, ETC.

IT MIGHT BE I WANT THE CLEFT PALATE BECAUSE IT LOCATES
HIM FOR ME, AS A CHARACTER, BASED ON A PARTICULAR PERSON
I KNOW. I'VE NEVER SEEN A POPULAR CHARACTER ALLOWED ONE
AND I KNOW ENOUGH FOLKS WITH ONE TO WANT TO REPRESENT
FOR THEM. IT FEELS RIGHT HERE. (ALSO CF. THE ACTOR JOAQUIN PHOENIX)

I'M WITH IT. FROM A VISUAL POV I THINK THE BIG BOTTOM
LIP IS DEFIANT, CHILDISH, ETC.—A LOT OF CHARACTER IN ONE
SMALL DESIGN ELEMENT. SO GO FOR IT!

TATTOOS—TEMPORARY DARK INK OR "WOAD" (WODE?).
BLUE DESIGNS, BODY AND FACE, RITUALISTIC AND CONSTANTLY
CHANGING—PERHAPS A NEW ARRANGEMENT FOR EACH SIGNI CANT
CHAPTER OR ADVENTURE. I PARTICULARLY THINK THEY WILL ADD
SOMETHING TO THE EYES AND MOUTH AREA, AN ELEMENT OF
MONA LISA MYSTERY AND FERAL BEAUTY. THESE WILL BE EASIER
TO SHOW OFF IN ANY COLOUR ARTWORK, BUT AS YOU CAN SEE
I'M ALREADY BEGINNING TO EXPLORE THEM HERE.

LOVE IT, SUGGEST THAT WE CONSIDER THE SAME FOR HIS **HAIR**.

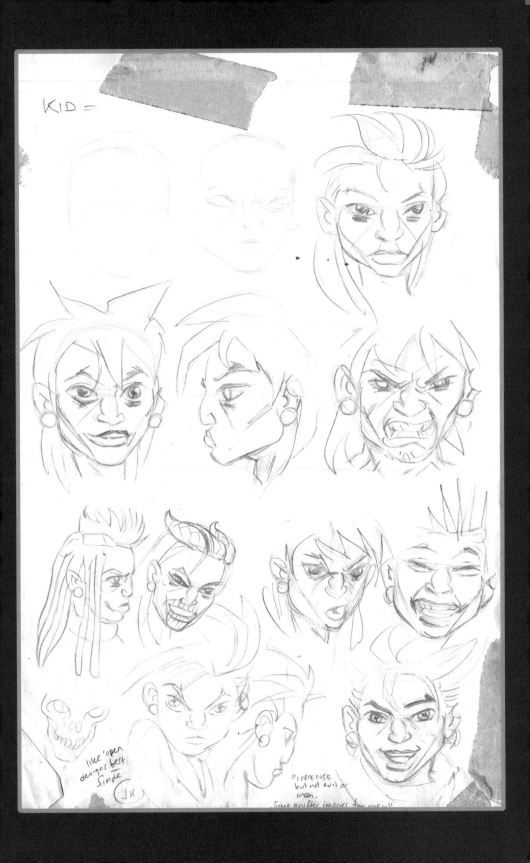

KID=

like 'open
designs best
Simple

JK

"INTENSE
but not evil or
mean.
some suffer images for me

His **HAIR** could work like a punk thing, in that some days it's a crazy mohawk, others it's a braid, etc. Use it to convey mood and intent. For some reason that reminds me of TANK GIRL—in a good way.

Adaptable hair, tats—check!
I nearly fainted when I saw pics of WILLOW SMITH (daughter of WILL, oh, SMITH (duh—I only just now got that!) and JADA PINKETT). She's remarkably on model for the direction we were already leaning in, especially with her half-shaved hairstyle—totally KID SAVAGE!

I was also put in mind of a favourite WEEGEE photo as a proto-model for KID, which is a portrait of a 16 year old in the back of a BLACK MARIA (police van), staring coolly straight at the camera lens as it noses through the mesh. KID's a killer, but looks blithe, like a wicked or fallen angel, his pupils almost see-through.

NAKED CITY © Arthur ("WEEGEE") Fellig

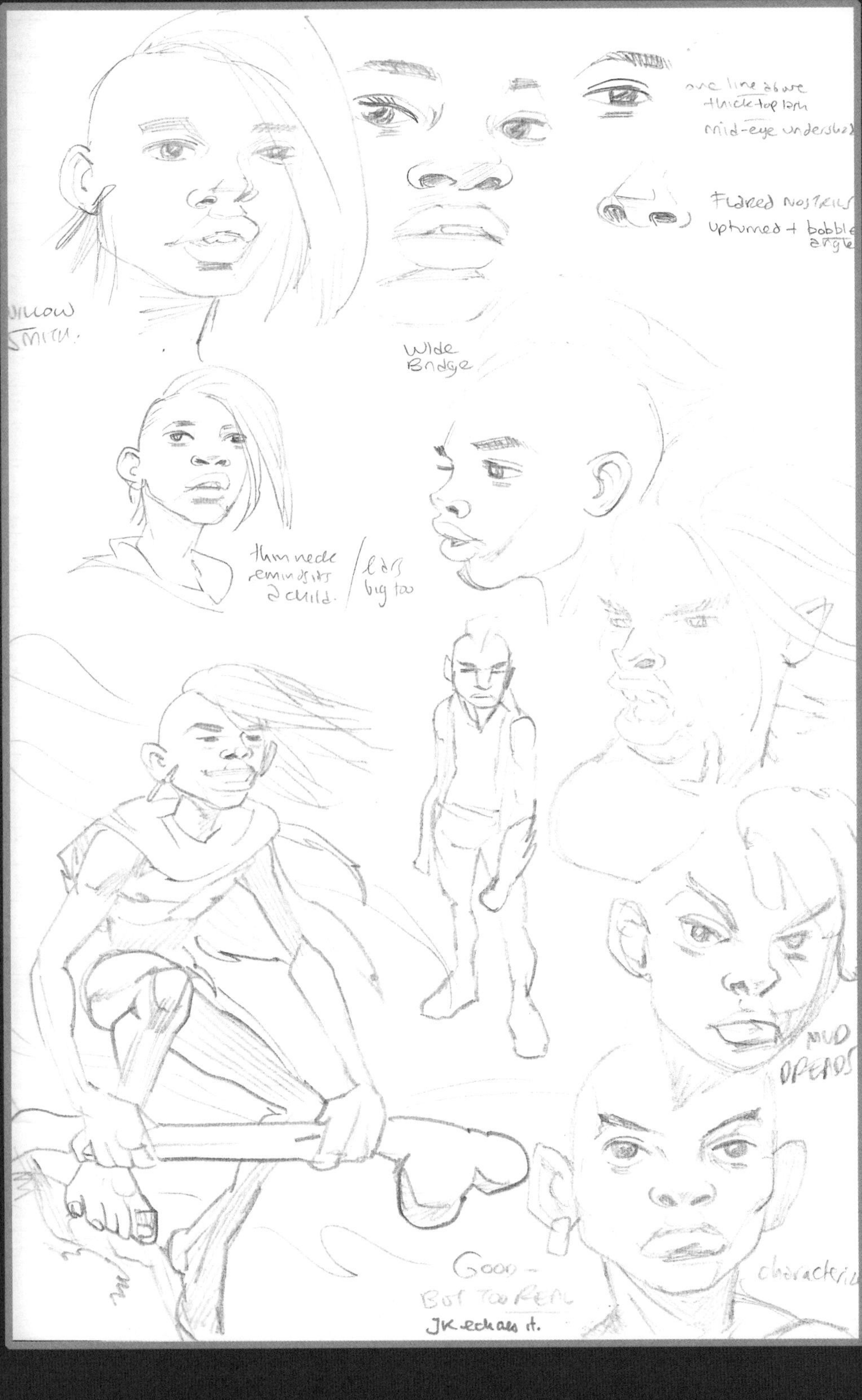
one line above
thick top lash
mid-eye undershad
Flared Nostrils
upturned + bobble
angle
Willow
Smith.
Wide
Bridge
thin neck
reminds its
a child.
ears
big too
Mud
Dreads
Good -
But too real
JK echoes it.

THE FIRST OF MANY PIN-UPS! I ALREADY SEE LOADS IN MY HEAD.* JUST FOR THE VERY FIRST TIME WE SEE HIM, MAYBE. CAN'T GO AROUND LIKE THAT ALL THE TIME—WE WANT TO READ HIS FACE.

* Referring to the image that became the cover of this first volume of KID, as well as a promo postcard...

AWESOME START! I HAVE TO TELL YOU—EVEN THOUGH YOU SAY IT'S TOO MUCH, THAT SHOT OF HIM WEARING THE SKULL IS PRETTY ("GOSH-DARNED") AWESOME! NOT TOTALLY INTO THE BEAR CLAW, AS I FEEL WE'VE SEEN IT, BUT...

WOLVERINE/FRIDAY THE 13TH'S FREDDY? AWARE OF THAT AS THE OBVIOUS, I WAS MORE CHANNELLING CAVEMAN DAYS AND A BIT BRUCE LEE VILLAIN (THE SLASHER GUY IN THE MIRROR MAZE—ENTER THE DRAGON) ≈ IT HAS MORE HONORABLE ASSOCIATIONS.

THE BEAR CLAW THING IS ALSO, FOR ME, A WAY OF WEIGHTING AND EMPHASISING HIS FORELIMBS, FOR DAMAGE, BUT ALSO LENDS AN INTERESTING BODY OUTLINE AND MAKES FOR HIS FIGHT STYLE. I THINK WHAT I'M ANGLING TOWARD, WITH THE BIG BONE TOO, IS A PRETTY UNSOPHISTICATED FIGHTING STYLE...
HE'S NO FENCER, NO PRINCE OF PERSIA. I WAS SEEING HIM AS A WHIRLY-GIG SLASHER AND STRAIGHT-OUT BLUDGEONER.

AMEN!

DAH HA HA, KID SAVAGE BELIEVES IN THE RIGHT TO BEAR ARMS!

WEARING THE SKULL AS BACK ARMOR IS PRETTY DARN SWEET. I REALLY RESPOND TO THESE BITS THAT I'VE NEVER SEEN BEFORE —NEW USES OF ANIMAL PARTS AND BONES, ETC. THE DIFFERENT COSTUMES/CAMOU AGE/ARMORS ARE REALLY COOL. I LIKE THE PHYSICALIZATION OF THE "WHAT I KILL I BECOME" IDEA.

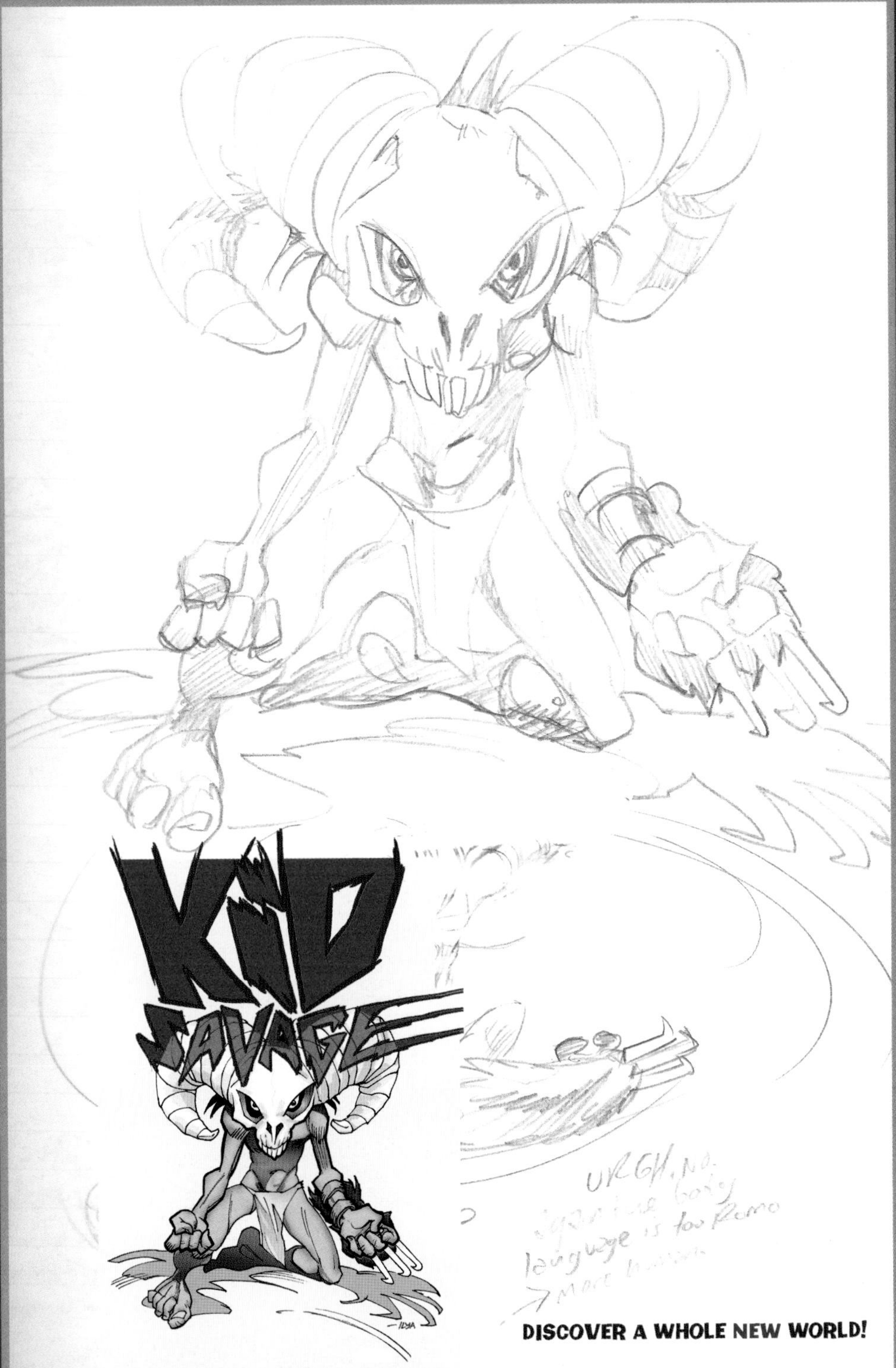

KID SAVAGE
URGH, NO.
language is too Remo
DISCOVER A WHOLE NEW WORLD!

KID IS THE MOST SOPHISTICATED AND THOUGHTFUL OF THE WHOLE CAST FROM A SPIRITUAL POV. HE DOES WHAT HE MUST TO SURVIVE, BUT HE LIVES THE SORT OF IDEALIZED NATIVE AMERICAN PHILOSOPHY THAT WE'RE ALL ON THIS PLANET TOGETHER, ALL BEINGS, AND IF YOU HAVE TO KILL ONE TO SURVIVE, THAT'S A SAD THING. BUT, YOU TAKE IT AS A GIFT AND HONOR THE DEAD BY USING THE BODY TO ITS FULLEST.

I'M AIMING FOR ALMOST A RHYTHMICAL APPEAL, IN TERMS OF THE STRETCH AND PULL OF CHARACTERISATION, AND SIMPLE SHAPES PLUS CONCENTRATIONS OF HEAVY DETAIL. MY STUFF HAS STYLISED ANGLES FIGHTING WITH THE SMOOTH.
IF YOU'VE GOT ANY CLEARER FOCUS ON THE FAMILY AND WHO THEY ARE, AND CRUCIALLY, WHAT AGES, THEN I'M ALL EARS...

FAMILY: THE STRANGE LAND (AND) THE STRANGERS IN IT.

(IN MY OWN HEAD, FROM WHAT YOU'D SAID, I HAD...) SPACE FAMILY ROBINSON IN A HARD ROCK AND FAST PLACE.

DAD: 30S, PROBABLY TALL AND HANDSOME, CLEAN CUT, BUT WILL CHANGE OVER TIME. THERE NEEDS TO BE SOMETHING OF A RACE BANNON FEEL TO HIM.

RACE BANNON? SORRY, WHO HE? OTHERWISE WITH YOU THERE.

YOU'RE KIDDING, RIGHT? RACE FORM JOHNNY QUEST? HE WAS JONNY'S TUTOR/BODYGUARD.

DAD JUST STRAIGHT OFF CAME OUT NOTHING LIKE THAT. SORRY. MY INSTINCTS ARE TELLING ME TO MAKE HIM NOT EVEN REMOTELY "HEROIC" LOOKING IN ANY WAY. MY THINKING WAS NOT TO UPSTAGE KID SAVAGE, WHO IS OUR HERO FIGURE.

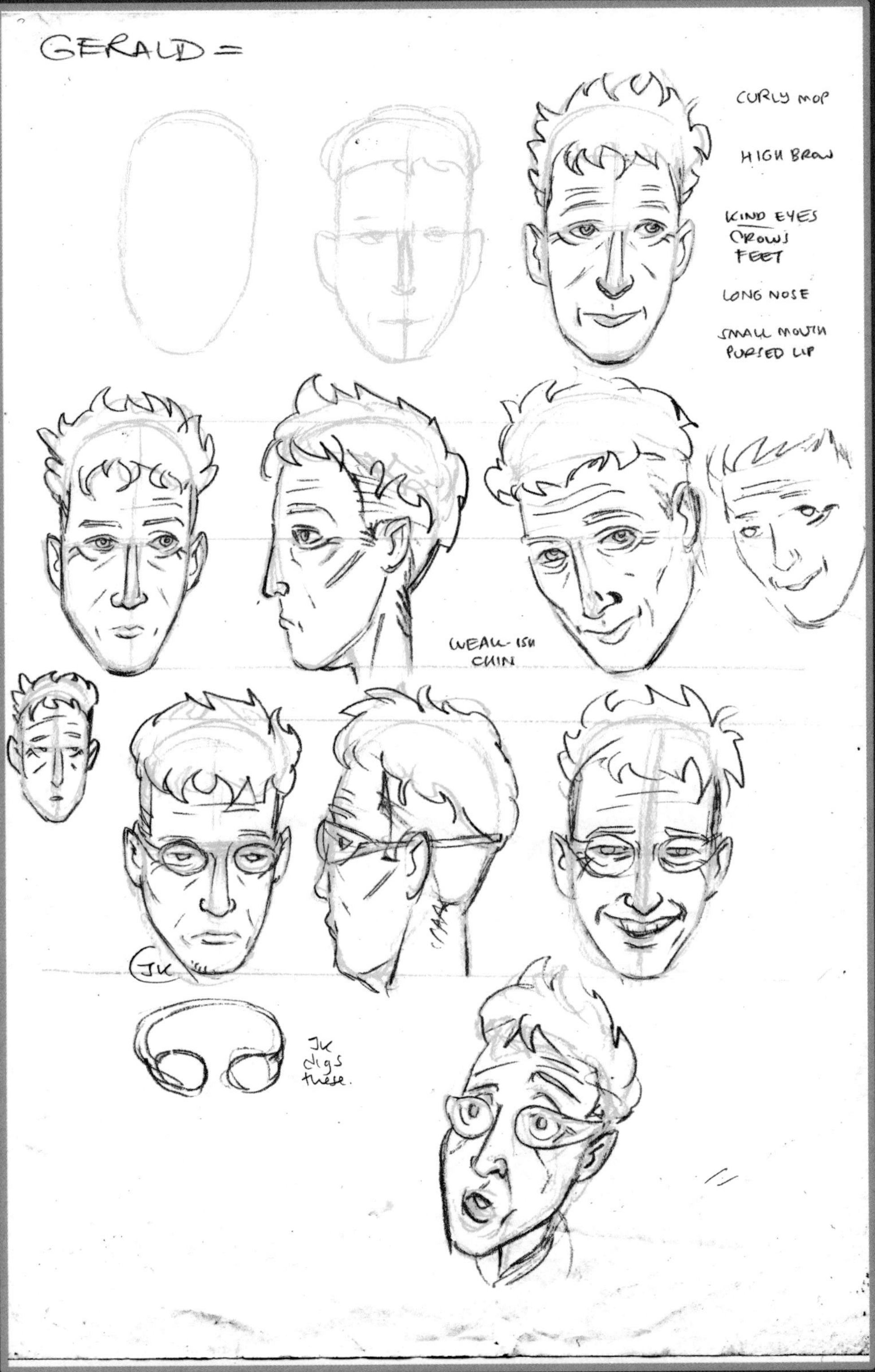
GERALD =
CURLY MOP
HIGH BROW
KIND EYES
CROWS FEET
LONG NOSE
SMALL MOUTH
PURSED LIP
WEAK-ISH CHIN
JK
JK digs these.

I'M WANTING THE FAMILY MEMBERS TO SEEM QUITE REAL,
NORMAL, EVERYMAN—IDENTIFIABLE WITH. THUS DAD SEEMS TO
ME TO BE CALLING FOR LESS THE ARCHETYPAL SQUARE-JAWED
HE-MAN OF 70'S CARTOONS, MORE A NEBBISHY ACADEMIC TYPE
(IF ON A DECENT ENOUGH FRAME). SAY, ELLIOT GOULD CURLS
MEETS ADRIEN BRODY. I'M HAPPY TO TAKE CLOSER DIRECTION
TO ZERO IN ON THE RIGHT CASTING, (I'VE YET TO HEAR HIM
SPEAK / SEE THE WAY THAT YOU ARE ACTUALLY WRITING HIM.)

BOY: WOULD BE SORT OF FUN IF HE WAS CHUBBY, AND LOST
WEIGHT DURING THE ADVENTURE. CLEVER, BUT NOT BOOK SMART.

I'M GOING FOR THE PUGSLEY TYPE, A REAL BUTTERBALL. HE HAS
A BOWL-CUT. A YEAR OT TWO OLDER THAN KID S, PROBABLY,
BUT NOT AS TALL OR ANYWHERE NEAR AS FIT AND STRONG.

SIS: LIKE HER BRO, SHE IS A KID OF SCREENS, TEXTS, VIDCHATS,
ETC. ABSOLUTELY KIM KARDASHIAN, POPULAR, PRETTY AND INTO
THE RAMPANT MATERIALISTIC BS OF OUR MODERN WORLD.

I'D LIKE TO DO HER QUITE BRATTY. SORRY, I DON'T KNOW KIM
KARDASHIAN. (I WILL GOOGLE THESE REFERENCES YOU MAKE BUT
I'D LIKE TO HEAR MORE OF WHAT THEY MEAN TO YOU, OR WHAT
YOU MEAN BY THEM, BEYOND THE NAMECHECKS.) FIM CHARACTERS
AND ACTORS I KNOW. TV I'M MOSTLY AT A LOSS (DON'T HAVE
ONE, DON'T WATCH BROADCAST TV, 15 YEARS NOW—JUST CATCH
UP WITH THE GOOD STUFF ON DVD). OLD BOY IN A BUBBLE!

SHE'S JUST A HOT SOCIALITE WHO'S FAMOUS BECAUSE HER
FATHER WAS OJ SIMPSON'S LAWYER. FAMOUS FOR BEING RICH
AND FAMOUS. THAT'S ALL I KNOW.

GIRL'S COMING OUT 16/17, CURVY/WILLOWY, AS TALL AS DAD.

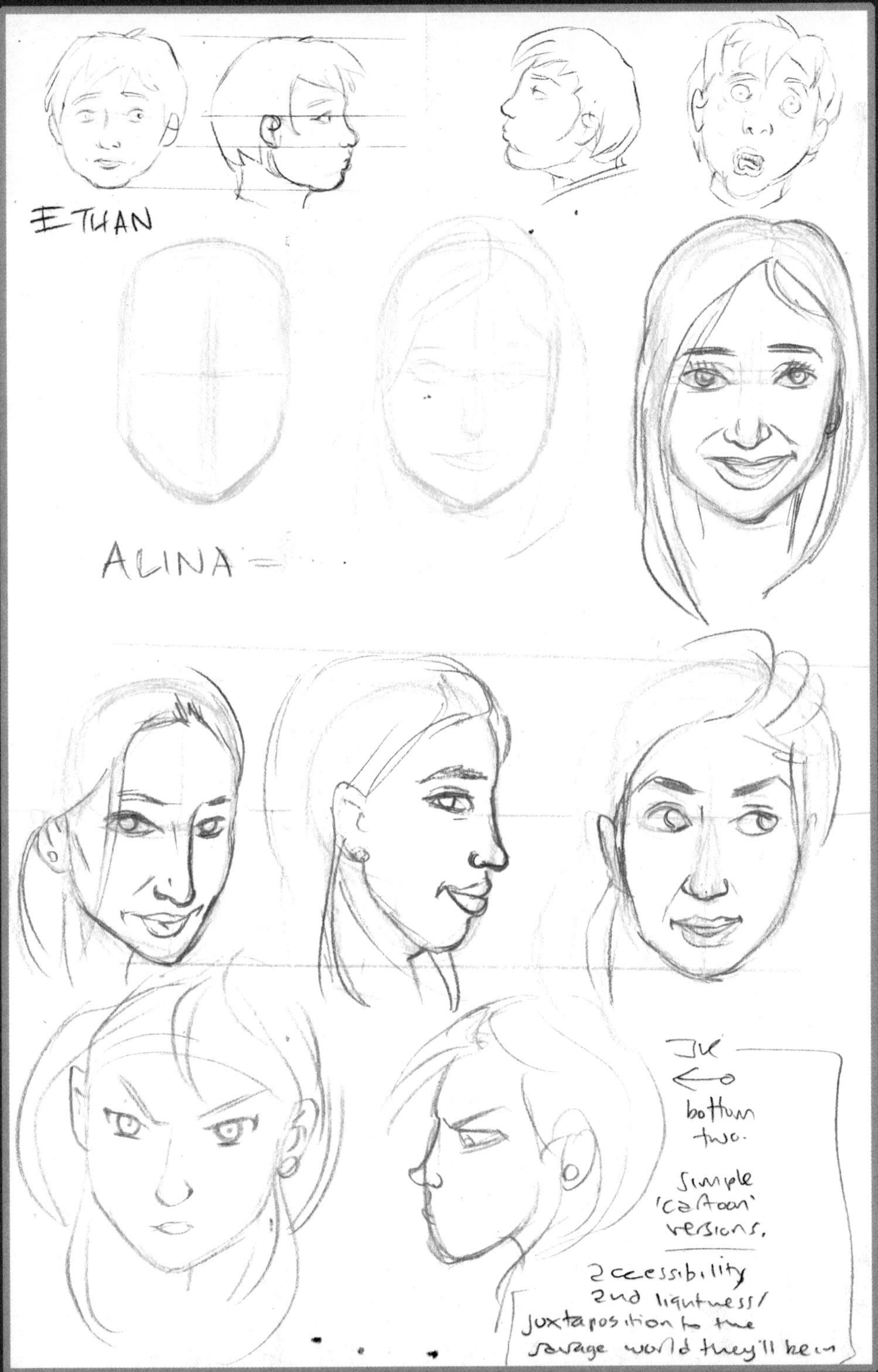

ETHAN
ALINA
JK
bottom two.
simple 'cartoon' versions.
accessibility and lightness/ juxtaposition to the savage world they'll be in

BOY IS WITHDRAWN BUT MORE EMO. GIRL DOESN'T KNOW HOW TO HAVE A DEEP RELATIONSHIP, BUT IS GREAT AT GETTING WHAT SHE WANTS. DAD IS LOVING UP TO A POINT, EASILY DISTRACTED BY HIS WORK. MOM IS THE BROKEN/DISTANT HEART OF THE FAMILY. SHE IS VERY SMART WHERE DAD IS CHARISMA AND LUCK. HE'S SAVVY—SHE'S BRILLIANT.

— "SHE'S FAST, HE'S WEIRD"? (" >)

DOG: IF WE WANT TO GET A GAG CHARACTER, SIS MAY HAVE BROUGHT ALONG A TEACUP CHIHUAHUA OR SOMETHING, THOUGH I PERSONALLY WOULD WANT TO SEE THAT EATEN IN ITS FIRST ISSUE—BUT THAT'S JUST ME.

NOPE. ME, TOO.

FOR THE FAMILY DYNAMIC, I'M SEEING UNI-TARD MAJOR MATT MASON TYPE ASTRONAUT GEAR, STRONG COLOURS, WITH PIPING DETAIL AND MULTIPLE POUCHES SORT OF THING. RIGHT BALLPARK?

YEAH, I THINK SO. I LIKE THE RELATABLE/ICONIC/PULP ELEMENTS WHEN WE CAN USE THEM TO GOOD EFFECT. THAT SAID, THESE ARE ASTRONAUTS OF OUR FUTURE, SO THERE CAN BE A STREAMLINED LOOK TO THEM, TOO. MORE FLOATING HOLOS AND HEADS-UP STUFF. KID'S MORE ABOUT NATURE AND MAGIC. THE FAMILY IS RELIANT ON SCIENCE.

YES, NEAT.

BOTTOM LINE IS, KS IS THE STAR, SO START WITH THE COOLEST VERSION OF HIM AND WE'LL CHANGE THE FAMILY TO SUPPORT.

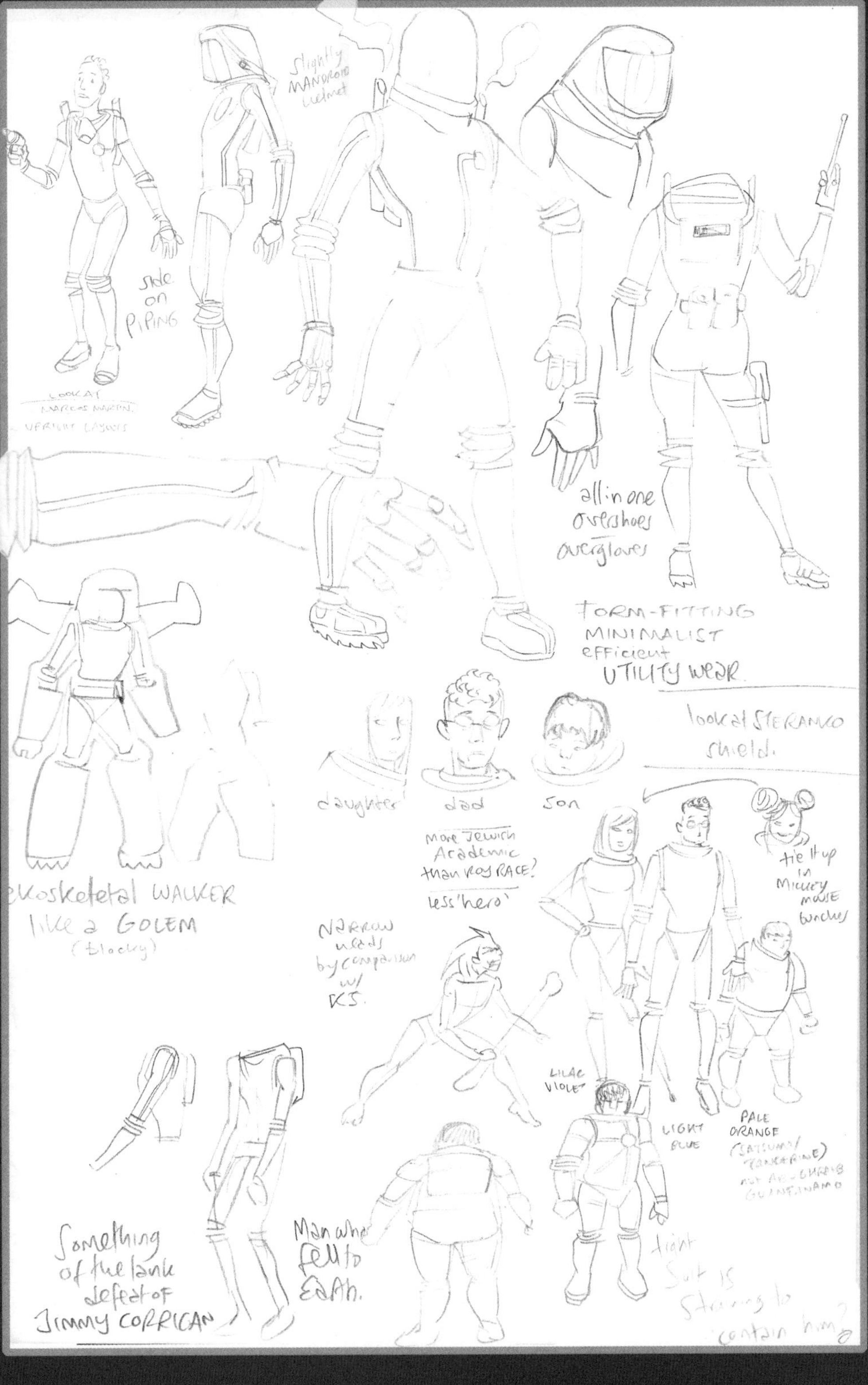
Slightly MANDROID helmet
side on PIPING
LOOK AT MARCOS MARTIN.
UPRIGHT LAYOUTS
all in one overshoes overgloves
FORM-FITTING MINIMALIST efficient UTILITY WEAR.
look at STERANKO shield.
daughter
dad
son
More Jewish Academic than ROY RACE?
less 'hero'
tie it up in Mickey Mouse bunches
exoskeletal WALKER like a GOLEM (blocky)
Narrow heads by comparison w/ KS.
LILAC VIOLET
LIGHT BLUE
PALE ORANGE
(SATSUMA/TANGERINE)
Something of the lank defeat of JIMMY CORRIGAN
Man who fell to Earth.
tight Suit is Straining to contain him?

LOVING WHERE YOU'RE GOING WITH THE FAMILY—THE SUITS
ARE DEAD ON, THE DUNE BUGGY, ETC. LOVE IT ALL. THE FIRST
IMAGE OF DAD HELPING THE DAUGHTER IS REALLY RIGHT TO ME.

IT'S WEIRD, FROM THE OFF I COULD SEE THAT POSE HE HAS THERE
—DAD CROUCHING A BIT PATHETICALLY IN HIS SPACE SUIT—AND
I COULDN'T THINK WHAT THE IMAGE ECHOING IN MY HEAD WAS.
I COULD SEE IT SO STRONG I COULD TASTE IT-SPENT HOURS
TRYING TO LOCATE IT IN MY HEAD. THOUGHT IT MUST BE JIMMY
CORRIGAN*, BUT NO, IT WAS CHARACTERS FROM END OF THE
CENTURY/TIME WARP. PLAYING AT POSTMAN'S KNOCK
I RIPPED OFF ONE OF MY OWN DRAWINGS!

* A comic by Chris Ware.

SHIP: WHAT I'VE DESIGNED SO FAR LOOKS A BIT LIKE AN
UNDERWATER AS WELL AS SPACE VEHICLE-OUTLINE A BIT LIKE A
ROLLERBLADE, INLINE SCATE, OR THUNDERBIRD 4 EVEN. THE
CENTRAL CORE IS BUILT AROUND SPHERICAL LIVE/WORK PODS (4
OF THEM, IN A LINE), LINKED BY LONGER BRACING CORRIDORS AS
WELL AS INTER-POD DOORWAYS (FOR INDIVIDUAL ACCESS/PRIVACY).
THE REST OF THE HULL IS BUILT AROUND THAT LINE OF PODS,
SO THAT IT PARTWAY RESEMBLES A SOYA OR EDAMAME BEAN
HUSK, OR A SUBWAY MEATBALL MARINARA. PLUS FINS, ETC.

ROBOT/BUGGY: WHAT I'VE COME UP WITH FOR THE ROBOT/
EXOSKELETON THING HAS THE CAPABILITY TO FOLD DOWN INTO A
ONE-PERSON BUGGY, TRANSFORMERS-STYLE (AS WELL AS 360
DEGREE ROTATABLE HEAD AND REVERSIBLE LIMS/EXTREMITIES,
FOR FAST CHANGES OF DIRECTION). BUT AS A WHEELED BUGGY IT
ONLY CARRIES ITS SINGLE PILOT. SO I'M THINKING OF DESIGNING
A SECOND, LARGER VERSION (FOR DAD) THAT COULD THEN
TRANSFORM-COMBINE WITH THIS FIRST ONE TO MAKE UP A
4-SEATER DUNE BUGGY...

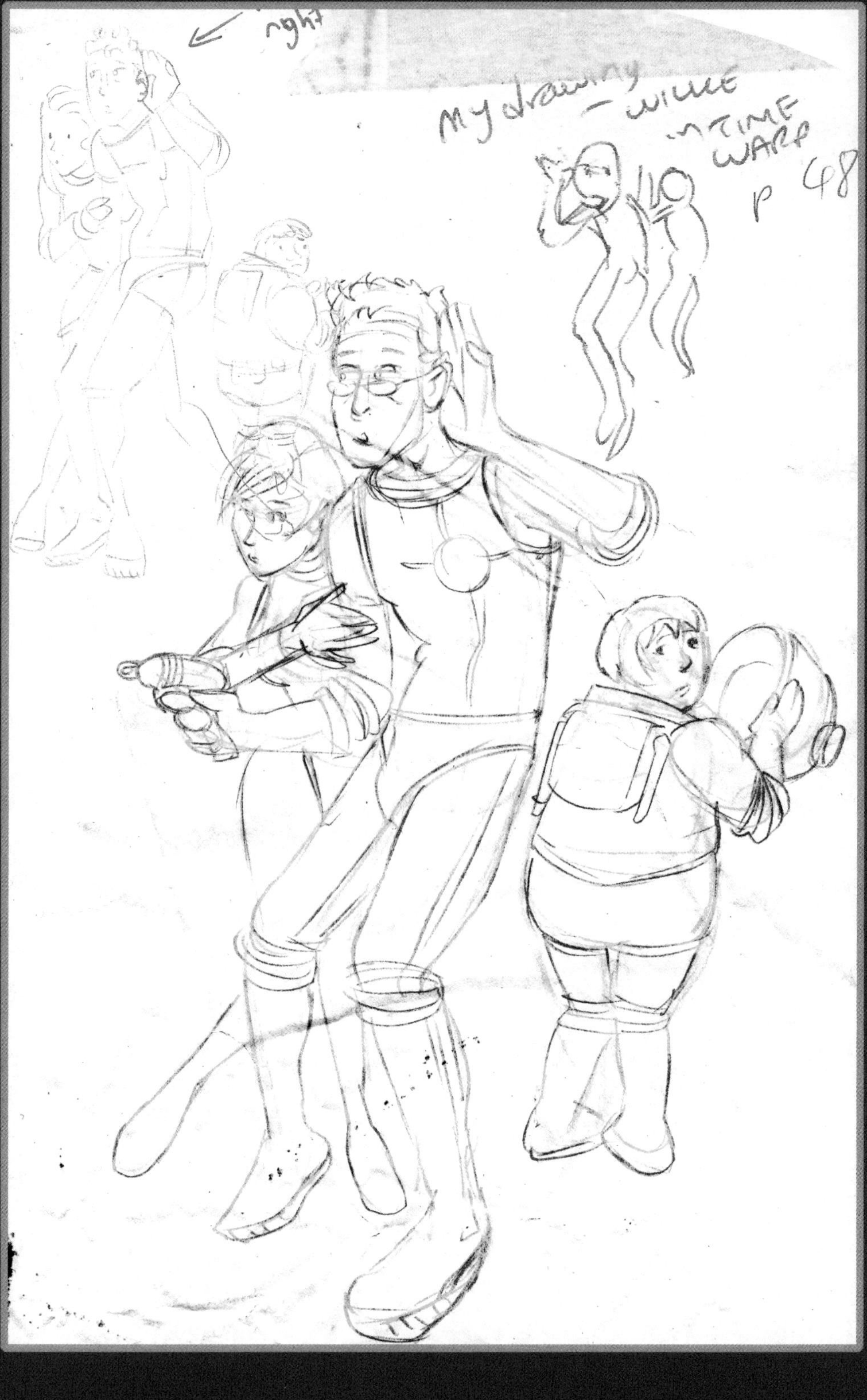
right
My drawing — WILLIE in TIME WARP p 48

They start off riding this big-wheeled space vehicle, except it's got an empty fourth seat—a significant absence where MOM should be, as a constant visual reminder that she was always meant to be with them.

ROBOT-SUIT DESIGNS: What I'm calling a GEOLOGICAL EXPLORATION MODULE or GOLEM (hence the squarish block head which I saw as primarily for protection, but also echoes the traditional appearance of a stone golem).

The ETHAN-BOT at the end of Chapter One gets trashed with the loss of the ship, leaving them with only the larger GERALD-BOT (perhaps as a two-person giant robot version of the earlier Ethan-bot, with either Ethan or Alina taking second pilot spot as the situation requires—leaving the other one of them exposed outside of the robot configuration). They make their getaway from the crash-site in the 4-seater vehicle form, only for it to later—surprise!—~~transform~~, uh, transmute into an even larger version of the Ethan-bot we've already met.

Have you seen or heard of RENE LALOUX'S FANTASTIC PLANET, BTW?* It occurred to me the other day when pondering about vegetation, while looking at a sculpture exhibition...

* A French animated film.

NO, I'LL CHECK IT OUT!

I immediately liked the flow of shorter, intense chunks, regular cliff-hangers and scene changers, but lots of splishy splashes (the short chapter thing was JACK KIRBY'S MODUS OPERANDI around the time of KAMANDI—perfect for youngers readers). Treat every chapter as our only and last, go in all guns blazing, give it all we got.

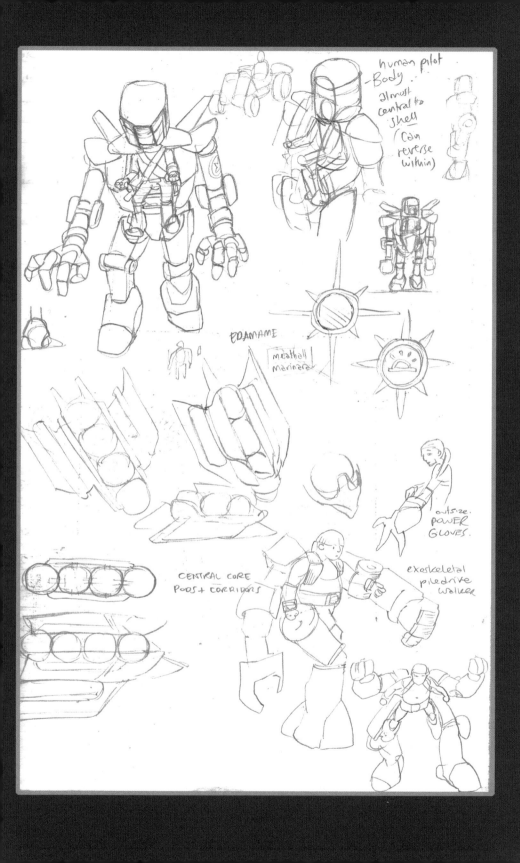

human pilot
-Body-
almost central to
shell
(can reverse within)

EDAMAME

meatball marinara

outsize POWER GLOVES.

CENTRAL CORE
PODS + CORRIDORS

exoskeletal piledrive walker

THAT'S HOW AMERICAN COMICS WORKED FOR ME AS A KID—SPOTTILY IMPORTED SNAPSHOTS OF SOME HIDDEN REALM THAT I FELT WAS GOING ON FAR AWAY BUT ALL OF THE TIME, WITH OR WITHOUT ME, SO I TREASURED THE GLIMPSES THAT I GOT OF IT, AND IN MY MIND PROBABLY EMBROIDERED THEM FAR BEYOND WHAT THEY ACTUALLY WERE. IT'S LIKE IN ATOMIC THEORY OR SOMETHING, WHEN ANY SINGLE PART ENCOMPASSES THE IDENTITY OF THE WHOLE. MODERN COMICS WITH THEIR HECTIC CROSSSOVERS AND SIX-ISSUE BITTY ARCS MISS THE SENSATION ENTIRELY.

THAT, I THINK, WILL BE OUR MAIN TASK—TO EVOKE ANOTHER WORLD OR WORLDS, EACH AND EVERY CHUNK LOADED TO SATISFY, SO THAT THEY ARE AS MUCH AS POSSIBLE A COMPLETE AND SATISFYING, NAY, GLUTTONISING MEAL, IN AND OF THEMSELVES. YOU JUST GET HUNGRY FOR MORE AND MORE...

I'VE BEEN THINKING ABOUT THE FIRST CHAPTER—READY TO ROCK IF YOU ARE. IT'S ALL KID AND MONSTERS UNTIL THE LAST PAGE REVEAL OF A "ROBOT" WHICH IS ACTUALLY ONE OF THE FAMILY EXITING THE SPACE SHIP.
THINKING ABOUT DOING IT GON*-STYLE, WITH NO NARRATION, BECAUSE I NEVER REALLY LIKE ALL THAT PURPLE PROSE ABOUT THE GRANDEUR OF THE WILD, ETC. PACING-WISE, I LOVE NICE, OPEN, BEAUTIFUL STUFF, BUT USUALLY FEEL GUILTY WRITING IT BECAUSE IT EATS UP PAGES. LONE WOLF AND CUB,** MEANWHILE, RUNS TO 24 VOLUMES, 5 OF WHICH ARE PROBABLY JUST ATMOSPHERE! SO THAT'S A LONG WAY OF SAYING GO FOR IT. I AM A FIRM BELIEVER IN THE AXIOM "THE PROJECT DETERMINES THE LENGTH", NOT THE OTHER WAY AROUND. HOPE THAT HELPS!

* Super-deformed Manga dinosaur action by Masashi Tanaka.
** Single-parent Samurai saga (well, okay, Ronin) by Kazuo Koike & Goseki Kojima.

SURE IT HELPS.

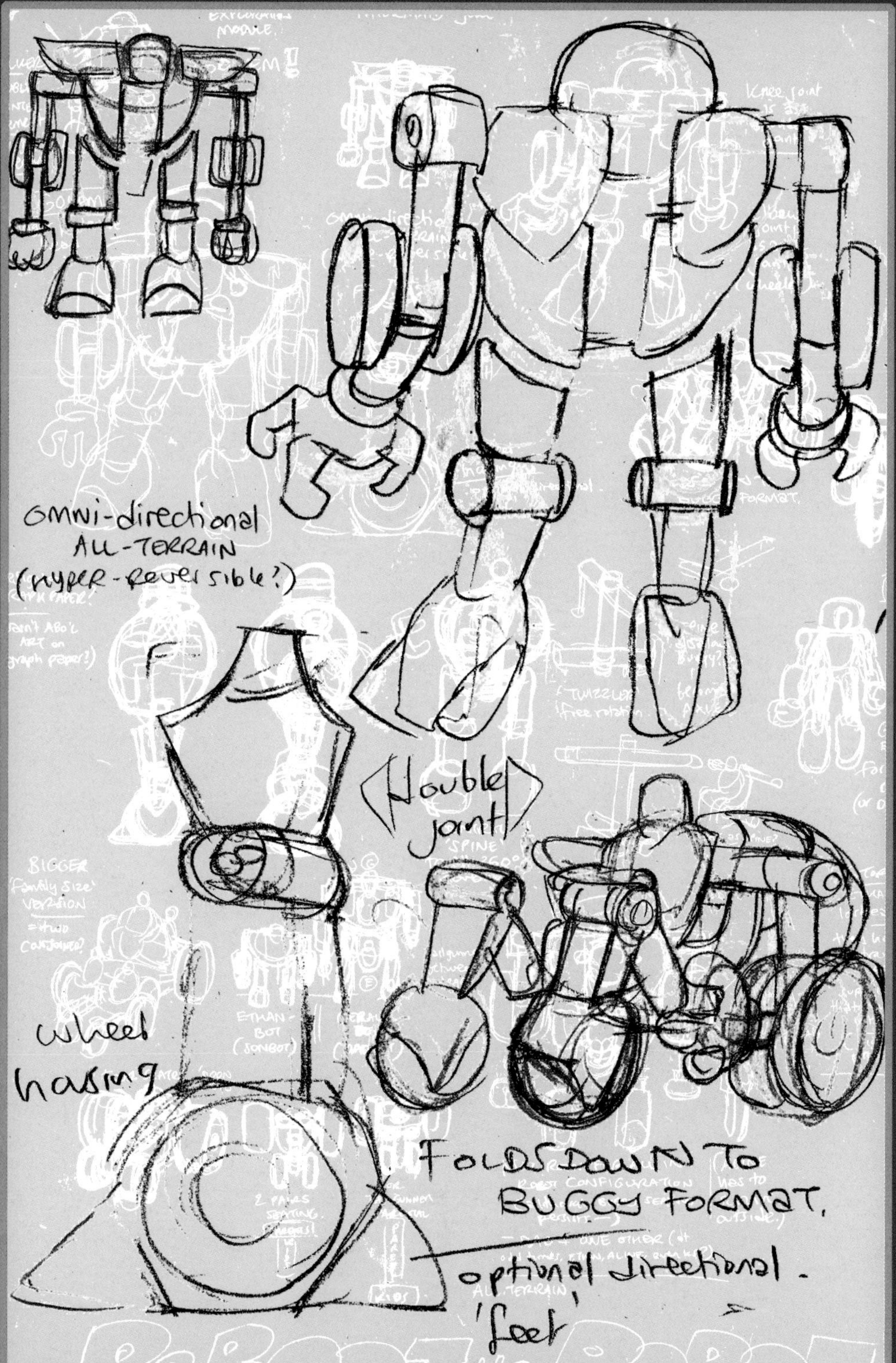
omni-directional
ALL-TERRAIN
(hyper-reversible?)
double joint
wheel housing
FOLDS DOWN TO
BUGGY FORMAT.
optional directional
'feet'

I'M PRETTY CONFIDENT OF HOW WE ROLL BY NOW, WHICH ALL ADDS TO THIS COLLABORATION. YOU APPRECIATE WHY YOU WRITE, AND WHAT IT CAN BE ABOUT—REAL RESONANCE BEYOND THE SURFACE FUN, THRILLS AND YOKS. THIS FEELS LIKE SOLID STUFF SO FAR ALREADY, AND WITH MORE LEGS THAN A MILLIPEDE... NO DOUBT, IT'S GOING TO BE STRONG AND AGGRESSIVE LOOKING— TAPPING INTO THAT "BOY ENERGY" THAT HAS THEM KUNF FU KICKING IN SUPERMARKET CAR PARS AND BODY-PUNCHING THEIR HAPLESS UNCLES AND FATHERS (THAT'S YOU AND ME, JOE. YOU KNOW THE BRUISES I'M TALKING ABOUT).

WHAT I NEED IS EMOTIONAL DEPTH. LAYERED CHARACTERS, AND A WORLD WITH GENUINE STAKES.

I'M YOUR MAN. GIMME ALL YOU GOT. I'LL GIVE IT ALL I GOT.

DELETED SCENES

ORIGINALLY, OUR STORY OPENED WITH A COUPLE EXTRA PAGES (SEEN HERE). THE MESSAGE WAS "KID ALONE IN HIS SAVAGE ENVIRONMENT", AND "MAN AS UNIQUE" IN A MUTATED WORLD. SO EVEN BEFORE WE GET TO THE ALIEN FAUNA (CREATURES) IN THE FRONT-LOADED ACTION SEQUENCE, WE TRIED OUT ADDING IN MORE ALIEN FLORA (PLANT LIFE) AND VIEWS OF THE LANDSCAPE.

CUT PAGE 3
BUZZ OF INSECTS IN AIR / INSECT FLIES TOWARD US OVER SUNLIT LANDSCAPE / IT IS LIKE A FLY CROSSED WITH A RAT! UGH!! / IT LANDS ON A VIOLENT, PINK FLOWER UN FULL BLOOM. / UNDERSIDE OF ONE LEAF, LURKS A CAT-SPIDER! / CHOMP. CAT POUNCES TO SINK FANGS INTO RATFLY.

CUT PAGE 4
CAT-SPIDER SITS IN MID-FLOWER DEVOURING ITS PREY / THE FLOWER SNAPS CLOSED ON THEM BOTH, VENUS FLYTRAP-STYLE / IT SQUEEZES, UNTIL BLOOD DRIBBLES OUT OF THE "FIST" FLOWER / BUNCHES OF THESE HANGING VAMPIRIC FLOWERS / PANNING DOWN INTO GRASSES BELOW.

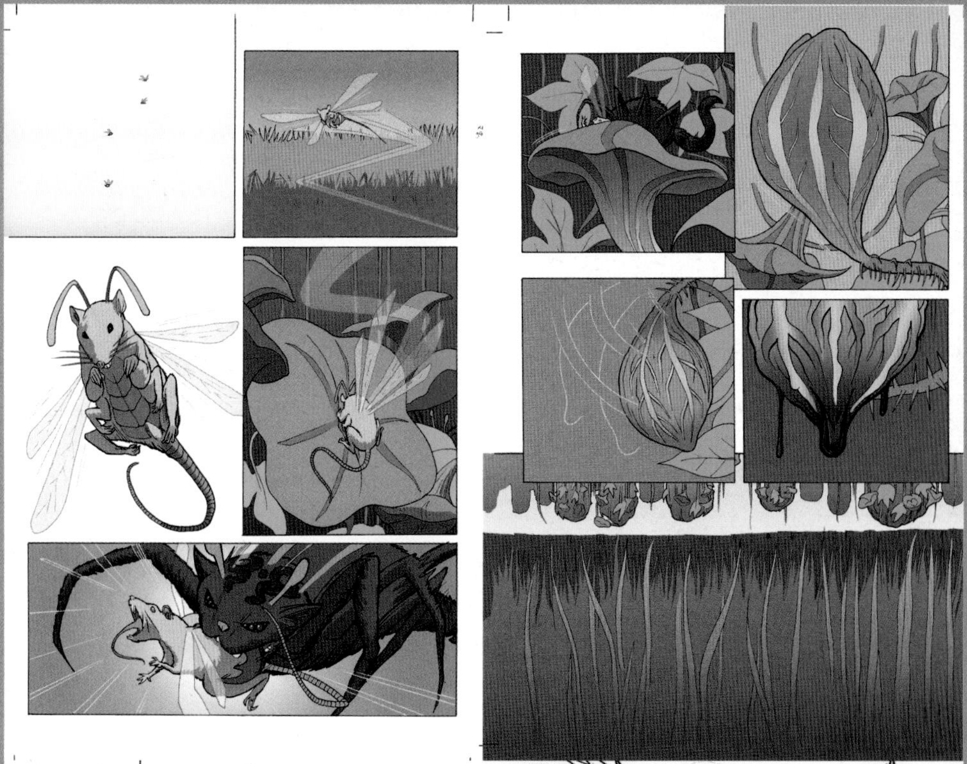

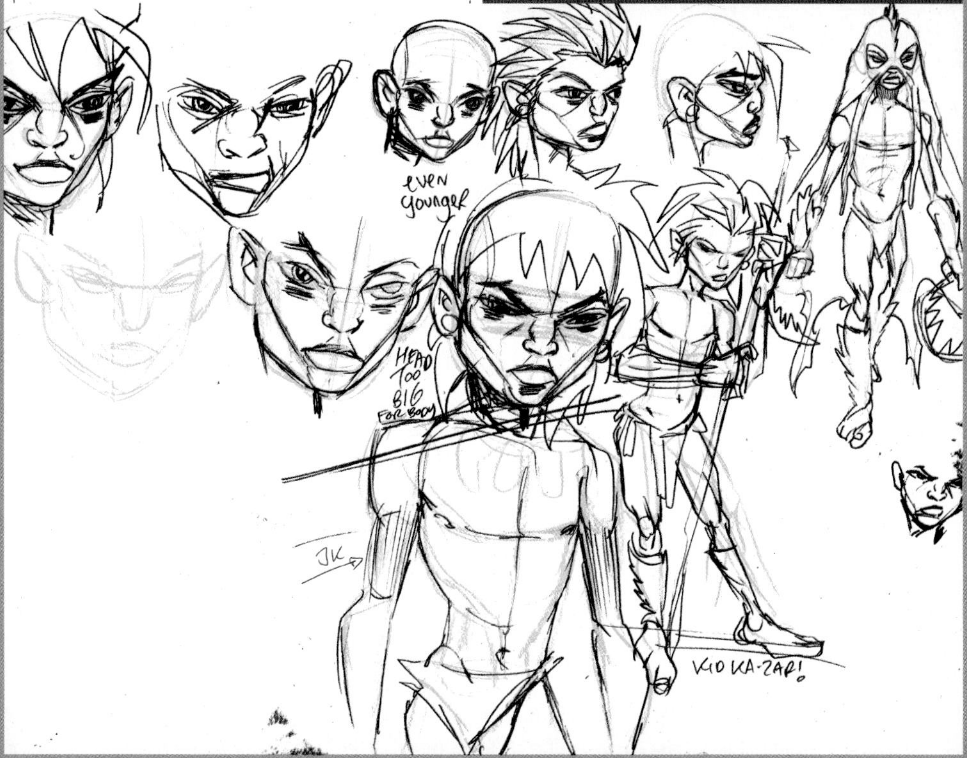
even younger
HEAD TOO BIG FOR BODY
JK
KID KA-ZAR!

JOE KELLY is a *New York Times* bestselling and award-winning author. He wrote the lauded graphic novel I KILL GIANTS, subject of a feature film currently in post-production and winner of the 2012 International Manga Award. His original graphic novel FOUR EYES was a YALSA "Great Graphic Novels for Teens" selection. Kelly's run on DEADPOOL remains the industry standard that greatly influenced the successful feature film. He returned to Marvel's SPIDER-MAN/DEADPOOL in 2016—one of the year's top-selling comics.

ILYA is a UK-based comic book writer and artist, published internationally by Marvel, DC and Dark Horse Comics in the USA, Kodansha in Japan, and numerous independent companies worldwide. Book titles include award-winning graphic novel series THE END OF THE CENTURY CLUB, Manga Shakespeare's KING LEAR, the MANGA DRAWING KIT and most recently, HOW TO DRAW COMICS: plus, as editor, MAMMOTH BOOK OF SKULLS, CULT COMICS and three volumes of BEST NEW MANGA.

GARY CALDWELL hails from Scotland and has worked in the comics industry for nearly two decades, initially as an artist (painting a JAMES BOND series for Dark Horse/Acme written by Don McGregor) before making a pragmatic decision to concentrate solely on coloring. He has since worked on a variety of strips for weekly UK anthology comic 2000 AD, most notably NIKOLAI DANTE with artist Simon Fraser (a lasting artist/colorist relationship having formed in the process). He continues to work for 2000 AD in addition to a regular role as colorist on Titan Comics' DOCTOR WHO: THE ELEVENTH DOCTOR title. KID SAVAGE is his first original work for the United States.

THOMAS MAUER is a German letterer and graphic designer. He has worked on a number of Harvey and Eisner Award nominees and winners, including the POPGUN and OUTLAW TERRITORY anthology series and Dark Horse Comics' THE GUNS OF SHADOW VALLEY. Among his recent works are Image Comics' COPPERHEAD, FOUR EYES and RASPUTIN, as well as Black Mask Studios' 4 KIDS WALK INTO A BANK. He recently finished lettering the World Food Programme's LIVING LEVEL-3: IRAQ and SOUTH SUDAN, comics which shed a light on the refugee and famine crises in these regions.